Pra..lf

'Tense, atmospheric and gripping. I adore Australian crime fiction and *Outback* doesn't disappoint. I eagerly await the next DS Walker thriller.'
Chris Whitaker

'*Outback* is a hot read, I highly recommend it.'
Lynda La Plante CBE

'Compelling, immersive and gripping, with a setting so vivid it's almost a character in itself.'
Becca Day

'A tense, twisty read that gripped me from its shocking start, immersed me in its sun-scorched landscape, then raced to its satisfying conclusion... Wolf is an architect of suspense.'
Sarah Yarwood-Lovett

'Nail-bitingly tense, *Outback* grabs you from the word go and doesn't release the pressure until the very end. A startlingly well-accomplished debut.'
John Marrs

'A dark, compelling read.'
Caroline Mitchell

Also by Patricia Wolf

Outback

PARADISE

Patricia Wolf

embla
books

First published in Great Britain in 2023 by

Bonnier Books UK Limited
4th Floor, Victoria House, Bloomsbury Square, London, WC1B 4DA
Owned by Bonnier Books
Sveavägen 56, Stockholm, Sweden

A CIP catalogue record for this book is available from the British Library.

ISBN: 9781471414657

This book is typeset using Atomik ePublisher

Embla Books is an imprint of Bonnier Books UK
www.bonnierbooks.co.uk

Prologue

She wakes with a start. Her bedroom is dark, too dark, and her heart is thumping hard in her chest. She can hear something. There's something here. She can hear it breathing, hear it coming closer. It's a bad dream, she tells herself. It's just a bad dream. I can wake up and it will all be OK. She forces her eyes wide open but the room is pitch-black and she doesn't know if she's properly awake or still dreaming.

Why is it so dark? She can't see anything, only shadows that make the room look all wrong. Her bedroom door must be shut. Mum doesn't usually close it, Mum knows she prefers it open, wants some light spilling in, doesn't like it when it's too dark. She's breathing fast. Everything feels wrong. The door shouldn't be shut, and she can hear something, breathing, grunting, panting, but it's so dark she can't make out what it is or where it is. She's trembling. The thing, whatever it is, is coming towards her. She'll pretend she's still asleep. Maybe it won't hurt her if it thinks she's asleep. Maybe if it can't hear her, it can't find her. She closes her eyes, doesn't make a sound, holds her breath, freezes, listens as hard as she can. Her heart is pounding in her ears.

There! She hears it again. It's not in her room, it's in the corridor outside. She keeps holding her breath for as long as she can and the noise comes and goes, sometimes quiet, sometimes louder, groaning, snuffling, squishy wet sounds. Like a big animal in the corridor, she thinks. It's sniffing and looking for her and it's going to come into her room and eat her up.

'Mum,' she tries to call, but her voice comes out in a whisper because she's so scared. She's definitely awake, she's not dreaming, it's not a nightmare. There's something out there. She curls tight into a ball, pulling her legs up and hugging Dotty against her chest. Dotty is a pink cat covered in white spots. She's soft and cuddly and she doesn't have claws like a real cat but maybe she can protect her from that thing outside.

As she lies there, her eyes open, straining into the blackness, trying to see, she hears someone cry out. Not a word, just a sound of hurt. Was that Mum? Is Mum OK? Has the thing found Mum?

'Mum?' she calls out. 'Mum?'

There's no answer. But the noise stops.

'Mum . . .' she calls again, a little louder. Mum always comes when she calls. She waits to hear Mum's footsteps, waits for Mum to open the door, to say 'Have you had a bad dream, Gabsy? Do you want a drink of water?' and come over and give her a hug.

She hears something coming but it's not Mum. The steps are too heavy, too stompy. Mum is quiet, soft. It's all wrong, everything is weird, nothing sounds right, nothing is normal. Not the thing outside nor the stompy steps, the closed door, the dark. It's almost as if her room has moved to a different house. The noisy steps come to a stop outside her bedroom door. She holds her breath, tells herself to be still. Perfectly still. Lie as quiet as can be. After a minute, she hears the thing stomp off again.

She's crying now but trying not to make too much noise. She hugs Dotty closer, tells herself this is a bad dream after all. A nightmare. It must be. She's been having them a lot this year. Mum says dreams can't hurt you. That you're in charge of your dreams and that if you don't like one you just say 'Go away, bad dream' and then you'll wake up. She whispers it out loud: 'Go away, bad dream' – but nothing changes. The room is still too dark, her heart is still pounding, the beast is still outside.

She wants to go back to sleep but she's too scared. She wants a drink of water and a hug from Mum. She thinks about calling out again but maybe the beast thing with the clompy steps will hear her and this time it might find her. Even if she is in charge of this dream, she doesn't want to risk it.

She wishes she could wake up in Mum's room, lying in bed beside Mum, telling her about the dream. Mum would make it all go away.

The thought of it, of Mum's arms around her, being warm and safe, the thing outside gone, the bad dream banished, is so comforting that she finds the courage to sit up. She sits there for a minute in the dark, holding Dotty close. She can't hear anything. Maybe the thing has gone.

Still holding Dotty, she swings her legs out of bed and waits, listening again. The air conditioner is on and blowing cold air across her bare arms and legs. She feels goosebumps on her skin and shivers. She can't hear the beast anymore. Now she's properly awake, the thing has gone and she's going to go and sleep with Mum. She stands and inches slowly across the room, her hand out in front of her to feel her way in the dark. When her fingers touch the wall, she slides her hand along to find the door. Just in case the thing is waiting outside, waiting to pounce, she does it slowly, quietly, trying not to cry, trying not to breathe too loud. She doesn't want it to hear her.

When she finally touches the cool metal of the handle, she's so relieved that she flings the door open. The hallway is gloomy but not as dark as her bedroom. The big light above the stairs is on and is throwing funny shadows down the hall. Her heart starts thumping again. She peeks out. She can't see anything scary.

Just ahead, towards the stairs, she can see that the door to Mum's room is shut but there is a shaft of light running underneath. Mum is awake, Mum will take care of her. She always makes everything better. She pulls Dotty close, takes a deep breath and then runs down the corridor as fast as she can and pushes open the door to Mum's room.

Chapter 1

Monday 6 March
4 a.m.

'This is triple zero. What is your emergency?'

'You have to help me. Please help me. They broke into my house, they tortured me and they've hurt my wife. I think she's dying. Oh god, there's so much blood. Please, I need an ambulance . . .'

'OK, sir, we're going to get help to you. Please tell me your address—'

'It's thirty-five Shipman Court, Macintosh Island. Please, please, I need an ambulance. My wife, she's been stabbed, she's losing too much blood, I can't make it stop . . .'

'Are you safe? Are there still intruders in the house?'

'No, no, they've gone. They tied me up . . . I got myself free but they've hurt my wife. Please, I need an ambulance.'

'Ambulance and police are on their way. What's your name, sir?'

'Owen – David Owen.'

'OK, Mr Owen, I'm here with you. Stay on the line, put me on speakerphone. Have you tried to staunch your wife's bleeding . . .'

Constable Anna Jones and her partner Dean Hammond are the first team to respond to the 000 call. Jones pulls the cruiser to a stop outside a big mansion in the swanky Macintosh Island neighbourhood, lights flashing, siren off. It's not a neighbourhood she knows well. This part of Surfers – with its big waterside mansions, quiet cul-de-sacs and wealthy residents – is not a crime hot spot. Even now the street looks peaceful in the pre-dawn dark. The only house with lights on is number 35, almost every window ablaze.

She takes her Glock out of its side holster and nods to Hammond. They're both constables but she's been in the force five years longer than him, so she's in charge.

'We'll go in, check what's going on, make sure it's safe for the ambos to enter,' she says, feeling a rush of adrenaline but trying to hide her nerves.

'Shouldn't we wait for back-up?' asks Hammond. Not for the first time, Jones wishes she had a more experienced partner. Still pimply, barely shaving and in this role less than six months, he's only on his first serious call-out – a home invasion, at least one victim seriously wounded. It's a potentially dangerous situation and she's happy that back-up is on the way, but they can't hang around.

'We need to get in there. It sounds as though there's a victim with life-threatening injuries,' she says.

Number 35 is an imposing place, architect-designed, modern, spread over two floors, sitting behind a white shoulder-height wall. The first sign that all isn't as it should be is the grey metal security gate, unlocked and swinging open. Jones and Hammond walk across a tightly mowed lawn dotted with palm trees, the fronds rustling in the night breeze the only sound they can hear. The front door is heavy teak, ornately carved. Jones pushes it gently with her foot, and it too swings open. She breathes deep, moves her gun into the firing position, arms extended in front of her, and steps into the hallway, a tall, high-ceilinged space brightly lit by a big glass chandelier. She can smell a heavy scent coming from a big vase of lilies on a glass console table beside her.

'Police,' she calls. 'Anyone home?'

'Up here, in the bedroom – we're in the bedroom.' A male voice, calling from a room on the floor above. It could be a trap; he could be lying in wait for them. She takes another deep breath and with a quiet movement of her hand directs Hammond to wait, to guard the front door; then, gun still drawn, she walks slowly up the staircase, the plush carpeting muffling the sound of her approach. As she gets to the top of the stairs she shouts: 'Armed police.'

'In here, in here . . .' The voice is shaky, coming from a bedroom to her right. 'It's David Owen, I called triple zero. My wife is bleeding. Please, we need help.'

Jones finds her courage, takes the last two steps quickly and turns into the room towards the voice, gun extended. Despite her experience, the scene she finds stops her dead in her tracks. She's in a bedroom, a large master suite, luxuriously decorated, lots of gold and white. A woman lies on the bed in front of her, arms and legs tied spreadeagled to the bedstead. Her chest and throat are a dark bloody mess. Pools of blood colour the covers around her crimson, and, where it has dripped off the side, it is coagulating in dark puddles on the wooden floor beneath. A man is sitting beside her. He's wearing a torn t-shirt also covered in blood. His face is ashen; his bloody hands are raised, trembling in the air.

'My wife, she's dying. Please. You have to help us,' he says.

'Is there anyone else in the house?' Jones asks, gun still drawn.

'No, they've gone, they've gone. My daughter is in her bedroom, she . . . she's sleeping. But please, my wife, she needs help now . . .'

Jones walks quickly over to a door on the far side of the room. It leads into a dressing room. She steps in, gun first; the room is empty. She can hear chatter on her radio, the back-up team arriving, a search of the ground floor beginning. She speaks into her radio: 'First floor, adult female, seriously wounded, adult male, also wounded.'

Turning to the man, she says, 'Stay there, please. I need to check the rest of the rooms.'

She goes back into the hallway. A pink-and-white soft toy is lying discarded on the floor, and a couple of steps further there's an open door to a room on the right. By the dim light of the hallway she can just make out a riot of pink and glitter and a young girl asleep, lying in bed, on her back. As Jones approaches the bed, she realises that the way the girl is sleeping is unnaturally tidy – her arms are tucked under the bedcovers, and only her shoulders, encased in a bright-pink t-shirt, are visible, her short blonde hair neat against the pink pillowcase. From closer still she can see that the girl's face is much paler than it should be, her lips blue, the skin a horrible white, and a cluster of small red spots, like a rash, on her face. She notes a second pillow discarded on the floor beside the bed.

She speaks quickly into the radio: 'I've got another victim, young girl, seven to ten years old . . .'

She needs to clear the house, ensure it's safe for the paramedics to enter. Her gun still raised, her urgency increasing, she checks the rest of the rooms. More bedrooms, a study – messy, papers lying on the floor, a wall safe with its door hanging open – a yoga room, two bathrooms, all empty.

'Top floor clear,' she says into the radio. 'Paramedics OK to enter.'

'Ground floor clear,' comes the reply, and moments later she can hear quick footsteps as the ambulance crew enters the house. Hammond is still standing with his gun drawn, face pale, at the bottom of the stairs.

'It's fine, all clear,' she says to him, and she notices his hand is shaking slightly as he holsters his weapon. 'Up here,' she calls to the paramedics. They are up the stairs and beside the bed in seconds. Standing behind them, Jones can smell the rusty tang of too much blood. The air conditioner in the bedroom is off, and the scent of slaughter and violence hangs heavy. Her stomach lurches and she forces herself to breathe through her mouth.

The two paramedics look at one another and something passes between them. Jones meets their eyes, and one gives a barely discernible shake of his head. The woman on the bed is dead.

A second ambulance team materialises at the door.

'There's a kid in the next room,' says Jones.

'Take us to her, please,' says the lead paramedic.

She turns and leads him to the girl's room, where the paramedics lean over the child. One takes her pulse, looks closely at her hand, then checks her breathing and tries to rouse her, tapping her on the shoulder, gentle but firm.

'Not responsive. She's breathing but her pulse is erratic, and she's unconscious. Her fingernails are blue.' He holds a small hand up to show her: the fingernails have a bluish tint. 'That and the rash on her face – it looks like she might have suffered a loss of oxygen. She needs to go to hospital now.'

A stretcher is brought up the stairs and then down again, the pair carrying it taking extra care with the girl, her small body heartbreakingly light.

Jones returns to the grim scene in the main bedroom. David Owen is kneeling by the bed, his face bloodless, eyes closed, holding his wife's lifeless hand.

'Mr Owen?' says Jones. He opens his eyes, looks at her, dazed, unseeing. 'Your daughter has been injured, Mr Owen,' she says. 'She's unconscious and she's being taken to hospital.'

Owen's eyes spark back into focus, and he clambers to his feet. 'Gabby's hurt? I looked in on her after I found Siobhan and she was fine, sleeping . . .'

'I'm sorry. She's unconscious. They're taking her to hospital.'

'I need to be with her. Where is she? Where are they taking her?'

She leads him from the room, closing the door behind her and calling for Hammond. 'Stay here,' she tells him. 'Don't let anyone in until CID or scenes-of-crime units arrive.' She turns to Owen. 'Gabby's in good hands, and I know this is the worst possible time, but we need to ask you some questions so that we can start—'

A paramedic appears beside them. 'Some of the blood on his t-shirt is from a stab wound to his chest,' he says quietly to Jones. 'He's been injured and he's in shock. He needs to go to hospital too.'

'How serious is it? We need to talk to him. We need all the information we can get so we can move on this.'

'I need to be with her,' says David Owen. 'I need to be with my little girl.'

Chapter 2

11 a.m.

DS Lucas Walker stands in front of the door, fiddling with the unfamiliar keys. His injured leg is throbbing after the two-hour drive from Brisbane to this temporary home in Surfers Paradise on the Gold Coast. He's on the fourteenth floor and there's only one door, 1401, so he's in the right place, but he can't get any of the keys to fit. The communal hallway is stuffy, with bland cream walls that match the ceramic-tiled floor. He runs his hands through his dishevelled hair and the mirrored elevator doors reflect his sorry state back at him. The bag that he's slung over his shoulder slides down his arm and hits the floor with a thud, landing next to the one he's already put down. He looks at the two of them lying there – the big black one badly packed, the zip barely closing over a bulge of clothes, the smaller dark-blue one equally full – and feels the sense of rootlessness he's been battling since his grandmother died climb up on him again. Apart from a couple of boxes that his ex-girlfriend Ellen is storing at her place in Sydney, if she hasn't already binned them, the two bags at his feet represent more or less all he owns in the world.

He wonders if he's made the right decision coming here. After his recuperation in hospital and weeks of intensive rehabilitation to help him walk again, he's finally been given the go-ahead to get back to work. Non-operational desk roles at this stage, but that will do. He's raring to get back on the job. But he's under review for his actions on his last case, actions that put a long-term undercover operation at risk, and he can't go back to his proper role until the review board delivers its findings. And if the board finds him guilty he won't be able to go back at all. That possibility is devastating. Policing is his life. His work with the AFP, putting away serious criminals at the top of the organised crime pyramid – there's nothing else he wants to do.

In the meantime his boss DCI Rutherford has given him a choice: act as a guest lecturer for a couple of sessions as part of a training programme for a group of Queensland Police drugs and serious crime coppers in Surfers Paradise, or take unpaid leave and wait out the review findings back home in Caloodie. Walker isn't ready for Caloodie without his grandmother yet – can't face the big empty hole that her death has left in his heart. It feels too soon, too raw. And it was a Hobson's choice, really. The AFP is under-resourced, and offering training to other forces isn't Rutherford's priority. But having a spare man on the ground gives the DCI a chance to do some important knowledge-sharing and earn some regional favours he'll no doubt call in later on.

It's Walker's idea of hell, standing in front of a whiteboard trying to teach others how to do the job he loves – a job that he does mostly on instinct and finds hard to explain. But he needs to do everything he can to win Rutherford back on side. So here he is on Queensland's Gold Coast for at least the rest of this week, staying in a flat that belongs to a bloke he barely knows while he trains a group of cops who probably think they know it all already.

He sighs, finds the right key at last and the door opens, smooth and heavy, into a small entrance that reeks of luxury, with a light-wood floor and walls painted in a warm caramel. Directly ahead of him is a vintage wooden console table with a bunch of fresh flowers in a big vase and another mirror that showcases his messy hair and the dark circles under his eyes. He hasn't been sleeping well, the pain in his injured leg, not to mention the possibility of losing his job, keeping him up at night. He shakes his head, trying to clear these endless looping thoughts, picks up his bags, closes the door behind him and turns left, towards a bright slice of light that is spilling into the hallway through an open door.

As he enters the flat proper, he comes to a stop. He's in an enormous living room with floor-to-ceiling glass doors that run the full length of the far wall and lead on to a large terrace dotted with potted plants and colourful sun loungers. Beyond is nothing but blue – the deep blue-green of the ocean meeting the lighter blue of the sky in a neat line at the horizon. The sun is bright and the entire room is washed in light that shimmers from its reflection off the water.

'Holy shit,' he says, a smile coming to his face. This is many degrees better than he'd expected. He'd come directly from the motorway to the block, negotiating the unfamiliar streets of Surfers Paradise and parking his ute in the underground car park, so he hadn't realised how close to the ocean he was. He hadn't been thinking about views on the ride up in the lift either, just indulging in feeling sorry for himself.

He breathes deep and looks around the room, taking in his good luck. Two big sofas sit at right angles to each other to his left, one positioned to look out at the water, the other facing a flat-screen TV. At the other end of the room a dining table sits in front of more big windows, this time with a view facing down the long stretch of coastline towards Burleigh Heads. White-sand beaches fringed by stacks of high-rises run for miles, the buildings casting fingers of shadow onto the shore, the waves curling white against the topaz-coloured ocean. More doors open into a fancy kitchen and two decent-sized bedrooms with a bathroom sandwiched between them. The views in the bedrooms are to the rear, looking over the homes and gardens that line the Nerang River and its tributaries to the hills of the hinterland beyond. Not as breathtaking as up front, but in any other building it would rate as pretty good. The last door he opens on the far left of the living room leads into a main bedroom, also facing the ocean, with its own floor-to-ceiling sliding doors on to the terrace.

'Holy shit,' he says again, and laughs, dropping his bags onto the gigantic bed. Maybe this training gig won't be so bad after all.

He opens the sliding doors, which glide at the lightest of touches, and goes outside. The terrace runs the full length of the flat and there are no neighbours above or beside it. The breeze is strong up here but not unpleasant. He walks to the edge and looks over the chest-high wall. The block is beachside; not even the Esplanade separates it from the sand. He can smell the ocean on the air, taste the salt and hear the muted sound of the waves breaking on the beach below. He stands, the sun hot on his shoulders, soaking up the view. As soon as he's sent a message of thanks to Craig, the bloke who owns the place, he'll go down and have a long swim. It'll be his first since his injury and, looking at the sea, he realises how much he's missed being in the water. The physio will be happy too. She's prescribed a routine of gym work and other exercises and recommended swimming as good additional rehab. His leg is better and the pain, though regular, is no longer constant. But he's a long way off being 100 per cent fit, and he'll be on desk duties for a good few months unless he follows the physio's advice.

He takes a couple of pictures of the view with his phone then sits, stretching his throbbing leg on one of the expensive-looking sun loungers, and sends one to Grace, his little sister who lives in Boston, and to Blair, his cousin in Caloodie. They've both been worried about him, and he wants them to know he's better and back at work. When he sends the photo to Blair, he thinks of Ginger, his auburn-and-white cattle dog who's still out in Caloodie at Blair's place, recovering from an injury of her own. He feels a bit guilty about leaving her there, but tells himself she's better off out bush, with a big garden and lots of kids to keep her company. Though he reckons she'd love a run on the beach, and smiles to think what she'd make of the salty ocean waves.

After a moment's hesitation he sends the picture to Barbara in Berlin too, with the same short message: *Working at the Gold Coast – it's a tough job but someone's gotta do it!*

He'd worked with Barbara on his last case and they'd formed a strong connection. It's more than three months now since he's seen her and he's been surprised by how much he's thought about her since she went home to Germany.

Sitting down, he finds the wind disappears completely, blocked by the wall of the terrace. The sun is hot, the sky is a deep pool of blue above him. He lies back, closes his eyes, lets out a long breath. Something tight inside him that hasn't unravelled since Grandma died loosens a little as he lies there in the warmth.

His phone pings, calling his attention. For a moment he thinks it's

Barbara and feels a twinge of pleasure that she's replied so quickly, but it's a message from Craig. He reminds himself it's the middle of the night in Berlin and clicks on Craig's message: *hope you're settling in OK mate*. Walker starts typing a reply then changes his mind, his finger hovering over the Call button.

He's only known Craig a few weeks. After the sensational end to his last case the media had had a field day and Walker's name and some old pictures of him had made the news rounds. Craig had seen the reports and fronted up to the hospital one visiting hour, looking awkward, carrying a Glad-wrapped basket of fruit from the shop downstairs. In his late fifties, tall and broad with a shaved head and muscular physique, his tan was the kind of nut brown that only people who live beside the ocean have. He was wearing expensive trainers, an even more expensive watch and a platinum wedding ring engraved with a tribal-style black pattern.

'Craig Ford,' he'd said, extending his hand, proffering the fruit basket. 'We never met, but I was a real good mate of your dad's. Least I'm pretty sure it was your dad – Bobby Walker?'

Surprised, Walker had nodded.

'You're the spitting image,' Craig had said, 'and I remembered he had a kid not long before he died.'

Walker had been bemused. His dad had died when he was two, killed in a car accident, and he couldn't remember anything about him. He'd never met anyone – family aside – who knew him. All Walker knows is that his dad had been a rugby league player, one of Queensland's best. He'd moved to Sydney to play professionally, and met Walker's mum, who was modelling part-time while studying for a mathematics degree. A few years later, his dad was dead at just twenty-seven and Walker was staying at his grandmother's place while his mum finished her degree and then moved to the States to do her doctorate. By the time he moved out to be with her she had remarried and they hadn't talked much about his father. He's only got one picture of his dad: wearing his footy team strip and holding him as a baby. It's in the boxes that Ellen might or might not be storing for him.

'Yeah, I was real good mates with your dad. We played footy

together in Sydney. He was a few years older than me and I really looked up to him. We had some great times. Man, those were the days, Craig had said, laughing. 'After your dad died, I lost contact with your mum. Not sure she thought I was the greatest influence. Your dad and I did enjoy a coldie or three. But when I saw your picture in the paper it was like looking at Bobby back to life. A bit older, but definitely Bobby. So I had to come and say g'day.'

They'd talked easily and Craig had visited a few times while Walker was in hospital in Brisbane, and then in rehab. Walker had suggested they get a beer together when he was going to be in his neck of the woods on the coast for a couple of weeks.

'Defo. You got a place to stay?' Craig had asked.

'Nah, I reckon they'll book me into a motel.'

'I've got a holiday flat that's mostly empty. We don't use it much – it's for mates or family when they visit the coast. Why don't you stay there?'

Walker had demurred but Craig had insisted.

'Look, you're Bobby's son. He was a really good mate and I'm happy to get to know you. It's empty anyway, so you'd be doing me a favour, looking after it. And you can use my gyms to do your physio and get fit again.'

After his football career had finished, Craig had come here to the coast and opened a chain of gyms, one of which is apparently just down the road from this flat. Gyms must be a money-making business if this place is anything to go by, thinks Walker as he presses the Call button on his phone. After a couple of rings, Craig answers.

'Lucas, g'day, how are ya? Did ya find the place? Settled in?'

'It's bloody beautiful, mate. Can't thank you enough.' Walker looks out at the blue-green water of the Pacific. 'I'm a bit speechless, to be honest.'

Craig laughs. 'Yeah, it's not bad. But you'll have to come visit me and Jess. Our place is even better. I'll take ya for a spin on the boat too. Gotta show you how we live down here on the coast. You might never leave. Have ya been to the gym yet?'

'Yeah, nah, I just got here. I'll head down in a bit. I might have a swim first.'

'Righto,' says Craig. 'Well, it's on the Boulevard, the road behind the Esplanade, five minutes' walk from the flat. You'll see the Iron Fitness sign. Ask for Dan when you get there, he'll see you right.'

'Will do,' says Walker. 'Thanks, mate.'

'No worries, anything for Bobby's boy. Hang on a sec . . .' He hears Craig calling out to someone, a quick muffled question, then he's back. 'Listen, Jess wants to meet ya. I've told her all about ya. Come to dinner at ours tonight. Nothing fancy – I'll drop a steak on the barbie, we can have a few beers.'

'Sounds good.'

'Righto, I'll text you the address. See you around six.' And with that, he's gone.

Walker stands at the balcony edge for a moment longer, savouring his good fortune, then turns and heads into the bedroom. The ocean looks so bloody good. Time for a swim.

Chapter 3

3 p.m.

After his dip – a welcome immersion in the warm salty water, buffeted by waves – he lies on the sand in the hot sun to dry, then showers in the flat and checks the route to the gym on his phone. He decides against driving. It's only a short walk but it'll help him stretch his leg and get his bearings and a better sense of the place he's landed in. It's his first real visit to the Gold Coast. His grandmother hadn't had the money when he was a kid to support summer holidays at the coast – though he'd never felt short-changed, loving the long days swimming at the waterhole with Blair and his mates or messing around, playing cricket and footy on the quiet streets and in the back gardens of Caloodie. But even though he doesn't know the place, it lives large in his cultural memory, as it does for all Queenslanders – the epitome of summer holidays and hedonism. It's a magnet to Aussies from all over the country and international tourists too, home to bikini-clad Meter Maids, the state's first casino and schoolies, that great Aussie tradition of kids finishing high school and spending a decadent booze-fuelled week celebrating at the beach.

He walks north along the Esplanade, a beachside road that's dwarfed by the high-rise buildings that line up, each bigger than the last, along the seafront. The Gold Coast is one of Australia's biggest cities and runs almost seventy kilometres in a slim line along the water, with most of the action concentrated between Southport in the north through Surfers, Broadbeach, Miami and Burleigh to Coolangatta on the New South Wales border. Surfers Paradise, where he's staying, is the thrumming heart of the region. The sand and the waves are better pretty much everywhere else, but Surfers' shopping, nightlife and its enticing edge of the illicit have helped it stride like a colossus over neighbouring areas.

The sun is warm, and he can hear waves crashing onto the sand over the sound of the traffic. Squat palm trees and spindly pines offer blocks of shade from the bright-white light, and the glass facades of the buildings, framed by the deep-blue sky, shimmer and glitter in the sun. Seagulls fly low, diving for scraps. Walker can smell sunscreen, sea salt, donuts being fried, and, despite his sore leg and his grief, he feels a touch of holiday spirit seeping in.

He reaches Cavill Avenue, the town's bustling main drag, and the mellow beachside energy dissipates. Even though it's March, summer nearly over and the kids well and truly back at school, the street is awash with waves of people rolling down the pedestrianised mall towards the beach. Boys with bare chests, towels slung around their necks, girls swinging their long hair and showing off brown legs in short shorts. Two lifesavers in their distinctive bright-yellow shirts, red shorts and red hats, their hair white-blond and salt-encrusted, meander against the tide, heading home after a day on watch. An electric scooter ridden by a woman sporting a floaty green dress and high platform sandals dodges a group of tourists in white straw panama hats with bulging daypacks, dragging rolling luggage.

It's all a very long way from Caloodie, thinks Walker, picturing its wide-open streets, quiet little stores, the laconic 'G'day's of the drinkers in the pub, the indigo sky that curves like an inverted bowl towards the red earth, the scalding heat, the sounds of the birds and cicadas in the trees.

He turns left, limping slightly now, heading away from the ocean, and after a few minutes left again onto the Boulevard, heading south. The vibe is immediately quieter and more workaday. This end of town has yet to be dusted with glitz. He walks past a tiny Thai restaurant sandwiched between a strip joint and a tattooist, a kebab kiosk, a massage parlour and a twenty-four-hour convenience store with a dusty display of beach umbrellas, bodyboards and Surfers Paradise branded caps.

Just beyond the convenience store he spots a big sign with Iron Fitness written in red letters below a barbell logo. Walker follows the signs up a flight of stairs and into a smart reception – a curving pale-wood desk in front of a large black-and-white close-up photo of a bulging bicep that covers most of the wall behind it. The desk is manned by a young woman with long blonde hair, wearing a tight red t-shirt emblazoned with the Iron Fitness logo.

'Welcome to Iron Fitness,' she says with a big smile. 'How can I help you?'

The name badge on her chest says *Nadine*. 'Hi Nadine. I'm Lucas Walker, a mate of Craig's. He said to come down and ask for Dan ...'

Her high-wattage smile gets even brighter. 'Oh yeah, Craig said you'd be coming in. Let me give Dan a call,' she says. 'Why don't you take a seat while you wait?' She gestures with a well-toned brown arm at a poppy-red sofa on one side of the room, beside a fancy-looking water cooler.

As he waits, Walker looks around. Craig is obviously doing well; the space is tasteful and expensive, much like the flat he's staying in. A double door opposite the sofa leads to the gym – Walker can hear the muffled sounds of music and the occasional clang of iron. He's barely cased the room before the double doors swing open and a big bloke, tall and well built, also wearing a red Iron Fitness t-shirt in what must be an XXL, pushes through and walks over to him, a smile on his face.

'Mr Walker?' he says. 'I'm Dan Anderson. I run the gym. Mr Ford said to look after you and show you round.'

'Call me Lucas,' says Walker, extending his hand. Dan encases Walker's hand in a huge paw but there's no iron grip, just a gentle shake. He sits down beside Walker and places a red folder on the table in front of them.

'What is it you want to do while you're working out here?' he asks.

Walker explains he has a leg injury, shows him the workout the physio has recommended. Dan studies it, asks a couple of questions, makes a few notes.

'Defo, you can do all that here and I can add in a couple more exercises that'll help, if you want,' he says. 'Let me show you the way everything works here today, then we'll set up a time for you to come in tomorrow. We should get that leg back in action pretty quick.'

He stands and leads Walker through the doors into a big weights room, with tall windows running along one side and a full wall of mirrors opposite. It's a serious gym, no treadmills or cross trainers, just plenty of weights, barbells and dumb-bells, kettlebells and suspension systems. Music is pumping, a tune heavy on guitars that Walker can't place, and the room exudes a scent of sweat overlaid with bleach. The only other patrons are two big blokes working out at the other end of the room. One, lying on the bench, is pressing a heavy barbell. The other, spotting him, calling encouragement: 'That's it, Nath – good on ya, mate. One more.'

It takes a good half-hour for Dan to walk him through the workout. He spends time checking that Walker is doing the exercises right, correcting a few positions. Walker is impressed with his professionalism and knowledge – the guy is clearly serious about his job – and he books himself a daily session with Dan, early each morning before work.

Afterwards he ambles home and then takes the ute over to Craig's place, which is only five minutes' drive away on the Isle of Capri, a residential island surrounded by the river and its tributaries, both natural and man-made.

Craig's house is a two-storey place behind a dark-grey fence with a fancy gate of twisted iron, which has a *Beware of the Dog* sign. Walker rings the bell and waves into the video camera. When the gate buzzes open he crosses a small front lawn of emerald-green buffalo grass and sees Craig's wife, Jess, standing at the front door. She's younger than Craig, about Walker's age probably. Her long blonde hair is pulled back in a loosely tied ponytail and she's wearing a white dress with a green palm leaf print that falls off one shoulder and drops to her ankles, flat gold sandals and pink-painted toenails peeking out beneath. At her feet a tiny dog, a mess of black curls, barks and yaps. If this is the guard dog, thinks Walker, I don't feel too threatened.

As he gets closer he can see that Jess has been crying. Her eyes are red, her nose too, and she's holding a damp tissue in her hand. She smiles at him, and he can tell she's trying to compose herself.

'I'm Jess,' she says. 'Come in. Craig's told me so much about you – it's great to finally meet you.'

She opens the door and he steps past the yapping dog, which immediately ceases barking and instead leaps insistently up against his leg.

'Down, Marty,' says Jess, but the dog ignores her, jumping and whimpering for attention. Walker bends down and pats the soft curls, wondering what Ginger would make of him. 'Marty! Put a sock in it, would ya.' Jess's voice aims for authority but she's half-laughing as the dog rolls on his back, presenting a stomach for a scratch.

Walker smiles. 'He's not much of a guard dog, is he,' he says, giving the proffered belly a quick rub before standing.

'Nah, not at all. All mouth, no trousers. We adopted him a few months ago. He's a miniature poodle – he's got proper papers and everything. His full name is Marcello but it's too la-di-da for him! We call him Marty.'

At the sound of his name the dog barks happily and Jess smiles again, looking more composed this time. She leads Walker through a large open-plan living room and out to a paved patio that overlooks the water – the river or a canal, Walker's not sure which. A big pool, complete with Jacuzzi, sits to the left, and a small rectangle of lawn on the right leads to a little sandy beach and a jetty, where a big white motor launch is moored. Craig, wearing bright-blue board shorts and a pale-blue t-shirt, is standing beside a barbecue on the far side of the patio, stubby in hand, looking out at the water. The barbecue is as overscale as the house and boat – more than a metre of sleek metal, with separate grill and roasting sections. A plate with a big hunk of raw meat sits on top of it. But Craig's face, like his wife's, is grim when he turns at the sound of their approach. He smiles at Walker, but the smile doesn't make it to his eyes.

'I'll get you blokes a beer,' says Jess.

'Ta, Jess,' says Walker. When she's out of earshot he asks Craig, 'Have I come at a bad time, mate?'

'Nah, yeah. Shit, we've had some really bad news. But stay, please, it'll help keep our minds off it.'

Walker accepts the stubby that Jess brings out for him and the three of them stand and make small talk, watching the water and sky turn orange as the sun sets behind the rolling hills of the hinterland.

The air is warm and sultry and it's peaceful – he can hear the water lapping against the boat and breaking in soft ripples on the sandy shore. A flock of parrots wheel overhead, flashing red, green and orange feathers, and as the dusk deepens, the fruit bats emerge from their sleep, fluttering and gliding across the darkening sky.

After a while Jess goes into the kitchen and comes out with a large bowl of pink tiger prawns chilling on ice. The three of them sit, she drinking white wine, he and Craig on the cold beers, peeling and eating the prawns, which are sweet, fresh and delicious, talking of football and fishing, of nights out with people he doesn't know, of Jess's love for fashion and the personal shopper business she's launched. It's a lifestyle that reminds him of Ellen and her Sydney friends: glitz, glamour and money. And although they're doing their best to entertain him, Walker can sense a dark undercurrent running between them.

When only a mound of pink heads and tails remains, Craig deems the barbecue hot enough to cook. He brings the piece of steak to show Walker. 'Wagyu,' he says. 'Look at that marbling.'

Walker laughs and shakes his head. 'It's all beef to me,' he says, but he has to admit the meat is delicious – buttery-soft and flavourful. The conversation, which has been fitful, falters as they eat and when Walker finishes his meal he says, 'That was great, ta, but I reckon maybe I'll call it a night, head off. You've obviously got a lot going on . . .'

'No, please, stay,' says Jess. 'Really, you're very welcome. It's just . . . we had terrible news this afternoon. A friend of ours has been murdered.' As she says the words she starts crying and Craig gets up and goes over to her, putting his arms around her.

'That's awful, I'm so sorry,' says Walker, standing to leave.

'Sit, mate, sit – please,' says Craig. 'You've got police connections, maybe you can help us make sense of it. A gang broke into our friend Dave's place last night, on an island not far from here. It's even more expensive than round here. They broke in, looking for cash or I don't know what, tied him up downstairs, tortured him, stabbed him and stole a couple of thousand bucks, all that he had in the house. Then they went upstairs and stabbed Siobhan, his wife.

They killed her. They even tried to kill his daughter Gabby and she's only eight years old, for Christ's sake. She's alive, thank god. When they legged it, Dave got himself free, called triple zero, but it was too late. Siobhan's dead.'

Jess is sobbing now. 'How could this happen?' she asks. 'We're not safe. No one is safe if they can come and kill people in their own homes like that.'

Walker is horrified at the story. A gang of criminals has murdered a young mother and attempted to murder a child. Home invasions are not unheard of on the wealthy Gold Coast, but this one either went badly wrong or there was something else at play. He feels sickened. And he's had poor Jess and Craig playing nice, hosting him for dinner while dealing with this . . . He sits silent for a moment, feeling their pain, wondering if there is any way he can help, but he doesn't have any contacts in the local force. Perhaps he can find out more at tomorrow's training session, but he's not sure and he doesn't want to overpromise. 'I'm not connected to Queensland Police,' he tells them, 'but I'm a hundred per cent sure they'll have a big team on it. They'll find the people responsible.'

'See, babe, that's what I said too,' says Craig.

Jess sniffs. 'Poor Gabby – her mum dead. Poor Siobhan. Imagine what she went through . . .'

'Come on, babe, don't think about it. Go inside, call your mum, relax. Lucas and I will clean up out here.'

After Jess goes inside, Craig gives the barbecue a quick once-over, removing fat and any tiny remnants of meat with a silver spatula. Walker starts stacking plates.

'Nah, leave it, mate,' says Craig. 'The cleaner can sort it tomorrow.'

They sit in silence, drinking their beers, the terrible story of Siobhan's death hanging between them. After a minute or two Craig says, 'Oh yeah, I almost forgot – I've got something I wanna show you. Hang on a sec . . .'

He goes inside and Walker sits in a sombre mood, looking at the dark smudge of river and the lights of the city skyline twinkling in the night sky, thinking about the terrible violence inflicted on their friends. A woman dead. A family destroyed.

When Craig emerges from the house, he's carrying a photo album, faded burgundy in colour with gold filigree edging. 'I dug this out for you earlier,' he says. 'Pictures from my Sydney days with your dad.'

Craig flips through the album, pointing out pictures of Bobby Walker and others. Walker soaks up the stories and the images of his dad, and others, in football team shots, relaxing in groups at the beach, at the pub, at barbecue nights like this one. An entire life Walker had never known about. In one picture he spots his mum and dad standing together, in their early twenties, young and beautiful, in Kings Cross, a part of Sydney he knows well. Not for the first time he wonders what his life would have been like if his father had lived, if he'd grown up in a family in Sydney instead of out bush with his grandmother and then in Boston, feeling like a foreigner at school and an outsider at home.

As Craig closes the album, Walker says, 'Ta, mate. I know it sounds strange, but I don't know much about my dad, who he was, what he was like. And having a chance to see these pictures, to hear your stories, it really means a lot to me.'

'I'm happy that we've met. Bobby was a good mate, and you're just like him. A chip off the old block.' Craig puts an arm around Walker's shoulders and picks up his phone. 'Selfie,' he says. 'We can add it to the album.'

Chapter 4

10.30 p.m.

Matt Monroe is gunning the car for all it's got. It's a top-of-the-range HiLux, just under a year old, and it's got plenty of grunt. He'd been cruising nicely, making good time, until he hit a traffic jam caused by an accident on the Toowoomba Bypass. No exits, no options, he'd sat there fuming for almost an hour, watching emergency services fly past on the hard shoulder, sirens blaring, the rest of the traffic at a standstill. When it finally got moving again, he was running late. He needs to be in Ipswich, an hour or so away, by 11 p.m. and it's almost 10.30 already.

It's taken him weeks to set up this meeting and he has to make a good impression. Ever since Stefan left Caloodie, an unexpected flit on a hot day last November, he hasn't had access to the drug supply he needs. His customers are freaking out, he's short of cash and Kelly is giving him all kinds of aggro about needing money for toys for Sienna, for clothes, not to mention the bloody rent. The number he'd had for Stefan was finished, a burner most likely, and it's taken him weeks to work his way up from the street grunt he could still contact to anyone with any power or influence. Finally he'd got hold of Nick Mitchell, one of the blokes closest to Stefan.

'You got a fucken nerve, Monroe,' Nick had said. 'You're neck-deep in shit. Stefan knows you fucken set him up.'

'What are ya on about?' Matt hadn't seen that one coming. 'I ain't set no one up. I'm a mate of Stefan's.'

'Well, the pigs found our Caloodie place and Stefan reckons it's you that squealed. So I'd back the fuck off if I were you, and don't remind him you still exist.'

'Listen, mate, I swear . . .' Matt had felt a cold sweat starting. He had to set the record straight. 'I never talked. I never would. I got plenty invested in this too. Please. Let me talk to Stefan. He knows me. He'll know it wasn't me. I can prove it. I want to keep dealing. I got plenty of customers up here. I wouldn't do nothing. I would never . . .'

In the end his pleading had worked. Nick had called him back a couple of days later to set up this meeting in Ipswich. Stefan is giving him another chance and he's going to buy three months' supply. He needs to prove his worth, his loyalty. Running late will look bad – disrespectful. He pushes the vehicle a bit harder.

His phone rings and he glances down at the screen. His mum again. He doesn't pick up. That's all he needs, more hassle from her. She'd been living with Stefan; she'd thought it was the real deal, the big romance, but Stefan had left her behind too, and no forwarding address either. She's got a week or so before the lease runs out on the house they'd been living in, no one to pay the bills and no way to earn any cash, so no doubt she's calling for a loan or, worse, wanting to move back in with him. He's not having that. He's living with Kelly now and one woman is more than enough. The phone rings again. He ignores it. It stops, then starts again. He keeps on ignoring it and she keeps on ringing. In the end, he bangs his hand on the steering wheel in frustration but answers it.

'What the fuck, Mum, I'm busy right now.'

'Kelly says you're on ya way to meet Stefan. Are ya out of your mind?'

'What's it got to do with you?'

He hears her breathe loudly down the phone. 'Look. Don't go near that bastard. They told you already, he thinks someone ratted him out to the cops and you're in the frame. I told him it wasn't you, but . . .' Her voice trails off.

'But he's not listening to you anymore, is he,' says Matt, pissed off and feeling vicious. 'He dumped you quick smart, headed back to the coast, found himself a hot young chick. Stay out of my business, Mum, you don't know nothin.'

'Fuck, Matty, it's you that don't know nothing. Just stay away from Stefan, orright.'

'No, it's not alright. How'm I supposed to make money? I've got Kelly and Sienna to look after. You've got no idea . . .'

He's about to hang up, he doesn't need this shit, when she says: 'Promise me you're not going to the coast, you're not meeting Stefan?'

'Shit. I'm not going to the coast and I'm not meeting fucken Stefan. Look, stay out of my life. Focus on finding yourself a new boyfriend and stay out of my business.'

He jabs the End Call button. He's nervous enough – the last thing he needs is her making it worse. He reminds himself that he's talked his way out of this situation, they're meeting him, they're supplying him, and he's gonna prove that he's solid.

It's gone 11 p.m. when the GPS directs him off the highway at the Dinmore exit. He doesn't know the neighbourhood and misses a couple of turns, driving too fast, stressed out. By the time he pulls in to the street it's 11.20. He slows down to check the place out. Most of the houses are dark – everyone in bed already – and the street is a dead end, finishing where it meets a strip of scrubby parkland, the lights of another suburb visible on the other side.

He spins the car around at the end of the street, kills the lights and engine. Number 12, the meeting point, is on his left, the second house from the end. It's a small bungalow, set back from the road. There's no fence to the yard, only a lawn of sorts that runs straight to the road. A rickety postbox is jammed into the dirt and a couple of battered wheelie bins on the far edge are tilting towards the kerb. The street is quiet; all he can hear is the rumble of traffic on the highway in the distance. Someone is awake in the last house – he can see the blue flicker of a TV screen through the front window – but it seems like there's nothing happening at number 12. There's a car parked in the drive, some sort of sedan, but no sign of any Harleys. Too noisy and obvious in a neighbourhood like this.

He pulls the sports bag that's lying on the passenger seat towards him and unzips it. The money is all there; he counts it one more time to be sure. He's borrowed from the bank, told them he was renovating the house, building a new kitchen. Haha. Jason and Pete put in a couple of grand each too. He's gonna build up a team, start to treat this seriously. Now that Stefan isn't in Caloodie, he can take the gear out there and further north too.

As he walks across the lawn to number 12 he notices a light in a side window and hears the air conditioner unit under the window rattling. His nerves fire up again. Sweat is running down his back and his chest, his shirt sticky, his hands clammy. He takes a deep breath and walks with as much swagger as he can to the door, bangs hard on it, telling himself to stop being such a pussy.

He hears steps approaching and the door opens. A big bloke, not someone he's met before, blocks the doorway.

'Yeah?'

'I'm Matt. Got a meeting with Nick.' His voice is holding up OK, just his hands feeling a bit shaky. He jams one in the pocket of his jeans; the other grips the bag a bit tighter.

The bloke in front of him moves fast, pushes him hard up against the wall. Matt drops the bag with a thud.

'What the fuck . . .'

The bloke jams an elbow against his throat. Matt can't get enough air, tries to move but he's pinned tight, hands frisking his pockets, his waistband. He feels the hands take his phone from his back pocket but leave his wallet. After a bit, the pressure against his throat eases, and the bloke steps back.

'He's clean,' he says.

Matt leans against the wall, breathing deep. He hears a door from the car on the driveway close quietly as he rubs his hand against his throat. A second bloke, another one he doesn't know, walks over from where he's been sitting in the car. Short, balding and bandy-legged, he looks like an ageing jockey. Matt stays focused on the bigger threat in front of him.

'Let's go,' says the big bloke, holding the door open.

Matt picks up the bag, his legs feeling shaky beneath him, and walks in. He hesitates as he enters but the big bloke pushes him hard between the shoulders and he half-stumbles down a short hall towards a light at the far end, emerging, blinking at the brightness, into a kitchen. The place is a dump, the doors to the units hanging loose, a manky blind over the window. There's a small table in the centre of the room, a wooden chair on each side, but no sign of Nick. The big bloke gives him another push in the back. 'Sit down,' he says.

Matt stands his ground this time. 'Where's Nick?' he says, half-turning.

The bloke steps forward, grabs his left arm and twists it hard and high behind his back, frogmarches him the three paces to the chair. 'Sit the fuck down,' he says.

'Fucksake.' Matt can hear a shake in his voice. He drops the bag on the floor and sits down. The big bloke moves to the end of the table and stays standing. Matt keeps an eye on him as he massages his arm. The fucker almost broke it. He's thinking about what to say next, how he should play this, when he feels a cool touch of metal against the back of his neck.

Stevie looks at the bloody mess on the kitchen table as Brains unscrews the silencer, his face impassive. Brains walks over to the holdall on the floor, unzips it, counts the cash, then drops the gun inside, zips it up again, lifts it with one hand, nods and walks back down the hallway. Not one word, the entire time. That's one ice-cold little goblin, thinks Stevie.

He calls Nick. 'It's done,' he says.

Nick grunts and hangs up and Stevie takes the tea towel that's lying on the sink, switches off the light, wipes down the light switch and the front door handle.

Brains's car is already halfway down the street as Stevie crosses the garden. It's a short walk to pick up his bike where he's left it on the other side of the scrub. He walks past the HiLux parked at the end of the street, the car the mark arrived in. He'd watched him from the front room, to see if the bloke had any company, made any calls. But Nick had been right: the bloke had no clue. Turns up, just him and his money, not even a blade, let alone a gun.

The car is brand new – even under the shitty light of the street lamp it looks pretty slick. Nick said to leave it; take nothing but his phone. But this vehicle is a beauty. Stevie looks around the quiet street. No lights, no noise. No one paying any attention. Fuck it, why leave the car for the cops. Or, worse, the fucking Banditos.

He goes back into the house, wrapping the tea towel around his hand to open the door, goes into the kitchen and pats down the body. He finds the car keys in the right-hand pocket of the jeans. The car will fetch a good price. He knows a bloke on the coast who'll buy it from him, no questions asked. Nick never needs to know.

Chapter 5

Walker wakes with a start, his heart beating wildly. He'd dreamt of being in a dank space, pitch-black, the smell of blood and death around him. He could feel the hard metal of a gun barrel jammed into the back of his neck. Then he heard Barbara screaming for help behind him. He'd wanted to turn, run to help her, but knew that, if he moved, the gun would go off and he wouldn't make it.

He lies there, calming himself by looking out at the ocean. Most nights he doesn't close the curtains, likes to wake up to a view of the water. This morning the sun isn't up, just a pale line of pink light on the far horizon, the water still indigo under the pre-dawn sky. Now that he's been in Surfers a couple of days, he's establishing a nice routine. He wakes early, has a swim and a workout with Dan, before starting the training course at the very civilised hour of 10 a.m. The group he's training are Queensland Police from both the Brisbane- and Gold Coast-based narcotics and organised crime squads. Yesterday morning he'd found himself surprisingly nervous, making notes, swotting over them as if he was back at uni preparing for an exam, but the group, a mix of more experienced cops and new recruits, is interested and easy to teach and their questions and discussions are engaging. The sessions are acting as a constant reminder of how much he loves his job, and how much he stands to lose, and he wonders if Rutherford knew this when he posted him here.

After work he'll have another swim then a beer on the terrace, watching the ocean turn from blue to indigo to black, before dinner and bed. The last two days have kept him busy, no time for thinking, but in the evenings his grief for Grandma and the fear of losing his job have still been running round and round in his mind. He's distracted himself by following the case that Craig and Jess told him about. It's made the news, of course, splashy headlines everywhere. Lots of stories about the family – Craig's friend, David Owen, a renowned sports doctor with big-name clients, a pillar of the community. Pictures of him with his wife and daughter, all smiling on the beach, at a barbecue, their normal life before it was cruelly upended. Queensland Police are asking for information, anything anyone might have seen or heard. Walker's sure they'll have a big team on this, but so far it seems there are no concrete leads.

There's media speculation that the attack might be linked to a spate of burglaries in the wealthy areas of Surfers, and real fears that the perpetrators might strike again. Walker has spent some time looking through the AFP database to see if he can spot anyone based up here who might have form for similar crimes. But it's a needle-in-a-haystack job without more information.

The sun is starting to rise. Walker gets up and goes out onto the terrace, listens to the ocean, the sound of it tumbling in and out against the shore, rhythmic and soothing. He knows nightmares can be part of the job, a way to let his mind process the things he has to deal with, but they are worse than usual at the moment. With his dream and in particular the sound of Barbara's terrified scream still playing on his mind, he checks the time in Berlin. It's early evening over there. He thinks for a minute, then presses the Call button.

She picks up on the second ring. 'Hello, Herr Walker.'

Hearing her warm, softly accented voice, he feels a smile come to his face.

'G'day, Barbara,' he says.

'It's so nice to hear you. How are you? How is your leg?'

'I'm alright,' he says. 'I'm back at work, just running a training course, but it's better than hanging around doing nothing. The leg's still a bit iffy but it's getting better every day. How about you?'

'I'm OK. Well, I'm a bit frustrated because I have to take time off work. The doctor says it is *posttraumatische stress* – I'm not sure how you say it in English – and that I need some weeks of rest. I told her that staying home is making me more stressed, but she doesn't listen.'

'That's no good,' says Walker, immediately worried for her. 'Why do they think you have post-traumatic stress?'

'I haven't been sleeping so good and I had a bit of an anxiety attack. I was interviewing a suspect at his home and . . .' Her voice trails off. He waits and after a second or two she says, 'Out of nowhere I thought he was going to attack me, lock me up. It was stupid, it only happened once, but they're insisting I take time off. But the thing is that working helps me forget.'

Walker empathises. He's felt better since he's been at the coast, mostly because he's had other things to think about, but he's still having the nightmares too.

'Yeah,' he says, 'I get it. I don't sleep so good either. That review at work still hasn't happened yet, and I could still end up losing my job.'

'You're still waiting? That must be horrible. But I can't believe they would ask you to leave after everything you did . . .'

'Well, "everything I did" messed up an undercover op,' he explains.

'Oh no, Lucas. I really hope it will be OK.'

He knows she understands, better than anyone, how much he loves his job and how much it defines him. They're alike in that way.

Afterwards, feeling better for having heard her voice, he walks down and takes a swim as the sun rises, the water warmer than the cool morning air, the waves low and somnolent as if they too haven't quite woken up yet. Then he goes to the gym, the first person there when Nadine opens up. He's so early today that he has time for a leisurely coffee and breakfast after his workout. He picks one of the cafés on the Esplanade overlooking the little park that abuts the beach and chooses a table outside. It's quiet, just one older couple, Victorians by the look of their pale skin and dodgy shorts, sitting at a table at the far end, not speaking to each other, staring morosely at the ocean. The coffee's not bad but the bacon and egg sandwich has nothing on the ones he'd get at the bakery in Caloodie; the bread isn't fresh enough and the filling is miserly, only one streak of bacon, not even crispy. But the table is catching the morning sun and he can smell the ocean and see the whitecaps of the surf, so he orders another long black, stretches his legs out and looks around.

Surfers Paradise lives up to its billing. The sun keeps shining, the days are warm, temperatures around 30C but without the humidity of Brisbane or the searing heat of outback Caloodie. And although it's a city, with plenty of high-rise blocks and busy streets, it doesn't give off a high-octane urban vibe. He reckons it's probably because the ocean is right there – you get unexpected glimpses of it all the time, the light reflecting off the water, smell the scent of salt in the air, hear the unbroken symphony of waves hitting the sand. Add in the palm trees, blue sky, bikinis and board shorts, the thongs – he smiles to himself as he remembers Barbara's confusion around the Aussie word, can almost hear her say 'Flip-flops are not thongs' – and somehow the place has a mellow energy. He gets flashes of a holiday vibe himself even though he's not feeling totally right yet.

As he drinks his second coffee, his phone buzzes. The caller ID says *Dan Rutherford*, and for a moment Walker toys with not answering it; then, steeling himself for the worst, he picks up.

'Alright, Walker?' says Rutherford. 'How's the training going?'

'Ah, yeah, pretty good, I reckon. There's some real good cops here, motivated to learn.'

'Yeah? Send me the names of the ones you rate the most. How's the leg?'

'Yeah, a lot better. I'm training at the gym and swimming too. Got another physical at the end of the month.'

'Good. Reckon you're up to taking on a small job? Nothing arduous, just desk work.'

The strength of Walker's relief surprises him. He'd expected to be in serious trouble, not offered the chance to work. He grabs at the olive branch with both hands.

'Absolutely, sir, one hundred per cent. You know how it is with these medics – they want me in better shape than I've been in a decade.'

'OK, good. Remember Matt Monroe?' As ever, Rutherford doesn't wait for an answer. 'Well, he's been murdered. Execution-style killing in Dinmore, out by Ipswich, on Monday night. Queensland Police are looking into it but given Monroe's links to the Vandals and to Stefan Markovich, I've asked that an AFP officer be part of the case. It won't be an operational role, purely overview. You'll sit in on the investigation and keep me up to speed with how it's proceeding. You'll need to get yourself up to Brisbane this afternoon. I'll send you the contacts now.'

'Righto,' says Walker.

'Good. But don't think you're off the hook for that stunt you pulled in Caloodie, by the way. The review board findings will be handed down Monday week at two thirty p.m. You'll need to be here in Canberra for that. You're a good cop; you might be a great one if you kept your head once in a while, but there's still a chance you're going to lose your badge.'

Chapter 6

11 a.m.

Walker focuses on Matt Monroe rather than his imminent performance review as he drives up to Brisbane to meet the detective in charge of the case. He'd set the trainees an assignment at the end of this morning's session – applying the techniques they've been talking about to their existing cases to see if they open any new leads – and they'll review the results at his final lecture on Friday afternoon. It's good timing – he's free to use the next couple of days to focus on the Monroe case and try to get back into Rutherford's good books.

He'd met Monroe, a bit player in the Vandals, one of Australia's biggest outlaw motorcycle clubs, on his last case. Monroe dealt in drugs and casual violence from his home in Hopeville – a small town in the state's west – and had been under suspicion in the disappearance of two young backpackers. Walker wonders what Monroe was doing in Dinmore, some 800 kilometres from home. Monroe's mother, Tina, is the girlfriend of Vandals leader Stefan Markovich, so he's well connected and perhaps he's moved up the chain of command.

Walker has more questions than answers by the time he parks his car in the staff car park at Queensland Police HQ and makes his way to reception, where he shows his ID and asks for the detective in charge, DI Ernie Cummings.

The young constable manning reception makes a call, then gives him convoluted directions to the homicide offices on the fourth floor. When Walker arrives, the room is jammed with people. All the desks are occupied, several officers are standing talking on their phones and a small group are clustered around a whiteboard in the far corner.

'I'm looking for DI Cummings?' he says to the woman sitting at the desk nearest the door.

She looks up from her computer, distracted. 'That's his office over there.' She points, then, seeing the empty space, looks around the room. 'You want the bloke in the blue shirt by the whiteboard . . .'

As Walker approaches, he sees Cummings is standing in front of a board filled with pictures from another crime scene. Most show a woman tied to a bed and covered in blood. He glances away out of respect, not wanting to be voyeuristic to her suffering.

'DI Cummings?' he says.

The man in the blue shirt turns; he's small, wiry, late forties, with a ginger moustache and red hair that's going grey at the sides.

'I'm DS Walker from the AFP. I've been told to report to you regarding the Matt Monroe case.'

Cummings nods. 'Right, yeah, I was expecting you.' He turns back to his team. 'We'll talk about this in the briefing. Follow me,' he says to Walker, leading him to his office. Once they're seated, the eyes he fixes on Walker are shrewd. 'So, you're from organised crime at the AFP?' he says. 'You knew Monroe?'

'That's right – well, I wouldn't say I knew him. I came into contact with him on a previous case.'

Cummings rifles through his inbox and pulls out a pale-green folder. 'Righto, well, this is the file so far. We haven't made much progress. We're flat out on a high-profile home invasion and murder inquiry that's sucking up all our manpower, so I'm glad to have you on the team for this one.'

Cummings must be heading up the Owen case, realises Walker, his interest piquing immediately.

'You'll be working this Monroe case on your own for the moment but let me know if you need any assistance,' says Cummings. 'We don't have much budget for forensics or surveillance, but maybe you can get some additional resources through the AFP?'

'Um, yeah, nah, I'm not sure . . .' says Walker, taken by surprise. This doesn't exactly tally with what Rutherford had outlined. Cummings is obviously bending procedure to take advantage of the extra manpower and the budget that might come with it.

'Goodo,' says Cummings, his mind already elsewhere. 'I'll leave this in your no doubt capable hands.'

Maybe, thinks Walker, he's being set up here. Being given the case so that any lack of results falls squarely on him and not on the local team. Or is he being cynical? Either way he's got his hands full, but as sitting around watching others work isn't his idea of a good time, he's happy that he'll have something to do. He follows Cummings back into the main room, which is even more crowded than it was before.

'We're a bit short on desks at the moment,' says Cummings, looking around. He turns to the harried-looking woman Walker first spoke with. 'Narelle, can you find somewhere for the DS to work? And give him access to the system too.'

Then he calls, 'Briefing, now – conference room,' and strides out. The room starts to empty, as the team follows Cummings out the door.

Narelle looks at Walker. 'Can you wait a few minutes? After the briefing half this lot will disappear and I can find you a desk. What systems do you need access to?'

Walker applies his motto of always asking for as much as you think you can get away with. 'All of it?' he hazards.

She tuts. 'Righto. I'll do that after the briefing as well. You might as well come with,' she says. 'It'll save me having to repeat the information to you later.'

Walker's pretty sure the briefing won't concern Monroe but he's interested in the Owen case, would like to get closer to it and is curious to see where the team are with it, so he follows Narelle as she marches away down the corridor. The room she leads him to is packed. Cummings is standing at a lectern, a few senior officers seated around a table in front of it, everyone else standing on the three sides of the room facing Cummings. The space gives off the smell of too many people jammed close together on a hot day, but Walker feels the familiar buzz of being part of a new case fire up inside him as he absorbs the energy and purpose that fills the room. It's good to be back at work.

Cummings starts talking, his voice low, forcing all other conversations in the room to quieten as everyone strains to listen. 'Right, quick recap on where we are with this case. We have a thirty-three-year-old woman dead, a young girl in intensive care and a traumatised father and husband, all victims of a brutal home invasion. The male victim, David Owen, was knocked unconscious, dragged to the living room, tied to a dining chair with cable ties then assaulted and stabbed, though not with fatal force. The adult female victim, Siobhan Owen, was tied up and fatally stabbed in her bed in what was a violent and angry assault. She has fifteen wounds to her throat and torso. No indication of sexual assault, though we're still waiting for the autopsy results. The murder weapon hasn't been found. Gabby Owen, eight years old, was knocked unconscious by a blow to the head. She was hit from behind with significant force by a blunt object, we think most likely a heavy wooden chess board, which has traces of her blood on it. Following that, an attempt was made to suffocate her with a pillow. She has both traumatic and hypoxic brain injuries and the chance of a full recovery is very much in question. I'll hand over to DS Lowrey, who interviewed the surviving adult victim, David Owen, for more details about the events of early Monday morning.'

A younger policeman, his trousers and short-sleeved shirt both ironed to perfection, stands to speak. 'First interview conducted on Monday with a longer follow-up yesterday,' he says. 'Victim is obviously distraught and confused, but his version of events is consistent. The family were asleep at home when he was woken by a noise downstairs around two twenty-five a.m. His wife didn't wake up, and when he went to investigate they must have jumped him from behind because he can only remember walking down the stairs then coming to, tied to a chair in the living room. He was threatened with a knife and cut several times, then stabbed in the chest. It's a minor wound, so I'd say they were only trying to intimidate him. They were asking for information about the valuables he kept at home but there wasn't much there. They took a Patek Philippe watch worth forty-five thousand dollars, and around five thousand in cash from the safe. They also demanded information regarding his bank account, which he gave them. The victim estimates that the attack took about an hour, during which time they threatened to hurt his family if he didn't give them what they asked for. He says he complied with all their requests, but they continued to threaten his family and were physically aggressive with him. He can't give much of a description of the culprits, he was falling in and out of consciousness, but says they were big blokes and that there were two of them. He thinks, given their accents, it's likely they were Pacific Islanders. When they left the house he was still tied up but after some time he was able to work himself free from his restraints. When he went upstairs just before four a.m. he found his wife tied to the bed, bleeding heavily, and called triple zero. Detailed autopsy and forensics will be with us by the end of today but the preliminaries suggest that we have found traces of a third person's DNA on Siobhan Owen's body.'

That's good news, thinks Walker, and there's a surge as others in the room start to ask questions. Cummings puts his hand up. 'Questions at the end, please,' he says, and nods to the younger cop.

'Yeah, well, we've only recovered very small traces at the moment, but it's enough to get a DNA profile. No match with anyone on the database, unfortunately. Aside from that, we've found some partial prints in the living room, but nothing we can use. There will be SOCO teams at the house again today.'

'Thank you, DS,' says Cummings. 'As you know, we've had a number of break-and-enters in the Macintosh Island area over the last three months, all of which seemed meticulously planned. They were timed when owners were away or out of the house and targeted specific high-value pieces. There has been no violence before so if this is the same perpetrators, it indicates a serious escalation. DI Bailey is heading up the investigation into those thefts, and I've asked her for her assistance.'

A tall woman in a skirt suit moves to stand beside Cummings. 'At this stage I'm not convinced this attack is linked to the previous burglaries, given the degree of violence, which is not typical of the other break-ins,' she says. 'In all the other cases there were indications that the thefts were highly targeted; usually it was art or jewellery that was taken, possibly even to order. The watch that is missing here is valuable but not in the same league. Previous pieces were worth hundreds of thou or more. But it may be that something went wrong and they didn't find what they were looking for, and that's why they resorted to violence. If these crimes are linked it is an extremely worrying escalation. Obviously it is highly plausible that they could strike again. I am making our case notes available and my team are on standby to assist.'

'Thanks, DI,' nods Cummings. 'DS Roberts, where are we with CCTV, video?"

'Nothing on CCTV yet, but that neighbourhood isn't heavily surveilled,' says a heavyset older copper wearing a crumpled shirt and playing with an unlit ciggie in his hand. 'We're looking at nearby roads but the house backs on to the river, so there's a chance they came and left by boat, in which case there'll be no trace. The house security system was cut at two fifteen a.m., which tallies with Dr Owen's timings. We've put a call out for any dashcam footage that might have been taken in the area but at that time of night, in that neighbourhood, well, it's very quiet.'

'Financials?' asks Cummings.

'Yeah,' says a slim guy wearing glasses on Walker's left. 'The stolen bank account details are being monitored – no one has tried to use the cards up to this point. The family's financials from first impressions are pretty solid. House is mortgaged and being paid monthly. The joint account shows income that's consistent with David Owen's role as a sports doctor. He has investments in stocks and shares of around four hundred and fifty thousand dollars. I'm still looking at the business account of his practice. His wife also has a separate account in her name, with just over six thousand in savings.'

Cummings starts detailing next steps, assigning jobs to various teams. The noise level in the room rises again until Cummings leans forward, taps something on the lectern and a picture of a young girl – her face deathly pale, her eyes closed, tubes coming out of her mouth and nose – appears on a large screen behind him. Walker's heart goes out to her. She looks so vulnerable, fragile, and something about her reminds him of his own sister, Grace, at the same age. Perhaps it's the blonde hair or the fact that with her eyes closed she could almost be sleeping. It reminds him of when Grace was a little kid and he came up to say goodnight and she'd already drifted off.

'This is Gabby Owen,' says Cummings. 'As I said, she is just eight years old. We believe she heard the attack on her mother, went to investigate and was knocked unconscious. She was carried back to her bed, where the attackers then attempted to suffocate her. It is sheer luck that she is not a second murder victim of this heinous crime. Gabby is in a coma in hospital at the Gold Coast. We've set a watch outside her room. There's a chance she might have seen something that puts her in danger, and that whoever tried to kill her might try again. I'll be looking for volunteers to take some shifts. Right now, though, we have to focus on finding the people responsible for this. We don't know to what degree the child will recover, but whatever the case, she'll be waking up to the news that her mum is dead, violently murdered. I know you're all a hundred per cent committed to finding these bastards but I need everyone to put in three hundred per cent. We have overtime hours. We have budget. We are dealing with men who will kill a woman, kill a child. We are going to find them, and we are going to put them away for a long, long time.'

Chapter 7

5 p.m.

The Monroe files are spread across Walker's dining room table. After the briefing the homicide room had been even busier than before, everyone feeling Gabby Owen's plight, taking Cummings's call to action seriously. Walker had quickly realised that there wasn't going to be any space for him and decided to take his work back to the flat. No one had objected. He's given his phone number and contact details to Cummings and Narelle – who seems to deal with the team's admin – and has also volunteered for a few stints sitting guard outside Gabby Owen's hospital room. It's just down the road from where he's staying.

'Bit outside your remit, isn't it?' Cummings had said when he offered.

'I want to help,' he'd replied. 'No one should have to go through that, poor kid.'

'Fair enough,' Cummings had said, adding 'Put him on the list' to Narelle, who'd promptly rostered him on a late shift tonight.

He logs in to the system for all the details on the Monroe case and discovers that Narelle has taken him at his word and given him broader access, including to the files on the Gabby Owen case. He glances through them, then forces himself to put it aside. Terrible as it is, there's a big team working the case, whereas the Monroe file is thin – only the initial police report, pictures from the scene and some light background on Monroe. He's got his work cut out, but it feels good to be back on a case.

The pictures of the crime scene show Monroe slumped over a table in what looks like a kitchen, the back of his head a gaping wound, blood and gore spattered on the table and the wall in front of him. He was found at 8 a.m. yesterday morning, when a realtor stopped by to value the place. Given the body's temperature, forensics estimate time of death to have been in the eight to ten hours before the body was discovered, so sometime after 10 p.m. Monday night.

As Walker examines the photos, it's clear he's looking at an execution-style killing. With Monroe's known links to the Vandals, there's an assumption that this is a gang feud gone wrong. The Vandals don't have much of a presence in the Ipswich area – it's the heart of Banditos territory – so perhaps Monroe was stepping on rivals' toes or he'd decided to switch allegiance and something went wrong. But Monroe was nothing more than a bit player in the Vandals, a prospect at best. If he went behind head honcho Stefan Markovich's back to start dealing with the Banditos, they would be unlikely to take him seriously. Unless he's moved up the ranks. Or perhaps his mum's connection to Markovich means that killing him sends a stronger message.

The police report contains a statement from Monroe's girlfriend. Walker remembers a slim young blonde in a short tight dress. There'd been a baby, too. He sighs. Monroe wasn't much of a bloke, violent and with a criminal record, but his murder will leave a major hole in this family's life and deserves as much attention as any other.

According to his girlfriend's statement, Monroe had driven to Ipswich for a business meeting on Monday evening. He hadn't shared any details of who he was meeting, but she'd expected him back early on Tuesday. He'd gone alone. She's given the number of a Jason Cheever, who she says was a business associate of Monroe's. His junior dealer maybe, thinks Walker. Monroe was clever enough not to hold the gear at home, so perhaps Cheever was the storage and distribution guy. No one has followed up the contact as yet. Walker dials the number but the phone is dead. A burner probably, and given what's happened to Monroe, no doubt Cheever has sensibly gone to ground. He calls a contact of his out west, Senior Sergeant Sarah Jordan, who he met on his last case. She's organised and professional and on the ground in Hopeville. As he'd hoped, she's happy to try to locate and interview Cheever for him.

Monroe had driven to Ipswich but there's no sign of his car at the site of his murder. Perhaps he'd parked it elsewhere and been driven to the execution site. Or his car has been stolen, possibly by whoever killed him. Walker remembers the vehicle, a blue HiLux with a sporting trim. Top-of-the-range, brand new when he'd seen it last November; it had stood out in the dusty front garden of Monroe's ramshackle home.

Walker makes a list of things to follow up. He needs to confirm who owns the house where Monroe was killed, and dig into the situation between the Banditos and the Vandals. Is there a territory battle going on? Perhaps the Vandals are building a presence in the Ipswich area. He'll put out a few feelers to see if he can locate the car too. If it's parked elsewhere it could provide a useful clue as to who Monroe was meeting. Finally he makes a note to ask Cummings to have someone interview Monroe's mother, Tina. He'd met her in Caloodie and it was all part of the fiasco that has him under review back in Canberra, so he needs to steer well clear of her and Stefan Markovich. But she's bound to have an insight into what's happened, and, given that she's lost her son, maybe she'll be more willing to talk now.

He fires off an email to Cummings and does some research into the Vandals and Banditos. There's been bad blood between the two clubs going back a long time, but no indication that things have escalated recently. Walker taps his pen between his teeth. Maybe the location of the killing is a red herring. Perhaps he's better focused on finding Monroe's car. He messages Cummings again and asks if it's possible to put out a bulletin across Queensland Police, requesting officers to keep an eye out for the vehicle.

He's mulling things over when his phone vibrates on the table. A message from Grace, his little sister in Boston. Not so little now – she's in her early twenties and at university – but she'll always be a little sister to him.

How's the beachside recovery going bro? she's written.

He thinks back to this morning's briefing, the little girl in her hospital bed, and feels a surge of protective love for Grace. Rather than texting a reply, he calls her.

'Hey, Lucas!' He can hear the smile in her voice as she answers. 'How's things, big brother?'

'I'm good, Grace,' he says. He doesn't want to worry her with the gory details of his recovery or his fears about losing his job. 'Getting better every day.'

'That's awesome,' she says.

'Well, I'm at the beach, nothing to do except sit in the sun, so . . .'

'Aaargh, stop it. It's freezing here and I'm way behind in my coursework.'

They chat, meandering around subjects, talking about everything and nothing.

'What's the name of the place you're staying in again?' she asks. He tells her. 'I knew it!' she says. 'A girl I know, Kaia Hale, she's in Surfers Paradise too. How weird is that? She just posted a pic on Insta that looks a lot like the one you sent me.'

'Ah yeah?'

'Listen, do you have time to meet her? She's from Hawaii and she's at college on a sports scholarship. She's a kitesurfer and she's amazing, like world number one or something. But she had a crappy year last year and she doesn't know anyone in Oz . . .'

'I don't know, sis,' he says. 'I don't think she'd want to hang out with an old codger like me.'

'I don't know what a codger is but I'm sure she'd like you. In fact, I know she would. And you'll like her. She's a lot of fun. Pleeease? For me?'

Walker sighs. He's never been able to say no to Grace. 'OK, OK. But only if she wants to. Tell her she can call me but don't pressure her into it!'

Grace laughs. 'I won't, I promise. But I'm jealous. I want to hang out with you too. Catch up properly. Not just texts and stuff.'

'Too right,' he says. 'Why don't you come over for a holiday in your summer break? We could go to Caloodie. It'll be winter here, and that's the best time to visit, when the weather's not too hot.'

'Hmm, maybe,' she says.

'I can shout you the flights – I've got a bit saved.'

'It's not that. It's just – I've never left the US of A.' She says it half-laughing, self-conscious.

'No worries, you'll be fine,' says Walker. 'I'll meet you at the airport and I'll take care of everything. Australia is a great country – you'll love it. I could take some holiday, we could hang out in Sydney for a bit then head out bush . . .'

'I always wanted to visit Sydney, check out the surfer dudes at Bondi,' she says, laughing.

'Well, I don't think you'll need my help with that!' He's laughing too. 'Afterwards I'll show you the real Straya, the proper country, the one you won't find at Bondi.'

Chapter 8

8 p.m.

Stefan Markovich is standing on his veranda, waiting for his three top lieutenants to arrive. He's had acreage here, on a hillside just outside the Reedy Creek township, for almost a decade. Set in the hills behind the Gold Coast, the house is big and comfortable, with all the mod cons including a private gym, a well-stocked bar with a billiards table, and a top-of-the-range infinity pool out front. You can see the pale-blue slick of the ocean when you're floating during the day, and at night the lights of high-rise buildings along the coast.

The block is surrounded by eucalypt woodland and light scrub, making it private and secluded, but it's still close to the action. He's got another place in Surfers that he uses at weekends, when he wants to bring a chick home or party, but this is where he spends most of his time. And he's bloody happy to be back in civilisation. For what he wants to do with the Vandals, moving the club in the direction of the seriously big money, it's better that they're down here, not stuck a million miles away out bush in Caloodie.

He's just got off the phone with the Banker. When he saw the call he felt a rush of adrenaline. The Banker usually avoids phones, paranoid as hell about being hacked or tapped or whatever. He's elusive all round, usually lets his lieutenants handle the day-to-day business. A personal call means either you're in deep shit or you're rising in importance in the organisation. The last call, after the Caloodie site had been exposed, was the former kind, and the Banker had made clear that Stefan only had one chance to put things right.

He's only met the Banker once, years ago – an older guy, dark hair going silver on the side, not tall, not built, not even dressed that well, just ordinary-looking, the kind of bloke you wouldn't pay a second's notice on the street. When Stefan was first introduced, he'd thought they were having a laugh, taking him for a fool; he couldn't believe that this was the Banker himself. But then he noticed the steel in the bloke's eyes and all the others pussyfooting around him, filled with nervous energy, the kind you get when you're near a big boss, the kind you can't fake. It was the Banker who'd come up with the plan to set up Pedro, the club's founder, on a trumped-up murder charge eight years back. Pedro was too old-school. He didn't mind dealing a bit of drugs but was mostly into riding and fighting, whoring and getting wasted. Not professional, didn't have a vision for the club and what it could be. The money that could be made. So the Banker got him sent down, and made sure Stefan had the support to take over in his place. Since then Stefan has prided himself on being on top of shit and running the club like a proper organisation, until the shitstorm in Caloodie damaged his standing no end.

When Stefan answered the phone just now, the voice – cold, hard – had cut straight to the point.

'Is the kitchen up and running?'

'Yeah,' said Stefan. He's called in all the favours he's owed, pushed everyone harder than he's pushed before, and they've found the perfect place. Discreet but accessible, in an area of light manufacturing where their production won't be especially noticeable and the vans won't attract any attention at all. 'I've found a site, imported the ingredients, and that cook you sent me is making the new recipe.'

'When will it be available in the restaurant?'

The Banker's paranoia means they avoid terms that might trigger AI recognition, but sometimes Stefan thinks it's a bit much. Recipe, restaurant, kitchen. Fucksake. 'From tomorrow,' he told him. 'In time for the weekend.'

There was a short pause. 'Good,' said the Banker. 'Make sure you keep it clean this time. We can't have another problem with rats.'

The Caloodie fuck-up was down to Monroe, the traitorous

fuck, who had squealed to the Feds about their last manufacturing operation. They'd had to pack up and get out fast, the Banker not happy at the inconvenience or the fact that the op was on the Feds' radar. But Monroe's gone now.

'Yeah, I've sorted that,' said Stefan.

'Good,' said the Banker, and hung up.

Coming after Caloodie, that's praise enough, and Stefan feels a surge of relief that he's redeemed himself. He's working his way up the ladder, almost at the top, and his share of the pie is getting bigger. The one black mark still against his name is the Fed that busted them, a narc called Walker. He's still out there. Probably back in Canberra. Markovich has shelved that problem for the moment, but he hasn't forgotten. And he's pretty sure the Banker hasn't either.

As he stands there he hears the dog out back start barking, growling, the clank of it pulling against its chain, and a moment later he hears the sound of a bike, even though it's still quite a way down the hill and hidden by the scrub. The house is hard to find – a private unmarked drive off the Tallebudgera road into what looks like bush. If you don't know the turn, it's easy to miss. The drive to the house is more than a kilometre long, which gives him and the dog plenty of notice if anyone unexpected shows up, and there's a back way out too, which no one else knows about. He only invites the blokes he really trusts out here and the three he's got coming today, Nick, Aaron and Wayne, he's always thought he could trust with his life. But now he's not so sure. Caloodie opened his eyes to the possibility of betrayal, and he's been more alert than ever since. Keep your friends close and your enemies closer, like they say.

The sound of the bike gets louder and he sees a shaft of light from the headlight spilling around the final curve and cutting across the large expanse of grass in front of the house, before the rider turns in to park beside his – the sounds of the bush returning as the satisfying growl of the engine cuts off.

It's Aaron Adams, his sergeant-at-arms. Aaron is a bit younger than the others, but he's as hard as they come. He grew up with an abusive father, learnt early to stand his ground and fight back, and he gives no quarter. Most of the members are shit-scared of him. The club is his life, the family he never had. Stefan trusts no one fully but he reckons if Aaron has turned, the whole club is fucked.

'Alright, boss?' says Aaron, climbing the stairs to the veranda.

Stefan nods curtly. 'Yeah. Had some good fucken news on Monday. We finally got rid of the rat that fucked up our last op.'

'Anyone I know?'

'I don't reckon you met him – Tina's son?' Aaron shakes his head. 'Low-level prospect from out west. No one important. But I want the word out. We don't let this kind of shit happen.'

"ken oath! Traitorous bastard. I'll spread the word,' says Aaron, raising his voice as two bikes, Nick and Wayne arriving together, ride across the grass.

They all help themselves to stubbies from the fridge in the bar then sit on the sofas in the living room.

Stefan kicks off the meeting, getting straight to the news. 'We're upping the ante. We got a new chemist that can make fentanyl, and we're gonna cut the meth with it.'

'Fentanyl – that's synthetic heroin?' says Aaron.

'Yeah. No need to grow poppies – it's totally chemical, man-made shit. You can cut it with coke or meth or even weed if that floats ya boat – and it's fucken potent, a hundred times stronger than morphine. A tiny amount can make us a shitload of cash. The junkies love that shit. A couple of grains gets 'em proper doped up.'

'If it's so fucken good, why isn't everybody doing it?' asks Nick.

'The Triads are doing it in Asia and the Mexicans have been at it in the States for a while. And everyone'll be doing it here soon, too. We're getting a head start. It'll bring us serious bucks. Especially as we're the first.'

There's a pause. They drink their beers, and Stefan watches them. After a moment he nods at Wayne Hopkins. He hasn't known Wayne as long as the others; he met him in Sydney when Pedro Silva was still in charge. They'd been mates, riding out and getting pissed and picking up women, and Wayne had been the first to back Stefan, even before Pedro went down. It was also Wayne who'd alerted him when Pedro's loyalists planned a counter-coup, and he'd followed

Stefan to Queensland, no questions asked. Unlike Aaron and Nick, Wayne knew almost nothing about the Caloodie op, just that Stefan was spending more time out there. Stefan trusts him enough that he's put him in charge of distributing the drugs beyond their Surfers heartland, but he's holding back the details of the manufacturing site. That's going to be strictly need-to-know this time. Just between him and Nick and the chemists on site.

'I've found us a new site where we can handle distribution,' says Wayne. 'It's on an industrial estate in Nerang. Busy place, lots of traffic going in and out all day. Plenty of noise and action, no one'll notice us, and it'll be easy to move the shit up north or interstate from there if we want to.'

'Good,' says Stefan, and Aaron nods too. Stefan looks over at Nick, who's not keeping up, just sitting there peeling the label from his stubby, rolling the bits of paper into balls before dropping them on the floor. 'You got a problem, Nick?' asks Stefan. Nick's changed these last few years. They've been best mates since they were kids, joined the club as prospects together, decades ago. But now he's got a missus and a couple of teenage daughters, a fancy house by the water in Coomera – proper bloody suburbia. He's the only one of them with a family. Maybe he's lost his taste for the fight.

Nick throws a small ball of paper at the stubbies sitting on the coffee table and looks directly at Stefan.

'Sounds iffy as fuck to me. I think we're buyin' ourselves a bunch of problems we don't need,' he says. 'We're doin' alright. We're making plenty of moolah. The gear shifts as it is. Why do we need to up the ante with fentanyl? It'll attract more attention from the pigs and more hassle all round. Business is good – I don't reckon we need it.'

'Fuck me, mate, when did you turn so gutless?' says Stefan. 'You want to start filing tax returns, register with ASIC?'

The others laugh. Nick doesn't. 'I reckon it's the Banker we need to be sorting out,' he says. 'He keeps most of the bucks while we take all the shit. Doesn't seem right to me.'

Stefan downs his beer, throws the empty into the big bin in the far corner of the room where it lands with a noisy smash.

'It's the way it fucken is,' he says. 'You don't like it, what are you doing here?'

Nick raises his palms in supplication. 'Yeah, nah, I'm just saying that we take all the risks. It's our blokes out there selling it, not theirs. What if we get busted again? Time we got ourselves a bigger share of the moolah, I reckon.'

Stefan grabs another beer from the bar, cracks it open and takes a long drink. 'We got to prove ourselves to the Banker after that fuck-up out west,' he says. 'Maybe then we can talk about a bigger share.'

Nick pushes himself up from the chair. 'I need a piss,' he says.

Aaron follows him out, saying 'Let's have a pissing contest' and laughing.

'Mate, you're disgusting,' says Nick, and Stefan can hear Aaron calling Nick a 'soft prick' as they go outside and piss off the edge of the veranda.

He turns to Wayne. 'Listen, keep the location of that distribution warehouse to yourself,' he says. 'After what happened out west, I want this tight, just between the four of us.'

When Nick and Aaron come back in, they drink a few more beers before calling it a day. As the other two ride off, Stefan asks Nick to stay for another drink.

'Yeah, nah, I gotta go, mate,' says Nick.

Stefan narrows his eyes. 'Fuck's the matter with you today?'

'It's Nat's birthday – we've got family round for tea. I'm already in the shit with Shell and she'll go crook if I'm home too late.'

'Fucksake, you need to put your old woman in her place,' says Stefan in disgust.

'She's alright,' says Nick. 'It's Nat's sixteenth, it's important.'

'Yeah, well, so is the club. You wanna remember that.'

As he rides home Nick thinks about Stefan's last instructions: to keep an eye on the new chemist at the production warehouse and to keep the location a secret, even from Wayne and Aaron. He's loved being a Vandal. It's about the bikes, sure, but it's always been about much more than that – the brotherhood, the money, the respect. He's been a member for more than twenty years and the club has been like a second family to him. But recently he's seen a different side. Stefan is stressed, trusts no one, always thinking someone is selling them out. The whole club has become darker and more unpredictable, more fucked up by drugs. The young members and prospects, with big chips on their shoulders, are more aggressive, more violent. Hooked on coke or meth, they think they're fucking Superman.

He's finding it harder to sleep at night, always looking over his shoulder, wondering if someone'll decide he needs to go, and bang, like Tina's kid out west, it'll all be over. Him and Stefan go back a long way. The early days were a laugh – riding bikes, fighting, drinking – and in the last few years they've grown the club into something serious. Serious risks and serious money. But the money has changed things, too. He's noticed that no matter how far back you go with someone it doesn't count for anything, really. The brotherhood isn't real. Any day your best mate could be your enemy, over a woman, a debt, some perceived lack of loyalty. Look at Pedro and Stefan, how that played out. And Stefan gave the order to get rid of Tina's son, for fuck's sake. Maybe he didn't like him much, but still. You don't have him fucking executed.

'You're only there to make money for them. They don't have your back,' Shell always says, and she's right – that's how it is. You don't make money, you don't make sense. It's the blokes at the top – Stefan, the Banker – they're the ones reeling in the funds while he's taking all the risks. Like Shell says, 'It's not Stefan who's going to jail, it's you. If you don't leave the club there's only two ways out – you're gonna end up in jail or in a grave.'

Now Stefan wants him right at the heart of things, right where they're making the gear. And it'll be harder than Stefan thinks to keep it under wraps. If he gets done running a fentanyl factory, that'll mean serious jail time. Nick doesn't want to end up in the bin. That's a young bloke's game. He's realised these last few years that he's got more to lose than the rest of them. He wants to be around when his girls get married and have kids. Wants a nice quiet life somewhere, not fighting and stuck in prison till he's a pensioner or dead. He's decided he wants out, wants to leave the club. But if he quits, Stefan will put a price on his head. He'd live in fear that someone would do a drive-by and kill him or, worse, one of the girls. If he wants to leave, he has to make a plan. He has to put some serious money aside and find a way to move them all a very long way away.

Chapter 9

Midnight

When Walker arrives at the ICU for his shift, the hospital is quiet. A few nurses at their station, the lights dim, the corridors empty. The constable sitting outside Gabby's room is happy to see him. She stands and stretches and says: 'I've been holding on to go to the loo for bloody ages. Give me five and I'll be back to brief you.'

Walker waits outside the ward for her to get back. 'Better?' he says, laughing.

'Bloody oath! Stay off the coffee, is my tip,' she says. 'Righto, so, there's been nothing much going on. Her dad's been to see her but otherwise no visitors allowed. Friends sometimes come by with a pressie or flowers but they're not allowed past reception. I don't expect anyone'll come this late but, if they do, check the gift, make sure there's nothing dodgy about it, no recording devices or cameras. Those bloody journos will try anything. No one other than family is allowed in the room. Photographers and journos have been a pain in the butt, but they shouldn't be any bother at this time of night, I reckon. Obviously no pictures or info, just kick them out.'

'OK,' says Walker. 'No one suspicious been hanging around?'

'Nah, not on my watch.'

Walker sits on the chair that's provided – it's comfortable enough – stretches his sore leg and relaxes. He's not the greatest at sitting still and doing nothing, too restless generally, but he's had a lot of time to practise during covert operations, and this late at night he finds it easier.

After an hour or so he gets up and takes a few steps in each direction to help ease the pain in his leg a bit. A nurse comes by to check on Gabby. He stands by the open door to the room while the nurse does her thing. The room isn't dark – the light of the hallway spilling in, the light of the machines and monitors, and another light above the bed somewhere emitting a soft bluish hue and illuminating the girl, small and fragile in the high hospital bed, attached to oxygen and various other tubes and monitors. Poor little thing, he thinks. The nurse obviously feels the same way; he sees her brush a strand of hair from Gabby's face and stroke her cheek.

'How's she doing?' he asks when she comes back out the room.

'It's hard to say,' says the nurse, whose name badge reads *Matilda McDonald*. 'She suffered a loss of oxygen and had a traumatic brain injury from a blow to the head. She's still in an induced coma but the doctors say the inflammation on her brain is slowly coming down.'

'That's great news,' says Walker. 'Do you think she'll be able to remember what happened when she comes to?'

'You cops!' says Matilda. 'That's all you want to know. Not "How is she going to feel that her mum is dead?" or "Is she going to be able to talk and walk?" Just "Will she tell us who did this?" If I had a dollar for every time one of you has asked me that already . . .'

'Sorry. You're right. Poor little kid. It's just that we really want to catch the bastards that did this to her and her mum. I guess that's why we're all asking.'

'I know,' says Matilda. 'But I wouldn't count on Gabby to help you. She has very serious, possibly life-changing injuries. There's no knowing with head injuries how well the brain will recover, and it could be a long road for her.'

'How's her dad doing?' asks Walker.

'Not that great, I don't think. He's a nice guy, he's always grateful for what we do, which is rare for a doctor. But he does go on a bit about how bad he feels. Typical bloke: it's all about him,' she says, then smiles to soften what she's saying.

'Is it OK if I sit in there with Gabby?' asks Walker. 'Or is it better that I stay out here?'

'Nah, yeah, defo. You can sit with her. Go ahead. I always think it's nice for patients to have company, that they can sense there's someone there, wanting them to recover. I'm sure it helps.'

When Matilda goes, Walker takes the chair and brings it inside next to Gabby's bed. He'd often sat beside his grandmother when she was sick, and he agrees with the nurse. There's something healing about it, for both parties. If he's going to be watching over Gabby, then this is as good a way as any to get to know her.

He looks at her lying there, the machine breathing for her, the sounds and beeps of the medical monitors and her smallness and aloneness in this. He feels for her and all that she's gone through.

'I'm Lucas. I'm looking out for you tonight,' he tells her softly. 'You can sleep, you're totally safe. Everyone here is taking care of you. Nothing bad can happen.'

He sits, thinking of Grandma, missing her wisdom, her smile and her hugs. He talks with her a little, tells her that he misses her, but hears only silence in reply. Then he thinks of Grace and smiles. He's looking forward to showing her Sydney and Caloodie.

'You remind me of my sister Grace when she was your age,' he tells Gabby. 'She also has blonde hair like you. Grace is coming to visit me. Maybe when you get better, you can meet her.'

Whenever Matilda comes back in, he stands and gives her space and waits outside the door. At this time of the night, this part of the hospital is not busy, only the soft tread of nurses and occasional doctors or orderlies. No visitors, no press, nothing suspicious. There's a vending machine just outside the room and he buys a Cherry Ripe to keep him going. When he gets back into the room he tells Gabby: 'I reckon you like chocolate too.' Her room is filled with soft toys and big cards and boxes and boxes of chocolates. Gifts from friends and well-wishers. 'When you get better you're going to have to share these, otherwise your teeth will fall out from all that sugar. Maybe you can share them with me. My favourite is Cherry Ripe, but I'll eat any of them, really.'

Around 4 a.m., he gets a coffee from the vending machine, but it tastes so bad that after a couple of sips he bins it. Matilda takes pity on him. 'We've got filter coffee in the staff room. I can bring you one if you like.'

'That'd be ace,' says Walker.

When she brings it to him, the scent of the coffee is strong in the small room, so he takes the chair back to the hallway to drink it.

'I'm going to sit outside now but I'm still looking out for you,' he says to Gabby from the foot of her bed. 'You're safe now. We are going to find the bad guys that did this, I promise. We are going to find them and lock them away.'

Chapter 10

Walker is under the beachside shower, washing salt and sand from his skin. He's only had a few hours' sleep after his shift at the hospital, but he forced himself to get up and head out, a swim more reviving than an extra hour in bed. The water of the shower is cold and fresh after the balmy ocean. The waves are low today, the water warm, salty and inviting. He put on his goggles and struck out beyond the break before turning and swimming perpendicular to the beach. It's harder than swimming in the pool – no black line to guide you, no mindless turning and turning again until your arms feel heavy and your chest tight. Here, on the rolling water, you have to keep an eye on your direction and watch that the waves aren't pulling you back in to shore. But today the surf was gentle, and the water and the exercise have cleared his head, washed the tiredness away. He'd let the Gabby Owen case run through his mind as he swam. He's not working on it officially and he needs to focus on solving this Matt Monroe killing, but he feels for the little girl and wants to see if there's anything he can do to help.

He stands drying himself, looking along the sand. The beach is quiet this morning. No surfers – the waves not inspiring enough; some other swell, some other beach, calling them away – just a handful of older men taking their exercise, marching purposefully up and down the hard sand, their bodies as brown and crinkled as walnut shells.

He pulls on his t-shirt and walks under the red metal arch and up Cavill Avenue towards the gym. The cafés are starting to open, sleepy-looking youngsters in vividly coloured t-shirts opening the doors of juice bars and coffee shops. The streets are quiet, a few locals dressed for work, not in the board shorts and thongs typical of visitors, hurrying along carrying takeaway coffees, but the tourists are still sleeping off their late nights. The only sound on the Boulevard is the hum of a pair of trams as they pass each other, heading in opposite directions.

The gym is busier today – half a dozen blokes, all big and ripped, lifting weights, watching themselves in the mirrors. Dan gets right down to it, putting Walker through his paces. It's the hardest workout he's had since he was injured and he's breathing heavily at the end. He realises he's still a long way from a full recovery. He's exhausted from his lack of sleep, and he'll feel this in his muscles and especially the dodgy leg later. Still, he likes working out with Dan – with the big man's professional help and encouragement, his leg is improving fast. He remembers the constant pain of the first few weeks, the way it throbbed and often bled, the scars leaking and seeping when he tried to put weight on it. It doesn't hurt that way anymore and there's no sign of infection, but the scar is still bulky, red and ugly. He's not all that vain, but he's happy that it's high enough on his leg that his board shorts cover it. He still has two tiny bullet fragments deep in his leg tissue, too, the docs having decided that removing them would cause more injury than letting them be. They shouldn't trigger any symptoms, but he sometimes imagines he can feel them, feel the scar tissue forming around them.

He'd been offered psychological counselling – standard procedure after an incident like the one that went down in Caloodie – and perhaps he should have taken them up on it, given that he's sleeping so badly, with the nightmares and all. But he reckons that being here at the coast, working out with Dan and with a job to get his teeth into, is better for his recovery than talking to a shrink.

When he steps back out onto the street, the weather has changed. The clear blue sky has gone. The air is soupy with humidity, the heat viscous, something you have to push through. Clouds are gathering, shades of grey and black. The pavement on Cavill Avenue is steaming, heat rising as he walks, the palm trees and spindly pines shivering in the wind.

The chill of the air-conditioned foyer at the apartment block is a relief. As he walks across the marble floor, the young receptionist at the sleek wooden desk on the left calls out: 'Lucas Walker?'

He nods. 'That's right.'

'Got a letter for you.'

Walker is surprised; not many people have this address. He picks up the envelope, plain white, A4, and takes the lift up to the top floor. The flat is hot and muggy. He'd left the balcony doors open for the sea breeze but the air blowing in is hot and thick.

He switches on the AC, slides the doors shut and opens the envelope. A note from his aunt Michelle flutters out.

> *Dear Lucas, here is Grandma's notice in the paper for you. So many people came to the funeral that we couldn't fit everyone in the church. It was a proper send-off. We missed you. I hope you are getting better. Come and see us soon, love Michelle.*

He reaches inside the envelope and pulls out a copy of the *Western Record*, the Caloodie local paper. It's been folded open on Classifieds and he sees his grandmother's small obituary. It's a quarter-page ad with a bold black border. There's not much to it, her name and dates of birth and death, *Beloved mother of Michelle and Bobby, loving grandmother to Blair and Lucas, great-grandmother of Zoe and Ruby*, and the date of her funeral. The funeral he missed. He reads it twice, three times, then drops the paper on the sofa. It's not much for a life filled with loving and giving, a life as deep and heartfelt as his grandmother's.

He feels an urge, deep and primal, to be back in Caloodie. With family. At home. The heat out there dry and burning, but the air easier to breathe. Walking in the bush with Ginger beside him, the swish of her tail, the endless horizon, the stillness. He could drive up there now. It's only nine, maybe ten hours. He'd be home in time for dinner.

From the back windows he can see a storm approaching from the hinterland. The hills in the distance are grey with mist and then invisible, the rain like a curtain closing off the view as it moves across the patchwork of houses and creeks, canals and developments. He watches the storm get closer, until big drops lash at the windows and a sheet of water comes thundering down. He goes out and stands on the balcony, sliding the doors closed behind him. The wind lashes the rain against him, a wall of water against his clothes and skin. In seconds he's utterly soaked.

He lets the warm drops pummel him, standing there for as long as the storm lasts. The water works its magic as always. As it subsides to a soft drizzle, the storm moving across the ocean and away, he strips off his wet clothes, throws them on one of the outdoor loungers and pads naked through to the bathroom. He showers under the rainwater shower, dries himself with one of the towels, soft and fluffy and as big as a blanket, then wraps it around his waist and goes to the kitchen to make a coffee, still half-toying with the idea of driving out to Caloodie. The sight of the Matt Monroe files on the table and the thought of Gabby, alone and badly injured in hospital, pulls him back to reality. He has work to do.

Chapter 11

1 p.m.

Despite his intention to focus on the Monroe case, Walker finds himself going through the Gabby Owen files. Cummings's team are pulling out all the stops. They'd started by looking into David Owen, a natural first suspect. But finding third-party DNA, along with Owen's injuries and the consistency of his story, points away from his involvement. Walker notes they've spoken to some of Owen's friends, neighbours and clients too. The reports are unanimously positive: he's 'charming and successful'; 'They're a lovely family'; 'They are always together, they seem devoted to each other.'

The spate of break-and-enter crimes is still the team's most likely lead, and as there's a very real chance the perpetrators might strike again, Walker can sense the team's urgency: they need to pin down the culprits, and fast. Though as Walker reads through the notes on the previous cases, he finds he has his doubts about the crimes being linked. This would be a monstrous turn of events for a group or individual who had previously gone to such careful lengths to avoid violence and detection. His instinct tells him that this was a different group of attackers.

Owen identified the perpetrators as Pacific Islanders and Walker wonders if they might have links to gangs like the Mongrel Mob or Black Power. He spends an hour or so going through the AFP database of known members of those clubs, looking for names whose location and criminal history might make them possible suspects. He whittles the list down to twelve. It would take him a day or two at least to track them down, establish alibis and reduce the list to a more manageable size. He makes himself a round of toast, torn with indecision as to his best next step. He keeps hearing Rutherford's voice in his head and, with the looming review on his mind, puts the Owen case to one side for the moment and turns his attention back to Monroe. He'll go through those names again later. Right now he needs to prove himself to Rutherford, and Monroe is the case that's going to do it.

He tapes photos from Monroe's murder scene on the wall of the second bedroom, alongside the Banditos logo, a picture of Matt Monroe and a question mark over Monroe's associate Jason Cheever, who the local police haven't been able to trace. He seems to have left Hopeville, no doubt putting as much distance as possible between himself and any connection with Monroe. Walker also pins up pictures of Monroe's missing car, his mother Tina and her boyfriend Stefan Markovich. That's pretty much all he has.

An email has come into his inbox from Cummings, with Tina Monroe's interview attached. When Walker met Tina during his last case she'd seemed confident, bolshie even, but the notes from the constable who spoke with her this time indicate she was angry and tearful, breaking down regularly. Walker reads her interview transcript:

Kelly, Matty's girlfriend, told me on Monday arvo that Matty was on his way to a business meeting. She reckons she didn't know where he was going or who he was meeting. She's a stupid bint. Whatever she's told your blokes, it's bullshit. Matty wouldn't take my calls. He always thought I was interfering. By the time I spoke to him it was late, gone ten on Monday night. He wouldn't tell me nothing, but he promised me he wasn't meeting Stefan. I haven't seen that arsehole since November. He left one day, didn't say where he was going and never came back. We had a whole bloody life together but just like that it was over. He changed his phone number, never called or nothing, that's how I figured out I was dumped.

He dumped Matty as well, that was the problem. Matty used to deal a bit of coke, a bit of meth to his mates, and

Stefan knew people down the coast who could supply him. But after Stefan finished with me, Matty couldn't get hold of him no more, couldn't get any gear. So, I guess he found someone else to buy from. Last week he took out a loan against his house. Borrowed twenty grand, so he must of been planning to buy big. He didn't have a bloody clue. He was just a jumped-up kid. Someone saw him coming. That money that he borrowed? Well, Kelly can't pay it back so her and the baby are probably gonna end up with nowhere to live. And they won't be with me because Stefan sure as hell ain't paying for nothing anymore. But Matty promised me he wasn't meeting Stefan. And your lot reckon Matty went to Ipswich. Stefan never did business in Ipswich. So whatever happened, it had nothing to do with Stefan.

The fact that Tina and Stefan have broken up means Matt Monroe's murder is starting to make more sense. If Monroe had been cut out of the Vandals' supply, he'd have had to start over, try to find somewhere else to buy the gear. Maybe he tried the Banditos and the deal went wrong. Monroe was a mouthy git and his mum is right: he wasn't a big player. Walker makes a note to check if anyone has dug into Monroe's financials. It seems plausible that he could have been killed for his money – there was no cash at all, certainly not twenty thou, at the house where he died.

The ballistics report has arrived in Walker's inbox too. Monroe was shot at close range, from behind. One 9mm-calibre Luger bullet, most likely fired from a semi-automatic handgun such as a Glock 19, was retrieved from the scene. Given the proximity of neighbours and the fact that no one heard anything, it's likely a silencer was used. The ballistics information and Monroe's missing car and cash make Walker think that this is something more than a business deal gone wrong. It has the feel of premeditation.

He's thinking it all through when he hears his mobile phone ping in the kitchen. He walks in to check it and finds two messages from an unknown number:

Hey, this is Grace's friend Kaia

be nice to meet up if you have time, maybe a drink later?

Walker puts the phone down, wondering how to answer. He's not that keen to meet Grace's friend; he's too busy with work, and entertaining a twenty-something stranger is low on his priorities. But if Grace was on her own somewhere far from home, he knows he'd appreciate someone looking out for her. He walks over and opens the fridge door, stares inside for inspiration, pulls out the ham, mayo and a tomato, then cuts himself two thick slices of bread and makes a doorstop of a ham sandwich. He eats it standing on the terrace, breathing in the muggy, salty air. The storm has blown over but the air is still as thick as soup, the sun moving in and out behind patchy clouds. When he finishes eating he replies to Kaia:

hey Kaia, sure thing, how about Salty Bill's on the Esplanade at 7?

That's early enough for it to be nothing more than a quick drink, and near enough to the flat that he can work until he goes to meet her. She texts back a thumbs-up emoji and he sighs. He's really not in the mood.

Focusing back on the case, he calls the real estate agent who discovered Monroe's body, to see if the homeowner might provide some clues.

'Christ, it was horrible,' says the agent. 'Keep having bloody nightmares about it. It's put me off going into empty houses, I can tell you that. The owner was an old bloke called William Shield. Lived there for forty years till he died a couple of weeks ago. His son, Michael, lives down in Sydney. He called me last week and asked me to value the place and put it on the market. It's gonna be bloody tricky to sell it now but. No one wants to buy a place that's on the news for murder.'

The old bloke's name isn't on any system, neither is his son's, but someone with the same surname, a Kevin Shield living in Inala, a

Brisbane suburb not far from Dinmore, comes up with a string of convictions, including assault and battery and drugs offences. Walker pulls up a picture of the bloke and the first thing he notices are his tattoos. One big design on his arm makes Walker pause: a large red V being cleaved by an axe. The Vandals marque.

Walker pins the picture of Kevin Shield to his wall of images and one of a 9mm Luger, too, then runs through the story in his mind once more. Monroe goes off for a business meeting and is killed in a house deep in Banditos territory. He's been frozen out of the Vandals club, so it could be that he was trying to buy drugs and negotiate with the Banditos and something went badly wrong. But the house has a connection to the Vandals and the way Monroe died, sitting at the table, shot in the back of the head with a silenced weapon, tells a different story. Monroe was none too bright, but he had a violent history and enough street smarts not to sit with his back to someone with a gun, especially not in the kind of situation where there are strangers, and drugs and money changing hands. He wouldn't do that unless he was relaxed, unless he knew them and wasn't expecting trouble . . .

All of which brings Walker back to the Vandals. But why would a small-time dealer like Monroe be executed by his own club, and who would benefit from it?

Chapter 12

5 p.m.

She's thirsty, so thirsty. Her lips are dry and cracked and her tongue is sticking to the roof of her mouth. Something plasticky-tasting is filling up her mouth and making it hard to swallow. She tries to open her eyes but they feel like they're stuck. That first-thing-in-the-morning feeling when your eyes are still full of sleep and you can't peel back your eyelids, but much worse – like they're glued shut with superglue. She really wants a drink. 'Mum,' she calls. 'Mum.' Or maybe she dreams it because Mum doesn't come.

Then she's in a dark corridor and someone is screaming, someone else shouting. She's scared, she cries out 'Mum!' and there's a big dark shadow, looming over her. She turns, trying to run back to her room, but the corridor looks different. Her bedroom door isn't there and she's running and running but the corridor keeps getting longer and longer. The shadow behind her is getting closer. It's just a bad dream, she says to herself, just a dream, and Mum says when you have a bad dream all you need to do is wake up. Wake up and Mum will be there. Mum'll bring me a drink of water. She forces herself to surface, swimming through blackness towards voices and lights.

'Mum,' she says again, and she hears her voice this time, a croak, a scratch. 'Mum.'

'Don't try to talk, love,' says Mum, and she feels moisture on her lips: water. The plastic thing is gone but her tongue is fat and raspy and dry. She puts it out for a few more drops. It feels so good.

'Thanks, Mum,' she says, and then she sleeps again.

The next time she wakes, it's quiet. Not dark but not light either. Her head hurts. She doesn't know where she is or what day it is.

She's in bed. But it feels wrong. And her head really hurts. After a moment she notices there's someone sitting beside her bed. Her heart starts to pound.

'Mum?' she says.

'It's Granny, darling. Don't try to talk . . .'

'I'm thirsty. My head hurts.' Her throat burns.

She doesn't know where she is. She's not in her bedroom, she's not in her bed. She feels confused and very scared. She starts to cry.

'Where am I? Where's Mum? Please, I want Mum . . .'

'You're OK, Gabby, you're safe. You're in hospital,' says Granny. 'Mum's not here. But you're alright, darling, I'm here . . .'

She can't think. Her head hurts. Everything hurts. The light in the room gets a bit brighter; it hurts her eyes but she's too scared to close them. Another woman arrives, moving around the bed, touching her face softly. She's not Mum but she has warm eyes and soft hands.

'Hello, Gabby,' she says. 'I'm Matilda, your nurse.'

'I want Mum.'

'I know, love, but I'm sorry, your mum isn't here right now. You're in hospital. You're safe. But you need to keep resting.'

A kind of warm feeling comes up her arm. She closes her eyes. The light is too bright. She's so tired. It hurts. She'll sleep, and when she wakes up again, Mum will be there.

Chapter 13

7 p.m.

Salty Bill's is heaving with people. Walker is waiting for Grace's friend, his mood grim. He has work to do and he'd rather be focusing on Matt Monroe than sitting here with a flat and ridiculously overpriced beer. The crowd isn't his type either – lots of young tourists, not quite schoolies but almost. Though that might suit Kaia, given she's only in her early twenties. Walker hopes not; he'd like to suggest they head elsewhere when she arrives. Try to find a place away from the seafront with decent beer and a more local crowd.

A server takes his empty glass. 'Can I get you another?' she asks. Walker shakes his head. Hopefully Kaia will be here soon.

He's looking around, keeping an eye out for her, not sure exactly what she looks like, thinking maybe he should check out her Instagram account. He's not sure what he's expecting. A kitesurfer, Grace had said, so some all-American blonde athlete, probably. There are plenty of young women that match that description here, but he doesn't want to approach random girls like some creep, so he stays seated, half-watching a woman make her way through the bar.

She's strikingly beautiful. Almost as tall as he is, slim but still curvy, her hair long and black and glossy, hanging halfway down her back in a silky curtain. She's wearing a red dress with a side split that offers tantalising glimpses of her long, tanned legs as she walks. She's the kind of woman who parts crowds: women make way for her, men turn to take a second look. She seems confident, walking to a table not far from where he's sitting, taking a seat facing the ocean and pulling out her phone. A waiter is immediately at her side.

As soon as she's given her order, a couple of blokes materialise at her table. They both have big muscles spilling out of tight t-shirts and plenty of tattoos. The kind of blokes he's seen at the gym.

'Mind if we sit here, gorgeous?' says one, pulling out the stool beside her. 'You waitin' for someone?'

She ignores them.

'Where ya from? You're not from round here, are ya?'

'You're a real stunner. Are ya looking for a boyfriend?'

Walker sees her shoulders tense and she turns in his direction, putting her back to the men at her table, still looking at her phone, typing a message. She's younger than he thought, early to mid-twenties, probably.

'Don't be like that, luv,' says one of the blokes. 'Can I buy ya a drink?' He puts his hand on her shoulder.

She turns her head and says loudly enough that Walker can hear: 'Don't touch me.' He registers the American accent and finally puts two and two together.

'Don't be a bitch,' says the bloke. 'I'm just tryin' ta be friendly . . .'

Walker is on his feet, makes eye contact with her, smiles. 'Kaia?' he says. 'I'm Lucas, Grace's brother. I've got us a spot.' He gestures with his hand towards where he's been sitting.

She looks at him, sizing him up, then stands and walks towards his table, without a look back at the men behind her. As Walker turns to follow her, he can hear the bloke behind him muttering, 'Bitch.' Walker's icy glare shuts him up.

He takes a seat on the far side of the table, giving Kaia space. 'Sorry I didn't recognise you right away,' he says. 'Grace didn't send me a picture.'

'It's OK. I don't need rescuing,' she says, 'but thanks anyway. It gets boring, being hassled.' The waiter is already back with her drink, something long and clear, maybe vodka and tonic, thinks Walker. She thanks him with a smile and raises her glass. 'Cheers,' she says, taking a long mouthful.

Walker orders another drink – can't face the flat beer, asks for a stubby.

'Would you like another?' he asks out of politeness. She's just got one, so he doesn't expect her to say yes.

'Sure,' she says. 'I'll have a double vodka tonic.' She drinks again and when she puts the glass down it's almost empty. She's obviously more nervous than she's making out, thinks Walker, and this makes it easier somehow, though he still feels momentarily tongue-tied. Kaia isn't at all what he'd expected. She seems much older than Grace, more worldly, more sophisticated, more contained. Grace still has the guilelessness of a teenager, whereas Kaia is every bit a grown woman.

'So, you're at university with Grace,' he says. 'She tells me you're a kitesurfer?'

'Yeah – well, actually, I've dropped out of college for a year. I'm focusing on the surfing, taking a break from studies.'

'That's why you're on the Gold Coast, right?' he says.

'Kind of. I'm on the professional tour. There's a competition further north in the Whitsundays in a couple weeks and I'm here to train some, rest some, drink some,' she says, smiling. 'You don't look much like Grace and you don't sound American either,' she says. 'You're her half-brother, right?'

'That's right. I'm an Aussie but I lived in Boston for a while as a kid,' says Walker. 'You know our mum is a mathematics professor at MIT?'

Her eyebrows go up. 'Seriously? You don't look like a math nerd.'

He laughs. 'I'm not, just my mum. And Grace too. She's a real brainiac.'

'Yeah? Actually, we didn't do any classes together. I met her through friends – sorority nights, you know.'

Walker doesn't know and can't imagine this world, Grace's world, but he nods, relieved to see their drinks arrive. Small talk isn't his thing, and as he doesn't have much in common with Kaia he doesn't know where to start.

'Grace is so cute – it's really nice of her to hook us up,' says Kaia, picking up her second drink. When she puts it down he notices the glass is half-empty again. She's going to drink him under the table at this rate.

His phone pings and he looks at the screen – a message from Barbara in Berlin.

'Sorry,' he says to Kaia, 'I need to check this.'

He opens the message and sees a picture of Barbara standing in the snow beside a frozen lake, everything around her white. She's swaddled in the biggest coat he's ever seen and a thick woollen scarf, both black. The only jolt of colour comes from a pair of fluffy earmuffs in rainbow shades that she's wearing instead of a hat. She's pulling a face at the camera and the message says *my recovery is not so hot as yours*. He looks again at the picture, laughs at her earmuffs and with relief at seeing her OK.

'Is that your girlfriend?' asks Kaia, glancing at the picture over the table.

'No, she's a friend. She lives in Berlin,' he says. He feels that he's being a bit dishonest somehow but he still struggles to categorise his feelings towards Barbara. They were colleagues on his last case, he definitely counts her as a friend, but if he's honest with himself there were times he would probably have liked to build it into something more. Still might, if she didn't live half a world away. He puts the phone back in his pocket.

The bar is getting more and more crowded. Walker's mind goes back to work, to the Monroe case and its links to the Vandals, not to mention the fact that he needs to start checking out the bikies who might have been involved in the Owen case. He'd like to ask Barbara what she thinks about that, too, but perhaps it's better not to mention it, given she's struggling with post-traumatic stress.

A girl pushes past him, her bag swiping the side of his head as she goes by, bringing him back to the moment. People are standing in big groups, jostling against his back, leaving half-empty glasses on their table. Someone spills a drink, just missing Kaia's dress but splashing her sandals and feet with beer.

'Want to go somewhere else?' he asks.

'Yeah, let's get outta here,' she says.

'We can check out The Island's rooftop bar,' says Walker. 'It's only a short walk.'

The minute they climb the white-painted stairs of The Island and emerge onto a large covered terrace with palms in pots, fairy lights and pale-wood furniture, Walker knows he's made a good choice. Lounge chairs cluster in groups around low tables, and there's a more sophisticated crowd here, well dressed and relaxed, and the beers even more expensive but cold, fresh and tasty. A DJ is spinning tunes. As Kaia looks around the space, Walker senses that this is her vibe. He orders drinks at the bar and Kaia finds a table for them in the heart of the action.

They sit, chat, and Walker decides she's alright. Fun, relaxed, easy to talk to, and despite being truly beautiful she doesn't seem arrogant or vain. He catches himself flirting a little with her on his third beer but reins it in quickly. She's his little sister's friend. He's looking out for her, not trying to date her.

The music ramps up and the bar gets busier, people laughing and talking, the noise rising. Kaia snaps a selfie of the two of them. 'We have to show Grace what she's missing,' she says, then goes to the bar and comes back with another round and two shots of tequila. 'Something to kick-start our night!' she says.

'Ah, yeah, nah, I don't think . . .' Walker is lost for words. He's 100 per cent not going to be drinking shots. She's had three, maybe four vodka tonics already – doubles. He's had the same number of beers, and he still has work to do. He's not planning to paint Surfers red, or even pale pink for that matter.

Kaia laughs and downs her shot. 'Come on, old man,' she says.

Her phone rings and saves him from replying. She looks at the number and says, 'I gotta take this', standing and walking towards the edge of the terrace.

He takes his shot glass and tips the contents into the nearest pot plant. He's going to have to close this down when Kaia comes back. He really needs to be focused tomorrow. He looks for her and sees her making her way to the stairs; maybe she needs the bathroom. As he waits for her to come back, he mulls over the Monroe case again. Solving it has to be his priority. It might influence the outcome of his review, which is only just over a week away now, so he'll have to move fast. Then his thoughts go to the little girl lying in the hospital bed, her mother brutally killed, and the list of gang members he needs to check out. Thoughts that make him impatient to get back to work and which suck any last remaining party mood out of him.

It's almost ten minutes before Kaia gets back. He's about to go and look for her when she appears with a couple of girls and two blokes in tow, all young, around her age. As Walker watches them approach, his police radar pings the boys as wannabe tough guys. With their short hair with tracks, tight jeans worn ankle-length and red trainers, they're doing their best to look gangster.

'I met these guys in the bathroom,' Kaia says, loud and happy. A couple of them nod his way, throw him a smile. 'Apparently there's a place near here with a night that really kicks off. Wanna come?'

Walker is relieved to be able to send her on her way with her new mates, though he feels a twinge of doubt about them and knows he'd have gone along to keep an eye on them if it were Grace. But, he rationalises, Kaia is an adult; he's done his duty and she's made some friends her own age, even if his internal radar reckons they might be a bit dodgy. But perhaps they're just posturing; playing at being harder than they are.

On his way home he wonders how well Grace knows Kaia, and if Grace, too, drinks this hard. He can't imagine it – if nothing else, Grace is younger for one and under the legal drinking age in the States. Still, maybe he should dig a little deeper into Kaia's life. Something about the evening doesn't sit right with him.

Back at home, he stares at the Monroe wall with a coffee to clear his head and then pulls up the list related to the Owen case. But he's too tired, and struggling to focus. He debates with himself about doing some background research on Kaia. He reasons that it isn't web-stalking. She's Grace's friend and Grace has asked him to keep an eye on her.

He googles her and finds that she has a glossy and professional website. It lists her rankings: Kaia was the world number one for two years running, winning her first world championship title when she was only nineteen. Walker whistles to himself in appreciation; she is obviously seriously talented. Her second winning year was followed by a very respectable placing of third, but then a year of virtually no wins. *Taking time out to recalibrate*, says the website. Perhaps she was focused on her university course. There is a *looking ahead* to the Whitsundays competition in late March. Nothing anywhere to suggest anything problematic.

The search also brings up a list of news reports. Alongside various interviews with sports and sailing sites, there's a *Daily Mail* story from a few months back: *Troubled kitesurfer Kaia Hale and bad-boy surfer Dillon Trevon split*. The story is a gossipy piece quoting anonymous 'concerned friends' who claim to be worried about Kaia's state of mind after the break-up. 'She put so much of her energy into Dillon that she lost her number-one spot and now he's dumped her for Lilli,' says one friend, sounding not so much concerned as gleeful.

There is a picture with the story too, captioned *Kaia and Dillon in happier days*, showing Kaia with Dillon Trevon, a muscled and tanned surfer with blond dreadlocks to his shoulders.

There are a series of links to stories about Trevon – the self-styled bad boy of surfing – which celebrate his wild lifestyle as much as his surfing skills. Beneath that are a couple of links to other stories about Kaia. Principally her loss of form, which is attributed to her relationship with Trevon. But it is the third link that catches Walker's interest. It notes her disappearance from the kitesurfing scene and speculates that she has gone into rehab.

Friends on the circuit say that Kaia Hale's poor showing in last year's season was largely down to her partying hard with her new boyfriend, surfer Dillon Trevon. Her father and former manager, Rick Hale, has apparently put his foot down. Kaia is believed to be in rehab at the expensive Featherstone Clinic on Maui, Hawaii.

The story resonates with Walker. Kaia had an addictive energy to her tonight – that's what sparked his concern. Not the drinking itself, but the pace, the focus of it. And the dodgy friends she'd made in the bathroom. If tonight's actions are anything to go by, thinks Walker, she's blown her rehab out of the water. He wonders what, if anything, he should do about it, before deciding that it isn't his business. He has other things to focus on right now: keeping his job, solving the Monroe case and looking out for the little girl still in a coma in the hospital.

Chapter 14

Friday 10 March
9 a.m.

David Owen wakes up, exhausted, at his mother's tentative knock on the door.

'Yeah?' he calls out.

'There's a policeman here to see you,' she says.

'Righto. I'll be down in a minute.'

He lies there a bit longer. He hasn't been able to sleep these last nights – the violent images of Siobhan's terrible death flood in the moment he closes his eyes. He's tried taking pills to help him sleep but they knock him out for too long, leave him feeling fuzzy around the edges, and he needs to be focused, in control, when he gets to the hospital to see Gabby. This morning it was 5 a.m. before he dropped off and his head feels groggy and heavy with lack of sleep, his eyes gritty with tiredness.

He needs to get up, go downstairs, talk to the policeman, then go to the hospital, check up on Gabby. They reduced her sedatives yesterday and she briefly came out of her induced coma. She was confused, distressed and in pain, so they upped the medication again and she went back under. He came home for a few hours' rest, but he feels worse, not better. He needs to go back, see how she's doing, but he can't get himself moving.

The last few days have broken him. Siobhan is dead, Gabby fighting to survive. During the hours he spends at the hospital watching Gabby lying there – unresponsive, unmoving – he's constantly fielding calls and texts, from his clients, athletes and coaches, expressing their sympathy, sending condolences. He appreciates those brave enough to talk to him in person. Some are so genuine and compassionate that in his more clear-headed moments he salutes their 'ticker', as he likes to call it. That indefinable heart and courage that makes an athlete great, lets them keep pushing for victory despite the sometimes insurmountable challenges they face. He's been asking himself quite often these last few days if he has the ticker to face this, to get through it.

There's no escape to home, either. The house is a crime scene, roped off and closed up. He'd thought about moving to a hotel but it felt too public, too visible, and the police, too, thought it would be safer if he was somewhere less accessible, so he's staying at his mother's while he looks for a place for him and Gabby, for when she's ready to leave the hospital. His mother's neighbours and friends are 'rallying round', as she says, bringing enough food to feed them for weeks – chicken casseroles, lasagnes and pasta bakes, cakes and biscuits – and while some have pressed their offering into his hands and simply walked away, others insist on staying, on accepting his mother's cups of tea, slices of cake. He can see them soaking up the atmosphere, sense their curiosity, the ghoulishness of it.

'So *awful*,' they say, and: 'It's unbelievable that this kind of thing could happen, *here*, on our doorstep.'

'How *are* you?' they ask with sad faces. 'How is poor little Gabby doing?'

'They must have been on drugs,' they offer. 'So much of it around – all the young ones are off their heads these days on god knows what.'

His mother seems to enjoy the attention but he's exhausted, stunned, grieving, and he rages at their morbid curiosity, their feeding on his loss. Usually he leaves the room to avoid them. He tries to rest, but his bedroom, the same one he had as a child, closes in on him, claustrophobic with memories. It's a guest room now with floral wallpaper and a double bed with chintzy covers, but it's still redolent with the frustrations and poverty of ambition that seeped through the house and infuriated and alienated him from his teens onwards. His parents had emigrated from Britain in the 1960s as Ten-Pound Poms. It was the biggest decision they'd ever made, the only risk they'd ever taken. His father, dead now five years, had been a mild-mannered man, thoroughly lacking in get-up-and-go. In his first week in Australia he'd found work running the payroll at a local construction company and had done the same job for thirty-eight years, 'man and boy', as he'd infuriatingly say, as if his lack of drive had something to commend it. His mother had thought she was better than their neighbours because she came from the old country – put on airs and graces as if she had more class than the Aussie mums, even though their house was the smallest on the street.

He'd gotten out as soon as he could, a scholarship to a boarding school, then university. He'd had to fight every step of the way, first to qualify in sports medicine, then to build his practice and attract the right athletes. He'd done it but it had taken work, hard work, and every ounce of his famous charm. When he'd grown his business big enough, made his first couple of million, he'd come back to the Gold Coast, Siobhan and Gabby in tow, and shown his parents what real success looked like. But now his house is a crime scene, Siobhan is gone, Gabby is fighting for her life in hospital and he's back here, drinking cups of tea surrounded by the wreckage of his life. It's like a nightmare that won't end.

When DI Ernie Cummings arrives at the house in Burleigh Heads where Owen is staying, he notes how much less impressive, how much more suburban it is than Owen's mansion. A small bungalow on a subdivided block, the house is 1950s, brick and a good twenty-five-minute walk away from the water. There's a small garden with a sandy, dry lawn ringed by flower beds filled with orange and yellow chrysanthemums, the blooms fading and wilted in the heat. Owen's moved a long way up in the world, thinks Cummings.

He's come himself to meet with Owen, rather than send one of his team, because he wants to take a better look at him, get a measure of the man. The evidence suggests Owen is innocent of the murder of his wife, but Cummings feels it would be remiss of him not to speak with Owen himself at least once, see how he's dealing with his wife's death.

An older woman, slim with grey hair, wearing white trousers

and a floral blouse, answers his knock at the door. 'I'm Susan Owen, David's mum,' she says, leading him into a living room. 'Would you like a cup of tea?'

Cummings declines and stands, restless, for the little while it takes Owen to arrive. The room is crowded – a forest-green three-piece sofa faces a large TV on a glass stand, and a shelf unit is filled with photographs and small ornaments. The coffee table has a floral runner and a bowl filled with potpourri that emits a sweet, artificial scent. It's all a long way from the tasteful wealth of Owen's Macintosh Island property and Cummings again finds himself admiring the man's obvious work ethic and ambition. And shaking his head once more at the brutal and unwarranted violence Owen and his family have been subjected to.

'Sorry to keep you waiting – I was asleep,' says Owen when he comes in and takes a seat on the sofa that seems too small for his large frame, too low-cost for his expensive style. He's wearing shorts and a navy polo shirt, his short hair damp and his face crumpled and pale. His eyes are red-rimmed. He looks exhausted. 'I'm all over the place at the moment. I spend all day at the hospital and then I can't sleep at night . . .'

'No worries,' says Cummings, taking a seat opposite Owen and placing a printout on the coffee table between them. 'How is Gabby doing?' The little girl has touched his heart and the rest of his team too.

'She's still in a critical condition in intensive care,' says Owen. 'But the medical team are cautiously hopeful that she's going to pull through. She's a real little battler.'

Cummings nods. 'Well, I won't take up too much of your time here. I just wanted to ask you a bit more about this series of text messages that we found on your phone.'

As Owen looks at the piece of paper on the coffee table, Cummings takes another opportunity to assess him. Owen is tall, six-two, and fit. He is broad-shouldered, blond and tanned – the tan of wealth, of time spent in the sun by choice, rather than the hardened skin of a man who works outdoors. His shorts and shirt are both Ralph Lauren. He looks beat, grieving, but he exudes a wealth and confidence that doesn't belong in this cluttered room.

'I'd forgotten about these,' says Owen. 'Or put them out of my mind, is probably more accurate.'

He's looking at a handful of messages from an unknown number, spread over a period of hours on a Thursday two months ago.

14.10: *She was only 25. She had everything to live for. You destroyed our family.*

16.25: *You killed our girl she was the light of everyone's life and u signed her life away for a few bucks how can u live with yourself u piece of shit*

18.50: *u still have your little girl we r all alone dont think we r going to let this pass u will get yrs*

21.00: *u will pay for what u did to us u fucking bastard*

Owen's shoulders slump and he rubs his hand across his forehead. 'I don't know exactly who sent these but . . .' He stops for a moment. 'An athlete that I was working with, a very promising young basketballer, she played for the Brisbane Capitals, the women's NBL team and for Australia, and had just signed a big-dollar contract with a professional American team. Very bright future ahead of her. She tragically died on court during a game in December. Rebecca Latu? Maybe you heard about it? Heart attack. Shocking and rare and totally unexpected. She only had a couple of games left on her contract with the team here in Queensland before heading to the US, and they wanted to get the most out of her before she left. She made such a difference to their stats – they'd never be in the play-offs without her. That day, she'd been complaining about feeling unwell so they asked me to check her over. I found nothing wrong, and I signed her off to play. Tragically that was the wrong decision, but there was no way . . . I was cleared of any wrongdoing in the medical tribunal that followed her death, but her family blame me. I assumed these messages came from one of them – they were sent on the day the tribunal findings came in.'

'Have you heard any more from them since you received these messages?'

'Not directly but they've been making my life quite difficult. They've written to the medical board asking for me to be struck off and made a formal complaint against me to the Australian Institute of Sport. They've been holding protests outside the Capitals' games, too, with banners calling me and the team management murderers . . .' Owen sighs. 'It happens in situations like this. It's understandable. A tragedy like that, people want answers. They want someone to blame.'

Cummings thinks Owen has a more forgiving attitude than he might have in the same situation. 'Did you report these messages when you received them?'

'No. I talked it over with the Capitals management and we felt it wouldn't help to involve the police. There was enough bad publicity around all this already. The Capitals reached out to her family and they never contacted me again, so I assumed it was all in hand.' Owen stops, bites his lip, looks at Cummings. 'You don't think her family had anything to do with what happened to Siobhan – to us – do you?'

'Well, there's definitely motive. And given that it was your wife that was killed, and Gabby that was injured, leaving you to mourn in the way this family is clearly mourning . . . it could fit.'

'No! Surely not. They wouldn't take it this far.'

'Are they the only people in your life that hold a grudge against you? Against your wife?'

Owen looks offended. 'This is very much a terrible one-off case. I've worked with hundreds of athletes during my career, and I've always had great relationships. Most of my clients are long-term and word of mouth.'

'Do you know Rebecca Latu's family? Would you recognise them?'

'I've seen them at the protests but I don't know them, not really, no. But I know they're Tongan, and I thought the blokes who attacked me had an Islander accent.' Owen pauses, thinking some more, recalling the night of the attack. 'Rebecca was tall,' he says after a moment. 'And her brothers are big men too. The blokes in the house that night . . . well, they were both built like brick shithouses. But . . . no.

I can't believe the Latus would take it this far. Would they?' Owen looks horrified.

Cummings shares his horror but he feels a surge of adrenaline too. This is the lead they've been looking for. They might have found the men responsible for this terrible crime.

Chapter 15

12 p.m.

Walker had woken with a bit of a hangover and, with work on his mind, had skipped the ocean and the gym and taken a swim in the pool at the back of the apartment block instead. The shade of the building keeps the water pleasantly cool and with the beach so close, no one else seems to use it. Narrow and around fifteen metres in length, it's designed for lap swimming. It's a bit short to lose himself in the meditative routine of forging up and down but he'd swum until his leg protested, and had felt refreshed and clear-headed afterwards.

He's been working the Monroe case but has hit mostly brick walls. Monroe's car hasn't been found and there's no forensic or fingerprint evidence at the house that they can use. His only tenuous lead, Kevin Shield, the Vandals member, did turn out to have a connection to the house used as an execution site – it had belonged to his uncle. But Shield has been inside since before Christmas, doing a stretch for aggravated assault. So he can't have had anything directly to do with Matt Monroe's murder on Monday night, though he would have known that his late uncle's house was empty and he might have told the Vandals that it could be used. It's a tenuous connection, and there's still the question of why they'd murder Monroe – insignificant and one of their own.

He decides to call Rutherford. Normally he wouldn't contact his boss unless there was something more interesting to report but he wants to tick every box with this case.

'There's a possible link to the Vandals with this murder,' he says, updating Rutherford on his findings. 'But I can't work out why they'd want to execute him.'

'That fits with our intel,' says Rutherford. 'We think Stefan Markovich ordered the hit, that he thought Monroe wasn't reliable. If we can get proof of Markovich's involvement, some kind of link that means we could pull him in, that would be a very good result.'

'Righto,' says Walker. It's helpful to know, but he wonders why Rutherford didn't share this earlier. Perhaps it's new info.

'Are you doing the legwork on this case, then?' asks Rutherford.

'Nah, yeah, I'm helping out, that's all.'

'You've recovered well enough for that?'

'Yeah, it's mostly desk work . . .'

'Righto. Well, don't let them make you shoulder the whole case,' says Rutherford. 'It's their bloody responsibility, not ours' – and hangs up.

Walker moves back to look at his case board. If Markovich had ordered Monroe's death, it makes sense that he wouldn't have him killed in Vandals territory, but he needs to find a way of proving it. He only has half an hour before he has to be back for the last afternoon of his training programme – not time enough to get his teeth into anything – so he clicks on the Gabby Owen case files for an update instead. He's happy to see that Cummings's team seem to have made a real breakthrough. Threatening WhatsApp messages from the family of a former client of Owen's who fit the profile of the offenders. It's a big development.

After he's wrapped up his final lecture on the training course, he walks home, looking at the ocean, wondering if he should have a swim, but decides on impulse to jump in the ute and drive over to visit Craig and Jess instead. He wants to see how they're getting on and if there's anything he can do for them. He knows the Owen case has hit them hard.

'G'day, Lucas,' says Jess when she comes to the door. 'Craig's not here right now – he's over at David's mum's.'

She looks bushed, with dark rings under her eyes, her face pale. Marty doesn't even pretend to bark at him, just runs over, asking to be patted. Walker bends down and ruffles his soft fur.

'Actually, I only came to see if you needed anything, if there's anything I can do to help?'

'That's sweet of you, thank you,' says Jess. 'Do you have time for a cuppa or a beer? I'd appreciate the company. I don't much like being home alone these days . . .'

'Sure thing,' says Walker, following her to the big airy kitchen that looks over the deck and the waterway beyond, where the last light of the day is colouring the sky pink and red. The kitchen's subtle lighting gives it a welcoming glow and the room is cool, cold almost. He feels a welcome shiver after the humidity of outside. He realises again how wealthy Jess and Craig are – the kitchen is seriously luxurious, with marble finishes and expensive appliances.

He makes a tea for them both while Jess sits on a high stool at the breakfast bar, sniffling into tissues from a box beside her, and Marty retires to a fluffy dog bed in the corner. Walker finds a packet of Tim Tams in the cupboard she directs him to and puts some on a plate. The action reminds him of home. Having something sweet and a cup of tea was always his grandmother's go-to, whether someone was upset or just visiting. It's the small things like this that press on his heart, remind him how much he misses her. For the first time since she passed, Walker feels her presence in the room, can hear her saying, 'Be gentle with her, she's suffering.'

He sits opposite Jess. 'Have a Tim Tam,' he says. 'My grandma always says you'll feel better if you eat something sweet.'

Jess nibbles on a biscuit then holds her mug of tea, for warmth against the chilly AC, or for comfort, perhaps.

'Were you very good friends with Siobhan?' he asks.

Jess looks at him, tears brimming in her eyes. 'Not really,' she says. 'She was quiet; she didn't drink much. I found her a bit hard work, to be honest. I often wondered what David saw in her. She was beautiful in her own way but he's so charming and outgoing and she was so mousy. She always looked a bit . . . drab. I really wanted to take her shopping. She'd have been the perfect client – she was crying out for a makeover, honestly. But she looked horrified when I suggested it and said David liked her clothes. As if he wouldn't like her looking a bit more stylish. Craig and David are good mates, so they came over quite a lot, but I usually spent more time with Gabby than with Siobhan. Gabby's a lovely kid and, well, we don't have any of our own, so it's always fun to spoil her. I can't believe they hurt her. Who would do that to a child? She's only eight, for god's sake. Animals. They must be animals.' She pauses, looks away. 'I've been to the hospital, but they won't let me see her. She's still in a coma and they don't know if she'll recover. I can't believe it. I still can't believe this has happened.'

Walker pulls another tissue from the box and hands it to her. She wipes her eyes, blows her nose. Takes a sip of tea. Composes herself.

'I've met the cop in charge of the case,' says Walker. 'He's good, and he's got a big team on it. They're following up a lot of leads and they're going to find the men responsible.'

'Really? Do they know who did it?' asks Jess.

'Not yet, but they will. They'll get justice for Siobhan.'

Jess nods, but she still looks despondent, and Walker thinks about how to take her mind off it for a while.

'How's the personal shopping business going?' he asks.

Jess perks up. She tells him about her first two clients, friends-of-friends who like her style, and the shops that she's taken them to, what they've bought. 'It's the best job ever,' she says. 'I get to go shopping and get paid for it. Honestly, I love shopping so much I'd do it for free, but it's good to have a bit of pocket money coming in. Not that Craig minds how much I spend or anything but, well, you know, it's nice to have my own money.'

They talk for a little longer until Walker, noticing the time, says, 'I should probably get going. Will you be OK – will Craig be back soon?'

'I hope so,' she says. 'I don't like being on my own anymore. What if someone breaks in here? Craig is signing us up with a new security firm. They'll evaluate everything and upgrade it if necessary and they also do regular night-time patrols. I don't feel safe without that at the moment.'

Walker reassures her that the house is safe and secure, but the truth is that Jess and Craig are vulnerable. It's difficult to fully secure a canalside home, and their wealth, and perhaps even their links to David Owen, could make them potential targets.

Chapter 16

6 p.m.

'I didn't do nothin' to the bloke, but you're fucken right, I wouldn't piss on him if he was on fire. He deserves everything he got. All he cares about is money. It's on him that Becky's dead. She told him she couldn't play that day. We was there when she told him how crook she was. An' he just says, "Nah, you're fine", didn't listen, thought he fucken knew it all. I didn't do nothin' to him but I'm fucken happy if someone else did . . .'

Cummings is watching through a two-way mirror as Rebecca Latu's eldest brother Josh is interviewed. Latu is a big bloke, late twenties, well built, his wide neck arriving at his shoulders in a meaty crease, an enormous chest visible under the basketball shirt he's wearing. His solid legs protrude from long, loose boxing shorts and his size fourteen feet are encased in high-top trainers. He has tatts running up his arms and down his calves, and his hair is shorn in an intricate pattern on one side. He's leaning back in his chair in the interview room, his bulk making the lawyer beside him seem weedy by comparison. Siobhan Owen wouldn't have stood a chance against him.

Josh Latu has owned up to sending the messages to Owen in January. 'They had an inquest into Becky's death but it was fucken rigged. Reckoned she died of natural causes. What a load of crap. Me and Mickey were so gutted we went and got shit-faced. I was legless, and I sent them messages to put the shits up him a bit.'

Cummings is flicking through Latu's form sheet as he listens. He'd been in and out of juvie for stealing cars and a couple of break-and-enters, and his sentence was extended, into adult prison, on account of a serious assault while in detention. Since he got out, six years ago now, he's kept himself out of trouble – visible trouble anyway. But when the team had talked to family, friends and neighbours, they'd got a clear sense that Josh Latu was not a man you messed with. Those people willing to talk had mentioned his capacity for intimidation, his short fuse, his rage and grief at the loss of his sister. He's got the means and the motive and he's capable of dishing out violence. Cummings is convinced he's the bloke responsible for Siobhan's murder.

'So you were at home, watching TV, on the night in question,' asks the DS in the interview room.

'That's what I said.' Latu is bored, untroubled.

'What did you watch, then?'

'Mate, you're gonna have to do better than that, aren't ya? Ya reckon I'm stupid enough to lie about being at home and not know what the fuck I was watchin'?'

'What was it, then?'

'It was *Fast & Furious 9* and I was streamin' it. Have a look at my telly, it's got a list of everything I saw on it. I went to bed around midnight and the next mornin' I drove over to my ex's place and took Mariah to school. There'll be plenty of people who can tell ya that's the truth.'

'Mariah's your daughter?'

'Yep.'

'How old is she, then?'

'What's it to ya?'

'Just answer the question, Josh . . .'

'She's seven.'

Cummings clenches his fists in triumph. Whoever did this, whoever killed Siobhan Owen with such violence and anger, didn't manage to do the same to little Gabby. He's pretty sure that means the perp has kids of his own, had some sort of sympathy for the girl that stopped him going all the way, stopped him hurting her the way he hurt her mother. Josh Latu fits again.

'Do you regularly take your daughter to school?' asks the DS.

'When I'm in the mood . . .'

'Or when you need to firm up an alibi?' Latu's lawyer looks like he's about to say something, but the DS presses on. 'But the fact is, Mariah isn't going to help you this time because between midnight and eight a.m. you don't have an alibi. No one who can vouch for you.'

Latu shrugs but doesn't say anything.

'You know this puts you right in the frame for this crime, don't you? From your place to the scene is less than an hour's drive. Plenty of time to go there, kill this poor woman, come home again and take your daughter to school. You've got motive, you've got form. You can see why we like you for this one.'

'Do you have any evidence to charge my client or are you going to keep speculating?' The weedy little lawyer finally summons up the energy to try to earn his fee.

'We have enough grounds to hold your client for further questioning. We've got a warrant to keep him in for another twenty-four hours.'

'Fucksake.' Latu sends the legs of his chair to the floor with a bang and crashes his fist on the table. 'I didn't fucken do it. It wasn't me. Youse can't pin this shit on me.'

Cummings walks down the corridor and nods to the DS now standing outside the interview room. 'Good work. Let him stew for a bit, and let's have a chat to the younger brother. I reckon he'll crack first.'

Mickey Latu is nineteen but if anything he's even bigger than Josh. Wider and taller but weaker too. None of his bulk is muscle: he's plump and soft-featured, his belly hangs low, even his arms – you'd need two hands to get round the tops of them but they're fatty, malleable, not the solid muscle that Josh sports. Unlike his brother, Mickey doesn't have previous either. He finished high school and has a job, working on a helpdesk for a software company. Cummings feels Mickey Latu is the key to this. Neighbours say Rebecca's death has affected him badly: he's turned to drink, he's missed so many days of work that he's in danger of losing his job, and he's frightened off his girlfriend with his outbursts of rage. And he looks a lot less at ease in the interview room than Josh does, his fingers drumming a beat on the table. He'll crack, reckons Cummings, who handles this interview himself.

'So, Mickey, you know why you're here?' he asks.

'Nah, not really. You tryin' to pin somethin' on my bro again? He's given that shit up. He's not running with no gangs anymore.'

There's no record of Josh Latu being a gang member but it's another black mark in the ledger against him.

'Your sister, Rebecca – she died a couple of months ago, no?'

'Yeah, so?' Cummings notes the change in Mickey Latu's demeanour. A tension comes over him; his shoulders tighten, his fists too. He might not have his brother's violent reputation but he's also quick to anger.

'Were you close to her?'

'Yeah. She was six years older and she was like a mum to me when we were growin' up. Mum wasn't around much – she's a drinker, you can't count on her for nothin'. Becky always made sure we had food in the house and she helped me with my homework and shit. She wanted us to do things different. Wanted us to have a life. Not like Mum and Josh . . .'

'Tell me about her.'

'She was a basketball player. The best. She was goin' to the States to make some proper cash. But she had a heart problem and we didn't know about it. This one game, she was feelin' crook, but the fucken doctor wouldn't listen to her, didn't believe her when she said she wasn't good to play. Told her she had to get out there. She died on the court. I was watching the game. I watched her fucken die . . .'

'I'm sorry, that's terrible,' says Cummings.

'Yeah.' Mickey Latu exhales loudly. Cummings can see that he's trying to calm himself down, trying to get his rage under control. 'Yeah, it's fucked up. She had her whole life ahead of her. If it wasn't for that fucken doctor . . .'

'You and Josh are pretty angry with him, with this doctor?'

'Fucken oath. Wouldn't you be? He killed our sister. He thought she was bludging but Becky never bludged a day in her life. She was totally motivated. But he didn't listen to her. He didn't even check her out proper. She's dead because of him.'

'Are you blokes angry enough to attack this doctor, hurt his family maybe?'

'I wouldn't mind bashin' his fucken head in. He fucken deserves it.'

Cummings decides to tighten the screws. 'We're looking for a couple of blokes who attacked Dr Owen, killed his wife, murdered her in cold blood, and hurt his daughter, just a young girl,' he says. 'You and your brother fit the description of the perpetrators and you've clearly got the motive. You're in the frame for this, Mickey.'

'No fucken way,' says Mickey Latu. 'You're taking the piss. I never did nothin'. And, like I said, Josh don't do that shit no more. He's got a kid, he's sortin' himself out.'

'Where were you on Sunday night?'

'Sunday? I dunno. Umm. At home. Yeah, at home.'

'You were at home all night?'

'Yeah, that's right. I was at home.'

'Were you on your own?'

'Nah, nah, my girlfriend Aimee was there. She'll tell youse I was at home.'

'Was she there all night?' asks Cummings. 'If we talk to her, what's she going to say?'

He can see awareness dawning in Mickey Latu's eyes; he looks like a rabbit in headlights, his eyes darting from side to side.

'I never did nothin',' he says. 'I promise youse, I never did nothin' to that woman.'

'We talked to Aimee,' says Cummings gently, 'and she told us that you are angry and devastated about losing Rebecca. That you were drinking that night. That you were threatening to hurt David Owen, to make him pay. That you smashed a chair and punched a hole in the wall. That she got so scared that she left and that when she tried to call you later, you didn't answer your phone.'

Chapter 17

9 p.m.

Walker parks his ute back at home and decides he'll walk into Surfers, find something to eat. Sensing her nervousness, he'd ended up staying with Jess until Craig got home and had found himself agreeing to go on a fishing trip with Craig and David Owen on Sunday morning.

'Dave needs a break, needs to think about something else,' Craig had said. 'Come with us, mate, it'll be good for him and for me. And I reckon you'll enjoy being out on the boat.'

Now, his stomach is letting him know it's time to eat. There's a pub he's seen that looks like it serves good beers and proper tucker. He walks there, orders the biggest burger on the menu with everything on it and a pint of Great Northern, and takes a seat at a high table by the open windows that look out across the footpath and street. The beer is refreshing and the burger, when it arrives, is massive. He eats it all, and the hand-cut fries that come with it, then orders another pint. The bar is buzzing but it's watching the Friday-night proceedings on the street outside that keeps him entertained.

Even this late, the road is busy with slow-moving traffic. A stretch limousine cruises by with a group of girls standing heads and shoulders out of a sunroof, one triumphantly waving a red bra in the air. A pedal rickshaw, its roof lit up with a string of flickering green lights, competes with the fairy lights that all the palm trees on the street are sporting like waistbands. A group of lads, a stag party probably, wander past dressed as superheroes – an Iron Man, a Ninja Turtle, a fat Batman leading a bedraggled Superman by the arm.

When he heads home, replete and relaxed, he finds his leg hurting quite badly. He didn't go to the gym today, caught up in work, distracted. He needs to stay on top of the regime if he wants to get back to full fitness. As he walks slowly along, he thinks about the dichotomy of this place. Families with kids and grandparents sitting at tables outside cafés, eating ice creams or drinking iced coffee topped with mounds of whipped cream. A few steps further, lairy youngsters dressed to the nines queue in front of nightclubs with names like Asylum and Lost Kingdom, and just beyond, right next to the police station, an addict is shooting up while his girlfriend, already loose-limbed in her high heels, wobbles then crouches down beside him.

Closer to Cavill Avenue he feels a shift in energy. The good-natured crowd, the laughter and joshing, is replaced by an undertone, a thrum of aggression, the unmistakable sound of a fight building. A Thai restaurateur and his waitress are rapidly packing up their outside tables and chairs, and a neighbouring kebab joint is pulling a grille down to cover the exterior window. Drinkers are gathering on the pavement outside the bars to watch as a group of men, half a dozen or more, shout and push each other. Some are still holding beers, others have put their glasses down, ready for a proper blue.

'Cops!' comes a shout from somewhere, and the crowd parts for three uniformed coppers, pedalling mountain bikes, one already radioing for a squad car.

Slowed by the crowd, Walker's standing there resting his aching leg when a woman appears at his right shoulder, reaches her hand out and grabs his arm. 'Oi! I know ya,' she says. 'You're that cop. The one that got shot.'

Startled, he pulls away before turning to look at her. He's only met her once before but he recognises her immediately – the blonde hair is tangled, not sleek, with dark roots showing, and her face is thinner, the lines around her mouth deeper, but there's no doubt in his mind: it's Tina Monroe.

'Do I know you?' he asks, playing dumb. He doesn't want her to think he's here for work, that he knows anything about her son's murder.

'Yeah, course ya do. I spoke with ya in Caloodie last year. Youse were looking for those missing backpackers and youse wanted to talk to Matt.' Her voice falters a little. 'My son, Matt Monroe.'

'Right,' says Walker, trying to sound as vague as possible. 'Well, we're a long way from Caloodie now.'

'Yeah.' She's looking at him, calculating, thinking. 'Are ya working down here now, then?'

'Not working anywhere, am I,' he says. 'Got shot, like you said. My leg's fucked. Look, I gotta go. Have a nice holiday.'

'I'm not here on holiday,' she says, her face tight.

'You live here now?'

'Nah, I don't live here. I'm visiting . . . a mate.'

He nods. 'Righto. Well, yeah, have a good one,' he says, and walks off, accentuating the limp, going slowly, hoping he'll convince her that there's no way he's working on anything with a leg this bad. But he curses his bad luck at bumping into her. Tina Monroe might not be dating Stefan Markovich anymore, but he'd bet his life that she still has contact with him, and if there's one person who doesn't need to know what Walker is up to it's Markovich. Though where the man himself might be is an open question. Maybe he's moved down this way, thinks Walker. Maybe she's here to see him.

He walks slowly down the Esplanade towards the flat, the limp more real with every step. The road is busier than usual. Lots of youngsters in pumped-up vehicles are making loops along the parade their night's entertainment. He sees a Porsche Taycan, a new one, windows down, music pumping loud, engine revving. A purple Ferrari with a young guy at the wheel. A Mercedes SUV, with a blonde driving and her friend riding shotgun. High-set four-wheel-drive utes, chromed and shiny, with mag wheels that have never seen a speck of dust let alone off-road duty. All with music blaring, brown elbows resting on open windows, checking each other out, seeing and being seen. Friday night on the strip.

As he approaches the roundabout near his place, the traffic slows. Most of the cars are heading further up the strip but a few are spinning round for a repeat view of the action on the Cavill Avenue corner. A bright-blue HiLux just ahead catches his eye. He stops. The car is the latest model and has a distinctive trim. He'd swear it's Matt Monroe's vehicle, the one that's missing.

He thinks back, visualising it in his mind: the hot dry garden in Hopeville, Barbara beside him, Monroe standing at the door, the vehicle parked in the shade to the left. Blue, the trim, exactly like that, racing-style. The traffic is starting to move, the HiLux slowly accelerating away, heading north. He grabs his phone, takes a couple of pictures, pulls one up on screen and uses his fingers to enlarge it. Good enough, he thinks. He can read the rego – he'll be able to pull up the plate and check if it matches Monroe's.

Back home, his aching leg forgotten in the scent of a lead, he accesses the database and enters the plate number into the system. It doesn't match Monroe's. In fact it belongs to a six-year-old Toyota Camry, a very different car. A few more keystrokes reveal that the Camry belongs to a Gold Coast resident named Adam Hughes, who has a Miami address a short drive away. What are your Camry's plates doing on a possible stolen vehicle, Mr Hughes? thinks Walker. He looks at his phone: 11 p.m. It's too late tonight, but tomorrow morning first thing he's going to go and have a chat with Adam Hughes.

Feeling energised at the possibility of a breakthrough, he checks the time in Berlin. Almost 2 p.m. on Saturday. He decides to call Barbara. She was with him at Matt Monroe's house last year – perhaps she can remember what his vehicle looked like, confirm his intuition.

'Hey,' he says when she answers. 'Listen, do you have a sec? I want to ask you something about a case I'm working on.'

'I'm on my third coffee with nothing to do and too much energy,' she says. 'Please, ask me! What case?'

He fills her in on the Monroe case and she remembers him instantly, as he knew she would. She is a natural cop, one of the best he knows.

'Do you remember his car?' he asks. 'When we interviewed him, in the yard of his house?'

She thinks for a moment. 'There was an old red sedan. And a new blue car, with a pattern,' she says. 'One like yours, with a trayback, but bigger. Higher.'

'Yeah,' says Walker, 'exactly. I think I saw it, here, tonight. A blue

HiLux. I also saw Monroe's mum, Tina. I reckon she's down here because of his murder. She knows more than she's telling the police. And I'm betting it's got something to do with Stefan Markovich and the Vandals.'

Chapter 18

11 p.m.

Tina Monroe is shaking with anger as she watches the curly-haired pig hobble away. She'd been having a drink at Kitty O'Shea's, building up some Dutch courage with a couple of gin and tonics, and had gone outside for a look at the fight that was kicking off. When it fizzled out, she'd been about to go back and order one for the road when she saw him. She recognised the hair first, a bit blonder now than the last time she met him, and then his outfit – moleskins and a shirt that screamed country bloke down the coast – had confirmed it. It was the cop that had fucked everything up. After he'd turned up in Caloodie, Stefan had decided that Matty couldn't be trusted and that he'd better up sticks and leave her behind. Now Matty is dead and she's on her own, and if there's anyone to blame for it it's that curly-haired arsehole.

He recognised her too. She saw it in his eyes. Pretended he didn't know her but then he couldn't get away fast enough. If she was a bloke she'd follow him, bash him up. Beat him to a fucking pulp for what he's done to her and her family. Wouldn't bother her that he's a cripple either. She clenches her fist, looks at the glass in her right hand, wonders if it would give her enough of an advantage if she went for him. But he's too tall, too big, even with the gammy leg. And where's she gonna do it, here in the middle of Surfers on a Friday night? Nah.

But the thought gives her pleasure and then, slowly, the beginnings of an idea. She stands outside the bar, people flowing around her, turning it round in her mind. Yes, it'll do nicely. It might help get her back into Stefan's good books, and it'll see that curly-haired pig get the bashing he deserves.

She leaves the glass on a table and goes to the ladies'. Catches sight of herself in the mirror on the way out and stops. She looks like shit. She digs around in her bag for a brush, runs it through her hair a dozen times until it looks sleeker – well, at least a little less scraggly. She needs a cut, a blow-dry, but she hasn't got the cash at the moment. She puts on some make-up, flips her hair upside down and back again and looks one more time. Better.

Stefan's Surfers place is at least a twenty-minute walk away but she doesn't have the money for a cab either, so Shanks's pony it is. It's a good few months since she was last there – with Stefan, on holiday, living the bloody high life, god, she misses their old life – but she remembers the way without any problem. She's hoping he's not at his big swanky house, the one in the hills. She's only been there once and can't remember the address at all. But usually on the weekend he's down here in Surfers, at least he was when they were together, and she's hopeful his routine hasn't changed.

The walk gives her time to think, which isn't a good thing. All that goes through her mind on endless repeat is Matty, the idiot, driving to meet someone, thinking he's a player but getting shot in the back of the head. Executed. She'd told the cops it wasn't anything to do with Stefan. She's still loyal; she's not ratting him out, even now, even for this. But she can't imagine that Matty would go and meet anyone else. He wouldn't know where to start. And there's no reason to think Stefan wouldn't be able to arrange something up Ipswich way. Probably he just didn't want it happening too close to home, she thinks bitterly – wants to keep the cops away from his business. He was always edgy about pigs, rightly so.

But some small part of her doesn't want to believe that Stefan would do that to Matty – to her. And she needs to know. She needs to know who killed Matty and why. So she's come to the coast, staying with Lisa Grogan for a couple of nights, and she's going to talk to Stefan. She didn't have much of a plan, but seeing the arsehole cop that caused it all has helped cement her intention. She's raging with anger and fighting back tears by the time she gets to Stefan's house.

The place is lit up like a Christmas tree, so at least he's at home. She looks at the house. It's not as big as his other place but it's still bloody lovely, everything you'd want, close to the beach and Surfers nightlife and even a private pool out back. She thinks bitterly of what she's lost, of how he walked out on her and left her without a word. She had everything, and now it's gone and so is Matty. Her heart is beating fast; she has to breathe deep to control herself. She can't roar up there, screaming at him. That's no way to get him to talk – he'll deck her one and close the door.

She slips her thongs off and fishes a pair of heels out of her bag. As she walks up to the door she feels a flutter of nerves. What if he's not alone? What if he's got another woman here? What if he slams the door or his fist in her face? She summons up her anger and plants her finger hard on the bell, listens to it chime, an elegant sound because even the fucking bell is expensive at Stefan's place.

When Stefan hears the bell, he thinks it's the pizza he's ordered finally turning up. He flings open the door, ready to give the delivery kid a heap of shit, and sees Tina standing there. Fuck. He hadn't expected she'd turn up, hasn't really thought about her since he left. He looks her up and down: she looks like shit. Her hair is a mess, sticking a little to her face, which is damp with sweat. Her eyes are red, mascara smudged everywhere, and she's lost weight. Not in a good way either. She looks old and tired and he wonders what he ever saw in her.

'Orright, Stefan,' she says, smiling at him, trying to flirt.

'What do ya want, Tina?' he says.

'I wanna talk to ya. I got some information you're gonna like.'

'Yeah?' Fucken likely. She's come about Matty but she ain't gonna learn anything here. He's bored already.

'It's about that pig, the one that busted youse in Caloodie.'

Stefan's interest perks up but he doesn't let it show. He glances at the wristwatch that cost more than Tina'll make in a lifetime. 'What about him?' he asks.

'Can I come in? It's bloody hot out here and I could use a drink.'

Stefan considers his options. He can't be arsed playing nice with Tina – she's history. But he wants to hear what she has to say about the cop and he doesn't have anyone else here tonight. He can always get rid of her when he's heard enough.

He stands aside and opens the door wider. 'I haven't got all night, so you'd better be quick about it.'

As she walks inside, the delivery guy rides up on a scooter, hoiks a crushed-looking pizza box out of his carrier and, leaving the engine running, walks towards them.

'Meat Lovers pizza for Stefan?' he asks.

'About fucken time,' says Stefan with a growl. The kid hands him the pizza and scarpers quick smart. Probably the fastest he's moved all night, thinks Stefan. The box is warm and greasy and with Tina standing there simpering at him he almost loses his appetite.

'Go and put this on a plate,' he says, thrusting the pizza at her. She takes it and marches off towards the kitchen. They spent plenty of weekends down here when they were together, so she knows where she's going. Stefan follows her, reflecting that from behind she looks the same as she always did, a good wiggle in her hips and radiating just the right hint of moodiness.

While he eats the pizza at the breakfast bar, she pours herself a big glass of wine and stands on the other side of the kitchen. Drinks it fast and pours another.

'So, tell us this story of yours, then,' he says.

'I'll tell ya, but I want some info from you as well. I wanna know what happened to Matty.'

That's what he'd fucking thought. She's got nothing for him, she's here to harangue him about that traitorous little shit. He eats another slice, makes her wait.

'What about Matty?' he says when he's done.

She looks at him with narrow eyes. 'He's dead. Shot in the back of the head in Dinmore. He was on his way to buy some gear and never came home.'

He can hear her voice catch, sees tears in her eyes. He'd never thought she had much time for that dickhead son of hers but blood obviously runs thicker than he'd expected.

'First I heard of it,' he says. 'Who was he buying from?'

'Don't give me this shit, Stefan. Youse are the only dealers he knows, the only place he was buying from.'

He's almost enjoying himself; she was always sexier when she was angry. 'Nothin' to do with me,' he says. 'And I ain't heard nothin' about it, so it wasn't Vandals business.'

She stands there, holding her wine, chewing her lip. 'Fair dinkum? He wasn't meeting youse?'

'Nah, I ain't heard from him since . . . I dunno . . . last year sometime, up in Caloodie.'

'I told the cops it was nothing to do with youse, I told 'em. But who the fuck was it? Who could he have been meeting?'

'I can look into it, ask around, if ya want,' says Stefan.

She steps towards him, puts her hand on his leg. 'Yeah, please, Stefan. I need to know. I need to know why my Matty died.'

He finishes the last slice of pizza, pushes his empty plate away. 'Get us a beer, would ya?'

She does what he asks. He takes a long drink. 'So, ya didn't have any information for me, then,' he says. He squeezes his left fist tight. He's going to clock her one for lying to him and then kick her out. He might still salvage this evening – call Aaron or Wayne and have a few beers, or maybe call a woman.

'Nah, yeah, I do,' she says. 'That pig, the curly-haired one from Caloodie? Well, I saw him tonight. He's in Surfers. He reckons he's not working. He's limping bad, got shot in the leg, didn't he? But he wasn't happy to see me. And I reckoned you'd like to know.'

Chapter 19

Midnight

Matilda is in the middle of her rounds when a scream reverberates along the corridor. The sound makes the tiny hairs on the back of her neck stand on end and she is in action, running, her shoes squeaking on the vinyl, before it even registers as a thought: Gabby.

She can hear the young girl, awake now, calling hysterically – 'Mum, Dad, nooo' – and crying. The policeman on guard outside her room, a pimpled young cop with a ruddy complexion and no common sense, is standing helplessly at the door to the ward, crippled with indecision. Matilda pushes past him.

'Mum, Mum, please – Dad, please,' Gabby is crying, thrashing around in her bed.

Matilda takes the girl's hand, pushes away a strand of hair that is stuck to her forehead.

'I'm here, love,' she says. 'You're alright, love.'

Gabby's not fully conscious, having a nightmare or perhaps a reaction to a drug she's been given, and she doesn't respond. Her skin feels hot and clammy and when Matilda looks at the monitors, her heart rate is too fast. She presses the button for medical assistance. Gabby has only just started improving, but she could be lapsing, having a seizure – any number of possibilities, given the extent of her head injuries.

The doctor, not one of Gabby's usual team, an intern covering the night shift, arrives looking harried, administers a sedative, makes a note in Gabby's medical records and departs. The little girl quietens down. Matilda wishes the policeman she met on Wednesday night, Lucas Walker, was here, not that young bloke out front. Walker is that bit older and more caring – he'd even sat in the room with Gabby.

She takes a few minutes herself to sit with her. If Gabby were her daughter, she would be here all day every day and all night every night. But Gabby's father usually doesn't spend the night. He's a doctor, so perhaps he has faith in the team. Or his grief, the loss of his wife, is all too much. In fairness he probably needs his rest and recovery. The day team tell her that he's always there in the morning for the medical conference, listening, asking questions, involved in the decisions, and that he spends hours by Gabby's bedside each day. The day nurses seem impressed with him. He's exhausted and devastated but is always polite and grateful and pleasant. He's the perfect parent – he knows enough about medicine and hospitals to not be unduly demanding but still stay fully involved.

As Matilda goes about her rounds she keeps a close eye on the little girl. She's slightly late leaving and when she makes her last visit before heading home, Gabby's father has arrived. She chides herself for her harsh judgement earlier. It's just gone 6 a.m. and he's standing at the foot of the bed reading Gabby's medical notes when Matilda comes in. He looks exhausted, dark rings under his eyes, lines deep on his forehead, but he's still a handsome man, exuding wealth. How is it that rich people always look good, she wonders. Is it genes or the result of years of pampering themselves and not having to work twenty-four-seven like the rest of us.

'She had a disturbed night, I'm afraid,' she says.

'What happened? What were her symptoms?' He has a doctor's voice of authority, not the usual parental fear and anxiety.

'She was distressed. Screaming. Calling for you. Calling for her mother. Her heart rate was up, her temperature too. The doctor administered a sedative . . .'

He nods. 'I saw that on the notes.' He walks to the side of the bed and sits, touches his daughter's forehead, feeling her temperature, then strokes her cheek and hair gently. 'I hope this isn't an indication of permanent brain damage,' he says. 'Personality changes, increased anxiety and fear, mood changes; they're not unusual after these types of brain injuries, are they.'

It's not a question, and there's no point softening the diagnosis; he's a doctor, he knows already. 'It's possible you're right,' she concedes, 'but I think it's too early to say. She might be reliving the trauma of that night, processing it. Or it could be a reaction to the drugs she's been given. You'll need to talk to the medical team.'

He looks over at her. 'What do you think? You spend quite a bit of time with her. Has she been lucid? Has she said anything to you?'

Now that she's talking with him properly, she can see why the others like him so much. He really listens to what she's saying, and he seems to value her opinion. She finds herself wanting to make him feel better.

'She's still on very heavy sedation and medication so it's really too early to say. Try not to worry.'

He nods. 'Thank you for looking after her. It's only because she has such good care that I can go home and try to sleep for a few hours. I should stay nights with her. I know her mum would if she . . .' His voice trails off. 'It's her mum's funeral today,' he says after a moment. 'And Gabby doesn't know, can't be there, might not get better.'

Matilda feels the pain he's going through; her heart aches in sympathy. 'We're taking good care of her,' she says, wishing she had more reassurance to offer.

'Thank you,' he says again, and gives her a tired smile. Despite her own end-of-shift fatigue, she finds herself smiling back at him.

Chapter 20

Walker is driving down the main highway that runs along the coast, looking for Adam Hughes's address. For the most part the road is lined with houses of varying sizes, their proximity to the relentless four-lane traffic seemingly no deterrent to those in search of homes near the beach. In between the suburban zones are various small shopping parades, comprising mostly of cafés, takeaways and drive-through bottle-os alongside tattooists, beauty salons and a surprising surfeit of tarot card readers. He misses Hughes's place the first time, has to chuck a U-ey when he realises he's gone too far. He's been looking for a house but the address turns out to be a small second-hand car dealership on the edge of one of the shopping districts. A half-dozen or so cars are parked on the forecourt, red-and-white *For Sale* signs plastered across their windscreens. They're of varying quality and age, mostly sedans, and none as high-end as the HiLux he saw last night.

The little Portakabin that serves as the office is closed, so he walks over to a mechanics' workshop to the left and calls out: 'G'day?'

After a moment a stocky bloke appears, wiping his hands on a filthy towel. He's wearing blue overalls marked with oil and grease and has dark hair pulled back in a ponytail. Tattoos run up his arms.

'I'm looking for Adam Hughes,' says Walker.

'Yeah, nah, he's not here at the moment. Should be back in half an hour or so.'

'Righto.'

'You wanna buy a car?'

'Maybe,' says Walker. He gestures with his head at the forecourt. 'Those the only vehicles he's got for sale at the moment?'

'Nah,' says the bloke. 'He's usually got a few more, doesn't have space for them all on the lot. Whaddaya after?'

'I'm looking for a ute. A HiLux, Triton – something like that.'

'Righto, I'll tell him. You wanna leave ya number, he can call ya back.' The bloke leads him into the workshop, rootles around on a messy desktop for a pen and writes down Walker's number on a bright-yellow Post-it. 'What's the name?' he asks.

'Donnie Young,' says Walker. It's a name he sometimes uses undercover.

'I'll get him to call ya.'

Walker finds a café down the road where he can wait for Hughes to call. The TV in the corner is tuned to a news programme covering Siobhan Owen's funeral from earlier this morning. The camera skims over the mourners, all in black on a somehow wrongly bright sunny day. He spots Craig and Jess, Craig looking sombre, Jess tearful, among the crowd arriving at the church.

The camera also catches DI Cummings, wearing a suit and tie. He brushes off questions and joins the congregation inside. 'Police say that two men have been detained for questioning and they are confident they are making progress in solving this horrifying case,' says the news anchor.

Owen arrives walking beside an older woman who the announcer says is his mother. Owen's face is ashen and tired. A photo of Gabby, smiling, sweet-faced, comes up briefly before being replaced by a photo of her in hospital, the same image that Cummings had shown the team earlier in the week. 'Eight-year-old Gabby Owen is still in a coma in hospital,' says the voiceover. Walker thinks of the little girl, wonders at her chance of recovery, lets out a sigh. Poor kid.

The report cuts to a picture of Siobhan Owen, smiling and pretty. She's about his age with shoulder-length strawberry-blonde hair cut in a neat bob, big blue eyes and a wide smile. Gabby looks just like her, only her hair's a little lighter. As the journalist recaps the story of her murder, Walker is reminded again of the violence of her death. A local MP is interviewed, talking about the safety of his constituents, the shocking spate of burglaries and thefts in Gold Coast communities, and the need for the police to put all their emphasis on solving this. 'People up and down the coast are scared. Frightened every night when they go to bed that their families could be next. We need to get these animals and lock them up.'

The picture switches to shots of the hearse arriving at a cemetery and long shots, from an enforced distance, no doubt, of the burial. 'A deeply sad morning,' says a reporter soberly, 'and the question has to be: can any of us feel safe in our homes tonight?'

The camera pans away from the reporter, across to the cemetery, where the crowd of mourners has gone and only one man, David Owen, sits on the ground beside his wife's freshly dug grave, his hands buried in the earth. As the camera pulls in closer, Walker can see that he's crying.

Walker orders a second coffee, puzzling over the Owen case. He can see why Cummings fancies the Latus for this – they have both motive and means – but there's something about the brutality of Siobhan's death, the ferocity of it, that is playing on Walker's mind. He feels his intuition flutter and closes his eyes, goes into himself, tries to interpret what it is that's bothering him, but all he can hear is the sound of the espresso machine and the conversation burbling around him and then his phone buzzing.

It's Hughes calling him back. 'Yeah, g'day. Look, I heard you were looking for a ute?' he says.

'That's right,' says Walker.

'I've got one you might like. A HiLux, almost brand new. She's got a few miles on the clock but I've had the workshop check it out and she's in good condition. You can come and take her for a test drive if you're interested?'

When Walker gets back to the car lot he's met by a bloke in his mid-thirties, compensating for a bald head with a bushy goatee. He's wearing white trainers and a short-sleeved white shirt tucked into pale chinos.

'G'day – Adam Hughes,' he says, sticking out his hand.

Walker shakes it. 'Donnie Young.'

'This is the vehicle I was talking about,' says Hughes, pointing to a blue HiLux parked outside the workshop. It's the same one Walker saw last night, with its bright colour and distinctive trim. He notices there are no number plates on it; the vehicle must be unregistered and perhaps Hughes was taking it out for a spin using his own plates last night.

He walks around the car, nodding and looking interested while Hughes rabbits on about engine size, four-wheel drive and load capacity. He opens the driver's-side door and gets in. With Hughes still talking, he snaps a quick photo of the vehicle identification number on the sticker inside the door.

'You want to take her for a test drive?' says Hughes.

'Ah, nah, not right now. I'm just looking around at the moment.'

Hughes starts talking prices. The figure he names is not unreasonably low, which makes Walker wonder if the car is legit and simply similar to Monroe's.

'It's the kind of thing I'm after,' he says, 'but I need to have a think about it. Chat to the missus, you know how it is. What time do you close?'

'I'll be here till two today. But give me a call if you want to come past a bit later. It's no worries.'

Walker drives straight home and enters the VIN into the system. The search takes seconds: the number belongs to a single-cab HiLux Rugged X four-wheel drive, registered October 2022 to Matthew Steven Monroe, Jubilee Avenue, Hopeville. There's no doubt about it, the blue HiLux on Adam Hughes's forecourt is Matt Monroe's missing vehicle.

Walker calls Hughes and sets up an appointment to meet him at the car lot at 1.30 p.m. He's hoping the workshop will be shut – he'd rather question Hughes when there's no one else around. He thinks it through a bit more, then he sends an email to Cummings. They'll need to arrest Hughes for dealing stolen vehicles and his possible involvement in Monroe's murder. Walker wants to interview him, but it will be Cummings's team that will handle the arrest.

Cummings calls him back within ten minutes. It sounds like he's in a car. On his way home from the funeral probably, thinks Walker.

'Yeah, look, I got your email,' he says. 'Good on ya, bloody good job. Nice to have some positive news to pass on to the super for a change. I've spoken to the Surfers blokes – they're going to send a couple of uniforms with you to handle the arrest.'

'Righto,' says Walker.

'I really appreciate all your hard work on this. Excellent.'

'Ah, yeah, no worries – just doing my job,' says Walker, taken by surprise. Working with Cummings is a pleasant experience. He's dished out two compliments in as many minutes. For Walker's boss, DCI Rutherford, to do the same you'd need to single-handedly close down organised crime in Australia.

Chapter 21

The sun is beating down from a solid blue sky, the shadows of the palm trees sharp and defined, when Walker arrives back at the car lot. There's no breeze and the heat reflects from the concrete and off the shiny metal of the cars. He's got two Gold Coast cops in a police cruiser parked down the street. He'll give them the nod to pull Hughes in when he's done talking with him.

As he'd hoped, the workshop is closed but the door to the Portakabin is standing open and Monroe's car is sitting out front. It's been washed and polished, Hughes obviously keen to get the sale. No doubt wanting to get a stolen vehicle off the lot as soon as possible, thinks Walker. He walks up the Portakabin steps and Hughes looks up from the desk with a smile on his face. A smile that fades fast when Walker flashes his AFP badge.

'We need to have a chat about that stolen HiLux,' says Walker.

Hughes's face goes pale. 'What are you talking about?' he says, but the quiver in his voice gives him away.

'Where did you get the HiLux, Mr Hughes?' says Walker, taking a seat in front of the desk, a position that puts him between Hughes and the door.

'Yeah, nah, you'll need to talk to the boss about that,' says Hughes. 'I just work here. I only sell the cars. I don't buy 'em. I don't know anything.'

'Mr Hughes, the car you tried to sell me this morning belongs to a man who was murdered on Monday evening. I have pictures of the car in Surfers Paradise last night, with a number plate registered to your name. And today you offered to sell it to me. By using and disposing of this vehicle, you can be considered an accessory to that murder.'

'What?' says Hughes, his face paling further, beads of sweat appearing above his upper lip. 'You pulling my leg? Like I said, I only sell the cars. I mean, I took it for a drive last night. I wanted to drive something a bit newer and nicer for a change, so I put my plates on it and took it for a quick spin. But I don't know nothing about no murder. Honest. Nothing.'

'In that case I'll need to arrest you for further questioning,' says Walker. 'As the victim was connected to organised crime, you'll have to come with me to the serious crime unit in Brisbane, where you'll be formally interviewed and charged. As you probably know, there are extremely harsh penalties for people who commit offences within the remit of serious organised crime. There are lengthy mandatory jail terms and you won't be entitled to parole. You are looking at a decade, maybe more, in prison.'

'No, mate, wait, wait,' says Hughes. 'I'm not the bloke you need. You need to talk with Mark Butcher. The bloke who owns this place. You met him. He runs the workshop. He bought the HiLux. He buys most of the cars on the lot. I only handle trade-ins on sales. He's the one with criminal connections, not me. He's a bikie, or he hangs out with a load of 'em. They bring their Harleys here for repairs or whatever. I was here on Tuesday morning when one of 'em dropped off that HiLux, but I don't know anything more, I swear.'

'Who brought the car in?' says Walker.

Hughes wipes the back of his hand across his face. Walker can see the sweat running off his bald pate and down his forehead. 'I can check the name that's on file,' he says. 'Mark gave me a sale sheet this afternoon, when he thought you might buy it.'

Walker nods and Hughes stands and goes over to a high filing cabinet behind the desk. He pulls open a drawer, flips through, and pulls out a pink Manila folder. He sits again and opens the folder. Walker can see that his hands are shaking.

'A bloke called Steven Purcell sold it to us,' says Hughes. 'That's who we've got down here. Steven Purcell, eighty-four Paradise Road, Southport.'

'And this Steven Purcell is a bikie?' asks Walker.

'I dunno, but I think so. He had the tatts, the look.'

'Is that his real name?'

'I dunno, honest. I never saw him before. I don't know him.'

Walker nods. 'But you knew the car was stolen.'

Hughes's shoulders drop and he puts his head in his hands. It takes him a while to answer.

'Nah, yeah, well, I thought it probably was. Mark didn't put it on the forecourt. It's a nice car, almost new, but he was trying to sell it on the quiet to a dealer down in New South Wales. He took the plates off, kept it parked out back. When you turned up today he thought he might as well see if he could sell it. He'd have got new plates, fudged the rego. Most people don't check the VIN when they're buying.'

'He does this a lot, does he? Handles stolen vehicles for bikies.'

'Yeah, sometimes. But it's got nothing to do with me. He has his contacts for that. I sell the legit stuff. My bit is legit, a front for the stolen stuff.'

Walker believes him. Hughes's nerves, his fear, his willingness to talk, none of it points to a career in illegal dealings. But he's mixed with a bad crowd here and he's about to find himself on the wrong end of an arrest warrant.

'I recommend you get yourself a good lawyer, Mr Hughes,' says Walker. 'Associating with Mr Butcher and his friends could end up with you serving some serious jail time.'

Chapter 22

2 p.m.

The little park in front of the art gallery is buzzing with people. The farmer's market stalls are set up on one edge, there are a few picnic tables on the grass and kids are playing in the shallow swimming area in the little ornamental lake. The sun is sparkling from the river on the right and the canal on the left and off the high-rise buildings of Surfers Paradise in the near distance. Against doctor's orders, Dave Grogan has just polished off an artisanal burger. It tasted pretty much like a normal burger – maybe the artisanal part is that it costs an arm and a leg. But whatever. He hasn't felt this good in a long while. Maybe ever. Lisa is sitting beside him on the grass drinking a smoothie; the girls are splashing in the water. It was worth getting shot, almost being killed. Worth the pain, worth the long recovery, the digestion problems that are going to plague him for the rest of his life, if only to get the hell out of Caloodie and land this posting in Surfers.

He should have been off the force, retired early because of injury, but someone up high had given him a lifeline, created this role for him in the local narcotics team. 'In recognition of your heroic efforts,' they'd said. It's purely desk work, managing the team, managing evidence, routine stuff. A bit boring but it's mostly nine-to-five, and on sergeant's pay, with a big cheque for his injury in the line of duty coming too. And best of all it's here, at the coast, with the lifestyle Lisa has always wanted. They've moved into a new house. It doesn't have a water view but it's only a few minutes' walk from the art gallery and the river and a short drive to the beach. The girls like their new school. And Lisa looks at him the way she did when they first met.

When his phone buzzes in his pocket he thinks it's Paul, a new mate. They've been talking about arranging a stand-up paddle session. But it's a number he doesn't recognise. He ignores it. A second later it rings again, and then a third time. Shit.

'I need to take this, babe,' he says to Lisa, pushing himself up to standing, feeling a pain in his stomach – the burger making him pay already.

'G'day,' he says.

'Alright, Grogan, how's Surfers treating ya?'

It's Markovich. Grogan feels his stomach twinge harder. 'What do you want?' he says.

'It's payback time,' says Markovich. 'You got your cushy posting, you got your promotion, you got yourself a life in Surfers. Now it's time to earn it.'

'What do you need?' Grogan says, feeling his palms getting sweaty around the mobile phone. It's all he can do to stop his hands trembling.

'That copper from Caloodie, the Fed, he's here on the coast,' says Markovich.

'Walker? What's he doing here?'

'That's what I need you to tell me. Find out what he's working on. Most likely he's here hoping to finish what he started up north, but that ain't happening. We aren't moving again and we are going to put a stop to him and his bullshit investigation.'

'OK,' says Grogan. 'I'll look into it.'

'Find out who he's reporting to and what he knows. And find out quick.'

As Grogan puts the phone back in his pocket, his stomach feels like it's curdling. He really shouldn't have had that burger. He wipes his hands on his shorts, bites his lip. He's standing there, thinking about Walker and what he might be doing down here, when his phone rings again. For fuck's sake, he thinks, but it's a work number this time.

'Yeah, g'day, Sergeant Grogan, this is Anna Jones,' says a young woman's voice in his ear. Jones is one of the more experienced constables at the station. She's ambitious, hard-working and clever but he doesn't much like her. Sharp elbows, he reckons. She'd be the type to whistle-blow at the slightest offence. 'We've had a call from serious crimes in Brisbane, says Jones. 'We're bringing in an offender for them, someone they believe was involved in a murder up Ipswich way. They found the victim's car in Surfers and apparently there's a drug connection. The duty sergeant thought you should know.'

Markovich slides the phone onto the coffee table and kicks back on the sofa. He's not sure Grogan is worth the money they paid for him – he doesn't have much ambition and he's gutless – but having someone on the narcotics team is useful. Grogan will be able to warn them about raids, pass on intel, keep them one step ahead. Perhaps he'll even find out something useful about this Walker bloke. But Markovich doesn't believe in relying on pigs, even the ones they pay off. He's asked Aaron to send out a message on the club's private Telegram channel, offering a big bounty to anyone who can bring Walker to them. Aaron's posted the cop's picture, the one from his old ID card that the Banker somehow managed to source. The club's members will be on the lookout for him. He won't stay hidden for long.

But the bigger issue is that the cop has followed him down here, found him so fast. Someone must be ratting them out. It might have been Monroe, but that little prick knew fuck all about his whereabouts or his plans. He'd thought about it all night, after kicking Tina out, putting names in the frame and discounting them. It could be someone in the lower ranks. One of those flash young fuckers, in it for the money and with no loyalty to the club, but they don't know anything worth telling.

Tina wouldn't have done it – she was too invested in the life he could give her, the life they were living, though maybe now, if she works out that he had Matt killed, she might change her mind. He needs to keep an eye on her.

The only three blokes that fully know his plans and always know his whereabouts are his closest mates. Aaron would rather die than sell out the Vandals. He has the occasional girlfriend, maybe a kid somewhere, but it's the Vandals that are his true family, his brothers, his life. He does a lot of coke and fuck knows what else, though. Maybe his drug habit has got him into debt and he's making a deal with someone. Markovich puts a mental question mark by his name.

Wayne is stalwart; he was one of the first to stand by Stefan when all the Pedro shit went down and he's committed and reliable. Does a bit of blow but nothing serious. Doesn't have family outside of the brotherhood, no wife or kids bitching in his ear. The idea that he's a mole – somehow Stefan doesn't buy it.

Nick is Stefan's best mate, but Nick isn't happy about this latest expansion and his missus Michelle is a nightmare. They've got two girls in high school and she's always nagging at Nick to spend less time at the club. Stefan would've dumped her years ago. She's probably the reason that Nick hasn't been riding out with them as much as he used to. Given all that, he needs to put a question mark by Nick's loyalty too.

His phone rings, vibrating across the glass top of the coffee table. It's Grogan, calling him back already.

'Yeah?' he says.

'You've got a problem. They've found Matt Monroe's vehicle in Surfers and they've linked it to the club. They're hauling someone in for questioning about his murder this arvo.'

Markovich curses hard under his breath. Why the fuck is Monroe's car here? He'd given orders not to take anything except the phone. Fucking clowns.

'Right,' is all he says. Never give the pigs more information than necessary.

'That's all you've got to say? What kind of fuckwit brings a car that belongs to a dead man to his back yard?'

Stefan wants to deck Grogan, all the more because he's right. 'Stay out of my fucken business,' he says. He hangs up, curses long and loud, then calls Nick. 'Who'd you send to Dinmore the other day?' he asks.

'We got Brains for the job,' says Nick.

Stefan thinks about it. Brains is a professional. He's hard, cold and clever and he doesn't take risks.

'Nah, not him. Who else?'

'I sent Stevie as muscle in case there was any trouble, but apparently it was a piece of piss.'

'The pigs have found Monroe's vehicle in Surfers. They've linked it back to us.'

'For fuck's sake,' says Nick. 'Fucken idiot.'

'Send him to Aaron,' says Stefan. 'He's getting more than a black eye for this.'

'Righto.'

'And if they pull Stevie in for it, he's going to own it and do the time. It's his fucken fault they're on our backs.'

'Yep,' agrees Nick.

'We got a bigger problem too. You see that picture Aaron sent round on Telegram?'

'Nah,' says Nick. 'Don't go on there that much.'

'Well, I got a tip-off last night. That pig, the one that shut us down out west, he's here. He's in Surfers.'

'What the fuck? How'd he know we were down here? We kept it tight.'

'You tell me,' says Stefan. 'I've put a bounty on his head, big bucks for anyone that knows where he is and brings him in. We need to figure out a way to shut this pig down for good.'

Chapter 23

5 p.m.

There's no one home at Steven Purcell's place. No one answering Walker's knock on the closed front door; no vehicles on the driveway. He walks round to the back of the house and finds a disused yard – pale, dry grass growing knee-high, a rickety Hills Hoist near the back door and a pit bull bitch, tan with a white heart-shaped patch on her chest, straining against a chain, her tail whipping in excitement, with that cheesy grin that pit bulls often have. She's so excited to see him that he walks over and strokes her, scratches her stomach, lets her lean against his legs. She whimpers when he leaves and he feels bad for her, tied up and ignored.

He goes back to the ute and waits. He's stocked up with chocolate milk, a ham and salad sandwich and a Cherry Ripe share pack that he manages to finish without sharing with anyone. He can wait all night if he has to. Just after 6 p.m., a little silver hatchback pulls into Purcell's driveway. A woman gets out, wearing black leggings and a baggy black t-shirt, and lets herself into the house.

Walker gives it a minute and then goes over and rings the bell. There's no answer, so he rings it again, keeping his finger on the buzzer for a long moment. This time he can hear steps coming to the door.

'Who is it?' The voice that calls out is shaky, tearful. 'Stevie's not here.'

'Police,' says Walker. 'Open up, please.'

He hears a chain being unfastened and a key turning in the lock. She opens the door a few centimetres and looks out at him. He holds up his ID and she opens the door more fully. She's in her thirties, shoulder-length black hair, wearing lots of black eye make-up that's smudged and messy, maybe from tears.

'Stevie's not here,' she says again.

'Where is he, then?' asks Walker.

She pauses, chewing at her lip. When she answers, her tone is angry, her face hard. 'He's in the Gold Coast Hospital. They beat him up. They beat him up real bad and then dumped him outside A&E. The hospital called me 'cause they found my number on his phone. I'm picking up some things for him and then I'm going there.'

When Walker arrives at the hospital, he finds Purcell in a short-term A&E ward. All of the ten beds are occupied, most with curtains drawn around them for privacy. Steven Purcell is sitting on the edge of the bed nearest the door, fully clothed. He looks like he's taken a proper beating, his face badly bruised, eyes swollen, his nose strapped with lines of white tape, likely broken, his head swathed in bandages. His arm is in a sling and the jeans and t-shirt he's wearing are torn and bloody. A nurse is standing in front of him, arguing with him.

'Please lie down, Mr Purcell. You could have concussion, you definitely have a broken wrist and your face is very badly bruised. It's all going to hurt like hell when that morphine shot wears off. You really need to spend a few more hours here. We need to observe you for a while longer before you can go.'

'Nah, I'm good,' says Purcell. 'When Leah gets here, I'm off.'

'I'm going to get the doctor,' says the nurse, 'maybe she can talk some sense into you.' He turns and pulls the pale-blue curtain around Purcell's bed. Walker steps away from the door to let him pass but the nurse stops and asks, 'Can I help you?'

'I'm here to talk to Steven Purcell,' says Walker, handing over his ID.

The nurse glances at it and hands it back. 'Good luck,' he says. 'Never met a more stubborn patient in all my years.'

When Walker opens the curtains, Purcell looks him up and down. 'I smell bacon,' he says, lip curled. 'Who told youse I was here?'

'What happened to you, Mr Purcell?' asks Walker.

'Came a gutser on me bike.'

'Looks more like you took a beating to me.'

'Whatever. Whaddaya want?'

'You sold a car that belongs to a man who was murdered earlier this week. What can you tell me about that?'

Purcell looks down at the floor for a long moment and says nothing. Walker's about to ask the question again when Purcell looks up and meets his eyes. His face is pale but there's a look of defiance in the jut of his chin, his fuck-you stare. He's aiming for cocky, but he doesn't quite get there; there's an undercurrent of fear that makes a lie of his arrogant pose.

'He owed me that fucken car,' he says. 'I lent him dosh, and plenty of it. Then he wouldn't fucken pay me back. We had a big blue and I lost it. I shot him. I didn't mean to fucken kill him . . .' His voice fades away. 'I took the car and sold it. He fucken owed me.'

By 8 p.m., Walker is in Brisbane. Purcell has been booked and Walker is interviewing him for his statement. The speed of Purcell's confession, the ease of it, took Walker aback and it still doesn't sit quite right with him. Purcell has enough of the facts, from a description of the house and kitchen to how Monroe was killed, but Walker knows he's lying about something, though he isn't sure what or why.

'Do you regularly go to meet associates with a silenced handgun?' he asks Purcell. 'Because that sounds like premeditation to me and I reckon a jury'll agree. You went to that house in Inala planning to kill Mr Monroe, to rob him of his money and his car. Premeditated murder gets a much longer sentence. You sure you want to spend the next fifteen years in the bin? You'll be an old man when you get out. Your life over. Unless there's something more you want to tell me? Like who ordered Monroe's execution?'

Purcell's face goes red; he half-stands from his chair. 'Nah, no way, it weren't like that. Youse can't say that. It just . . . We had a fight, that's all.'

Conscious of Rutherford's desire to find a way to connect Markovich with the crime, Walker puts some more pressure on Purcell. 'It looks like an execution to me, Stevie, and I reckon that's what you'll go down for. You'll be away for a long fucking time. But if you give us some information, tell us who ordered Matt Monroe's execution and why, well, there might be a deal in it for you. You'll do less time.'

'Youse have got no idea.' Purcell looks sick, pale. 'I'd be a dead man.' He shakes his head. Walker sees him make a decision. 'It went down like I said. We had a blue, I shot him, took the car. That's it.'

After the duty sergeant takes Purcell away to the lock-up, Walker makes sure there'll be a doctor on call for regular check-ups over the next twenty-four hours. He doesn't want Purcell claiming that he'd had concussion and been forced into confessing something while he wasn't at full capacity.

That done, he walks up to the homicide team incident room to debrief a delighted Cummings.

'Bloody well done,' says Cummings. 'We've got him and the two blokes for dealing stolen vehicles, booked them as accessories to murder, too. Good for our stats and gets the super off my back for five minutes.'

Walker will take the win, too. Purcell is off the streets, Monroe's murder is more or less resolved, and he's in Cummings's good books. He reckons he'll get points from Rutherford too, especially if they can convince Purcell to implicate Markovich. Let him go to court, get his long sentence, sit inside for a bit, and maybe he'll change his mind about taking this one for the Vandals team.

He looks around the incident room. Even though it's Saturday evening there's still a big team hard at work, but the atmosphere is subdued. Cummings notes his gaze.

'They're frustrated. We're certain it's the Latus – they're perfect for this. I'm convinced they're involved. But we can't break them; they're both staying adamant. We've got a warrant to search their homes and vehicles first thing tomorrow. We've applied to hold them for another twenty-four hours but the clock's ticking. We have to find something, anything, to put them at the scene and we have to find it fast, otherwise we'll have to let them walk.'

'What about that spate of break-and-enters?' asks Walker. 'Any links that way? Doesn't one of them have form?'

'We haven't found anything to link those cases yet,' says Cummings. 'But Josh Latu, the one who's got the record, he's apparently had gang links in the past.'

'Oh yeah?' Walker is intrigued. 'I pulled up a list of gang members with possible links to the Owen case the other day. I haven't checked them out yet but maybe one of them has a connection to Josh Latu. Maybe that's a way in? If you want, I can send you the list for your team to take a look at . . .'

'Yeah, good one, that'd be helpful, ta,' says Cummings. He looks at Walker appraisingly. 'How much longer are you up this way?' he asks.

'Another week or so, I reckon,' says Walker. He'll be staying at the coast at least until his review on Monday week, but he doesn't share that detail with Cummings.

'You working on anything else, now that you've sorted this Monroe murder?'

Walker shakes his head.

'Well, if you're going to have some spare time, maybe you can help us out with the Owen case. I appreciate you sitting shifts at the hospital but I reckon you might have more to offer. Why don't you have a look at the files? Maybe a fresh pair of eyes will spot something new.'

Chapter 24

10 p.m.

The queue for the nightclub is long and slow-moving and Walker is having serious second thoughts. He's back in Surfers, his belly full of a generous serving of pad Thai that he ate at the little restaurant near the gym. He's emailed the list of gang members to Cummings and, with some time to kill before his next shift at the hospital, he'd texted Kaia. She's messaged him a couple of times since their drinks on Thursday, but he hasn't had a chance to reply and he wants to check she's OK.

He's agreed to meet her at this club on Orchid Avenue, but the queue is full of much younger patrons, not one of them over twenty at his guess, and he's fully regretting his decision. Barbara would laugh if she saw him now. He should have gone home and read through the Owen case notes again, in the hour or so before his next shift at the hospital. But he's promised Kaia, so he pulls out the $10 for the door and goes in. The noise and the heat assault him the minute he enters – music pumping, people shouting to be heard, a long queue at the bar, the whole place jammed full. It's hot and sticky and sweaty and close and he's the oldest by at least a decade. He pushes through the crowd, looking for Kaia, and sees her with another girl, both of them coming back from the bar, holding drinks. He follows them with his eyes to a booth in the far corner then fights his own way to the bar and, eventually, heads over with a drink of his own, a tonic water in deference to his upcoming shift.

There are four blokes and a couple of other girls at the table with Kaia, all around her age. The blokes set his antennae on edge again. He knows their type. On the fringes of the criminal world, dealing a bit of coke or meth to pay for their cars, their clothes, their girlfriends.

As he walks towards them he sees one slip a wrap of something, coke most likely, to one of the girls, who disappears towards the toilets.

He catches Kaia's eye and she smiles and waves to him. He puts his drink on the table and she says something he doesn't hear, then drags him around the table, shouting over the noise to introduce him to the group. The blokes nod, the girls smile, but no one is that interested in him. Kaia pulls him down to sit beside her, and leans towards him, animated and chatty. He only catches a few snatches of the conversation but smiles and nods and it seems to be enough. She's full of energy, moving in her seat to the music, but he's struggling to find any enthusiasm for the place or for her friends. When he finishes his drink he's only been there twenty minutes maybe; he looks at the melee around the bar and decides it's not worth having another.

He bends down to Kaia. 'Listen, I can't stay. I have to go and do some things.'

'Oh.' She looks momentarily disappointed, then she smiles and says, 'Just give me a second.'

She slides in beside the guy on the other side of the table. Walker subtly watches as another wrap changes hands and then Kaia, too, heads off to the bathroom. As he waits for her to come back he feels his full age. Most in the crowd are drunk, swaying in the arms of friends, the boys trying to swagger but tilting, the girls as unsteady as baby deer in their high heels.

When Kaia gets back she says, 'Let's go, then!' and he realises she's misunderstood him.

He has to explain: 'No, no, I have to go to work, I'm not going partying. I just came to say hello.' He sees how disappointed she is.

'You're blowing me off! You don't like me . . .' she says, pouting.

'I have to work,' he says. 'Maybe we could meet tomorrow, have a swim or something?' He wants to talk with her about her friends and the drugs, try to temper her habit a bit. It's not really his business, but once a cop, always a cop.

'Yes! I'm going to hold you to that,' she says and, unexpectedly, leans in and kisses him on the lips. Walker moves back in surprise, extricates himself from the kiss. Kaia is beautiful but she's very young – she's Grace's friend and he doesn't have any feelings for her.

'Just friends,' he says, gently. He sees a look of embarrassment cross her face. 'See you tomorrow?' he asks, and she nods but doesn't say anything, and turns away, back to the group.

Outside, he takes a deep breath, relieved to be in the fresh air, the back of his shirt wet with sweat, his ears ringing, rebuking himself for meeting with Kaia. Her kiss has thrown him. It hadn't entered his mind that she would consider him as anything other than an older-brother type. He hopes it won't be too awkward when they meet tomorrow.

He drives over to the hospital and is sitting outside Gabby's room, his mind still preoccupied with Kaia and her dodgy friends – she's a good kid but he can tell she's on a bad path – when, out of nowhere, Gabby starts screaming.

She's in the corridor, walking towards Mum's bedroom door. The corridor is dark but there's light shining behind the door and she knows Mum is inside. She runs forward but as she's about to push the door open, she stops. There's something bad behind there, she can feel it. She stands, trembling with fear and cold. She should turn away, go back to bed. Before she can move, the door swings slowly open and almost against her will she looks into the room. A black shape, monstrous and wolflike, covered in blood, is crouched on the bed above her mum. As she watches, it leans forward, clamps its jaws around her mother's throat. Blood flows, spurts, sprays, and she screams, as loudly as she can, with every fibre in her body: 'Nooo, leave my mum alone!'

The wolf-animal turns. Its yellow eyes stare at her; its mouth is open and bloody, its sharp teeth gleam in the light. With a loud snarl it leaps from the bed and lopes towards her. She turns, starts to run, but her legs won't operate, they don't obey her instructions. The corridor stretches for miles in front of her, the door that leads to the safety of her room is far away. She tries to force herself to move, but her legs are stuck, heavy, she can barely drag them behind her. The wolf is coming, it's coming, she can feel it breathing on her neck, and then, with a single leap, it's on her back. She screams as she waits for its jaws to bite down hard on her head, her neck.

'Gabby, Gabby, you're OK. You're safe, love, you're safe.' She can hear a voice from far away.

'Mum, Mum!' she's screaming. 'Run, Mum! Run! No. Don't hurt her, don't hurt her.'

'It's alright, love, you're safe. It's alright, nobody is going to hurt you.'

She swims into light, a face above her, a woman but not her mum. It's Matilda, the nurse, hugging her. Through her tears she sees a man at the door and cries out in terror. Matilda turns to look and says, 'Don't worry, love. That's your policeman. He's here especially for you. It's his job to look after you. He makes sure you're safe and that there's nothing that can hurt you.'

'I want my mum,' she says. 'Please, I want my mum. I want my mum.'

Matilda holds her close and after a few minutes, when Gabby is a bit calmer, unwraps her arms and says: 'I'm going to get you a drink of water and something to help you sleep. I'll be back in a minute.'

'No! Don't leave. I'm scared.'

The policeman at the door comes into the room. He's big and tall and has a lot of very curly hair. 'My name is Lucas and I'll be here to look after you,' he says. 'No one is going to hurt you.'

Lucas has kind eyes and broad shoulders, and his arms have strong muscles. 'Can you fight a wolf?' she asks him, sniffing.

'I bet I could beat a wolf one-handed,' he says. He curves his arm up and his muscles get even bigger and pop out from under the sleeve of his t-shirt.

'What about a shark?'

'For a shark I might need two hands, but I'd definitely win. I'm a beaut swimmer,' he says. 'Was it a shark in your dream?'

She shakes her head. 'It was like a wolf. It had yellow eyes and sharp teeth and it was on the bed eating my mum.' Tears spring into her eyes. 'I want my mum . . .'

He sits on the side of the bed and holds her hand. 'That wolf – I'm going to find him and I'm going to take him away and lock him up in jail and he's never going to bother you again. The next time you see him in a dream or anywhere, you call out my name. You call out "Lucas" and I'll come and fight him off, one-handed.'

She nods her head. 'OK,' she says.

Then Matilda comes back, and Lucas stands up and says, 'I'll be here all night. Sitting just outside the door. No wolf is coming through tonight or any night.'

Walker is sitting outside Gabby's room, his mind going over and over what he's witnessed. Something about this case has got under his skin from the start. Grandma had always believed in listening to your dreams, in letting your subconscious, your instinct, show you things you might otherwise miss. Gabby's dream is very likely revisiting the night that her mother was killed. He knows there's a clue, prompted by Gabby's dream, that is tugging at his brain. His mind is trying to lead him somewhere, but he can't quite follow the thread of the idea to its source.

As he thinks about it, he realises he doesn't know much about Siobhan Owen. Despite Siobhan being the victim, his attention has been more focused on David Owen and how his wealth or his profile might somehow have invited the attack. He wonders how much the poor kid saw of the attack on her mother and how much she remembers. The fear he saw in her eyes is haunting him.

The doctors have been firm with Cummings about not interviewing Gabby until she's much further on in her recovery. Walker feels for the little girl, what she's going through, but if she can remember something it could help them put the criminals who did this away. Meanwhile, he wants to find out everything he can about that wolf. See how it likes being the one who is hunted.

Chapter 25

1 a.m.

When Nathan Brown saw the picture of the cop on the club's Telegram group, he recognised him right off – he's seen him working out in the gym and knows he's mates with the bloke that owns the place. Before he made a call to the club, he thought about how to handle it. How to do it right. The bounty money would come in bloody handy, but more than anything he wanted to up his standing in the club, earn membership, maybe get to work with Aaron on enforcement.

He knew he could go straight to the top, to Markovich, earn some kudos with the big bloke, but on reflection Nathan decided he'd call Aaron with his info. It turned out to be a good decision: the information made Aaron look good with the boss and Aaron has invited him to the clubhouse, bought him a beer and they've done a couple of lines of coke together. Everyone is asking him questions about the copper and he's enjoying being the centre of attention. But then Markovich fronts up and Nathan feels a shiver of fear and doubt run through him. Markovich is a giant and he's moody with it. If he fucks this up, if he's got the wrong bloke or something, he's history.

Markovich kicks everyone else out of the back room aside from Aaron and Nathan and they sit at a table by the bar. Nathan tells the story again, how he's seen the bloke in the gym, how he's good mates with the owner. He holds it together, keeps the tremor out of his voice, the coke helping fire up his confidence.

'What's this place called?' asks Markovich.

'Iron Fitness,' says Nathan. 'Bloke called Craig Ford owns it. He's got a few places, in Surfers, Broadbeach, Main Beach. They're all about the weights. None of that yoga or CrossFit bullshit. That pig you're looking for – he works out there sometimes. I've seen him once or twice this week, early in the morning.'

'You're sure it's him?'

'Yeah,' says Nathan. 'It's him alright.'

Stefan is happy they've found the cop, but he's not convinced by the bloke that's telling him the story. His well-built upper body slices into a neat waist and then down to puny legs. His biceps, broad shoulders and muscled chest are so overblown that they remind Stefan of Popeye. He's wearing tight jeans and his legs are as slim as a girl's. It looks bloody stupid, like he'd topple over if you gave him a push. Youngsters these days have no fucking idea; it's all about how they look on Instagram, thinks Stefan.

'You reckon we could take him out at the gym?' he asks.

Nathan blanches. 'Ah, yeah, nah,' he says. 'They got security cameras and receptionists and shit so it wouldn't be that easy.'

'What about outside?'

'Nah – um, it's in the middle of Surfers and I've only ever seen him in the morning when it's light and there's people around.'

'If we're gonna knock off a pig we need to be smart about it,' says Aaron. 'Can't go in blasting away.'

'You got any ideas, or you just into stating the fucken obvious?' says Markovich, his face dark. Nathan can feel himself starting to sweat but Aaron stays calm.

'We need to find out where the pig lives and maybe get a bit more info on this Ford bloke,' says Aaron. 'We need a way in, find a way to take him out in a place that isn't so obvious.'

'What do you know about Ford?' Markovich asks, turning a moody eye on Nathan.

'He's an ex-footballer. Bit dodgy. Got a juice factory somewhere – you can get roids at the gym if you want.'

'He deal in anything else?' asks Markovich.

Nathan looks shifty. He's part of the club, so he shouldn't be buying from anyone else. 'I dunno. They reckon you can get other gear there, but I never tried.'

'Yeah, he deals,' interjects Aaron. 'I asked around after Nath called me and one of our blokes makes regular deliveries to his gyms. More than personal use. Mostly coke but MDMA, meth too. Reckon he sells the gear through his gyms.'

'Right. That's a way in,' says Markovich. 'Aaron, dig the dirt on this Ford bloke. You' – he jabs a finger at Nathan – 'find out where the pig lives or where else we can nail him. You don't get your dosh until we get him, so get fucken movin'.'

Tina Monroe is looking at the little plastic bag filled with pale-blue pills that she's been carrying around in her bag since Stefan gave it to her last night.

'Here, a goodbye present,' he'd said as she left the house, throwing it over to her, not even bothering to get up from the sofa.

She'd looked at it, recognised the pills as meth. 'I'm not using anymore,' she'd said.

He'd shrugged. 'So sell 'em, then.'

They've been in her bag, tempting her, ever since. But she needs the money more than she needs a hit. The trouble is, she's never sold gear and doesn't know where to start, and she's staying with Lisa Grogan whose husband is a cop, for fuck's sake.

She decides she'll ask one of the Vandals members to buy it from her. She knows a few of them and they're less likely to rip her off, given her connections to Stefan. She takes a cab over to The Three Arms, the pub that the Vandals use as a clubhouse since the cops closed their proper place down. The locals know better than to go there unless they're connected to the club. Stefan is hardly ever there, so she's not going to run into him, but it's Saturday night so hopefully there should be a few members in having a drink, getting rowdy. There'll be someone she knows and someone who'll buy the gear for sure.

But the clubhouse is quiet when she arrives. Just one bloke behind the bar, wiping glasses, who watches her approach, not smiling, bar towel in hand. Aaron Adams is at a table in the corner with a young bloke she doesn't know. They're in deep conversation so she leaves them to it, orders a gin and tonic and waits. She's on her second before Aaron pays her any attention. He gives her a funny look, but she smiles at him and beckons him over.

'Alright, Tina. Wasn't expecting to see you here,' he says.

Bad news travels fast, she thinks. 'Well, Stefan and me might be finished but that doesn't mean I can't come here for a drink, right?' She puts on a bright smile.

He shrugs. 'Free country, I guess.'

'Look, Aaron, Stefan gave me some gear when I saw him yesterday but I'm not using anymore and I want to sell it. Wanna buy it from me?' She pulls out the little plastic bag and shakes it enticingly.

He reaches out, grabs her wrist, looks at the bag in her hand then lets her wrist go. 'You and Stefan are good, then? No hard feelings.'

'Nah, course not,' she says.

He gives her another funny look. 'I don't want the gear, but Nathan might take it off you. Nath, come here a minute.'

The young bloke swaggers over. He's one of those pumped-up, muscled-up types. Looks bloody stupid, like a floating toy where someone's inflated the top half but not the bottom. She gives him her biggest smile anyway.

'You wanna score some meth?' she says. 'I'll give you a good deal for the whole bag.'

'This is Tina Monroe – she was Stefan's old lady for a while,' says Aaron.

'Monroe?' says the young bloke. 'You related to the dead rat? Wasn't he a Monroe?'

Tina feels her stomach cramp at the mention of Matty. Aaron is looking directly at her, a mean-looking grin on his face. 'Yeah,' he says. 'That's right. But you know Stefan. It don't matter if it's his old lady's kid or not – rat's gotta go.'

Tina is finding it hard to breathe; her hands are shaking, her face feels hot and then cold. 'Stefan reckons he didn't have nothin' to do with Matty dying,' she says, but she hears the tremble in her voice and in that moment she knows he lied to her. Lied to her and bought her off with a bag of pills.

'Matty sold out the club. He got what was coming to him,' says Aaron, his voice hard. 'You should take your shit and get the fuck out of here if you don't want some of the same.'

Her hands still shaking, she picks up the drink in front of her, sculls it, then turns and walks towards the door. Her legs are wobbling, her heart is a block of ice in her chest. If she had a gun on her she would turn around and shoot Aaron right in the face. Blow a hole in that ugly mug of his, the same way they killed her Matty.

When she gets outside she turns left into the car park, leans against the side of the building and pukes twice, bringing up the gins and the beers and pizza she had at Lisa's before she left. A couple of bikes roar in and park up, but no one pays her any attention. She pulls herself upright and wipes her forearm across her mouth, then fumbles for her phone and calls a cab.

In the back of the taxi, she takes the first tab of meth. By the time the cab drops her outside Stefan's house she's flying, she's raging, she's on fire. She rings the bell, bangs on the door, but he doesn't answer.

'Come out, you lying arsehole!' she's screaming at the building. 'You killed him, you fucken coward, and you were too gutless to tell me. He never ratted on no one. You're a fucken murderer.'

Chapter 26

The sun is rising – the pale-blue sky streaked with golden morning light, the air coming off the water soft and cool – as Walker stands on Craig's jetty. He's only had an hour or so's sleep and he's fighting a bone-deep fatigue, but he's forced himself up. He wants to meet David Owen. Maybe he'll find an insight into the case in this more casual setting. He'd pulled up the case files and pored over the injury and the blood spatter reports when he got home from his shift. Whoever murdered Siobhan Owen knew exactly what to do with a knife. It's as if they wanted to watch her suffer.

Why would the Latus – assuming it was them – direct all their anger towards Siobhan, he wonders. Something about it feels off; his internal radar is pinging alerts at him that he can't quite decipher. With Cummings's team focused on finding a way to implicate them – the hope is that today's search of the brothers' homes and cars will throw up traces of blood or DNA or a weapon – Walker's decided he'll use his time to try to understand who Siobhan Owen really was.

Craig's boat is a cruiser, close to forty feet in length, the bow wide, curved and open, with a section designed for sitting. 'Jess and her mates always sit up there, posing in their bikinis,' says Craig, walking up behind him, then stepping past him and onto the boat, stowing an Esky and the fishing gear in the cockpit. Walker follows him on. The cockpit is covered and has an open L-shaped seating area at the rear. There's a cabin below with a small galley, heads and a couple of berths. At the far stern is a casting deck-cum-swimming platform.

It's an expensive boat, but Walker likes that it's clearly seen some use. This isn't a boat for mooring in a marina. It's clean and well maintained but emits the scent of salt, sunscreen and sea.

Craig has brought a Thermos filled with coffee, and Walker is happy to find it strong and fresh. Craig pours two cups and then a third as they see David Owen walking across the garden towards the jetty. It's the first time Walker has seen Owen in person and he looks him over with interest. Owen is tall and tanned with blond hair cut close to his head, wearing khaki-coloured shorts, a red polo shirt, brown leather deck shoes and an expensive-looking watch. As he climbs aboard he nods at Walker and says 'Morning' to Craig. He's freshly shaven and smelling of cologne, but his eyes are tired and there are dark circles curving beneath them. Up close, Walker realises that Owen is older than he'd thought, late forties at least. Much of his face is unlined – the artificial smoothness of plastic surgery, thinks Walker. Only a few small lines around his eyes and mouth and greying hair at his temples give his age away.

Craig passes him a coffee and says, 'This is Lucas, the friend I was telling you about – Bobby Walker's son.'

As Walker and Owen shake hands, Owen says, 'I didn't know your dad, that was before my time with the Rabbitohs, but Craig's mentioned him. I hear he was very talented.'

Craig asks, 'How're you doing, Dave?'

Owen shakes his head. 'Not good. I can't sleep. It all keeps going round and round in my mind.'

Still holding the Thermos, Craig gives Owen a half-hug. 'I know, mate,' he says.

Walker's thinking of the little girl in hospital last night, her terrifying nightmares – feels a terrible sadness for her and for the man in front of him. What Owen has lost, what he's going through, is brutal and horrific.

'How's Gabby?' asks Craig.

'Better, thank god. They're reducing her sedation and the swelling on her brain has gone down. But she's very distressed, especially at night. She wakes up screaming in terror and her doctors aren't sure if it's because she has brain damage or if she saw something and her brain is trying to process the memories through dreams. Christ, I hope to god she didn't see anything. It's bad enough what she's going through. I still have to tell her that her mum is dead. I don't know how to do it. I popped in earlier when I couldn't sleep, to give her a hug, but it's so hard to see her like that. It brings all the horror of that night back to me.'

They must have just missed each other, thinks Walker, but he decides against mentioning his presence at Gabby's ward. There's nothing to be gained by it; it'll look like he's asking for thanks. He listens with interest to the doctor's assessment of Gabby too. Personally, he's certain Gabby had a dream – she seemed otherwise coherent when he spoke with her.

'Do you still want to go fishin'?' says Craig. 'We won't keep you away from Gabby for too long.'

'Nah, yeah, you're alright. My mum is going in today, giving me a break. She'll sit with her, read her some stories – Gabby loves that.'

The sun is brighter, birds flying low over the water, the temperature beginning to rise, as Craig casts off from the jetty and they motor slowly along the canal and into the Nerang River and past the brightly coloured HOTA gallery on the bank opposite – 'Bloody eyesore,' says Craig, but Walker likes it. It adds a bit of personality to an otherwise bland residential area. On each side of the river are houses, some grand and extensive, others more suburban in scale, playing at being mansions. The design of favour is a rectangular cube over two levels with lots of glass. The backs of the plots are virtually identical – a deck with dining table and chairs, and, where space permits, a small pool. As they head downriver the houses get even bigger.

'This is where I live, where it happened,' says Owen to Walker, pointing to their right. 'Just behind these places. They call it Millionaires' Row.'

'Right,' says Walker. He figures Owen needs to think about something else, not the house in which his wife was murdered and he and his daughter attacked, so he asks a few questions about the area. 'Who mostly lives here, then?'

'Oh, you get all sorts,' says Owen. 'We even have movie stars.' He points to a house with a roof that looks like a ski jump. 'That's Jackie Chan's place. You know, the actor? We're almost neighbours.'

'Nice,' says Walker, though truth be told he doesn't really like the area. The houses are colossal but also bland and, Chan's aside, mostly characterless. A lot of them look unlived in. Holiday homes, probably. It helps explain why the area is a target for thieves: wealthy people and empty homes an irresistible lure.

They motor under a bridge and past a marina, yacht masts clanking in the early-morning breeze. The river traffic is light; a couple of canoeists paddling along is all they see. As soon as they leave the river limits Craig opens up the engine and the boat rises up out of the water. The wind blows Walker's hair and he can feel the ocean spray on his skin. It's too noisy for conversation. Owen joins Craig in the cockpit and Walker stays seated at the stern, enjoying the freshness of the breeze, half-dozing as they motor east for half an hour or so, directly out to sea. When Craig cuts the engine, the coast is a thin slice of land barely visible in the distance.

'There's a reef here – it's only forty-five metres or so deep,' says Craig. 'It's not really the right time of year but in winter you always catch something – snapper, trag jew, flathead. But even if we don't land anything, a bad day fishing is still better than a good day doin' anything else!'

A north-easterly breeze is blowing. It's pleasantly cool and the chop is light, the boat barely moving on the water. Craig baits and casts the rod for Walker, Owen does his own, and then Craig opens a round of beers for them, ice-cold from the Esky. It's just gone 7 a.m., but Walker's timing is all over the place after his night shift, so he takes one.

Craig works hard to keep the conversation going, rattling on about footy, fish they've caught on previous trips, and the form and prospects of some of the athletes that Owen works with. Owen doesn't say much but he seems to relax as time goes on. They're out there for a couple of hours. Craig is the only one who catches anything, a couple of small snappers, each time shaking his head and throwing them back.

Around 9 a.m., the wind picks up and the swell rises, too. Craig looks at the clouds gathering further out to sea.

'The forecast said there's a storm coming mid-morning,' he says. 'Looks like it might be early. Best we call it a day, head in, I reckon. There's nothing doing out here anyway.'

Walker nods. 'Mind if I have a quick swim first?' he says.

'Knock yourself out,' says Craig.

Walker pulls off his t-shirt, dives in and finds the swell higher and the current stronger than he'd expected. The water is clear and refreshing. He can see rays of sunlight sinking deep into it, colouring it that unique mix of green and blue that typifies the Pacific. He swims for a few minutes, directly away from the boat, thinking all the while of the forty-five metres of ocean falling away beneath him and the fish it might contain. He can't really relax or get into a rhythm so he turns and heads back, fighting hard to swim against the current, which is dragging him in the opposite direction. The boat seems a long way away and he's not getting any closer. He's relieved when Craig turns the boat around and brings her slowly alongside him. When he pulls himself up the ladder he's out of breath.

'Not sure I liked that much,' he says as he wraps a towel around his shoulders.

'I'm not surprised, that's a bloody strong current,' says Craig. 'You wouldn't get me in there for a million bucks. I don't mind getting into a pool or preferably a Jacuzzi now and then, but you can keep the ocean, thanks. There's big sharks out here.'

He revs up the engine and they turn for shore, the clouds behind them gathering in volume and darkness. By the time they're back on the river the rain is coming down, fat drops bouncing off the surface of the water, striking a drumbeat on the roof of the cockpit. They have to run across the grass to the house, where Jess is waiting for them with a breakfast of bacon rolls and more coffee.

Walker notices that Owen's mood deteriorates again when he's back on land. He hears him saying to Craig, 'What am I going to do without her? She was my life.' Walker eats a couple of bacon rolls, fighting to stay awake. He's properly bushed, the nights without sleep taking their toll. When he tunes back in, Owen is saying: '. . . when someone dies you find out all sorts of things about them that you didn't know. Siobhan had a bank account with six thousand dollars in it. I didn't even know she had it. Did you know anything about it?' he asks, turning to Jess.

'Me? No, Siobhan and I didn't really talk about money. She must have been saving up to buy something for Gabby. Or for you?'

'That's what I figured. I always gave her everything she needed so I reckon maybe she wanted to buy me a special present for my fiftieth – it's coming up next year. That'd be the kind of thing she'd do. Give me a treat I wasn't expecting . . .'

Walker is a little surprised that Owen didn't know about his wife's account, though she might have been the kind of person who really wanted his birthday gift to come out of the blue. The conversation rings a bell, but his head is too fuzzy with tiredness to make the connection. He files it away to follow up later.

'I didn't see her family at the funeral,' says Jess. 'She's got a sister in Sydney, right? I was expecting her to be there.'

'Nah, she wasn't that close to her. They'd fallen out and haven't spoken for years.'

'Still,' says Jess, 'she should have come.'

Walker hadn't known about a sister either. He makes a note to check what the files say about Siobhan's family.

Craig wipes his mouth on a napkin and changes the subject. 'I think there's some cricket on. A Twenty20 match. You want to watch it? I've got the seventy-five-inch in the games room.'

Owen nods, and takes another bacon roll. Craig turns towards Walker, eyebrow raised in question.

'Yeah, nah, mate – thanks, but I've got to go. I'm meeting a friend later.'

Owen and Craig disappear down the corridor and Walker finishes his coffee, standing in the kitchen with Jess. He can see his reflection in the windows: he looks bedraggled, tired, out of place in the luxurious space. He needs to go home, catch a couple of hours' sleep, but the thought at the edge of his mind that's been nagging at him is still hovering. Why was Siobhan Owen killed in such a brutal way, while David Owen, the likelier target, was barely injured? Perhaps the Latus wanted to make him suffer by taking away the people he loved the most, but it still seems off to him somehow. Jess knew Siobhan well – maybe she can give him some insights.

'Thanks for brekky,' he says to her. 'But I need to go home and hit the sack. I was keeping watch outside Gabby's room last night and I'm knackered.'

'Really? Did you see Gabby?' asks Jess. 'How is she?'

'She's OK. She's been having nightmares. I think perhaps she remembers something from the attack.' Then, seeing Jess's eyes filling with tears, he adds, 'She's getting better, though. And she has a great medical team looking after her and police protection around the clock.'

'I don't usually do it, but I've actually been praying that she's going to recover,' says Jess. 'Will you see her again?'

'Yeah, I do a shift every few nights, whenever they need cover.'

'Can you do me a favour?' she asks. 'I want to give her something. Come with me.'

He follows her. It's the first time he's been upstairs in the house. She leads him to a bedroom, a luxurious space decorated in aquamarine and pale cream, and through into an adjoining room that turns out to be a walk-in wardrobe, with shelves and hanging spaces on three walls. The clothes are neatly folded or hanging, many in dry-cleaning sleeves, the shoes stacked in boxes. The vast majority seems to be Jess's. A small chaise longue near the window has a black dress draped across it and a big dressing table is topped with make-up and perfume, jewellery hanging from the mirror and spilling from an ornate Thai-style wooden box. Softly lit and scented with Jess's perfume, the whole space reminds Walker of an upmarket boutique.

Jess is searching in a box in the far corner and emerges with a soft toy, a little dark-grey elephant, a bit bedraggled, with a pink stomach and paler grey trunk. 'Gabby loves this,' she says. 'It's mine from when I was a kid and she always played with it when she came to visit. Can you give it to her for me?'

'Sure,' he says, taking it. 'Listen, I was wondering, is there anything to suggest that Siobhan might have had problems with someone?' he asks Jess. 'Someone who disliked her or anything like that?'

'What? No. I don't think she had many friends, let alone enemies. David and Gabby were her life. She never even came to girls' nights out. She only came out if David was there too.'

'What did she do for a living?'

'Nothing. Well, you know, just house stuff. She was a nurse, but she gave that up when they moved up here.'

'Did she do any volunteering or anything?'

'I don't think so,' says Jess. 'David wasn't really keen on her getting a job. He thought Gabby needed someone at home and he works long hours, so I think he also likes being able to come home and have everything taken care of. She's the real mothering type – you know, a great cook, even makes cakes and biscuits and a dessert with dinner kind of thing. They don't have a cleaner and their place is always immaculate. Gabby adores her and she really spent time with Gabby, not just letting her sit with an iPad or in front of the telly or whatever.'

'Do they have any financial problems?' asks Walker. Then he adds: 'Sorry for all these questions – I'm going into cop-mode.'

'No worries. And yeah, nah, not at all. Dave makes really good money. His clients are all elite athletes, guys who swim for Australia or play for the Wallabies and whatnot. Their house is fancier than ours. Although Siobhan still always acted like she had no cash. It drove me a bit mad. You know those people who are loaded but never spend anything? Well, that's her. I remember once, I went over to drop off a casserole dish they'd left here or something, and I convinced her to come shopping with me. She was a nightmare. She'd left her bank card at home, and she had like fifty dollars in her purse and wouldn't have lunch or anything. I don't think she even bought a coffee.'

'And you think they were happy in their marriage?'

'Absolutely. They were hardly ever apart. She said David would text her like thirty times a day to make sure she was OK. Proper lovebirds! Like I say, David and Gabby were her life. And she took really good care of them. I don't know how David will cope. Poor guy. He's devastated. I think he feels guilty that he survived and she didn't. He was such a mess at the funeral . . . It broke my heart.'

Chapter 27

1 p.m.

Walker wakes from a kind of half-sleep, feeling almost worse than before he lay down. The storm that pelted down most of the morning, thundering and roiling through his daytime dreams, has passed. The room is cool, the dim light of the day filtered by the heavy curtains, but he is wide awake, restless and hungry.

He makes himself pasta with tomato sauce and lots of chilli, cracks open a beer and opens his laptop. He's made a promise to Gabby Owen and to himself. There has to be a way to find the men responsible for hurting a small girl and killing her mother.

He starts by watching the body cam footage from the first officer on the scene, PC Anna Jones. He sees the Owens' house, lights blazing in the dark night, the open front door, the sound of David Owen calling out as Jones goes slowly upstairs, her gun drawn in front of her. She enters the main bedroom: Siobhan Owen's bloodied body is tied to the bed, spreadeagled. David Owen is kneeling beside her, also covered in blood. 'Please. You have to help us,' he says.

The video shows another room – a walk-in wardrobe similar to Jess's, with suits and jackets and shirts hanging in neat lines, sports gear against another wall. The video moves again, down the corridor and into Gabby's room. It looks like Gabby is sleeping, tucked up in bed, but when the PC walks closer, Gabby's deathly pallor, her blue lips, become apparent. He hears the PC calling for medical assistance as she rapidly checks the rest of the upper floor: a spare bedroom, a book-lined study with a safe, the door swinging open, a slew of documents lying on the floor, a pair of bathrooms and a small room with only a yoga mat and a big plant in the corner.

The video from downstairs shows a trail of bloody drops leading from the bottom of the stairs towards a living room where a dining chair is lying on its side in front of the sofas. It's out of place, moved from its position at the table that sits on the far right. Four black cable ties lie around the chair, broken and torn. There's more blood on the carpet near the chair. The camera moves into the kitchen, which is in darkness. A light turns on and the camera is still for a moment. The space is sparkling clean – a bowl of fruit sits on the counter beside a bottle of wine and a wine glass. It's a glimpse of the family's peaceful daily life before the intrusion of violence and horror.

He spends an hour or more in a detailed reading of the case files, and when he sees the messages that Owen received from the Latu brothers, he can see why Cummings has them down for this: they have form and they hold a grudge. They are a strong lead, the likeliest perps, but, given the resources Cummings already has focused on them, Walker decides he can add more value if he steps away and looks afresh at what happened that night. He goes back to the feeling that's been prickling in his mind since Gabby's dream – what is Siobhan's story, why was she so brutally attacked? Perhaps there's something in her background that can help him find another way into this case.

He reads through the file the team has put together on Siobhan. She had worked as a nurse and masseuse in sports medicine – that's how the couple met – but she hasn't worked since they came to the Gold Coast. She's estranged from her family. Her parents are dead, but she has one sister, Flora White, who lives in Sydney. David Owen had told the team that Siobhan and Flora hadn't spoken for years. According to Owen, Flora had been jealous of Siobhan's lifestyle, of their happy marriage and of his wealth. She'd been constantly asking Siobhan for handouts, and belittling her – calling her a gold-digger who'd only married for the money. When Siobhan and David moved to Queensland, Siobhan had taken the opportunity to reduce contact. Cummings's team had contacted Flora, and she'd confirmed that the last time she'd spoken to Siobhan was six years ago. She'd been devastated at the news of her sister's death but still bitter that her sister had broken contact with her.

We were close, you know, maybe because Mum and Dad died when we were so young. I was only eighteen and she was twenty when it happened. She looked out for me, helped out with money when I needed it, and I stayed with her for a couple of months after I broke up with one of my exes. But then she got herself a new family, she had Gabby and Dave, she didn't need me anymore and she just dropped me. As soon as she went up to Queensland, that was it. She made out that her life was too boring, that I wouldn't be interested in hearing from her. As if! She had this great life on the coast and lots of cash and before she left she said I could come and visit anytime. But that never happened. I wasn't good enough for her anymore. She hardly even bothered to send a birthday text. And when she changed her number, she didn't even tell me.

Siobhan didn't seem to have a lot of friends either. David Owen suggests Jess Ford is one of her closest mates. Walker thinks of Jess's slightly dismissive attitude and feels sorry for Siobhan. She obviously didn't make friends easily.

She had no income of her own, but Walker notices the personal bank account that David mentioned this morning, with just over $6,000 in it. It looks like Siobhan's been saving for years – the account was opened in 2018 and she's been putting in $100 or so most months ever since. There's no money going out, so she must be saving up for something specific, as Jess suggested – but if it was for David's fiftieth, she's been saving up for it a bloody long time, reflects Walker.

It's also with a different bank from the couple's joint account, which is the day-to-day spending account, by the looks – the balance hovering around $13,000. All the bills come out of there and most of the regular spending. The really big money is in David Owen's private and investment accounts, and there's a credit card in his name with a balance of $8,700 in debit. He pays it off every month, various items related to his business, golf and other sports equipment, a subscription to a wine club, a purchase from an upmarket shoe brand and men's grooming products. Nothing to attract attention, but Walker looks at it for a moment longer. He can't put his finger on why it doesn't feel right, but he files it in the back of his mind alongside his mental twinge from earlier, regarding Siobhan's savings account.

He looks at Siobhan's phone records next. The team has put together a massive file of information, hundreds of pages, ranging from call logs, messages and emails to social media accounts, pictures and internet history, even to-do lists and calendar information. There's page after page of location data too – historical geolocation data, cell phone tower data, Wi-Fi connection information. It makes his head hurt looking at it all. He's wondering where to start when his phone rings and he sees Barbara's name on the screen.

'G'day, Barbara.'

'Hello, Lucas,' she says. 'I'm not bothering you, am I? I've been lying awake for hours and it is driving me crazy, so I thought I'd call for a chat.'

'Nah, yeah, it's all good . . .'

'How's your day going? I hope you are not going to tell me the sun is shining and you have a beach view.'

'Well, I do have a pretty beaut view. The weather isn't too bad but the waves are even better. I'll be going to the beach for a swim with a friend a bit later. I can send you a picture if you like.'

'No thanks! You should not torture someone suffering through winter in Berlin with pictures of beaches.'

He laughs.

'Do you remember our swim in Caloodie? And the barbecue afterwards?' she says. 'Your family were so nice to me . . .'

Walker does remember. He and Barbara floating in the waterhole, the hum of cicadas, calls from a flock of noisy galahs. They'd lain on the blanket in the shade with a picnic, throwing sticks for Ginger. Afterwards they'd gone to his cousin Blair's birthday barbie, everyone there, including his grandmother, the sun around which they'd all orbited.

'Ah yeah, I remember. It was my grandma's last family barbie.' Saying it out loud makes his chest hurt.

'Oh, Lucas, that's right. I'm so sorry. Are you missing her a lot?'

'Yeah,' he says. 'Yeah, I am. I haven't been back to Caloodie. It won't be the same without her.'

'She was very kind and warm and generous. You have a lot of her in you.'

The thought warms him. He can almost hear Grandma saying 'That girl knows what she's talking about', and laughing. 'Thanks, Barbara,' he says.

'I feel a long way away from Caloodie this morning,' she says. 'It's cold and dark and raining here. I'm still off work and I'm really bored. How are you getting on with your case?'

Walker fills her in on the Monroe arrests. 'I'm helping out on a home invasion now,' he says. He gives her the details.

'Poor woman and that poor little girl,' says Barbara. She thinks for a moment, and he waits. 'You say the wife was killed but the husband is OK?' she asks. 'In my experience in these cases the husband is the first suspect, no?'

'Yeah, that's right, but in this case they've ruled him out. There's third-party DNA on the wife's body and he was attacked too. Tied up in the living room and stabbed. They also stole some money and a watch from a safe. And there are suspects who have a grudge against him and who have form . . .'

'If the grudge is against him, why was she the target?'

He explains the Latu story. 'But yeah, I'm wondering too if maybe there's something we're missing about Siobhan Owen that might give another way in. I'm looking into her at the moment, but she seems to be an ordinary stay-at-home wife, no obvious red flags.'

'I wish I was working this case with you. Anything to keep me busy and off the red wine.'

He laughs. 'Nothing wrong with a glass of wine or two. But it would be great to have you here – we did make a good team.'

She's quiet again, thinking. 'Why don't I help you from here? You can send me the case records. You know how good I am with details. Maybe I can find something new.'

'You're supposed to be resting,' he says. 'If they've got you off duty it must be for a reason.'

'You are supposed to be recovering, too,' she says. 'And you are running all over for this. I will just look at the files.'

Walker has to laugh. She never lets him off the hook if she wants something.

'Fair point,' he says. 'But I can't send them to you. That's not allowed.'

'Why? I'm fifteen thousand kilometres away. I'm not going to invade the privacy or talk about it with anyone. I will be a consultant to you. You don't even have to pay me.'

He laughs again. 'Bloody hell, woman, I'd forgotten how bossy you are.' He thinks about it for a moment, remembering from their last case how good she is at following up on details, at persisting with a line of inquiry, not being derailed by others' scepticism or doubts.

'I can't send you the case notes, but how about I give you Siobhan's phone records and maybe you can find something there?'

'Hmm, OK,' she says. 'I guess that will have to do.'

Walker smiles. After he hangs up he shakes his head at his capitulation. Barbara reminds him of his grandmother. They're both physically small but stronger-willed than anyone he knows.

Chapter 28

3 p.m.
Kaia has texted him: *wind is really good I'm going to go to Narrowneck for a sail come and meet me there for that swim you promised.*

He's tired and getting nowhere and a swim will do him good. He leaves the files on the table and walks along the beach to meet her, still thinking about Siobhan. He knows he's missing something but the harder he thinks, the further the thought retreats. He forces himself to tune out, focuses on being beside the ocean, feeling the warm water rushing around his bare feet, the sand wet beneath his toes, small shells crunching underfoot as he walks. The storm has blown in some bigger waves that are crashing in messy curls across three or four breaks, the water dun-coloured from the sand they're stirring up. When he arrives at Narrowneck he spots Kaia absorbed with putting her board and sail together. She doesn't notice him and he watches her, smooth and practised and confident in her movements. She launches the kite into the air, the sail instantly full and straining in the wind as she walks it towards the water, her board under her arm. When she reaches the water's edge she drops the board into the shallows, slides her feet into its grips and lets the wind and the sail pull her up. She's moving in an instant, skimming across the tops of the waves. As she takes off she morphs into a different creature, a being at one with the water, the wind, the waves.

Walker sits on the sand, watching the triangle of her sail, a deep yellow with a fat white stripe across the centre, leap and fly, become a tiny speck far out to sea, then return. He sees her shift her weight, lie low to the water, and the board turns seaward again in a smooth, effortless movement, flying across waves, rising into the air, landing and racing off across the white-capped water. It's beautiful to watch someone so in control, in total mastery of air and water and self. Three more sails, then four, join her, racing each other far into the blue.

In the sunny aftermath of a wet morning, the beach is busy and the rectangle of water between the lifesavers' red-and-yellow flags is full of swimmers. The kids are covered up, wearing long-sleeved rashies against the sun and big-brimmed hats. On adult skins he notices an epidemic of ink. A butterfly on a bum cheek, a dragon climbing across a thigh, a Native American warrior on a bicep. Under a rainbow-patterned beach umbrella beside him, a mother is giving her two kids fruit juice and sandwiches from an Esky, her right arm a sleeve of tattoos. With no tattoos of his own, he's the odd one out.

Tired from his all-night shift, he lies back, letting the sun warm his skin, and drifts into a doze, soothed by the noises of the beach. The sound of the waves, of children playing, people's voices coming in fragments on the breeze, tinny music, barely audible, from a group of teens off to his right. He must fall asleep for he's woken by a shower of cool drips onto his face and chest. Kaia is standing above him, shaking her wet hair over him. She looks exhilarated, her eyes shining and a smile on her face. Her board is pulled up on the sand beside him.

'Hey,' she says, 'are you sleeping or are you swimming?'

He shakes his head awake. Lying in the hot sun has made him feel dehydrated, sunburnt, and he needs to cool off. 'Definitely swimming,' he says.

'Come on, then,' she says, turning and running with big steps into the water. She's diving under the waves and swimming out before he manages to get himself to his feet and jog over to join her. He's a good swimmer and happy to be in the ocean, but she's like a mermaid, half-human, half-fish. The scorching heat of a Sunday afternoon has brought a big crowd to the water, but all the other swimmers are standing waist-deep, ducking nervously under the rollers or being swept helplessly off their feet, laughing and shrieking as the waves pound in. Kaia dives through the waves and swims out, some inner signal seeming to tell her when another crest is coming, and she's past the first break in a quick moment. The smile on her face when he reaches her lights up her eyes. Her skin is glowing, her hair a long dark waterfall down her back. He hasn't seen her so alive, so relaxed, before.

'It is so good to be in the ocean,' she says as she looks towards the incoming swell. The water is warm, the sky blue; the clouds of the morning's storm have mostly dispersed. In harmony, they dive through a wave that's cresting a few feet above them.

'Can you bodysurf?' she asks.

'Nah. I grew up out bush – this ocean stuff is all new to me.'

'I'll teach you!' She gives him rudimentary pointers. 'Can you touch the bottom?' He nods. 'OK, so turn your back to the wave. When it gets close, use your feet to push off, swim as fast as you can and then, as soon as the wave begins to lift you, push your arms forward. I'll show you.' She half-turns towards the shore, looking over her shoulder at the incoming waves. They float over a couple and on the third she says, 'This one.' He can't really see what she does, but the wave catches her, or she catches it, and she flows with it, only coming to a stop close to shore in the shallow white water. When she swims back out, she says, 'Your turn.'

He tries. He misses the first one – he doesn't have the acceleration, or doesn't time it right. She tells him to wait out the next one and then says, 'This one, now – swim.' He pushes off, swims hard, and the wave picks him up. He thrusts his arms forward like she does and lifts his head, surrounded by water, feeling the energy of the ocean propelling him, the drop and the bounce of the break and then a tumble on shallow sand, exhilarated by the feeling of being one with the waves, of riding the ocean.

They spend an age in the water and he learns to shape his body for the best result, putting his head down in line with his leading arm, streamlining his entire body from his fingers right through to the tops of his feet and toes, for a longer, more controlled ride.

Kaia is different out here. There's no artifice, no pretence. She's childlike in her pleasure at being in the water but also improbably capable. 'If we had fins we could catch the bigger waves further out, but without fins you need to be able to push off the bottom. The good bodysurfers are amazing,' she says. 'They can slow themselves down or speed up, just using their body, and they ride the biggest waves.'

His fingers and toes are like prunes when they finally throw themselves on their towels in the sun, his leg throbbing, his heart beating with exertion, a little breathless from the exercise. She's fitter than he is – a better swimmer too.

'Did you learn how to do that in Hawaii, then?' he asks.

She props herself on an elbow, facing him.

'I can't imagine what it must be like to grow up far away from the beach,' she says. 'My name, Kaia, it means "ocean", and I've always been happiest in the water. My family always says I learnt to swim before I could walk, and I was playing in the waves before I started school. My pop, my brother, me – we all surfed. Then, when I was thirteen, I tried kitesurfing and it was like coming home. I found the thing that I was supposed to do. There's nothing better in the world.' She looks at him and smiles. He can imagine six-year-old Kaia riding the waves, he's seen that energy in her today. But now, looking more closely, he can see her eyes are tired and have dark circles underneath.

'How was last night?' he asks.

'Oh, it was so much fun. It totally kicked off. After the club we went to another friend's house on the beach at Mermaid. We ended up partying until this morning – I've only had a couple hours' sleep. The others are probably still there but I had to get back because my parents check up on me and if I'm not at the hotel or training, they give me so much hassle it isn't worth it.'

'Why do your parents want to keep track of you?' he asks.

She lies down, looks up at the sky. A bank of clouds is building above them, the humidity rising, the wind hot. 'My pop was my manager for most of my career and all he thinks about is the circuit and winning,' she says eventually. 'No fun, no life, just training all the time. It was too much, I wanted to do my own thing, so I got a new manager. And then I met a guy too, and we had this amazing thing going on. But my mom and pop never liked him. They thought he was a bad influence because I was having fun for a change, living a real life. Dillon, that's my ex, he's a professional surfer. A really good one. And he totally understands how it is on the tour. How being in the water, competing, is so amazing, the best thing you can ever do. But then there are hours and days of hanging around and being super-bored. He did drugs and sometimes we did some together. Nothing heavy, you know, just a bit of fun. Then I went home to Hawaii to see my family for Christmas and I had a wrap of coke in my bag. I'd totally forgotten about it until they found it at customs. My pop pulled some strings so that it stayed out of the papers, but I had to go to rehab, do community service. My parents fired my manager, and they told Dillon it was over too. I'm allowed back on the circuit this year, but I said I'd quit if my pop insisted on coming with me. My parents only agreed to let me come if I call them every day to make sure I'm training and not having fun. But it's kind of lonely being here alone. I guess I didn't realise. I haven't been away on my own before.'

She sounds defeated, anguished. Walker resists the urge to reach out and hold her hand.

'Well, you've got me. I can be your Aussie big brother – you can call me anytime . . .'

She props herself up on one elbow again. 'Big brother?' She looks at him, a question in her eyes.

He looks her in the eye and nods. 'You don't want an old man like me,' he laughs. 'But I'm here for you, Kaia.'

'I don't know about that,' she says as she lies back down. 'But it's good to have an Aussie big bro.'

They lie in silence for a while. He looks at the ocean, watches the sunlight bouncing off the water, then hiding behind the clouds that are building fast. Another storm is on its way.

'You're a cop, right?' she says after a while.

'Not exactly. I work for the Federal Police but I'm an analyst – a desk jockey.' The lie is so familiar, it comes out without thinking.

'I remember you said you're a math genius,' she says. He wants to explain that it's his mum, not him, who's the mathematician, but it suits the story so he lets it go.

'Do you do drugs?' she asks. 'I guess cops don't.'

'No,' he says. 'I don't.'

'Because they're illegal? Or because they're bad for you – your body's a temple and all that?'

'Mostly because of the harm they do. Not just to users,' he says, 'but the whole way along the chain, from poor farmers in Latin America who are terrorised by the cartels, to the organised crime and violence that goes with distributing drugs right here in Australia. And, of course, the damage it does to your body and the pain and criminal behaviour that comes with addiction. Using drugs recreationally might seem like fun in the moment but you're supporting a whole world of violence and crime.'

Kaia is quiet. She doesn't say anything in reply, and Walker gets the feeling she wants him to drop the subject. Later he'll ask himself if he shouldn't have pressed harder, if it would have made a difference if he'd dug a bit deeper and taken the time to listen to her properly.

Chapter 29

7 p.m.

Aaron has spent most of the day checking out Craig Ford, starting with a prospective member's tour of his Main Beach gym, where he managed to clock Ford himself.

'That's Craig, he's the owner,' the young receptionist who'd shown him round had said, pointing out Ford – older bloke, late fifties – sparring in the boxing ring. He's not that tall, less than six foot, but in good physical condition for a bloke his age, with muscled arms and strong legs. From his size, Aaron guesses he must have been a forward back in the days when he was playing footy.

In the interests of being a bit less visible, Aaron is driving his half-sister Amelia's car today rather than using his bike. She's got a little red Merc hot hatch that has been the cause of so many speeding tickets she's about to lose her licence, so he reckons he's doing her a favour by keeping her out of it for twenty-four hours. He sits in it, in the underground car park, waiting for Ford to emerge from the gym. After half an hour or so Ford comes down and gets into a blood-red Range Rover. Aaron follows him to Broadbeach, where Ford parks outside Mamasan, the fancy Asian restaurant, for a few minutes before a good-looking blonde emerges and jumps in beside him.

He follows them to the Isle of Capri, the same island where Stefan has his Surfers place, and down to Gibraltar Drive, one of the nicest waterside streets, watching as they park in the driveway of a modern two-storey house. There's a small park a couple of blocks down from their place that opens on to the canal. Aaron pulls over and walks across the grass to look back along the water. It's almost dark now but he can see there's a big boat moored outside Ford's house too. Whether it's the dealing or the gyms, the bloke is doing well.

He gives it a couple of minutes then walks up to the house. The doorbell is one of those video-operated ones, so he goes back to the car and roots around in the boot. Sure enough, there's a Mike's Delivery-branded paper bag in the back. His sister is addicted to the company's expensive groceries and ready meals, and always has a heap of their bags in the house. The one in the car is full of empty bottles; Amelia must be recycling them or some shit. He tips most of the empties into the boot, then walks back to the house and rings the bell, standing out of sight, only his shoulders and chest visible on the screen.

'Hello?' It's a woman's voice.

'Delivery for Craig Ford,' he says, lifting the Mike's Delivery bag into focus. As he'd hoped, it works a treat; Ford must be into this bullshit too. The gate buzzes open and he cuts across the lawn to the front door.

The woman he'd seen climbing into the car opens the door. She's got a heavy gold bracelet on one arm, a couple of big diamonds on her fingers, and at her feet a yappy little mongrel of a dog that won't stop barking. It's closer to a rat than a dog, thinks Aaron, resisting the urge to kick it back down the posh-looking hallway behind them.

The woman puts her hand out for the bag, half-smiling, not really looking at him. 'I hope Craig tipped on the app, 'cause I don't have any change, sorry,' she says.

'Yeah, nah, I need to have a word with him,' says Aaron, holding the bag out of her reach. She looks at him properly for the first time and gets nervy fast.

'Just a sec,' she says, going to close the door. He steps forward, jams his leg and hip against it, using his bulk to stop her from shutting it all the way. She looks at him again, biting her lip.

'Craig,' she calls. He can hear a tremble in her voice. 'Craig, there's someone here to see you.'

Ford strides down the hallway towards them, his step faltering only slightly when he sees Aaron standing in the doorway.

'We know each other?' he asks, putting himself between Aaron and his wife.

'I reckon so. Your fella buys the gear from us,' says Aaron.

Ford turns to his wife. 'Give us a minute, babe, this is business.'

She leaves, happy to be out of it, thinks Aaron, taking the yappy mutt with her. Ford steps outside and closes the front door behind him.

'What are you bringing this shit here for? I don't do business at home.'

'We like to know where all our customers live,' says Aaron. 'In case there are any payment problems or loyalty issues.'

'Yeah, well, you've made your point, so fuck off and leave me and my wife alone.'

Aaron drops the bag he's holding, steps forward and punches Ford hard in the solar plexus. He doubles over, struggling to breathe. Aaron pulls his knife out of his back pocket and pushes Ford up against the wall beside the front door. He holds the knife against Ford's throat, pulls it along, making sure it nicks the skin. Ford's face goes pale; he's still trying hard to get enough air into his lungs.

'Now I've made my fucken point,' says Aaron.

Ford nods, or tries to. He's too scared to move.

'The thing is,' says Aaron, putting the knife away but staying up close and personal, right in Ford's face, 'we need your help. We got a problem with one of your mates – Walker, his name is. He's messing with our business and we need to talk to him about that, set him straight on what's what. Normally we'd pay him a visit but he's a pig, and we don't want any problems with the pigs – they have a habit of giving us aggro. So you need to tell your mate Walker to come and see us on the quiet. You can figure out the details, but we need to see him this week. Alone. Unarmed. Not expecting any trouble. Got it?'

Ford nods, mute with fear.

'Good. If he doesn't show, I'll be back to see you, or maybe I'll pay a visit to that pretty missus of yours. And if you think about telling the pigs, think again. We got a bloke inside that keeps an eye on things for us, lets us know what's going on, who's doing what. You call them, we'll know about it. And then it'll go extra hard on you and your missus.'

He steps back onto the grass. 'When you've sorted it, call your regular dealer, let him know when Walker's coming to see us. Do it quick – we're not in the mood to wait.'

Ford, with a trembling hand to his throat, nods once more.

By the time Aaron arrives at Stefan's Reedy Creek place, it's raining again and how. The driveway has been taken over by rushing streams of water and muddy potholes. The Merc barely makes it up to the house. A curtain of water is thundering down from above, smashing onto the veranda roof with a noise like being inside a beaten drum. Stefan and Nick are inside and the humidity, the heat, the storm must be aggravating them both – a moody edge fills the room.

'Alright?' says Aaron.

Nick keeps his mouth shut. Stefan chugs his beer down. 'Get us another one,' he says as Aaron goes to the bar for his own. Aaron brings back one for himself and one for Stefan. Nick can sort himself out.

Using his palm, Stefan crushes his empty tinny flat onto the coffee table. 'Fucken Tina kicked off yesterday,' he says. 'Came round mine in the middle of the night, shouting and screaming outside, high as a fucken kite. She even smashed her fucken car into the garage doors. Stupid bitch. She keeps that up, she'll be going the same way as her prick of a son.'

Aaron takes a sip of his beer. 'She was at the club, too, trying to flog some gear. I sent her on her way.'

'Fucken right,' says Stefan. 'Next time give her a hiding.'

They sit for a moment, drinking their beers, the rain thundering on the roof above them.

'Wayne coming tonight?' asks Aaron.

'Nah, he's got some family shit in Sydney, some aunt of his died or something,' says Stefan. 'Let's get on with it . . .'

'We're selling heaps of the new gear,' says Nick. 'The druggies come back more often and they're buying more as well. They reckon it feels fucken great when they're on it and real shit when they're down.'

Stefan nods but his mind isn't on sales of the gear. 'What did you find out about this Ford bloke?' he asks Aaron.

'I put the shits up him,' says Aaron. 'He's not as hard as he likes to think he is. And he's got plenty to lose: big house, nice boat, expensive missus. Still, I reckon he might need a bit more incentive to take us seriously.'

'Is there any leverage there?'

'Plenty,' says Aaron. 'He's got a fancy boat tied up at the back of his place. We could easily get to it. Sink it.'

'Nah. Let's hit him where it really hurts,' says Stefan. 'Torch one of his gyms. Make a bigger statement.'

'I'd say the Surfers gym would be our best bet,' says Aaron. 'Nathan, the bloke that spotted the pig, he's a member there.'

Stefan thinks of the skinny-legged prospect. 'You reckon he's up to it?'

Aaron nods. 'Easy way for him to earn his spurs,' he says. 'Leave it with me, I'll sort it.'

Chapter 30

9 p.m.

A storm has arrived. Rain thundering down, so heavy that Walker can barely see the ocean from his windows. As night falls, the lights of the city, usually vivid and bright against the dark sky, fade in and out of vision, obscured by low cloud and the wall of water that is crashing down from above.

Because a visual approach always helps him to think more clearly, he takes down the Monroe case notes from the spare room wall and pins up pictures of Siobhan, David and Gabby Owen. He adds Flora's name and the year she last spoke with her sister, 2018. He puts up a copy of Siobhan's bank statement. Also opened in 2018, he notes. He stands and looks at it all, thinking. A clue, a memory – something is pricking at the back of his mind. The TV is on in the living room behind him, the noise a distraction. As he walks over to find the remote and switch it off, the news comes on.

'This is the Gold Coast News,' says the anchor, a well-coiffed woman in her forties smiling at the camera, her long hair artfully blow-dried. 'A woman who has allegedly gone on a twelve-hour crime spree – stealing a vehicle, causing malicious damage to property and robbing a store – was arrested late this morning at a hair salon in Surfers Paradise.'

Walker stops to watch the story, laughing despite himself at the woman's brazenness in stealing a vehicle and robbing a store before calmly going to the hairdresser.

'The woman is alleged to have stolen a silver Mercedes-Benz from outside a Surfers Paradise club early on Sunday morning,' says the anchor, over images of a high-end nightclub. 'Over the

161

course of the night, Queensland Police received multiple calls from the public who had spotted the vehicle driving erratically and at high speeds. The offender is also accused of smashing the vehicle into the garage doors of a home on the Isle of Capri at around four a.m. and creating a disturbance before abandoning the car in a shopping centre car park this morning. The same woman then allegedly stole cash from a takeaway till before she was spotted having her hair done at a salon. She was found to be in possession of considerable quantities of methamphetamines. Police have named the woman as forty-one-year-old Tina Monroe, from Hopeville in the state's west.'

Walker stops in his tracks. Tina Monroe went on a wild drug-fuelled binge on the same day as Purcell's arrest for the murder of her son. The news moves on to a different story and Walker mutes it and goes to search for more information online. The story has been covered in one of the local papers but there are no additional details. He wonders if Tina heard about Purcell's arrest and the fact that Matt had been killed by a Vandal came as a shock to her, enough to send her off on one. She'd been adamant in her statement that the Vandals weren't connected to his murder.

He sits for a moment at the dining table, thinking about it. They can use this, he's sure of it. If Purcell won't talk, Tina might be more willing to testify against Markovich or at least share any information she has, if she believes the club is implicated in her son's death. He fires off an email to Rutherford, with a link to the story.

Not sure if you saw this but Tina Monroe, Stefan Markovich's ex-girlfriend, went on a bender after we arrested Purcell. Qld Police have her in detention. She might be more willing to talk to us about Markovich/Vandals now? Happy to interview her.

He goes back to look at the Owen case but exhaustion is setting in. He hasn't slept properly for almost thirty-six hours. He's certain he's missing something obvious. Something that's still hovering at the edge of his knowing but not coming forward into clarity.

He's too tired. He decides he'll pay a visit to the Owen house in the morning, check out the scene of the crime; perhaps he can find something to unlock the clue he knows is there, but still can't quite see.

Chapter 31

3 a.m.

It takes a moment before Matilda clocks the sound of the alarm. The ICU is quieter at night, fewer family around, fewer staff too, but there are always at least a half-dozen if not the full complement of ten patients on the ward, and there are always the beeping, buzzing and humming noises of various systems operating, and occasionally the louder alerts of a change in some patient's vital sign or other. The noise is so constant she doesn't really hear it anymore.

But now the beeps, escalating in sound and urgency, filter into her awareness and she leaves the patient she's been checking on and goes out into the corridor. The sound is coming from Gabby Owen's room. The chair outside, the one the young cop is supposed to be sitting in, is empty. Matilda hopes he's already inside, calling for medical help, but when she gets to Gabby's room her worst fears are realised. There's no sign of the cop, there's a pillow lying on the floor beside the bed and the little girl's oxygen stats are right down in the danger zone, her heart rate too.

Matilda checks Gabby's airways, her breathing. All clear. She administers oxygen and presses the emergency medical call button. Slowly Gabby's blood oxygen level stats rise. A doctor arrives and takes over, and after a few minutes heart and oxygen levels are back to normal.

'What the hell happened?' asks the doctor as he looks through Gabby's notes.

Matilda can't be sure and the young cop, who's returned stuttering and red-faced, admits he was having a coffee in the staff room and doesn't know either.

She points to the discarded pillow. 'This was lying on the floor beside the bed.'

'Why does she have a non-regulation pillow?' The doctor is looking for someone to blame.

'Her dad brought it in earlier,' says Matilda. 'A memento from home. Apparently she always sleeps with it.'

Gabby had been cuddling the pillow when Matilda first came on shift, with a lovely smile on her face. 'It smells like home,' she'd told Matilda, and had fallen into an easier and more restful sleep than she'd had for days. Full marks to Dad on that one, Matilda had thought.

'Well, it looks like she's almost smothered herself with it,' says the doctor. 'Patient's responses are still not back to normal so make sure she doesn't have it in bed with her again.'

Matilda nods. It's possible that Gabby pulled the pillow on top of herself and with the sedation and drugs she's receiving her body's instinct didn't kick in and wake her up. But then again, it's possible this was deliberate too. Gabby's in hospital because someone tried to smother her; perhaps they've tried again. That's why there's a policeman sitting outside her door. Or there's supposed to be.

'Did you see anyone go in or out of this room? Any doctors, any nurses, anyone at all?' she asks the young constable.

'No,' he says. 'But I . . . I went for a coffee. I was gone for a few minutes.'

Once more, Matilda wishes the other copper was here. Walker. She trusts him with Gabby's life, but this pimply kid not at all. On impulse she digs out Walker's number. He gave it to her earlier in the week. 'In case Gabby needs anything,' he said. The other nurses teased her that she had a beau – maybe a couple of them were even a bit jealous. She let them think what they liked, but she believed him. He's really invested in the little girl's recovery.

Walker parks the ute outside the hospital and walks down one flight of stairs to the security room on the lower ground floor. The night guard is sitting there, coffee cup resting on his belly, feet on his desk, flicking through a fishing magazine.

Walker shows him his ID. 'Can I look at the CCTV footage for the ICU reception desk?' he asks. 'There was a patient emergency and I want to check something.'

Theoretically it's not possible for just anyone to gain entrance to the ICU. There's a reception desk you need to sign in at and the doors into the wards require a key card for entry. But at night the reception isn't manned and a key card isn't that hard to get. Walker's got one for his guard shifts, as do medical staff, families of patients, orderlies, cleaners and so on. But there's a CCTV camera that covers the reception and it should show them who has gone in and out.

'No worries, mate,' says the guard, bringing his feet to the floor with a thump. 'What time?'

'From two thirty a.m.,' says Walker.

The guard finds the time and presses Play. Nothing happens for a good while, then at 2.41 the lift doors slide open and a figure steps out. It's a man, wearing the white coat that denotes medical staff, with matching white Crocs and, incongruously, a black cap above an N95 surgical mask. He keeps his head down and steps quickly out of shot. He knows where the camera is, thinks Walker.

'Can you rewind? I want a closer look.'

The suspect is well disguised. Only his size, tall and broad, gives away that he's even male. There's nothing visible – no hair, no facial features – that would identify him.

'Can you let it play a bit longer . . .' asks Walker.

A few minutes later, at 2.45, the constable who's supposed to be on guard outside Gabby's room appears, walking away from the ward, in conversation with a nurse. The ward entry doors are almost closed when Black Cap reappears and pushes through them. He's been waiting for his chance, thinks Walker, cursing the young cop's lack of professionalism. He needs a major bollocking.

At 2.51 Black Cap appears again, a glancing shot. He doesn't take the lift. Not long afterwards the constable also passes by, on his way back. Walker notes with fury that he's been gone almost ten minutes.

'Is there another way out, if you're not taking the lift?' asks Walker.

'You can take the stairs,' says the guard. 'But they only exit on to the ground floor or the underground car park. The other floors are locked at night.'

'Do you have CCTV on those floors?'

They watch the CCTV for both areas but Black Cap doesn't make an appearance. 'He could have taken the pedestrian exit out of the car park direct from the stairs – there's no cameras there,' says the guard.

'What about the camera inside ICU?' asks Walker. There's another camera inside the ward that points down the corridor. They should be able to see if Black Cap goes into Gabby's room.

'Yeah, nah, actually we've got a problem with that. It went out at nine p.m. tonight. They sent someone to check it out, but it needs to be replaced. Totally fucked. Won't get a new one until the morning.'

'How come it went out?' asks Walker. 'Could it have been tampered with?'

The guard shrugs. 'No idea, mate. They can probably let you know tomorrow.'

Walker would bet that it was deliberately broken. With the broken camera, the suspicious stranger on the ward and the pillow beside Gabby's bed, he is starting to believe this could have been a well-planned attack on Gabby Owen, made that much easier by the constable's absence. If it hadn't been for the patient alarms and Matilda's rapid response, the perp might even have got away with it. Walker goes outside to place a call to Cummings. He feels certain their worst fears have been confirmed. Someone has tried once more to silence Gabby Owen.

Chapter 32

Monday 13 March
8 a.m.

DI Cummings is forcing himself to breathe deeply, fighting an inclination to bang his fist on the table and insist on the bloody matter. He's been sitting with David Owen and Gabby's medical team – at a small round table in a consulting room a couple of floors below the ward where Gabby is slowly recovering – for over an hour now. Cummings has taken the heat that's due for the apparent attempt on her life last night. The constable involved has been severely reprimanded and will face further disciplinary action. His lax approach could have led to Gabby's death. Cummings acknowledges the mea culpa and promises that more rigorous policing will be in place moving forward. But there are hospital failings, too. The intruder had access to the ICU for six minutes, undetected. And in Cummings's opinion, the whole scenario is all the more evidence that they need to interview Gabby and soon.

'We need to speak to her as soon as possible,' he says. 'She's a witness to a crime and it's possible that she's seen something of material use to solving this case. This incident proves that we need to find out what she knows so that we can take whatever steps are necessary to keep her safe.'

The medical debate as to whether the girl is well enough to be interviewed, complex conversations regarding the extent of her recovery, goes mostly over his head, but the outcome seems to be that Gabby is doing as well as can be expected. She's experiencing some mood swings, occasional anxiety and panic attacks, and has been on sedatives to keep her calm, but no cognitive damage has been detected; though, as the neuro specialist argues, that probably can't be fully measured until further down the line.

'So does that mean we can interview her? Later today? We have specialist officers trained to interview children – it won't be invasive...'

'That may be the case,' says the resident psychiatrist, interrupting him. 'But you don't have specialists in interviewing children who have sustained life-threatening head injuries and who are in a delicate stage of their recovery. We don't want to make Gabby feel even more threatened or vulnerable. She doesn't even know the whole story of what happened that night. She needs time and space to get better.'

The debate starts up again but this time there's a general consensus. The girl needs to be left in peace. Cummings knows he's fighting a losing battle, but fight he will.

'We urgently need to talk to her,' he reiterates. 'She may be able to identify the blokes who murdered her mother. It's our best way to get them off the streets as quickly as possible.'

The search of the Latu brothers' homes hadn't turned up any evidence connecting them to the Owens and they'd had to be released yesterday evening. He's got teams watching both brothers' movements, so he's confident it wasn't one of them who attacked Gabby, but the timing of it, coinciding with their release from custody, is telling.

'A further attack can't be fully discounted,' he says. There's a moment of silence as the doctors consider this.

The lead consultant turns to David Owen, who has been listening but not saying much. 'What would you like to do?' asks the consultant. 'As her father, this is ultimately your call.'

Owen had, understandably, been coldly furious at what he called 'a complete failure of policing further endangering my family', and Cummings has been unable to do anything more than apologise. It hasn't made an ally of Owen, and he clearly doesn't feel he owes the police any favours because he now shakes his head. 'I think it's too soon,' he says. 'Of course I want to find the people who did this, who hurt Gabby and killed my wife, but Gabby's recovery is my first priority. I still need to tell her that her mother has died. That will be totally devastating for her, and after last night I don't think we should add any further stress on her right now.'

The doctors around the table nod. 'Agreed – it's not in her best interests at the moment. We'll reconsider in two days' time,' says the lead consultant, gathering the papers in front of him into a neat pile and pushing his chair back. There's a general hum of conversation. The meeting is over. Cummings exhales in frustration but there's nothing he can do.

David Owen stands and walks over to the lead consultant. 'Just a heads-up – I've decided I want Gabby to come home as soon as possible. I think she'll be safer there. I've found an apartment for us with excellent security, much more secure than it is here. And I think she'll recover more quickly and naturally in a home environment. I'll hire a day nurse to look after her, and with my medical training she'll be fully supervised. I really want this to happen as soon as possible.'

'Noted,' says the consultant. 'Let's see what the next couple of days bring . . .'

It's not even 8.30 a.m. and Walker is sitting in his ute outside the Owen house when Cummings calls him.

'I've just come from the most embarrassing fucking meeting of my life,' says Cummings bluntly. 'That young PC, wandering off for a coffee, chatting up a nurse or some bullshit – he'll lose his bloody badge if I've got anything to do with it. We're ramping up the security, obviously, but they still won't let us interview Gabby. Say she's too fragile. When you sat with her on Saturday night and she spoke with you, did she say anything that could be useful?'

Walker thinks through his conversation with the little girl. 'Yeah, nah, not really. She had a nightmare, a wolf attacking her mother. From what she said, her mother was on the bed, the attacker above her. She only spoke of the attacker in the singular . . .'

'That's what forensics say, too, just one person,' says Cummings. 'She didn't give you anything descriptive? No idea of what the person looked like?'

'Nah, she didn't say it was a person. She said it was a wolf.'

'Look, you reckon you could chat with her again? Maybe pay her a visit during the day. We've had to let the Latus go – we don't have enough evidence to hold them. But if Gabby can ID them or give us something, anything, that indicates it might have been one of them . . .'

'I don't know. I don't have experience interviewing kids, and she's still pretty crook.'

'Not an interview – nothing formal, of course – just a quick chat. See if she says anything. We really need her. Otherwise I've got nothing solid I can pin on the Latus.'

Walker can sense how frustrated Cummings is. 'I'll see what I can do,' he says.

'Nice one, appreciate it.'

Walker sits for a moment thinking about Gabby. Maybe Matilda could chat to her; she seems to have a close relationship with the little girl. He gets out of the ute and stands in the drizzle, looking at the house in front of him. Even on this damp, grey morning, it looks plush and luxurious, a wide sprawling mansion spread over two floors and taking up a double-size block.

The house is still a designated crime scene and a soggy-looking constable is huddled under an umbrella outside the gate, deployed to keep media and other gawkers away. Walker shows his ID. 'I'm helping DI Cummings and he's given me permission to have a look around.'

The constable checks his ID and lets him in. 'SOCO has finished for the moment, but you'll need to wear the usual gear,' he says.

Walker slides covers over his shoes and puts on disposable gloves. Seen in daylight and in real life, the house is more imposing than he'd expected from the body cam footage. High ceilings, big windows, and so much space. Even the entrance hall is wide and light, the luxurious feeling only slightly marred by the sickly scent emanating from a bouquet of dying lilies in a vase on the hall console table. A host of petals have fallen to the floor beside the table, their pollen staining the wood a reddish yellow.

The stairs to his right, which curve up to the first floor, are sweeping, grand. He walks up, goes to the end of the hallway and starts in the study – a big room with a high-spec office chair behind an expensive-looking desk, and a designer armchair upholstered in black leather with a matching footstool, positioned to look out the large windows at the view across the water. The safe beside the desk is open and empty, robbed of its contents, some $5,000 and a ruinously expensive Patek Philippe sports watch. The room speaks of wealth and success: a red-patterned Turkish rug covers the wooden floor and a striking work of art by a well-known Aboriginal artist takes up half the wall opposite the desk. Another wall is covered with signed sports memorabilia; Walker recognises the names of some of Australia's most successful athletes across basketball, tennis, golf, football and swimming.

The room opposite the study is much smaller, less than a third of the size. It is unfurnished – only a plant in the far corner beside the window, which looks over the street. A small portable yellow speaker stands on the floor beside the plant and a blue yoga mat is rolled up in the corner.

There are three swanky bedrooms and two bathrooms that remind Walker of an upscale hotel – elegant but lacking in personal touches. The exception is what must be Gabby's. A pink electric toothbrush with a cartoon princess on the handle and three small white rubber ducks with rainbow-coloured tails sit on a shelf above the sink in her bathroom. Her bedroom is tidy, no toys on the floor, no clothes spread around. A shelf of books with a Barbie sitting on top, a small desk with an iPad on it, the screen riven by a deep crack. He glances at a basket of toys and notices that several are broken – a doll with its arm missing, a wooden doll's house, the rear smashed in and clumsily repaired. Perhaps old favourites that she hasn't been able to let go, he thinks.

Aside from the bloodstained bed, the main bedroom is neat too, as are the en suite and the walk-in wardrobe. One side of the wardrobe is dedicated to sportswear – tennis outfits, golf shirts, running gear, basketball shoes and balls, snorkels and togs, football guernseys. On the other side are Owen's shirts; there must be fifty or more, all pressed, hanging alongside suits and trousers and casual jackets. There are drawers and shelves with jeans, shorts and t-shirts, folded and neat, a few jumpers – all cashmere, notes Walker – and a rack of shoes, ranging from formal black brogues to slip-on sailing shoes, trainers and a pair of brown leather Birkenstock sandals. The man is clearly a bit of a clothes horse. On the third side of the rectangular room is a more feminine presence: a rack of dresses and skirts, some formal, some more casual, hanging above high-heeled sandals, casual flats and trainers. Beside them, shelves with folded pastel-coloured t-shirts, sports bras and leggings, shorts and jeans.

He walks back downstairs and follows the trail of blood into the living room. In the daylight it's possible to see that the room opens up on to a large garden overlooking the canal, with a pool and a jetty, though no boat. Cummings's team is right to think it would be easy for intruders to gain access to the house from the canal. The cable ties have gone; the chair is upright. The kitchen, as it was on the video, is neat and tidy and silent.

He stands for a while in the kitchen, thinking. He still can't put his finger on what is gnawing at him. He walks slowly around the house one more time, but the harder he looks, the less he sees.

Chapter 33

9.30 a.m.

Walker is sitting in traffic, heavier today because of the rain, when the image comes into his mind from yesterday – of Jess looking for the soft toy to give to Gabby. They'd been in Craig and Jess's dressing room, and he remembers the pieces of jewellery spilling from the decorative box, the piles of make-up and bottles of perfume, the hatboxes, the row upon row of sandals and shoes, silk scarves and other accessories. The room had been filled with her things. By all accounts, David Owen is wealthier than Jess and Craig are, but Siobhan's belongings were negligible by comparison. Her corner was sparse, and he can't recall seeing much in the way of jewellery or make-up.

He thinks back to the en suite bathroom. He remembers seeing shampoo and shower gel in the shower but few if any lotions and creams or make-up. He'd always teased Ellen, his ex, about her oversize toiletries bag, which went with her even if she was only away for the weekend. It might be that Siobhan wasn't that kind of woman, but the more he thinks it through, the more he decides that Siobhan is virtually invisible in the house. Even the wine bottle in the kitchen had a solitary glass beside it.

He recalls with a jolt that he's never heard Owen mention his wife as an individual, as a woman who must have been terrified in those last moments as she was brutally killed, a woman who has lost her chance to live a full life, see her daughter grow up. Siobhan seems to be a shadow, a woman who only existed in the presence of her husband. All the pieces come to him in a horrifying rush as he remembers Jess talking about Siobhan not having money, giving up her job, never coming out on her own . . .

The case that has been hovering at the back of his mind comes to him. It was years ago, when he'd first started at the AFP. A woman in Canberra murdered by her partner. Liz Kent, that was her name. She'd disappeared out of the blue one day – her husband had reported her missing. They'd found her body three weeks later, beside a bush track that she'd regularly walked along. She'd been strangled, dumped, lightly covered with brush.

There'd been no history of violence in the relationship and beyond the initial checks they hadn't suspected her husband. But the woman's family had been convinced of his guilt. They'd outlined her isolation, his total control of her life. He'd driven her friends and family away with jealousy and suspicion. He'd gaslit her and her family – claiming the problems were down to her behaviour – and he'd controlled everything from what she ate to what she wore. Siobhan Owen, too, had lost contact with her sister, had few friends. He remembers Jess saying that she hadn't wanted a makeover, not because she liked her own style but because David Owen did.

He remembers that Liz Kent had an account in her own name with just $50 in it. The figure had been heartbreaking to Walker. She'd had as little financial autonomy as a child. Siobhan Owen had more than that in her account but compared to her husband it was relatively little. The other accounts were all solely in Owen's name and even the credit card statement, the purchases, were his personal expenditure, nothing of his wife's.

Coercive control. That's what they'd called it in court. A kind of domestic abuse that isn't necessarily physical but is more about socially, financially and mentally isolating the victim. It's a deceptively dangerous and insidious type of abuse and, he remembers, often ends in violence and murder, particularly if the victim decides to leave.

When Liz Kent had finally had enough and tried to leave, her husband had killed her – not wanting to lose control of her, needing to claim even her death. Siobhan had been saving money in a personal account, an account that David Owen hadn't been aware of. Could she have been preparing to leave too? And could Owen have discovered that and reacted with such violence that he killed his wife and nearly killed his own daughter?

* * *

'I reckon David Owen might be lying to us,' says Walker. It's lunchtime and he's sitting in Cummings's office. Cummings looks like he hasn't slept in days, his face drawn, his cheeks erratically shaven.

Cummings listens to Walker as he outlines his theory, but he looks unconvinced. He scratches at the bristles on the edge of his chin, then shakes his head. 'I mean, we obviously considered Owen as a suspect, but there's not a shred of evidence that he killed his wife. First, there's DNA that shows there was at least one unknown person involved in the attack on Siobhan Owen, and domestic violence rarely involves other parties. Second, he was attacked himself, and third, there are credible suspects that hold a grudge against him. There's also no evidence that Siobhan Owen wasn't happy in her marriage, or that he's ever been violent towards her.'

'Coercive control isn't just about violence. It's more subtle than that,' says Walker.

'Yeah, I know, but I don't reckon this is the case here. I've met the bloke. Owen doesn't need to coerce anyone. He's loaded, he's good-looking, he's charming, he's a doctor – he works with Australia's leading athletes, for Christ's sake. He's every woman's dream. And he's a stalwart member of the community. He's not the type.'

'If you look at the signs, there are some real red flags here,' says Walker, as one of Cummings's team knocks on the door, waving a piece of paper.

'I'll add it to the list of theories we're following up,' says Cummings, taking the paper and glancing at it. 'It wouldn't be the first time that a bloke killed his missus, but Owen deserves a bloody Oscar if he did,' he says, still with half an eye on the document he's reading. 'Look, we've checked everything out – his story holds. There's nothing out of order in his life, in his business, in his finances. We've gone through all Siobhan Owen's phone calls and her online searches, and there's nothing to suggest she was involved in an abusive relationship or that she was trying to leave him. We're focusing our efforts on the Latu family. They have a grudge, they have a motive and they have form . . .'

'But the level of violence, the number of stab wounds. That feels personal.'

'It's pretty personal for the Latus. They blame David Owen for the death of their sister.'

That's true, thinks Walker. He has one last go. 'Have you checked David Owen's alibi for last night? If I am right, Owen could be a danger to Gabby. He could have tried to hurt her again.'

'No, I haven't checked his bloody alibi. His daughter was nearly killed, and I had to apologise to him that our bloke wasn't doing his job properly, wasn't looking out for Gabby like we'd promised. Look, thanks for all your help, DS, I do appreciate it. But this is not the direction our inquiry is going to be taking.'

Chapter 34

1 p.m.

Walker has found himself an empty desk next to Narelle, who is typing ferociously, not looking at the keyboard, reading the screen as she writes. Slightly mesmerised, he watches her fingers flying across the letters, hitting them with hard, audible clicks. When she finishes and looks up, he says, 'That typing's pretty impressive.'

'You need something, DS?' she asks.

'Yeah, nah, I'm good,' he says. 'Just looking through the forensics on this case.'

'Well, you do that,' she says. 'I don't know about you but I'm busy here.'

Feeling like a naughty schoolkid who's been caught bunking off, Walker opens the forensics report and looks through it with new eyes. It is not enlightening. Owen's DNA is everywhere, as you'd expect in his own home, but there's nothing untoward, or if there is it's impossible to distinguish from the day-to-day. And there was DNA from an unknown assailant found on Siobhan's body, a factor that points sharply away from Owen's involvement.

The only fact in the report that catches Walker's eye is a one-liner that he'd missed the last time. Forensics had detected alcohol in Siobhan's pillow. Deep in its centre, the pillow was wet with some kind of alcohol. Walker remembers Jess saying that Siobhan wasn't a drinker. Maybe the attacker had been carrying booze and spilt it, which might also account for the violence of her death. Mickey Latu had been drinking heavily that night; perhaps he was still drinking when he attacked Siobhan. But if it soaked through to the centre of the pillow, that suggests a lot more than a small spill. He reads

Siobhan's autopsy and discovers she'd had a very high blood alcohol level, approaching point one five. That would have been enough to make her very drunk, particularly as someone who wasn't a regular drinker.

He finds Cummings back in his office. 'I'm curious about Siobhan Owen's blood alcohol content,' he says. 'It's point one five, but a friend of hers told me she's not a drinker . . .'

'That's not what her husband says. He claims she drank regularly and heavily at home, sometimes even to the extent that she couldn't pick Gabby up after school. He tried to keep her off it when he could, but she'd hide the booze and sometimes he wouldn't notice until it was too late. According to him, she'd been drinking that night. Passed out quite early, he says.'

Walker can't quite square the image of Siobhan Owen hitting the grog until she passes out with the same Siobhan Owen described by Jess – quiet, reclusive, with a life built around Gabby and her husband.

'What was she drinking?' he asks.

'Vodka,' says Cummings. 'She'd been drinking since the afternoon and passed out by ten p.m. that night. Probably that's why she didn't hear the break-in – she'd have been unconscious. In a way it's a blessing. She would have been too drunk to be properly aware of what was happening. She might not even have been conscious during the attack.'

Walker knows that vodka, odourless and colourless, is often the alcohol of choice for those who don't want their drinking to be obvious. Perhaps that's why Jess didn't realise that Siobhan had dependency issues.

On his way back to the Gold Coast, Walker decides to pay a visit to the state's morgue and forensic services team. He finds it on a busy road, just off the M3 highway, about fifteen minutes' drive from the Roma Street HQ. There's no obvious signage, only a simple Queensland Government-branded plaque stating the address: 39 Kessels Road. Behind a small bank of trees is a series of modern-looking buildings. It's an extension of the hospital further down the road, and with the innocuous-looking sign and the bland, squat, rectangular buildings, it could simply be a campus of offices or medical labs, which, in effect, it is. There's a CSIRO research team based there, some government biosecurity labs and, at the back, the Forensic and Scientific Services department and morgue.

Walker doesn't have an appointment and it's Monday afternoon, a busy time post-weekend. He has to wait half an hour, and when the pathologist comes to meet him he can see she's stressed. She's carrying an armful of folders, her mobile phone jammed between shoulder and ear, talking animatedly. She sees him and heads over, still talking. When she ends the call she says, 'G'day, I'm Maria Marques, the forensic pathologist. Sorry to keep you, but it's a madhouse here today. I can only give you five minutes – we'll have to walk and talk.'

'No worries, I just have a couple of quick questions about Siobhan Owen, the woman who was killed in the home invasion. The DNA you found on her body—'

'I hope you're not building your whole case around that?' Marques interrupts him. 'As I explained in the report, forensic technologies have become so highly sensitive that the amount of DNA required for analysis has become very low. A sample of about sixteen cells is all that's needed. The DNA sample we found on Siobhan Owen wasn't quite that small, but it wasn't big enough to warrant identification on its own. Humans shed tens of thousands of cells every day and shed DNA transfers easily between people and objects. You can pick it up from a handshake or touching a doorknob. It might be that Siobhan Owen didn't even meet the person whose DNA we've found – she could have picked it up from pushing around a supermarket trolley that was touched by someone else.'

'But wasn't the trace found on her body rather than her hands?'

'OK, so say she hugged someone – it could have been transferred like that, for example.'

'I've always thought DNA evidence is a bit more foolproof than that,' says Walker.

'It is very useful, up to a point. But to really be certain we need a bigger, more significant sample than we found on this victim. Investigators can be a bit too eager to use the evidence from minute amounts of DNA, but it's not impossible for secondary transfer to falsely place people at the scene of a crime. You just need to be aware of that.'

'OK,' says Walker, filing the information away. 'One other thing. I also saw that Siobhan's blood alcohol level was very high.'

'That's right,' says Marques. 'Toxicology showed it was close to point one five, if I remember correctly. Probably would have been higher before death, as I understand she stopped drinking before ten p.m. and time of death is somewhere between one a.m. and three a.m.'

'The thing is, our witness statements say that Siobhan Owen wasn't a drinker. That she rarely touched the stuff. Did you do a full internal examination? Did you notice if her liver or kidneys had any signs of her being a heavy drinker?'

Marques slows then comes to a stop, eyes cast upwards, thinking about this last question, remembering. 'No,' she says eventually. 'I didn't. I did a full external and full internal examination on Siobhan and I put samples in for histology too. I don't think I've had the histology report back yet, but I don't remember noticing any damage. And if she was a regular drinker at those levels, I'd definitely have seen it. I could smell the alcohol in her system when we performed the autopsy. She'd drunk a very significant amount that night.'

They start walking again, towards a bank of lifts in the far corner of reception.

'Look, I can't be certain, and I don't want to give you false information,' says Marques briskly. 'I need to double-check my notes and the histology. I'm on my way to a meeting now but I'll let you know later this evening.'

'OK, but it's really quite urgent,' says Walker.

'Yeah, yeah, everything always is,' says Marques. 'I'll send it as soon as I can.'

Chapter 35

3 p.m.

When Walker reaches the outskirts of Surfers, the clock in the ute reads 2.20 p.m. He recalls the name of Gabby's school, St Anne's Primary, and looks it up on Google Maps. He doesn't remember seeing anything in the case notes to suggest Cummings's team have visited the school, though no doubt someone from victim support services will have been here to help Gabby's friends and teachers. But as he's heard conflicting accounts of the type of person Siobhan Owen was, maybe the principal at the school can tell him more about her.

He parks, then sprints through the rain and through the first door he finds, into a hallway with classrooms running off it. The place has the smell of school: kids, sweaty shoes and the remnants of the tuck shop lunch: meat pies, hot dogs, tomato sauce. The halls are quiet, the kids in class, and he follows the signs to the school office. A receptionist, standing and talking at the open door of the principal's room, turns when he knocks on the small shield of safety glass that separates the reception from the corridor.

'Can I help you?' she asks.

He holds up his ID. 'DS Walker. I'm part of the task force looking into Siobhan Owen's murder, and I wanted to speak with your principal.'

'Send him in, Shirl,' calls a voice from the office beyond, and Shirl, looking a little piqued that her authority as gatekeeper has been overridden, opens a swing gate and waves him through.

Valerie Simpson, according to the name plaque on the principal's desk, is a woman in her mid-forties dressed in a grey silk blouse and navy skirt, her dark hair cut in a neat bob. She looks at him with clear eyes that seem like they wouldn't miss much and Walker has a schoolkid-in-trouble feeling for the second time that day.

'Are you with VictimConnect?' she asks, gesturing Walker into a seat in front of her desk. 'Poor Siobhan and poor Gabby – it's been a terrible shock to all of us. We've appreciated your officers' help and support.'

'Yeah, nah, I'm part of the team that's looking into Siobhan's death, and I'm trying to get a sense of the kind of person that Siobhan was. We've had some conflicting reports. I thought that, as you knew her, perhaps you can tell me a little bit about her?'

'I didn't know her all that well, I'm afraid,' says Valerie Simpson. 'Gabby has been a student here for almost five years so of course I met Siobhan, but she always kept herself a bit separate.' She purses her lips and thinks. 'From what I could tell she was quiet, shy, a bit of an outsider. Not part of the mums' social group, though she and her husband always turned up and helped out at the fete and on sports days. Gabby's father is the opposite – very outgoing. He could charm the socks off anyone. Gabby herself is a good student and quiet, like her mum. We asked her parents in for a teacher conference a month or two ago because we felt Gabby was retreating into herself more than usual.'

'Did you ever get the sense that Siobhan Owen struggled with addiction issues?'

'No.' The answer is definitive. 'We do have some families here where drugs or alcohol are a problem but not Siobhan. Or she hid it exceptionally well. She's quiet, yes, but she's also very reliable, always here to pick up Gabby on time, always attended sports and family days and so on, and that's unusual if addiction is an issue.'

'She never missed any days picking up Gabby?'

'I've never been made aware of her unexpectedly not turning up. I know Gabby's father would come and pick her up once in a while, but as far as I recall it was never the case that we had to call him because Gabby hadn't been collected by her mum. And we do have to do that sometimes with a few other families who are a little more . . . chaotic, let's say.'

'How often would David Owen collect Gabby?'

'I can't tell you exactly – I'm not usually at the gate and I'm not paying attention to individual kids unless there's a problem there somewhere, but I'd say it was rare. Perhaps once or twice a term.'

The conversation is confirming the picture of Siobhan that Jess painted, too. A quiet person, who kept to herself. It contradicts the autopsy evidence and, disturbingly, David Owen's description of his wife.

'Righto, thanks very much,' says Walker. 'You've been very helpful. Appreciate it.'

As they stand and shake hands, Valerie Simpson looks at the clock. It's a few minutes before 3 p.m.

'If you want to find out more about Siobhan, there is one mum she sometimes spoke with. Maggie North. Her daughter Mia is in Gabby's class and they're friends. Maggie will be here picking up her kids – I can introduce you if you like?'

Walker accepts the offer and walks with her to the gate of the school. A cluster of parents are standing just inside the gate, sheltering from the heavy rain under the covered walkway that leads to the teaching block. Valerie Simpson walks up to a slight woman with curly hair, wearing pink sneakers, green yoga trousers and a pale-green singlet top.

'Maggie, do you have a second?' The principal looks around, perhaps conscious of other parents watching them, and gestures towards the school block. 'Can we talk a bit further on?' she says. 'Just for a bit more privacy.'

The eyes of the other parents follow them but with the noise of the rain on the roof of the walkway, they won't overhear anything much.

'This is DS Walker,' says the head. 'He's part of the team looking into Siobhan Owen's death and wanted to ask you a few questions?' When Maggie North nods assent, she says, 'Righto, I'll leave you to it', and strides back down the pathway towards the school.

Maggie North turns towards Walker. She's in her early forties, he'd guess, perhaps ten years older than Siobhan. 'What would you like to know?' she asks. 'Siobhan was such a lovely person. I can't stop thinking about what she must have gone through. It's just unbelievably horrible and tragic. How can I help?'

'You knew Siobhan well?' says Walker.

'Well, we're friends, but mostly because our girls are friends, so we saw each other when Gabby came over to our place to play or Mia went to theirs. And we'd say hello in the afternoons here sometimes.'

'What was she like?' asks Walker.

'She was a lovely woman. Quiet and shy, but very caring. A couple of months ago I had the flu and my husband was away with work. She picked up the kids and took them to her place and made them dinner. And she brought me a big pot of soup and some home-made biscuits and even went to the chemist for the medicines I needed. She always remembers birthdays and brings a card and she makes the best cakes . . . We baked together for the school fete once. Well, she and the girls did the baking, while I made the tea and washed up. I'm not much of a cook. It's a shame we didn't do things together more often, but she was quite hesitant about accepting invitations . . .'

'Did she talk about her family to you? About her sister or her husband?'

'No, Siobhan keeps— kept herself to herself, really. It was mostly just chat about the kids and school, you know?'

'Did Siobhan ever seem drunk to you when she picked up Gabby? Or did she miss picking her up on some days – maybe Gabby's dad picked her up instead?'

Maggie North gives a shocked half-laugh. 'What? No, never!'

'You don't need to protect her,' he says. 'We really need the truth – it can help us find the people who did this.'

'It is the truth. I never saw Siobhan drunk or tipsy or anything. I can't even imagine it. She was totally reliable. She was always here on time to meet Gabby. I work on Tuesdays and Thursdays and sometimes if I'm running a bit late she'll wait with my kids till I get here. I would have trusted her to pick up my kids anytime. I don't know if she drank at home, but she'd never pick Gabby up under the influence. Gabby's dad only picked her up once in a blue moon. He works, so it was always Siobhan.' She stops and thinks for a moment. 'Though, maybe I am missing something. Gabby's dad would often text Siobhan when she was here, check that she'd met Gabby, that everything was OK. I said he was very protective, but she said it was because she was a bit flaky sometimes. So maybe she did drink. I don't know, she never seemed flaky to me.'

Walker wonders if Siobhan was unreliable or if David Owen wanted her to feel that she was, to justify his control.

'How did Siobhan seem to you in the days before her death? Did you notice anything unusual? Was there anything worrying her?'

Maggie North thinks about it. 'No. In fact, maybe the opposite. She was always a bit of a worrier. I didn't see her smile or laugh that much. She always seemed a bit nervy. But the last time I saw her, waiting for the kids on the Friday before it happened, she seemed more energised than usual.'

'Did she say anything at all that day? Anything to give you an idea of why she was feeling good?'

'I don't really remember. We talked about our weekend plans, I think . . . That's right. I was taking the kids to Brisbane to see their grandparents and she said David was going to be out on Sunday with friends, sailing or golfing or something, and she and Gabby were going to have a girls' day together. That was more or less it.'

As she finishes talking, a shrill bell pierces the calm of the afternoon and a stream of kids in the red-and-grey uniform of the school flows past them, at first just a handful, then a growing number washing around them, damp and full of energy, walking, running, pushing and shoving, laughing and talking. 'Mum, Mum . . .' A girl pushes against Maggie North's legs. 'We made bickies in home ec – I brought us bickies for afternoon tea.'

Walker takes his leave. 'Thanks for your time, Mrs North,' he says.

She nods, distracted by her daughter and a smaller boy, the same curly hair as his mum, who has also arrived at her side. Walker turns to go, walking against the tide of children who part in eddies around him.

'Mr Policeman, Mr Policeman . . .' It's the curly-haired boy, pulling at his arm. Walker looks down and he points towards his mum, who beckons him back.

'There is one thing,' says Maggie North, when he's back in front of her. 'It's probably not important but she gave me a new phone number that Friday. She said she was changing her number, and this was the new one to reach her on. She had a new phone too, a silver iPhone. She showed it to me. It wasn't the latest version, but it was newer than the one she normally used and she was really happy with it.'

Chapter 36

5 p.m.

When Walker arrives back at the Owens' house, the damp-looking PC has gone. There's no police presence outside; perhaps the rain is heavy enough to deter nosy bystanders. Walker curses under his breath. He's spoken to Narelle and she checked the evidence log for him. The phone they have for Siobhan Owen is a battered-looking Samsung, not a silver iPhone, and the number, too, is different from the one Maggie North has given him. He wants to have a look for Siobhan's new phone, and is wondering why David Owen has given them her old one. He wants to check a few other things at the house too. There are clues here that will help him piece things together, and now that he has more information, he thinks he knows where to find them.

The gate is open so he jogs across the garden to the front door, the rain so heavy that even just a few short metres leave his hair and shoulders damp, and knocks hard. He's hoping there's a police presence inside. Surely Cummings wouldn't leave a crime scene unguarded. He hears footsteps, and when a woman constable opens the door he flashes a smile of relief.

'G'day,' he says, badge in hand. 'Lucas Walker, AFP. I'm helping out on the Owen case. I need to check a couple of things here.'

She checks his ID, lets him in and gives him the protective gear to put on. He starts by looking for the vodka that Siobhan had been drinking the night she died. It takes an age but eventually he finds it, hidden behind cleaning products in a cupboard under the sink, only an inch or so left in the bottom. The location matches what Owen had told Cummings, that Siobhan hid the evidence of her drinking. Even so, Walker wants to get it checked out. Beside the bottle is a small red plastic funnel. He thinks for a moment, then bags them both as evidence.

He starts hunting for Siobhan's new phone. He calls the number Maggie North gave him, but an automated voice tells him the phone is switched off. He searches the upstairs rooms first. He spends a long time going through all the bedrooms and the study. In Gabby's room the box of toys catches his eye again. He looks gently through it. There's a smashed-up plastic phone that someone has tried to tape back together, the pretty wooden doll's house he noticed this morning, glue running in a thick line a third of the way across the roof and down the back, a broken plastic camper van, the roof squashed in, which looks like it's been dropped or stood on. Gabby is hard on her toys, he thinks, or someone else has broken them. The latter thought makes his heart sink – it could mean there are two victims of David Owen's controlling behaviour.

He goes downstairs and keeps searching for Siobhan's phone, but after more than an hour has nothing to show for it. There's no sign of it anywhere. He needs to ask Cummings to organise a proper search, he thinks, outside in the canal too, perhaps. He looks for the constable, who is sitting in a folding chair near the front door.

'I'm done now,' he says, reading her name on her shirt. 'Thanks, Constable Jones. Could you submit these as evidence and ask for them to be analysed for DNA and fingerprints?'

'Will do, sir,' she says, taking the bags with the bottle and funnel. She looks at him. 'I thought all the forensics had been done. Have you found something new? Are there some new leads?'

'I'm an extra pair of eyes, looking at the case from a different perspective,' he says. 'Let's see if anything comes of it. Could you ask forensics to make this a priority?'

She nods. 'Righto, absolutely.'

Something comes to him. 'Are you Constable Anna Jones?' he asks.

'Yeah, I am.'

'You were first on the scene here, right?'

She nods. 'Yeah.'

'I've read your report, but could you walk me through what you found again, now that we're here together?'

She takes him through the house and how they'd searched it, where they'd found David and Siobhan, Gabby. As with her written report, he's impressed with her clear memory and eye for detail. At the end of her description, standing at the bottom of the stairs, he asks: 'Is there anything, anything at all, that jumped out at you that night, that caught your eye? Any little detail that seemed off or surprising?'

She looks at him, indecision in her eyes. 'I'm not an investigator yet so, you know, I'm not really trained in looking at crime scenes.'

'I understand, but when you're the first on the scene you have a unique perspective. It's a living, breathing space, everything is still in motion, not set in aspic like it is now. And sometimes there's something that you notice, either then or when you think about it later, that prompts a little question inside you . . .'

She nods, thinks for a while. 'Yeah, well, one thing I did think was a bit weird was that Dr Owen was sitting beside his wife, on the floor, holding her hand. He wasn't trying to save her life, trying to staunch her wounds or whatever. He's a doctor, so he must know what to do. But maybe he'd already realised it was too late.'

She's perceptive, thinks Walker. Owen wasn't frantically trying to save any lives, neither Siobhan's nor Gabby's, which goes against every principle of his training and medical oath. Not to mention his role as husband and father. You could argue he was in shock, perhaps, from the attack he'd suffered, but Walker's not so sure.

Jones thinks a moment longer, then leads him into the kitchen. 'There was a back-up team that checked down here, but while my partner and I were waiting for CID and SOCO teams to arrive, I had a look at the living room and then I came into the kitchen too,' she says. 'There was nothing here. It was untouched.'

Walker nods, remembering the footage from the body cam.

'I stood here for a minute, catching my breath. It had been a tough night. The crime scene – it was violent, horrible, the worst I've seen. And the poor little girl, too. The rest of the house – most of the rooms had been invaded. You know, the bedrooms, the study and the living room, even the hallway had blood through it. But when I came in here it was quiet and, well, normal. They hadn't come in here. You could tell. It felt like the only room in the house that wasn't violated,' says Jones. 'So I stood here for a minute and I heard the dishwasher running. I didn't think anything about it at the time, but later on I thought it was strange.'

'Why's that?' asks Walker.

'Well, we arrived at the scene at four ten. I was probably in the kitchen at four thirty, something like that. Dishwasher programmes usually run for two, maybe three hours? That means the dishwasher was put on at the earliest at one a.m. But most likely later because it wasn't finished, it was still in the washing phase – I could hear it running. That's pretty late to switch a dishwasher on.'

Walker nods. Owen had said that Siobhan had gone to bed early, and that he'd been asleep when the intruders broke in at 2 a.m. Perhaps he'd put the dishwasher on just before going to bed. He walks over and pulls it open. The dishwasher is still filled with its clean load from that night, and it emits a stale, slightly bacterial scent. Plates, a pan, a salad bowl, pasta bowls and a smaller pink plastic bowl with a unicorn design fill the bottom rack. Cereal bowls, glasses and mugs, one with *World's Best Mum* written on it, are stacked in the rack above. Walker spots a third rack, a slim one right at the top. It's filled with cutlery: wooden spoons, an egg flipper and a pasta server with a pink plastic handle. There is also a knife. A large wood-handled chef's knife, twenty centimetres long perhaps, with a broad blade coming to a sharp point.

Chapter 37

10 p.m.

She's so tired but she's trying to stay awake. She can't go to sleep. If she sleeps something bad might happen. She remembers another night, going to bed, waking up, hearing a scary noise, calling for Mum but no one came. Then ... the corridor, the light in Mum and Dad's bedroom and— No, she can't remember, she doesn't want to look behind the door. It's too scary. Her stomach hurts. Her head hurts. She's scared. She wants her mum.

Matilda comes in to check on her. Matilda is nice. She gives hugs and she reads her all the cards from her friends. 'They miss you,' she says. 'They all want you to come back to school.' She wants to go back to school, wants to go home, but most of all she wants her mum. Matilda gives her a big smile but when she looks at her it changes to a frown and she says, 'What's wrong, Gabby? Does something hurt?'

'No,' she says. 'But Mum isn't coming to visit and I'm scared. When can I see my mum? When is Mum coming to visit me?'

'There's been an accident and that means she can't come to see you,' says Matilda. 'If she could be here, she would be. She would want to see you and hug you and she would be so happy at how much better you are. She loves you very, very much.'

'Is she alright? When can she come?'

'I don't know, Gabby,' says Matilda. 'But I do know that she really, really loves you. Now, it's almost eleven p.m., which is very late. You go back to sleep, and your dad will be here when you wake up.'

She tries to sleep but every time she closes her eyes the wolf is back in her dreams and it's hurting Mum and there's blood everywhere and she screams and the wolf growls and chases her down the dark corridor and she can feel it grab her around the neck and she can't breathe, she can't breathe. She cries out, her arms pushing it away, and she's awake and there's nothing there. She's crying, not loud, but she can't stop, and after a minute a man pokes his head around the door to her room. She sees his curly hair. She's met him before. He's Lucas, the policeman who guards her door.

'Hello, Gabby,' he says. 'Are you OK? Do you want me to call the nurse?'

She shakes her head.

'Is everything OK?' he asks again.

'I'm scared,' she says. 'Is there something under the bed?'

Lucas comes into the room and gets on his hands and knees, looks under her bed. Then he walks over and looks carefully behind the table with the presents and flowers; he even opens the little cupboard beside her bed. Then he stands at the end of her bed and gives her a salute.

'I can report, Miss Gabby, that I have searched your room and it is totally safe. There's nothing under the bed or anywhere. And I'm here to look after you. You can go to sleep. I'll be sitting outside or, if you like, I can sit in here with you. And if you wake up and feel scared, you just call out for me and I'll come and check again. OK?'

She nods. 'I dreamt the wolf was hurting Mum again . . .'

Lucas nods. 'Do you want to talk about it?' he asks.

She looks at him. He has a nice face. Perhaps she could tell him. But Mum says we can't tell, or Dad will get cross. She won't tell. She shakes her head.

'OK,' he says. 'I'll be right outside. You call anytime you need me.'

The constable covering the next shift arrives early and Walker is grateful for the chance to get some extra sleep. Before he goes, he looks quickly into the room. Gabby is sleeping. Matilda had given her something and there'd been no more nightmares. He tells the constable who's taking over to say hello to Gabby when she wakes up, to tell her Lucas will be back tonight.

'Will do,' says the constable. 'Poor little thing. Does she know about her mum yet?'

Walker shakes his head. 'I don't think so,' he says. But as he walks down to the ute he wonders if that's true. He thinks Gabby is starting to recall the night of the attack. He had a feeling that she was keeping something from him when he spoke with her earlier. If her nightmares are starting to reveal the truth to her, and if what Walker suspects happened that night is right, it puts her in very real danger.

Chapter 38

Walker wakes. He hasn't closed the curtains and the rising daylight is bringing him out of a dream. He's slept briefly and badly. When he came home from the shift at Gabby Owen's bedside he went through the case notes again, putting together a more complete picture of what he now thinks really happened that night. The longer it takes for him to prove his theory, for them to solve this case, the greater the danger she's in. He needs to convince Cummings, but he has to wait for the forensics on the vodka bottle and knife. Until then it's nothing more than conjecture and Cummings has made it clear he needs concrete evidence.

He pads over to the windows and looks out. A heavy grey mist and rain clouds obscure his view of the sea. The air is cool on his bare chest. He goes back to bed, puts a couple of pillows behind his back, switches on the morning news. The rain, which has been non-stop for days, seems to be getting heavier and is making headlines.

'A rain bomb,' announces the weatherwoman with something approaching relish, 'is sitting above South-East Queensland.' Created by unusually warm oceans and some kind of low – Walker misses the exact details – it is dumping unprecedented amounts of rain onto the state capital and southern coastal areas, including the Gold Coast. Brisbane has had the equivalent of a year's worth of rain in less than two days. Chaos has ensued, the news filled with images of swollen rivers, flooded streets and cars floating down suburban roads. One home on a steep slope has been washed away into the river, a shocked-looking homeowner in borrowed pants explaining he

195

escaped in his undies from a rear window, everything else gone. The climate crisis feels very real this morning, thinks Walker. No longer limited to the outback's terrible drought – age-old water systems drying out, grasslands turning to dust – but something that's affecting urban Australians. He thinks of Caloodie and his cousin Blair and the ranchers whose livelihoods have been destroyed. Perhaps now that a larger and more vocal electorate has been affected, those in charge will take the climate more seriously.

His thoughts turn to Kaia. It was well after 2 a.m. before he went to bed last night and he'd been fast asleep, waking with a start to the sound of his phone ringing. He grabbed the phone in the dark, instinct taking over, answering without looking at the caller ID.

'Yeah?'

He heard the sound of rapid breathing, the sound, too, of the storm, rain and wind, and then a sob. Turned the phone to look at the screen, illuminated in the dark. *Kaia*.

'Kaia? Are you OK?'

'Nooo.' It came out as a wail. 'I'm lost, Lucas. It's dark, it's raining so much and I got totally wet and I went inside the wrong building and I've lost the others, and I don't know where I am, I'm, I . . .'

'No worries, you're OK. Where are you? Describe to me where you are.'

'I don't know. It's dark and there's a big storm. I can't see anything, and I lost the others. I can't find them, I'm on my own.' She's crying, big gulping sobs.

'OK, we'll sort this out, we'll get you home.'

'No, no, I need to find the party. I need to go back.'

'Tell me what happened, and I'll help you find them.'

She started a long story, not making much sense. 'I was with Martin and Toby and a few others. I can't sail, the beach is shut, it's raining. We went to the casino, blackjack and roulette, I'm so crap. Not the high roller. It was funny' – she giggles a bit through her tears – 'we were dancing in the rain. Then we went to Toby's place because he's always good for a party. But I lost them. I lost them.' She is crying again. 'I don't know where they are. I don't know where I am. I need to find them, Lucas. I don't want to be on my own.'

'No drama – send me your location and I'll come and pick you up—'

'No! You're not listening to me! I don't know where I am. I'm lost.'

'I'm listening. I want you to open Maps on your phone, and I'll talk you through it.'

She sniffs loudly. 'You're not listening,' she says.

'Can you open the Maps app?'

There was a pause and then: 'Toby!' She screamed the name. 'Toby!' Walker held the phone a little further from his ear.

'I found them, I found them!' She was half-laughing, half-crying. 'I gotta go, I found them, I gotta go.' And then she hung up.

When he looked at his phone again, he saw it was 3.30 a.m. Thinking of his promise to be a big brother to her, and knowing what he'd do if Grace were in the same situation, he sent her a message. *All OK Kaia? Let me know if you need me to pick you up, doesn't matter what time, just call.*

Afterwards he fell into a restless sleep, half an ear out for another call from Kaia. He dreamt of rain, then of the ocean pounding the city, waves as high as buildings flooding the streets. He was standing on a footpath, waves curving over him, trying to dive through them, under them, but they were too fast, too big. One crashed down on him and he was underwater, turning over and over. When he came up for air he saw Kaia in the water beside him, reaching her hand towards him, saying, 'Help me, Lucas', but another wave crashed over them and he was tumbling, turning, and she was gone. When the wave finally released him he emerged into a calm ocean, the shore a long way away. And no sign of Kaia anywhere.

Now he checks his phone again but there are no more messages from Kaia, his last message to her still unread. He remembers that she texted him some pictures earlier last night and scrolls up again for a look. A group of youngsters sitting on a roof terrace somewhere, hair wet, clothes too, by the look. Kaia smiling and raising a glass to the camera. He recognises one of the blokes from the nightclub, holding a bottle of bourbon in one hand. In another shot the same group are on an L-shaped sofa, the photo a bit blurred but it looks like there's a bag of pills and maybe a line of coke too on the coffee table in front of them.

He needs to talk to her, today or maybe tomorrow when she's over her hangover. She won't like what he has to say but it needs to be said. She needs to take her parents' advice, go back to rehab. She won't regain her form, won't reclaim her life, living like this.

He takes a long hot shower then makes and consumes three rounds of toast and Vegemite and two rounds of extra-strong coffee. He hasn't slept well and needs to wake up. While he's eating, he checks his email. Maria Marques, the pathologist he met yesterday, has sent him a message.

> *You were right. Siobhan Owen doesn't have the hepatic histology that I'd expect of a regular drinker – the liver isn't enlarged and doesn't exhibit steatosis (fatty liver), steatohepatitis (alcoholic hepatitis) or cirrhosis.*

His stomach twists as he reads it. He thinks he's worked out some of what happened to Siobhan and Gabby that night, and he knows he's in a race against time.

When he's ready to leave he spends a few minutes looking for his mobile phone, finally finding it hidden under a stray pillow on his bed. He's received a flurry of texts from Kaia in the last half-hour. The first is a selfie in which she doesn't look herself, her pupils dilated, her smile off-kilter. Then a stream of messages:

> *martin and toby are losers*

> *party a total downer*

> *still raining i hate it here*

> *my life is shit i always fuck things up*

Followed by a series of duck emojis and a crying face.

He starts to type a message, thinks better of it and presses the Call button. Her phone rings and rings but she doesn't answer. He thinks about calling again but she's probably sleeping. She needs the rest, he decides, and it's probably better to wait until he can talk with her in person anyway. He'll invite her to dinner, ask her more directly what drugs she's using, try to talk her into rehab or at least pulling her foot off the party pedal for a while. He can see why her parents are worried. She seems to have been partying for several days straight and she's obviously not in a good place.

He stops the lift at reception on its way down. He can hear the rain driving against the big plate-glass windows and the floor by the doors that lead to the street is a couple of inches deep in water. A cleaner, mopping desperately, is struggling to keep up with the inflow.

He walks over to the receptionist. 'Shocking weather,' he says.

'Yeah, and it's been throwing it down like this since Sunday arvo, non-stop. Not natural, is it?'

'Nah, it's not,' agrees Walker. The rain feels biblical – a flood, a purge. 'Any mail for me? Lucas Walker. I'm staying in the penthouse.'

The receptionist checks the numbered mailboxes behind his desk. 'Sorry, nah, nothing. But we haven't had this morning's delivery yet. Rain disruption.'

Walker is conscious of an undefined feeling, something unfamiliar, as he goes down to his ute. He sits for a moment before he starts the engine, thinking about it. He's homesick, he realises with surprise. For the first time in decades, since he moved to Boston when he was just a kid, he's homesick. Homesick for Caloodie, for the quiet streets, the peaceful bush, the wide arc of the indigo sky, the bird calls, the sweet mangoes in his grandmother's back garden and the swish of Ginger's tail against his leg. He misses Blair's laconic good humour, and most of all he misses Grandma, her biscuits, her hugs, her love-filled home. He breathes out a big sigh. He'll go home. As soon as he's finished here, as soon as he knows what the outcome of the review board is, he's going home.

The decision cheers him up. He accelerates out of the covered car park then slows as he reaches the road. The rain is like nothing he's seen, sheets of it coming down from the leaden sky. He can barely see the neighbouring high-rise buildings, hidden behind the heavy rain and low clouds. The roads are covered in water, which sprays high behind the ute, and muddy puddles fill every depression on the verge. Even in the heart of Surfers Paradise the streets are almost empty of other vehicles.

His phone buzzes a few times but he ignores it. The roads are dangerous enough in this weather without driving while distracted. When he hits a traffic light on red, he glances down at it. Another set of messages from Kaia. He pulls over into a servo on the next corner, switches off the engine and picks up the phone. The first is a voice message and when he listens to it he's shocked. He can barely recognise her voice – it's so slurred, so slow, he struggles to make sense of what she's saying. He immediately wonders what she's taken.

'Hi Lucas, n'you call me, I wanna talk can't sleep . . . feel bad . . . sorry you know sorry I took so much shit. I know I shouldna . . . but wanna sleep. last one, promise, last one. gonna stay clean as clean as clean. giz a call alright?'

A series of text messages:

u mad?

Call me puleeze

The rest are nothing more than a jumble of letters: *badsas simnot nea otrmore sting abeioscnthhhhh*

He hits the Call button; her phone rings and rings and rings. Then voicemail kicks in. He tries again, and a third time. No reply. As he leaves her a message – 'Call me, Kaia, I'm here, please call me' – Walker has a very bad feeling in the pit of his stomach.

Chapter 39

9 a.m.

The rain is drumming on the roof of the car, so loud Walker can't hear his own thoughts. He's torn with indecision but his gut feeling about Kaia is getting worse. Before he does anything more on the Owen case he needs to speak with her. He looks up the phone number of the hotel where she's staying.

'Sorry, sir, there's a Do Not Disturb on that room,' says the receptionist. 'I can't connect you. Can I take a message?'

'Look, I'm really worried about my friend. She's texted me, she's feeling crook and she's alone and upset. Please, try the room, see if she'll take my call.'

'I would if I could, sir, but there's no way to interrupt the Do Not Disturb. It's set up that way.'

'Can you put me through to someone? Your manager? This is really important.'

He hears her huff down the phone. 'Please hold,' she says.

He waits an age, the hold music interminable, a discordant plunking in his ear. He needs to get to Kaia. He switches the engine back on.

'This is Melissa King, front-of-house manager. How can I help you?'

'Ms King, this is DS Lucas Walker from the AFP. I have an urgent request. A young woman, Kaia Hale in room seven-oh-nine, has been trying to get in touch with me. I need to speak with her as soon as possible. Can you try her room? I know she'll take my call if you contact her.'

'I'm sorry, sir, as my colleague told you we can't bypass the phone system.'

'Look, this is a police matter,' he lies. 'I really need to speak with her.'

There's a long pause. 'As I can't verify that with you, unfortunately I can't put you through. If you want to send an officer over, we can take them up to the room.'

He breathes out an angry sigh. 'I'm on my way. Please could you ask someone to go and check on her, make sure she's OK?'

There's a pause. 'OK,' she says. 'I can send a porter to the room to check.'

'Can you call me back, let me know her status?'

She takes his number. 'There's a lot going on right now,' she says. 'The flooding means we have a lot of guests who can't get home, people who are stranded and distressed. I'll get someone to knock on her door, but I can't promise I'll get back to you quickly.'

What should be a twenty-minute drive to Kaia's hotel takes almost double that, Walker's already slow progress impeded by closed roads and enforced detours. When he pulls up under the high-roofed driveway in front of the hotel the relentless drumming of the rain on the roof of the ute is finally stilled, but as soon as he steps out into the damp air the noise is back, so loud he can barely hear the surf on the beach out front. He gives the ute's keys to a doorman in the tan, blue and white uniform of the hotel, who holds out his hand for them as Walker jogs by.

He runs into the foyer and across to the lifts, presses the button for the seventh floor. Nothing doing. An expensively dressed couple join him in the lift, both giving him a suspicious side-eye.

'I think you'll find you need a key to operate it,' says the man.

'Fucksake,' says Walker, exiting the lift and walking quickly to the concierge desk. He's got his badge in his hand, flashes it at the guy before anyone says anything. 'Police,' he says. 'I urgently need to speak to one of your guests. Kaia Hale, room seven-oh-nine. I have reason to believe she needs medical attention.'

A flicker of concern crosses the concierge's face. He takes the badge, checks it and hands it back. Picks up his phone and dials.

'The room's on Do Not Disturb,' says Walker.

'That's right, sir,' says the concierge.

'I know because I called an hour ago, and no one would take my request seriously. I've had to come myself to check on Ms Hale.'

The look of concern is more visible now. The concierge picks up the phone again and says, 'Can you send a porter over, please?' A moment later one of the young blokes from the door is at his side. 'Take DS Walker to room seven-oh-nine, please,' says the concierge. 'If you need to open the door you have my permission to override the Do Not Disturb.'

When they get up to room 709, there's a small red light above the key card reader.

'It's on Do Not Disturb,' says the porter.

'For fuck's sake, just open it, mate,' says Walker. 'It's urgent.'

The porter holds a card to the reader, which beeps twice, then the red light flashes. After another long moment it turns green; the porter pushes down on the handle and the door opens.

'Ms Hale, this is housekeeping. Good morning, Ms Hale. Housekeeping,' the porter calls out. He is standing in front of Walker in the room's short hallway. The bathroom to the right and the bedroom ahead are in darkness, only a small chink of light from behind the heavy curtains where they don't quite meet in the middle.

'Kaia,' says Walker loudly, 'it's Lucas', and he pushes impatiently past. He can vaguely see a shape lying on the bed but there's no sound from Kaia. Most likely she's fast asleep. He turns back to the porter, lowering his voice – he doesn't want to wake her, but he needs to check she's OK. 'Can you turn a light on, please.'

'She's sleeping, sir – I think we should leave . . .'

Walker holds in a curse. He walks slowly towards the bed, his feet catching on clothes strewn on the floor, half-trips, puts a hand in front of him, feels his way along the edge of the mattress. When he gets to the bedside table, he reaches across it, feeling for the lamp, and then along the base of the lamp until he finds the switch. The light bathes the bed in a gentle glow. Kaia is lying on her back, the sheets pulled up to her shoulders. But he can tell instantly that something isn't right. Her mouth is slightly open, slack; her eyelids, too, don't look fully closed and her tanned skin is pale. He reaches over to touch her arm. Her skin feels cool. He can hear his heart beating loud in his ears.

'Turn the lights on now,' he says over his shoulder to the porter. 'She's in trouble.'

The porter hesitates.

'Turn the fucking lights on!' shouts Walker. The porter moves back into the hallway, and a second later the lights come on. In the brighter light Kaia's face looks even paler.

Walker reaches over, shakes her gently by the shoulder.

'Kaia?' he says. 'Kaia, can you hear me?'

There's no response. He feels at her wrist for a pulse, then her throat. Nothing. He checks for her breathing: can't hear anything, can't see her chest moving up and down, nothing.

The porter is standing at the end of the bed, his face anxious.

'She's not breathing. Call triple zero,' says Walker. 'We need an ambulance now. Is there a doctor in the hotel?'

The porter runs over to the desk on the other side of the room, picks up the phone. 'We need a doctor urgently, room seven-oh-nine,' he says into the phone. 'And call triple zero. We need an ambulance.'

Walker starts chest compressions, pushing firmly downwards and then releasing. He's hoping Kaia hasn't been unconscious, unresponsive, for long. If he can keep the blood pumping around her body and into her brain until help arrives, she can recover. He pushes down firmly and repeats. After about thirty compressions she's still not breathing. He tries rescue breaths, tilting her head back, pinching her nose, blowing steadily into her mouth for two breaths. Nothing. He goes back to administering compressions again.

'Does the hotel have a defibrillator? We need a defibrillator,' he says to the porter, who is back at the end of the bed, watching in shock. 'Call reception, find out if there's a defibrillator in the hotel.'

He's counting compressions when the doctor arrives – an older man. He's casually dressed, a mauve short-sleeved shirt with a polo-playing horse rider logo embroidered on it and long navy shorts, but he's carrying a brown leather bag and Walker can tell he's been running; he's breathing hard.

'I can't find a pulse,' says Walker. 'She's not breathing.'

The doctor takes over from Walker, pressing down on Kaia's chest. Walker stands there, watching, helpless. Kaia's face is so pale, her lips blue. She's cold, that's what he thinks. She's ice-cold.

Chapter 40

10 a.m.

Nathan Brown is working out. He's benching weights so heavy his arms are shaking. Lifting in sets of thirty. Pushing it hard – twenty-six. This is the day – twenty-seven. The day he's been waiting for – twenty-eight. The club has finally asked him for help, and if he does a good job, he's going to make member – twenty-nine. He can feel the blood pumping, his veins standing hard against his forehead, his heart beating under his chest – thirty. He holds the weight a moment longer, feeling the pressure, the pain of it, then drops it with a clang back into the power rack, lying back, covered in sweat, his singlet and the skin on his back sticking to the plastic cover of the bench.

It's early morning and the gym is quiet. Aaron has told all Vandals to stop using Iron Fitness and it's kept the blokes Nathan usually works out with away. There are a couple of young blokes spotting each other in one corner and another bloke, on his own, who's spent the last half-hour posing with weights and taking mirror selfies. The pig isn't here but he reckons Aaron will be happy there's a few others at least. They want to send this Ford bloke a message and the more chaos there is when he starts the fire, the bigger the message.

He sits up, looks around. The others are engrossed in their workouts, not looking like leaving, so this is as good a time as any. He pushes through the door that leads from the gym into the changing rooms. These, and the adjacent reception, are the most luxurious areas of the gym and both have wooden floors. The sauna, in a far corner of the changing rooms, isn't used much and is made of wood too. He can cause a bit of damage here.

He opens his locker, digs out a little bag of pills. These are the latest mix, Aaron told him. New formula. Faster, harder, better than before. Pills are best for a job like this – the rush takes longer and is more controlled. He takes one, thinks fuck it, tips another into his hand and drops that one too. He's got a few minutes till the high kicks in. He grabs his t-shirt out of the locker and pulls it on over his vest, his heart already beating fast, his hands shaking a little. He's not sure if it's down to the exercise or the adrenaline rush or the pills taking effect.

His sports bag is stuffed with goodies. He pulls out the handful of newspapers and the big bag of chips he bought at the local newsagent's this morning and moves the changing room bin, a big round metal thing as high as his thighs, to beside the sauna. He takes the lid off and stuffs half the newspapers inside and lights the corner of the crisp packet. Crisps are the perfect accelerant: they burn well and don't go out quickly. When he was a kid, he and his brother set their grandmother's sofa on fire using a much smaller pack than this, so he reckons it'll start nicely. It takes a few seconds before the flame from the lighter gets the crisp bag smouldering. As soon as it does, he drops it onto the newspaper and puts a bit more paper lightly on top. It'll take a few minutes to get fully going, which gives him time for the bigger job. He heads out past reception, leaving the main doors open as he goes. A through-draft will help the fire build.

He walks past the lift and takes the stairs. The gym is on the first floor, above an escape room franchise called Heist and the car park in the basement. The stairs are mostly only used by staff and some of the fitness freaks that work out here.

'Take the stairs for some free exercise,' one loser had said to Nathan a few weeks ago while he'd been waiting for the lift. Nathan had stared him down so hard the bloke almost bricked himself, but he'd remembered it when Aaron had asked him about the chances of causing a bit of mayhem with a fire. He scoped it out, and he's come up with a plan. The stairs from ground floor to first floor are covered with dark-blue carpet tiles and he reckons they'll catch pretty good.

He can feel the meth kicking in now. A rush, a kick, a divine intervention of power, of strength. He takes a small can of diesel out of his bag, pours it along the side of the stairs as he walks down. He is invincible. He wants another draught of air to keep it all moving. He tries the door marked Staff that leads into Heist. Not locked. He pushes it open. There's a heap of boxes filled with paper and files just inside. You little beauty, he says to himself.

He tips a heap more diesel across the papers and boxes and drops a match on top. The flames jump high, almost burning his hands and arms. He dances out of their reach and lights the diesel on the stairs with another match, then takes the concrete stairs to the basement two at a time and walks through the car park and out the side door for pedestrians. He forces himself not to run. There's no CCTV here but still, he needs to be calm, doesn't want to draw attention.

His Harley is parked a block away and it's raining like a mongrel but he doesn't care. He feels his exhilaration build as he reaches the bike, climbs on and rides off. He's done it – he's gotten away with it. Once he's on the highway, away from the scene, he accelerates. The bike matches the speed of his mind: he's at one with the road, with the wind, the rain, the storm. He's flying. Exhilarated. Free. A fucking legend in his own lifetime.

Nadine West has been online since she started her shift on reception this morning, trying to rearrange the details for Ryan's thirtieth birthday party this Thursday. They'd planned a barbecue, but the rain is supposed to hang around for days and she doesn't fancy cooking for twenty-five friends and family in her shitty little kitchen. The problem is that no one wants to go out in this weather either. She found a pizza place that'll deliver but Ryan thinks pizza is a bit lame. She's trying to think of other options that'll work for everyone, half-nods goodbye to the bloke leaving, then notices belatedly that he hasn't shut the doors. She calls out, 'Sorry, can you shut the door, please?' but he's already gone. She looks at her phone: 10.14. She needs to come up with a plan before her shift finishes at twelve. She leaves the doors – she'll get up and close them in a minute – and gets back to tapping on her keyboard, googling for inspiration.

It takes a few minutes before the smell of smoke reaches her. As she looks up, the fire alarm in the stairwell goes off, with a violent scree-scree-scree that causes her heart to accelerate. There's smoke coming in through the open doors. It must be downstairs. Shit. She runs to the doors and closes them, the alarm still screaming, the noise only abating slightly with the doors shut. She hears a shout, a half-scream, and a bloke runs through from the gym. 'The fucking changing rooms are on fire.'

Nadine looks to the front doors she's just closed. She'd have sworn the smoke was coming through there. She runs over and pulls the fire extinguisher from its brackets. Two other blokes push through the doors from the gym. 'Evacuate!' she's shouting at them. 'You need to evacuate now.'

She looks at the fire extinguisher, can't really remember the training in how to use it. You just pull the pin, she thinks, and push down on the handle. It's easy. She pulls the pin and pushes with her hips on the door into the changing room. As it opens, a sheet of heat engulfs her. She can smell her hair burning. Her fingers press down on the fire extinguisher. It emits a jet of foam, not lessening the heat much, then there are hands pulling her back, a wet towel over her hair, the heat subsiding.

'Are you OK? Are you OK?' They're around her, anxious looks on their faces.

'Yeah,' she says. The smell of her hair burning is horrendous. Her hands, her arms, are red and stinging. She runs to the water cooler, sticks her hands underneath, trying to stop the burning. One of the blokes brings his bottle of water over and pours it over her arms, another opens the main doors.

'For fuck's sake, the stairs are on fire. We're fucking trapped.' She can hear hysteria in their voices. The smoke is acrid, burning; the men are coughing.

'Shut the doors now,' she shouts as loud as she can, finding a tone of authority. 'Shut them now.'

They're milling around, not listening. She runs over, closes the doors, wincing at the pain in her injured hands.

'The lift – we'll take the lift.'

'Not the lift,' she says. 'In case of fire, we can't use the lift.' She runs back to the reception desk, dials 000.

'Fire brigade, we need the fire brigade – we're trapped. The stairs are on fire and the gym too. It's Iron Fitness on the Boulevard at Surfers. There's four of us and we're trapped.'

Chapter 41

10.15 a.m.

The doctor is still giving Kaia chest compressions when there's a commotion at the door of the room and a staff member appears holding a defibrillator in a dark-brown box.

'Take over from me, please,' says the doctor to Walker.

Touching Kaia, he feels again how cool her skin is. She's still not breathing. 'Come on, Kaia,' he says under his breath. 'Breathe for me.'

The doctor peels off the defibrillator's sticky pads and attaches one to Kaia's chest, the other a little lower by her ribs. 'Stand back,' he says, and Walker stops, lifts his hands from Kaia's chest.

The machine beeps and speaks in a robotic voice: 'Evaluating heart rhythm' – then a moment later: 'No heartbeat detected.'

Walker looks at the doctor. 'What does that mean?'

'Keep going with the compressions,' says the doctor, then, turning to the hotel staff, 'Clear the room, please. Find out where the ambulance is, tell them we have an unresponsive patient, no heartbeat, and then wait outside the door and bring the ambos directly in when they arrive.'

While Walker is pressing down on Kaia's chest the doctor feels for a pulse then shines a small torch into her eyes. Walker is close enough to see her pupils are tiny and unreactive.

'How long has she been unresponsive?' the doctor asks Walker.

'I don't know. I'd only been here a few minutes before you arrived. She messaged me earlier, an hour or so ago, confused and feeling unwell.'

'I'll take over now. Can you open the curtains, please.'

They swap places and Walker goes quickly over to the windows

211

and opens the curtains. The wind is blowing rain against the building. Hard streaks of water lash the veranda and Kaia's bikini, which is hanging, wet and scraggly, on a soaked sun lounger. The storm has turned the ocean a sickly hue, the crashing waves foamy brown.

Walker turns back to the bed, the doctor still pressing down on Kaia's chest, watching her face. As the light of the day washes into the room, Walker sees the pale, unnatural colour of her skin and has to breathe deep to suppress nausea.

Back at her bedside he notices for the first time a small orange-topped pill bottle lying on the floor beside the bed, on its side and empty. He picks it up. Endone, an oxycodone painkiller. Her name is typed on the label on the front.

'Endone,' he says to the doctor. 'Maybe she took too many of these?'

They swap places again. For a moment Walker feels a twinge of hope – Kaia's skin is warmer – but as he adjusts his hands he realises it's only where the doctor has been pressing down. The rest of her is still cold. The doctor checks the pill bottle, then walks quickly back to his bag. Walker watches as he draws something from a vial with a needle and, working quickly, injects it into the muscle of Kaia's upper arm.

'Naloxone,' he says to Walker. 'It's an antidote to opioids, can help the patient keep breathing or start breathing again. It's an uncertain treatment when the patient doesn't have a pulse but it's all we have right now.'

Walker keeps pushing on her chest. 'Come on, Kaia, come on.' He's not sure how long he keeps pressing before he feels a hand on his arm. The doctor is standing close beside him.

'You can stop for a minute,' he says. He has his stethoscope in his hand and when Walker steps back, the doctor holds it against Kaia's chest for a long moment, then checks again for her pulse, before placing her arm gently on the bed. He brings out his torch and directs the light to her eyes.

Walker hears him exhale.

'No palpable carotid pulse, no heart sound, no breathing detected,' says the doctor. He turns and looks at Walker. 'I'm very sorry but there's nothing more we can do.' He looks at his watch. 'I declare life extinct at ten twenty-four on Tuesday March fourteenth.'

Walker feels his knees wobble. He sits on the side of the bed, touches Kaia's cold cheeks, pushes a strand of hair away from her face, holds her hand.

The doctor gives him space, stands at the desk, writing something in a notebook. Time slows for Walker. He doesn't know how long he's been sitting there when he hears a noise outside the door and then a team of two paramedics come into the room, moving fast. They slow as they see him sitting on the bed beside Kaia and look to the doctor, who gives a shake of his head.

'I'm Dr Kyle, hotel resident. I was called to the room at five past ten, found the patient unresponsive, possible opioid overdose. I gave her a dose of Naloxone and we administered compression for more than fifteen minutes. At ten twenty-four I heard no heart sounds for thirty seconds, no breath sounds for thirty seconds, detected no palpable carotid pulse and declared life extinct.'

Walker is dazed by the words – so bland, so clinical. This is Kaia they're talking about. Beautiful, vibrant, athletic, alive. He can see her flying across the waves, running on the sand, laughing and smiling.

Dr Kyle, who has been conferring quietly with the paramedics, turns to him. 'This is a reportable death, I'm afraid, so we'll need to call the police and then take her to a coroner. Are you family? Can you make a formal identification?'

Walker shakes his head. 'No, I'm not family – she's friends with my sister. I've only known her a short while. I don't have her family's contact details but she's from Hawaii. Her parents live there, in Hawaii, I think. Her name is Kaia Hale. She's a kitesurfer, quite famous.' He pulls out his badge. 'I'm with the AFP. I can secure the room until Queensland Police get here, and I can give them a full statement too.'

The three medics confer quietly, then leave him. 'We'll wait outside,' says Dr Kyle.

After they've gone, Walker shuts off the feelings that are rising inside him and goes into professional mode. He looks around properly for the first time. The room is a bit of a mess; clothes and shoes lie strewn on one side of the bed in front of the mirrored wardrobe. It looks as though Kaia stepped out of her dress, shoes and bra and left them where they fell.

He walks to the other side of the bed and pulls open the drawer of the bedside table. A sleep mask, contraceptive pills and a pair of AirPods in their white case. There's also a small Ziploc plastic bag, filled with a dozen or more pills, pale blue, circular, stamped with a raised M logo. But for the plastic bag holding them, they look like standard prescription meds. Walker photographs the bag and tips two of the pills into his palm and sniffs them. They have a vaguely bitter, medicinal scent to them. He pulls a tissue from the box on the bedside table, wraps them up and drops them into his pocket.

Underneath the bag is a prescription, a repeat, for more Endone. He looks at the details – issued by Dr David Owen. The name makes him start, but Owen is a sports doctor so it makes sense Kaia would have been in contact with him. He snaps a photo of the script on his phone, then puts the prescription back under the bag of pills and closes the drawer. He's pretty sure Endone is a very strong opioid, designed for severe pain, but he doesn't recall Kaia mentioning any injuries. One more question to ask David Owen, he thinks.

He walks quickly around the rest of the room. Hotel brochures and room service menus are lined up with military precision on the desk. The low table between two armchairs in front of the windows has an almost empty glass of white wine on a coaster, an open tin of Pringles crisps beside it.

As he goes back to sit on the bed beside Kaia, he sees her iPhone lying on the floor, half-hidden under the bed. He picks it up gingerly, using a tissue, holding it by the sides. The screen flicks into life at the movement and he sees his messages, piled up one behind the other. Another stack of messages, too, from someone called Toby, only the last visible: *Kaia fucksake pick up u got all the gear.*

Walker debates with himself for the merest moment. He's seen Kaia unlock the phone a few times . . . He thinks back, pictures the movement of her fingers, tries once. Nothing. Tries again. On the third try, the screen unlocks. Her WhatsApp icon shows fifty-six unread messages and calls. Along with his, there are dozens unread in various groups and, at the very top, nine missed calls and a handful of messages from a Toby Stone. Walker looks at the bloke's profile picture, recognises him from the bar. The wannabe gangster. He adds Toby's details to his own phone and snaps a few pictures of the messages Toby sent Kaia.

He's not sure exactly what has caused Kaia's death. Whether she took too many of the prescription Endone or if the mix of Endone and whatever else she took last night was a fatal combination. Either way, it seems like this Toby bloke supplied her with illegal drugs. He is at least partially responsible.

Before he puts the phone back on the bedside table he goes to Settings and removes the screen lock passcode. This way Queensland Police will be able to use the phone to find her parents' contact details, and the messages from Toby will be useful for them too, if they decide to open a full investigation into her death.

Afterwards, he holds Kaia's hand for a few minutes, then leans over and kisses her forehead before pulling up the bed sheet and covering her face with it. 'I'm sorry, Kaia,' he says. 'I'm so sorry I wasn't there for you.'

Chapter 42

By the time Walker has debriefed the local police it's mid-afternoon. The rain hasn't lessened. He drives along the Esplanade to his place, the ocean invisible and muffled by the sound and force of the rain. Back home he takes a shower and puts on a sweatshirt and jeans. The air is still muggy and warm, but he's feeling chilly, shivery. He needs to call Grace, tell her what's happened, but he can't face it yet. Can't face her grief, can't face owning up to having failed to look after Kaia, failed to protect her.

Instead he texts Toby Stone.

Kaia gave me your gear and asked me to give it back to you. You about?

The reply is quick in coming.

About bloody time flat 803 281 hedges ave mermaid

The message has the effect of adding unnecessary fuel to Walker's anger towards the young dealer. The address Toby has given is a short drive away, a new high-rise building on a road near the ocean at Mermaid Beach. Walker follows an older woman through the door into an expensive-looking lobby, lots of marble and mirrors and a bank of lifts. She looks at him with undisguised hauteur but doesn't say anything. The block and its location in this expensive part of town means Toby is either a rich kid, using and dealing drugs to his mates, or he's a bona fide dealer.

The lift takes him to the eighth floor and when Walker buzzes the bell for the apartment the bloke from the bar, bare-chested this time, wearing long denim shorts covering most of his skinny legs, opens the door. Up close his air of arrogance is magnified, and Walker can see that he's young, mid-twenties probably. His look switches to unease when Walker barges past him into the flat, deliberately putting in a bit more force than necessary as his shoulder connects with Toby's chest.

'What the fuck?' says Toby, rubbing his chest and following Walker into his living room.

'Nice place you got here,' says Walker, looking around the open-plan living room. He recognises the grey L-shaped sofa and the big glass coffee table in front of it, powdered with the telltale white dust of a cocaine addiction, from the pictures Kaia had sent him yesterday. 'You must make pretty good money dealing the gear?'

'Um, yeah, nah, this is my dad's place,' says Toby. 'Um, look, I don't deal. I just want my gear back. I don't know why Kaia took it with her.'

'That right?' says Walker, getting up close into the bloke's personal space. Toby steps back, until he's standing against the hallway wall. 'Where'd you get your gear, then?'

'What's it to you?' Toby summons up some balls. 'Just give me back the shit Kaia took.'

Walker's rage intensifies. All he can see is Kaia, lying there, not breathing, the life gone from her features, alone in her hotel bed. He grabs Toby by the throat, squeezes tight, holding him against the wall.

'Kaia is dead. She's dead. She died taking the pills you gave her. That makes you guilty of manslaughter, you little piece of shit. So you better tell me where you got it from.'

The kid is struggling for breath. 'Uh . . . It's from a guy I know at the gym.'

'What's his name?'

'It's Craig – Craig Ford.' Toby is trying to free himself, still struggling to breathe; the name comes out squeaky.

In the shock of hearing Craig's name, Walker lets the kid go. Toby falls to his knees, hands on his throat, gasping for air, looking up at him. 'Kaia's dead? She can't be . . . She . . . We . . . I only saw her this morning. She was here – we were partying last night.'

The kid is shocked, scared even. Nothing less than he deserves.

'She's dead,' says Walker, pushing away the image of Kaia, cold, pale, alone. 'Don't lie to me – where did you get the gear?'

'I swear – I swear it's from a bloke called Craig Ford. He owns a gym and he sells to members. He's usually got a bit of everything – MDMA, meth, coke, weed, whatever. This gear, it's a new kind of meth. But we only took a little bit, we didn't go crazy. She can't be dead. She can't be . . .'

When Walker parks in front of Craig's place the rain has stopped but heavy streams of water are running along the gutters and across Craig's pale-sandstone driveway and the trim lawn is disappearing under deep puddles of water. He rings the intercom, nods into the camera and the door buzzes open. Jess opens the front door, her eyes red, her face swollen from crying.

'Thank god you're here,' she says.

'What's happened?'

'You didn't hear? There's been a fire – a terrible fire. Nadine is in hospital, the Surfers gym is totally destroyed. Craig's been down there with the police all day.' Her tears start again. 'It's horrible, Lucas, horrible.'

'How did that happen?' asks Walker.

'They don't know but it started so fast and burnt so hard that they think it was lit on purpose. Who would do something like that? There were four people in there, trapped. The fire brigade pulled them out. They have smoke inhalation but thank god they're OK. Nadine has some burns – she's in hospital under observation. She was a hero. She did everything right. She put lots of towels in front of the doors, she saved them . . .'

Jess is sobbing but Walker doesn't have any words of comfort to offer.

'Is Craig still at the gym?' he asks.

'No, he's in the back yard. He's trying to fix the garden and the jetty; everything's been destroyed by the storm.' She opens the door to let him past. Marty starts yapping when Walker steps in. The dog can probably sense his anger.

Walker strides down the hall and through the pristine living room. The pool outside is overflowing, streams of water running down the sloped grass towards the river, which is brown and turgid from the storm. Craig is crouched at the riverbank, pulling at the small metal jetty, which has torn free of its mooring and is tilting dangerously into the swirls of water around it. His boat, too, looks like it's about to bob loose in the fast-moving water. As Walker approaches, Craig loses his footing, slips onto his haunches, his hands automatically loosening their grip to break his fall. The jetty gives a creaking groan and slides into the water, bobbing in slow circles, half-submerged. Craig scrabbles to his feet, cursing, the back of his shorts brown and muddy. He turns, sees Walker.

'Give us a hand with this, would ya?' he calls.

The sight of Craig, the man he'd trusted, his father's friend, *his* friend, who'd taken him under his wing, helped him but lied to him and killed Kaia, ignites a fire of rage in Walker. He takes the final few steps towards Craig in fast strides and, when he gets within reach, swings his arm back and lands a solid right hook on Craig's chin. Craig falls backward, his feet slipping on the muddy grass, and lands with a thud on the ground. Walker is on top of him, grabbing him by the shirt, hauling him to his feet. Craig, groggy with the impact of the punch and the fall, holds onto Walker's forearms.

'What the fuck?' Craig is shaking his head, twisting to get free.

'You killed her,' says Walker through his teeth. 'You sold those pills and now she's dead and I'm going to make sure you pay for it.'

He can hear Jess screaming, 'What are you doing? Leave him alone!' and from somewhere behind him, the dog barking excitedly, dancing around his feet.

'You better tell me exactly what drugs you deal and where you get them, and you better tell me fast or I'll flatten you again.'

Craig is coughing. 'I don't know what you're talking about. What are you talking about?'

'Kaia Hale, the kitesurfer from Hawaii – she died this morning of an overdose. I found the pills that killed her. The illegal ones that you supply. I got your name from her friends; they're going to give evidence against you and the cops are going to haul you in. But first you're going to tell me where you get the drugs.'

'It's nothing to do with me. I didn't sell her anything illegal. I don't even know who she is.'

'Leave him alone – I'm calling the police, I'm calling the police!' Jess is hysterical and Walker comes to his senses, the red mist of rage cooling. He drops his hold on Craig.

Jess backs away from him. 'Leave him alone!' Her face is a red mess of tears and shock.

Walker puts his hands up in supplication. 'Fine, I'm going,' he says, stepping away from them both, taking slow steps across the garden, trekking a mess of muddy water, grass and leaves through the living room and down the hall.

Chapter 43

5 p.m.

Gabby can't get her head around what Dad is saying to her. He wants to talk about Mum, about why she hasn't been to visit. He sits on the bed, holding her hand, telling her, 'I'm sorry, darling, Mum isn't coming to visit. There was an accident and . . . she died, Gabby. Your mum died.' He starts crying. She's never seen him cry before and she watches in horrified fascination as the tears run down his cheeks.

'What?' she asks. 'What do you mean . . .'

'The night you were hurt, Mum was hurt too. You're getting better but she couldn't. She's in heaven now. She can't come to visit. She's gone.'

She's gone, she's died, she's in heaven. Gabby hears the words but they don't register, don't make any sense. 'When is she coming back?'

'She's not coming back. She can't come back. I'm sorry, darling, but she can't come back.'

Mum isn't coming back. She's not coming to visit. She won't give her a hug and make it alright. Gabby starts crying too. 'But I want to see her. I want to see her . . .'

Dad leans over and hugs her tight. 'I know, Gabby, I know. I want to see her too.'

She pushes him away. 'I want Mum. I want my mum!'

He hugs her again and this time she lets him. They sit there together, crying and crying, and she can't breathe, she can't think. Her head hurts so bad and her stomach and her heart. She can't breathe. She sucks in air, chest heaving, pulling, but she can't breathe. She's gulping for air, faster and faster, but it's not working.

A nurse comes in and says, 'She's having a panic attack', and Dad

221

moves away. The nurse holds her hand and says, 'Watch me, Gabby, watch me. Breathe in when I put my arm up – that's it – and now breathe out when I put my arm down. That's it, Gabby, good girl. Breathe in when my arm is up, and slowly – that's right – out when my arm is down.'

They do that for a while and when she can breathe again they give her something to make her feel better. She feels sleepy, feels her eyes closing, fights against it.

'I saw him,' she says. 'I saw him. He was hurting Mum. I saw him . . . The wolf . . .'

When she wakes up, Dad is still there and he's talking to a lady doctor she hasn't seen before. She remembers what he told her. That Mum is dead, that she's gone, she's not coming back, and she starts crying again. She wants her mum.

Dad comes over and holds her hand. He turns to the doctor. 'It's too soon. I told you it's too soon. This will only upset her more.'

'I'm here to help, Dr Owen. I won't upset her.'

Dad makes his cross face, but the doctor doesn't notice. Gabby breathes hard and stops crying. 'I'm OK, Dad,' she says.

He looks at her; he's still got his cross face on. 'This is Dr Shiller and she's going to talk to you for a bit,' he says, and goes and stands by the presents table.

Dr Shiller has very short silver hair and blue eyes. She says she's a feelings doctor and that Gabby can talk to her about anything she wants. She asks Gabby questions about school and her friends, about normal things like her favourite games to play and if she likes drawing and colouring. Then she asks, 'How are you feeling right now?'

Gabby thinks about it and says: 'I'm really sad. I want to see Mum. I miss her.'

Dr Shiller asks her questions about Mum and they talk about how Mum makes the best cakes and how she's a good runner and that Mum likes reading and how she can do all the voices in a book when she reads a story.

She asks Gabby about Dad too. 'How do you think your dad is feeling right now?'

Gabby looks over at him, then she says, 'I think Dad's sad too.'

Dr Shiller nods. 'I'm sure he is,' she says. 'He wants you to get better and he misses your mum a lot.'

They don't say anything for a while. 'Is there anything else you want to talk about?' asks Dr Shiller.

Gabby shakes her head.

'What about the wolf?'

Gabby shakes her head.

'Are you sure?' asks Dr Shiller.

She nods. 'It's just a bad dream,' she says.

Walker is relieved to arrive for his shift, the now-familiar hospital corridor offering respite from the image of Kaia that is running on an endless loop through his mind.

Matilda, the night nurse, pulls him aside. 'Gabby is very upset. She's been told about her mother's death,' she says. 'Poor love. I don't know how you can ever get over something like this.'

Gabby has also been assessed by a child psychologist and found to be responding as well as can be expected emotionally and physically, but deemed still too upset for a police interview. Cummings will be frustrated, but Walker thinks she's been through so much, she doesn't need to relive her nightmares further just yet.

'You'll have to sit out here,' says Matilda. 'Gabby's dad has decided to spend the night. He's hoping it will help her feel safe, keep her calm.

Walker looks in and can see David Owen on a chair beside Gabby's bed, his head resting against the wall, neck at an uncomfortable angle, legs stretched out in front of him. He looks like he's asleep. Walker doesn't share his fear that Gabby may be in more danger with her father in the room. He moves his chair to the opposite wall of the corridor and leaves the door to Gabby's room ajar. From this vantage point he can see if David Owen makes any moves.

Time passes slowly. About an hour into the shift David Owen wakes. Walker watches him stretch and rub his face. He pulls out his phone, looks at the time and stands, moving out of sight towards his daughter's bed. Walker is up in an instant, knocks lightly on the door and goes in. Owen, standing by Gabby's bed, turns towards him.

'She's OK. I woke up and wanted to check . . .' His voice trails off as he sees Walker. 'Lucas? What are you doing here?'

'I'm part of Gabby's protection team,' says Walker. 'Didn't Craig tell you? I'm in the AFP.'

'Ah, yeah, nah, he didn't say. Well, thanks very much, you know, for watching over her. I'd say you'll be an improvement on the last bloke.'

'How is she?' asks Walker.

'She's OK – she's sleeping at last. We told her about Siobhan today. I didn't think I'd live a day worse than the one Siobhan died but today was terrible. Having to tell my daughter about her mother. No parent should have to go through that. Your lot need to find the people who did this.'

'The team is hard at work,' says Walker. 'They've got a few good leads . . .'

Owen shakes his head. 'Yeah, well, I've heard that before,' he says. Then, a second later, his voice more conciliatory: 'Sorry. I'm very tired and today has been a terrible day. I think I'll go home, try to get a few hours' sleep. I can see Gabby is in good hands here.'

After Owen leaves, Walker, who has been putting off his call to Grace, works out the time difference – it's 10 a.m. in Boston; Grace should be awake. He needs to tell her about Kaia. He braces himself for her pain, full of the knowledge that he didn't do as she asked: he didn't take good enough care of Kaia, didn't keep her safe. He looks at the little girl on the bed in front of him and promises himself that he'll do better for her.

Chapter 44

Wednesday 15 March
7 a.m.

Walker should be tired but he's too wired. He's barely slept. He couldn't still his mind, couldn't stop thinking of Kaia's lonely death, his failure to save her and Craig's betrayal. At least his conversation with Grace wasn't as hard as he'd expected. She was shocked and tearful, but she didn't blame him. 'Kaia had some problems,' she said. 'It's not your fault.'

He's worried for Gabby too. Matilda has told him that David Owen wants her to be discharged soon, that he thinks she'll recover better at home, back with friends and family. But Walker is far from convinced. If anything she needs extra protection, particularly if she starts to more fully regain her memories of that night.

He stands at the bedroom windows looking at the ocean. The rain has eased, pieces of blue sky appearing among the grey clouds, but there'll be no swim today. The ocean is a bilious mix of green and brown, flecked with foam. The sand on the beach is grey, covered with foam, which heaves and breathes like a living thing, and other debris – logs, torn palm fronds, pieces of furniture and smaller pieces of indistinguishable plastic, jolts of red, blue and yellow on the dull sand.

He brews a coffee, but the bitter flavour burns his throat and hurts his stomach. He makes a round of toast, spreads it with butter and Vegemite then can't swallow it, his appetite gone. He's moving out of here this morning – won't take another night of hospitality from Craig. He's put all the files he's been working on neatly together, taken down the case details from the wall and put them on top of his clothes in his big sports holdall.

He opens his email: still no news from forensics on the knife and vodka bottle. But there is a message from Barbara.

Can you send me David Owen's phone records? I just want to check something . . .

Walker hesitates. This is really against regulations, but he rationalises that Barbara is police, too; she's completely trustworthy and maybe she's found a way into this case. He attaches the files she's asked for with a note:

Here you go Barbara. Are you on to something? Give me a call, let's discuss . . .

He tips his half-drunk coffee into the sink and decides he'll start by going to the Surfers police station. He needs to ask Anna Jones to chase up the forensics results, and the local team are handling the inquiry into Kaia's death too. They might have the toxicology report by now. Perhaps they can tell him more about exactly what caused her death.

He leaves the keys to the flat on the hallway console, puts his gear in the ute, then walks to the police station. It'll be easier than trying to negotiate the flooded city centre by car. When he reaches the Boulevard he's met with a police cordon that forces him to make a short detour. He's turning back on himself when he realises the police cordon is concentrated outside Craig's gym. It must be the fire that Jess had been talking about.

He joins a group of bystanders under the awning of the small supermarket on the other side of the road and looks up at the gym. He can't see much. A few dark streaks of smoke damage on the facade of the building; the windows of the gym and the doors to Heist also black from the heat and smoke. The door to Heist and the other to the staircase are both open, a handful of firemen going in and out.

Walker hasn't given the fire much thought until now, but if it happened yesterday and the fire teams are still here, it must have been a hell of a blaze. Arson seems the likeliest explanation, the building not being an obvious fire risk. Arsonists love to watch the mayhem they've caused, he thinks instinctively; it could be that the firesetter is here now. He scans the group – three teenage boys balancing on electric scooters, a middle-aged woman clutching a plastic bag of groceries and talking on her mobile phone, a couple of older blokes in animated discussion, a journalist talking to the PC manning the cordon. No one obvious. He looks up. The street is surrounded by high-rise residential blocks. It'd be possible to see what's going on from a hundred apartments. Or perhaps it was deliberately set by Craig himself. Walker would no longer put it past him.

He turns away. This is not his problem.

When he reaches the station he shows his ID to the constable at reception and asks for Anna Jones.

'Yeah, nah, we haven't got those forensics back yet,' says Jones, apologetic. 'I did ask for it to be prioritised so it should be later today.'

Another day is too long, but at least Gabby is safe in hospital.

He asks about Kaia's death and Jones refers him to the narcotics team. 'I'll get someone to come and talk to you,' she says.

Walker decides that, if they don't have it already, he'll give them Craig's name. He's only waited a couple of minutes when the doors from the back of the station swing open and a uniformed officer walks out. Walker looks up and his eyes widen in a moment of shocked recognition. The man at the doors is much thinner, the shirt no longer straining at the stomach, his ruddy complexion paler and his face marked with a host of lines that weren't there before, but there's no doubt about it: it's Dave Grogan.

He'd last seen Grogan in Caloodie, during his previous case. Grogan had been the constable in charge of the remote region, and Walker had thought him ineffective and unreliable and hadn't fully trusted him. He's shocked to see him here. It's clear that Grogan recognises him too; he stops in his tracks before forcing a smile that's not far from a grimace.

'DS Walker? Fancy meeting you here,' he says, proffering his hand.

'Constable Grogan,' says Walker, then, noticing the bars on the uniform, 'Sorry – Sergeant. Congrats on the promotion and the recovery. You're looking good.'

'Ah, yeah, ta,' says Grogan. 'Getting better fast and managed to land myself a desk job down here. It's bloody lovely being on the coast and not stuck out bush. What brings you to town?'

'I was asked to help out on a training course while I'm waiting for the physio to sign me back on to active duty. Thought I might as well have some time on the beach while I'm recovering, but I hadn't planned on all this rain.'

'It's a shocker,' says Grogan. 'Where are you staying, then? You got friends here?'

'Yeah, nah, I'm at a motel in Surfers. Reckon I'll only be here a couple more days. The training's over, and if this weather keeps up there's not much point in hanging around.' He pauses then adds, 'Believe it or not, you're the second person from Caloodie I've seen this week. I bumped into Tina Monroe on Friday. Have you seen her around town too?' Walker is digging – Tina and Grogan's wife were friends, last he heard.

'Oh yeah?' says Grogan. 'Nah, I'm not sure what Tina's up to these days.'

Walker's ears prick up. That wasn't the question he'd asked. He'd bet Grogan is lying to him, that he knows Tina is in town.

'What can I do for you today, then?' asks Grogan.

'A good friend of my sister's, a young kitesurfer name of Kaia Hale, overdosed and died yesterday. My sister is really cut up about it and I wondered if you might have some information. Has the toxicology come back yet? There were some dodgy pills in her drawer . . .'

'Yeah, nah, the full toxicology will be a couple of days, I reckon. But the pills, yeah, we've seen them before. They're fairly new on the street. A powerful meth, started turning up in the last week or so. We sent some for analysis and seems it's been cut with fentanyl. We've had a couple of overdose deaths already.'

'Shit,' says Walker. 'That's no good.' In fact, it's very bad news if the synthetic opioid that's wreaking havoc in the States has arrived on the Gold Coast. He wonders how much Grogan knows, whether the narcotics team has any leads as to who is manufacturing and distributing this new gear. 'I didn't think we had much of that,' he says. 'Isn't that a Mexican narcos thing?'

Grogan nods. 'Yeah, that's right. Looks like it's made its way across here.'

'Where's it coming from? Who's selling it? Anyone here have links to the Mexicans?'

Grogan's eyes dart sideways then back to him. 'Hard to know,' he says. 'It's probably coming in from Asia somewhere . . .'

Either Grogan doesn't know or he's not telling. Walker files the information away, wondering if it could be linked to the Vandals. Perhaps that's what they were doing in Caloodie – experimenting with fentanyl.

'Righto, well, thanks. And, look, I've got a tip-off for you,' says Walker. 'I went and had a chat with some of Kaia's friends yesterday and got the name of the bloke that gave her the drugs. He's called Toby Stone. He lives down Mermaid Beach way and deals to a young crowd. Maybe your blokes might want to bring him in? Maybe he can give you some info on the gear.'

Grogan feels a sharp pain in his stomach as he watches the AFP cop limp out. The bloke knows. Walker knows he's crooked. He doesn't know how he's worked it out, or when, but Walker's look of shocked recognition had telegraphed a message loud and clear: he can't trust him. And fucking Tina. He hadn't been happy to see her, had told Lisa they needed to cut ties with her. She's not linked to Markovich anymore but still – it won't look good if it comes out that she and Lisa are mates. Walker, the arrogant prick, had to let him know he knows.

This cock-and-bull story about his training course, his friend the dead surfer and her shitty little dealer – Grogan doesn't buy it. Markovich is right. Walker has come here to chase down the Vandals, chase down their meth. And now Walker knows that he's here too. Shit. Shit shit shit. Grogan breathes deep, summoning up clarity. They're finally living their best life, the life Lisa deserves, the life the girls deserve, the life he fucking deserves. He's not risking it. He'll do whatever it takes. He pulls his phone out of his pocket. Markovich can take care of it.

Chapter 45

11 a.m.

Aaron takes Shaun, one of the club's enforcers who loves nothing better than stacking on a blue, when he pays a return visit to Craig Ford. Not that he couldn't handle Ford on his own with one hand tied behind his back, but Stefan wants a show of force. Wants to scare the shit out of the bloke, make sure he gives up the pig without any more fuss. They've had inside information this morning that the pig is here to close them down. Stefan wants him taken care of, fast.

They get lucky: the blood-red Range Rover is parked on the street, the big double garage doors are open. Ford is cleaning up after the rain, sweeping water and mud out of the garage and into the gutter of the street. When he sees them pull up, bikes revving, his face pales. Aaron can see him debating whether to run or close the garage doors, but he has his bike up the driveway and into the garage before Ford can get himself into action. Shaun parks outside, angling his bike across the drive.

Aaron dismounts, Shaun too. Ford steps back, holding the broom in front of him like a shield.

'Your mate didn't call us,' says Aaron. 'You didn't listen to me, did ya? I told ya, if he doesn't call us, you're gonna pay.'

'Look, it's been a bad time, there was a fire at the gym . . . I haven't had a chance—'

'You reckon that fire was a fucken coincidence?' Aaron laughs. 'Nah, it was a little message. We wanted your mate to pay us a visit. He didn't turn up, so we torched the place. If he doesn't get in touch with us in the next twenty-four hours, you'll find more than your gym on fire. Next time we'll come closer to home. I reckon that missus of yours would squeal like a pig if a couple of our boys turned up for a ride.'

Ford takes a step towards them. 'Leave her out of it. Don't even fucking think about it. She's got nothing to do with any of this.'

Aaron nods at Shaun, who walks over to Ford, rips the broom out of his hands and clobbers him with it, a series of hard whacks across the shoulders, chest and – as Ford puts his arms up for protection – the forearms and face. Ford shouts with pain and steps back, Shaun following him, broom raised.

Aaron puts his hand up: 'That'll do for now,' he says to Shaun. He turns back to Ford: 'You do what we fucken ask or there's plenty more where that comes from, for you and your missus.'

Ford is whimpering. 'How'm I supposed to get him to visit you? He won't turn up to meet you without a good reason, will he? He's not an idiot and he's fucking clean as a whistle. He won't go picking up drugs.'

Aaron looks at him. 'Tell ya what. You can pay us a bit of protection money. To make sure we don't torch another one of your gyms. I reckon twenty grand should do it. Get him to deliver it.'

Walker has picked up his ute but is undecided as to his best next step. His phone is buzzing with calls and a series of messages from Craig that he's ignored. He's thinking instead about his conversation with Grogan: fentanyl is seriously bad news. He needs to talk with Rutherford.

'Morning, sir,' he says when Rutherford picks up the phone. 'Did you see my email about Tina Monroe?'

'Yep. I've put someone on it. I don't want you pinging up on Markovich's radar again.'

Fair enough, thinks Walker, though he keeps it to himself that it might be a bit too late for that. 'I wanted to update you on some other developments,' he says. 'A . . .' He pauses. A friend? An addict? 'A girl I know overdosed yesterday. She died, and it turns out the pills she took came from a new batch of meth that's hit the streets up here. The local narcotics team tells me that it's cut with fentanyl and they've had a few other overdose deaths already. I've got a sample of the pills – I can send them to you.'

'Do that,' says Rutherford.

'The local blokes say the gear is coming in from Asia but I don't know. Why would they bring it in here, not into Sydney or somewhere? I was thinking, maybe there's a Vandals link? Maybe that's what they were doing out west. If Tina Monroe is here, there's a good chance Markovich is too. Maybe he could be making the gear down here now.'

There's a moment's silence. 'Yes,' says Rutherford. 'That's a possibility.'

'If the Vandals are using fentanyl, we have to shut down their production,' says Walker.

This time the silence at the other end is even longer. 'Alright, look, Markovich has moved down that way and they're ramping up their manufacturing capabilities,' says Rutherford eventually. 'This is beyond confidential. I'm only telling you because you're close to the case and I know you – whatever you do, don't go charging in there and fucking things up again. We've got a bloke undercover who is getting close to the very top of the club. He's discovered that the Vandals aren't running this drugs op on their own. They have high-level organised crime backers who are providing cash and chemists and helping the club to upgrade their production and cut their meth with fentanyl.'

Walker feels a deep well of respect for whoever is doing that undercover job. He's been in deep undercover in the past, and he knows that to have gotten that close to Markovich, to the top echelon of the club, will have taken years of work and balls of steel.

'We can't go in and close this down. Not yet,' says Rutherford. 'Our bloke's been working this for a long time, and we're close to the very top of the organisation. That's the result we want. Until then, we don't make a move.'

'How long is that going to take?' asks Walker, thinking of Kaia, of others like her. 'How many people are going to die? You know how serious this is in the US – they have tens of thousands of deaths.'

'This operation is bigger than a few dead addicts,' says Rutherford. 'This is a long-term infiltration and we're aiming to disrupt Mafia-level leadership. Since Ironside they've cut back on using smartphones, they're wary of being hacked, so we have to get this intel the hard way.'

Walker had been part of Operation Ironside a few years back. His own arrests were just one part of the hundreds of organised crime offenders who were brought down after their encrypted communications were hacked by the FBI and AFP. Tonnes of drugs and millions in cash were seized. It was a nationwide operation and had a major impact on organised crime across Australia, but it had alerted criminals to the risks inherent in mobile phone communication.

Rutherford is still talking. 'I can't compromise our undercover guy and the bigger operation by closing their manufacturing site. But as you're up there, see if you can find out what's happening on the streets, who their main dealers are. If we can piece together some of their distribution chain, we can feed that to the local narcotics team and try to slow them down that way. I know it's far from ideal, but this operation is five years in the making, Walker, and I won't shut it down now, not when we're so close.'

After the conversation, Walker comes to a decision about the rest of the day. He doesn't have the forensics on the Siobhan Owen case yet, only hunches, and Gabby is in safe hands in hospital. But the Vandals drugs are out there now, killing people like Kaia. As Craig is dealing this deadly meth, he must have some link to the club. If he can find out who Craig buys from, perhaps there's a way to use that connection to get the names of their big dealers. He can pass that information to the local narcotics team, or, given his distrust of Grogan, perhaps to the team in Brisbane instead. He met a couple of intelligent and committed blokes from the squad on his training sessions. That could help slow down the Vandals' distribution as Rutherford has asked.

Before he does anything else, he needs to find somewhere to stay. He drives up the highway towards Miami and pulls in at the first motel he sees. It's painted pale blue and pink with a big triangular sign out front in an old-style font that gives it a 1960s vibe. But all the character ends at the exterior. The room is small and bland and, when he sits on the bed, instead of the breathing roll of the surf all he can hear is the endless traffic thundering along the highway.

He comes up with a plan. He will use Craig to get the names of other dealers, those higher up in the Vandals network. He would have given Craig's name to the narcotics squad, but he doesn't trust Grogan to do the right thing, especially if there is a Vandals link. And although he's going to make sure that Craig does time for his involvement in Kaia's death, first he needs to get some information so that he can disrupt the Vandals' supply chain.

Craig has been trying to reach him for hours now; Walker's been ignoring his calls and messages. He pulls out his phone – six missed calls and a heap of messages.

Can you call me? We need to talk

Please call me Lucas, its urgent

It's not about last night. I'm not angry. I know you were upset about your friend

Please Lucas I really need to talk to you!

Chapter 46

David Owen is standing firm. 'She's my daughter and I know what's best for her. You've said yourself that she's made a remarkable recovery. Now I want her to come home and complete her recovery there. It's safer, for starters: it's a well-secured block and no one knows we're there, not like this circus. And I think it's a more conducive environment for her mental health. She's dealing with the death of her mother. She needs me, she needs her grandmother, she needs her friends and a normal life. I'm a doctor, I know how to read the signs. If she seems to be deteriorating, I'll be the first to know.'

The consultant paediatrician is undecided. 'I agree it's beneficial to get back to a home setting but the neurologists want to keep monitoring her. The effects of a head injury like this can be long-lasting and intermittent. She's better today, but it might not be the same tomorrow . . .'

'We'll schedule regular appointments for her to be assessed,' says Owen. 'But I'm taking her home today.'

The psychiatrist, Dr Shiller, is an ally. 'I think Gabby will do well at home. She's emotionally stable, considering what she's been through. I've talked to her about the new apartment she's moving to. She needs to connect with friends and get into a routine, with a view to going back to school as soon as possible. The greater the normality in her life, the better her mental health prognosis. With her father's care and regular appointments – I'll be visiting her twice a week for the next month – I think it's a good idea.'

After a moment, the consultant nods assent. Gabby is recovering well and they need the bed for other patients, there's no debate about that. And her father is a doctor. She's in the best possible hands.

Granny is helping her get dressed. She hasn't said much but her back is stiff and Gabby can tell she isn't happy. While Gabby puts her t-shirt on, Granny says, 'I think you're rushing this, David.'

'Well, you'd know, being a doctor and all,' says Dad.

Granny sets her mouth in a straight line but doesn't say anything else and Dad goes over to look at the toys, chocolates and flowers. 'I don't think we need all of these,' he says. 'It feels a bit over the top. Why don't you pick two or three of your favourites and we'll donate the rest to the children's ward. And leave the flowers, too, they're funereal.'

Granny looks at Gabby, who says, 'OK.' Granny doesn't understand that Dad likes it better when you agree with him. When she's put on a pair of leggings and her favourite sneakers, she sits on the edge of the bed. She's not sure she wants to go home. She'll be alone. Mum won't be there. And she'll miss Matilda.

Matilda says that Mum is with Gabby in spirit, that every time she thinks of her, Mum will be right there beside her. Sometimes it works; sometimes she can hear Mum saying 'Love you, Gabsy' and smiling. But mostly she doesn't let herself think about Mum too much, because she keeps remembering things that don't make sense. Things that frighten her. Her stomach hurts thinking about it.

'Are we staying with you, Granny?' she asks. Granny's house is smaller than theirs and Dad always frowns and makes his lips tight when they visit, and says 'Thank god that's over' when they leave. But Gabby likes it. She and Granny look at pictures of Dad when he was a kid, or they watch telly together or pick flowers from the garden to put in a vase on the table. Granny reads her stories too.

Granny doesn't get a chance to answer. 'No, we are not,' says Dad. 'We have a much nicer apartment of our own. Now, come on, choose a couple of these.'

She stands up. Her legs are wobbly and Granny has to hold her arm and help her walk. She picks out a rainbow-coloured unicorn with a glittery pink horn and a black-and-white cat with a long fluffy tail. She already has Olly, the elephant that Jess gave her, packed in with her things. Granny packs some of the chocolates, giving her a wink, while Dad goes out and comes back in with a wheelchair with a bright-yellow frame. She sits in it, puts Olly and the other toys on her lap, and he pushes her to the door. Matilda isn't on duty but she's come to say goodbye and give her a big hug.

Then they're going down in the lift to the entrance, and she and Granny wait while Dad brings the car around. Dad carries her to the car, and she has to close her eyes when they drive because the light is bright and there's so much to see and it hurts her head after the days and nights in the hospital ward.

They don't go to their normal house; Dad says they can't go there yet, that they're going to spend a while somewhere new, with fewer bad memories. He drops Granny at her house, and she leans over to the back seat and gives Gabby a hug and a kiss. 'I'll see you tomorrow, darling,' she says. 'I'm coming to visit first thing and I'll be with you all day.'

'Don't come too early,' says Dad. 'Gabby needs to rest. I'll call you and let you know when it's a good time.'

Then Dad drives to the new house. They don't talk on the way. She hopes he's not in a bad mood but when they arrive he says, 'Here we are!' and he sounds happy. It's a high-rise building, not a house. There's a lift and then a corridor that gives her goosebumps and not in a good way. It doesn't have a garden, but it has a balcony that looks at the ocean.

'This is only temporary. A new place for the two of us to have some time together alone,' says Dad.

Her bedroom has a big bed, too big for her, and none of her things, but there is a TV and Dad has bought her a new iPad. The old one got broken that night, but she doesn't want to think about it.

'My toys aren't here,' she says.

'No, but hopefully we can go and get them soon,' says Dad, 'or we can buy new ones.'

He makes her a sandwich with cheese and Vegemite and gives her an orange juice but he doesn't know that she likes juice watered down with fizzy water, that it's too strong and bitter on its own.

'Can I have some fizzy water in this?' she asks.

'Umm, I don't think there's any fizzy water.' He looks in the fridge. 'No. Do you want some normal water in it?'

'Mum always makes it with fizzy water,' she says. Saying it out loud, saying 'Mum', makes everything worse. Mum isn't here and she isn't coming back. That's what Dad said and that's what Matilda said too. 'She's watching over you from heaven,' said Matilda. But she doesn't want Mum to be in heaven – she should be here. She starts to cry. 'I miss Mum,' she says. 'I want to see her. I want to see her.'

Dad comes over and gives her a hug.

'Mum's gone,' he says after a while. 'We've got to look after each other now. I don't have anyone else either. I only have you.'

She cries so long that her nose fills up with snot and she can't breathe, and she doesn't want to eat. She can't taste the orange juice so she drinks it but afterwards her stomach pains are worse. Dad makes her a bed on the sofa and puts on the TV, but she can't watch it. Everything hurts because she misses Mum so much. She wants to be back at home, proper home, playing in her bedroom, knowing Mum is downstairs making dinner. But when she thinks of her bedroom, when she thinks of home, she starts to feel really scared. The corridor, the light from Mum's bedroom, the blood everywhere. Then running, running, and the shadow chasing her, getting bigger and closer.

She hugs a pillow to her chest and half-watches *The Loud House*, wishing she had ten sisters, or even one sister. Wishing she wasn't here alone, without Mum, in this weird place that isn't home. Dad is in the other room, talking on the phone, and after a while she falls asleep. When she wakes up it's dark, the room is gloomy, just the blue light from the TV, the sound turned low, and she doesn't know where she is.

'Mum?' she calls out. 'Mum!'

She can hear Dad talking somewhere and she remembers that Mum isn't here. She starts crying. Dad walks into the room, a finger to his lips, shushing her, still talking on the phone. He switches on a light. It makes the room brighter but outside darker and she feels more scared, the nightmare shadows coming to chase her even when she's awake. She thinks of the policeman with the curly hair, the one who told her he was standing guard, keeping her safe.

'Is the policeman going to be outside my room tonight?' she asks when Dad comes over, his phone off, a drink of water in his hand for her.

'Policeman? No. Why would you need a policeman?'

'He was outside my room in the hospital. I was having nightmares and he said he was there to protect me.'

'Protect you against what?' Dad is standing in front of the sofa, blocking her view of the TV.

She pushes at his legs. 'I can't see the TV,' she says.

He doesn't move. 'What do you need to be protected from?' he asks in his serious voice.

'I was having a nightmare,' she says. 'I was being chased and I couldn't run away and the policeman said he was there to look after me. To make sure no one would hurt me.'

'Well, you're at home now and you're safe and you don't need any policeman. I'm here, and I'll take care of you.'

'I can't see the TV,' she says again, and he slowly moves out of the way.

Chapter 47

5 p.m.

Walker rings the bell at Craig's place and it's Jess, as always, who opens the door. Her face is pale and, unusually, without make-up, her hair pulled back unevenly, and she's wearing leggings and a t-shirt rather than her usual colourful dresses. When he sees the way she's standing, keeping her distance, a wary look in her eyes, fear even, he feels a rush of shame for his actions yesterday.

'I'm sorry, Jess,' he says. 'I had a terrible afternoon yesterday. A young girl died, a friend of my sister's, and I couldn't save her. But that was no excuse for how I behaved. I'm really sorry. It won't happen again, I promise.'

She looks at him for a minute then her shoulders slump and she nods. 'He's waiting for you,' she says. 'He's on the boat. I can't get him to talk to me, to tell me what's going on.'

The boat is sitting high in the water, the river still swollen from the rain washing through it. Craig has managed to attach it to a neighbour's pontoon; his own jetty has disappeared, part of the flotsam the storm has washed into the ocean. Craig is sitting in the L-shaped seating area at the rear of his boat, staring at the deck. Three empty beer cans and his phone are on the table in front of him. He raises his head as Walker approaches but the bonhomie, the smile, the usual garrulous greeting, are all absent. It looks as though Craig might have been crying too. There are bruises forming on his face and Walker feels another twinge of guilt. He hadn't realised he'd hit him that hard.

'Thanks for coming, Lucas,' he says. 'I know you're upset about

241

your friend, but it was nothing to do with me. I didn't sell her anything.'

Walker knows at this moment that any mateship he'd felt towards Craig has gone. He feels nothing but disgust for the man. 'You're dealing drugs and your pills killed Kaia. Whether you sold them to her direct or to someone who gave them to her, you're responsible for her death.'

Craig doesn't seem to hear him, doesn't acknowledge what Walker's said. 'You have to help me,' he says. 'They burnt down my gym and they're saying they're going burn this place down too. They say they're going to do it when we're asleep in our beds.'

'Who?' asks Walker.

'Two bikies. They rode up here this morning, beat me up.' That explains the bruises, thinks Walker, slightly relieved they're not down to him. 'They told me the gym was just a warning. They're going to kill us. You have to help me. Please.'

Craig's self-pity enrages Walker. 'This is what happens when you deal with these kinds of people, Craig. You buy their drugs. You get rich off this shit and you don't care that your drugs kill people. Kaia was twenty-three years old, she had her whole life ahead of her.'

'Didn't you hear what I said, Lucas? They want to kill me, kill Jess.' Craig is close to tears.

'Why? What have you done that bikies are setting fire to your gym and threatening you?'

'I dunno, I dunno. It's all got out of hand. A few years ago a mate of mine was getting divorced and it was costing him a lot. He gambles all the time too, horses, pokies, you name it, and he was struggling. He needed to make some fast cash, so he started dealing. He made a shitload of moolah. It was unbelievable. He convinced me I should do it too, sell through the gym. He's the one who buys the gear – from the bikies or whoever. I give him an order, whatever the members want: bit of weed, coke, MDMA. I'm comfortable with it because, you know, everyone takes drugs. Everyone. It's not a big deal. And it's not like I'm a junkie or the type of dealer that means my missus can't walk down the street and feel safe. I only sell to members, to normal people. It's civilised.'

Walker is asking himself how he ever liked this bloke. Did Craig's connection to his father blind him to his selfishness, his complete lack of a moral centre?

'But now the bikies want a bigger cut. They're coming direct to me, they're saying I have to pay them protection money. They're asking for twenty thou. If I don't give it to them they'll hurt Jess, they'll burn down the house too. You have to help me, mate. I'm in way over my head and I don't know how to deal with these people. I can't tell the cops or I'll have to tell them about the drugs and then I'll end up in prison and these bikies will fucking kill me. You have to help me, please.' Craig is openly crying now. 'I need someone to deliver the money for me. Please. Please help me. I can't do it.'

Walker feels disgusted. Craig is incapable of owning his mistakes, of acknowledging his guilt, his complicity. Walker wants to see him do time with every fibre of his being. Craig's taken a young woman's life, he deals class-A drugs, and he has zero remorse. He deserves a stint in the bin.

But first, this situation offers Walker the chance to slow down the Vandals. If he can meet with Craig's dealers, get them on tape extorting him and selling gear, he can give the intel to Rutherford and Queensland Police. It will help take a few – hopefully top-level – dealers off the streets. Upset their distribution without compromising the undercover op.

He looks at Craig, trying to push down the loathing he feels. 'Maybe I can help you,' he says. 'But we're doing this my way and on my terms.'

Craig nods. 'Yeah, mate, yeah.'

'What're the names of the blokes you're dealing with?'

'No idea,' says Craig. 'They never introduced themselves.'

'What do they look like, then?'

'Big, covered in tatts, typical bikies. The bloke in charge, he's bald, lots of face tatts, taller than me, shorter than you – bulky. His sidekick was a big bloke, six-three maybe? Long hair, beard.'

'Right, make sure you tell them I want the bloke in charge there. I'm not handing off the money to his sidekick. When are we gonna do this?'

'Tomorrow. It has to be tomorrow. They said I should call them and set it up.' Walker nods and his acquiescence helps Craig regain some of his usual bluster. 'Righto. Good on ya. Ta, mate. Really, ta very much. Let's go in; I'll make the call and we'll have a beer or a JD or something,' he says.

'I've got a few more questions first. What does David Owen have to do with all this?' asks Walker.

'Dave? Nothing. I send him clients sometimes, that's all, when blokes at the gym want steroids. He writes the scripts. But he's got nothing to do with the gear.'

'He doesn't deal drugs?'

'Nah. He doesn't even use them. He's a bit of a control freak, doesn't like to get too loose.'

'What about prescription opioids?'

'Ah, yeah, nah, I wouldn't know. I mean, you'd have to ask him. He probably could write you a script. Is it for your leg?'

Craig is deliberately misunderstanding him but Walker lets it pass. 'You need to get Jess out of here,' he says. 'Even if we sort this, it's not safe for her to be here.'

Craig nods. 'Yeah, you're right. We should shoot through, take a holiday somewhere for a while.'

'Nah, Craig, you're not going anywhere,' says Walker. 'You need to stay and deal with this.'

Craig bites his lip but nods.

When they walk into the house through the kitchen side door, Jess looks at them both with hope.

'Can I get you a beer or something?' she asks.

'A beer, thanks, babe,' says Craig.

Walker shakes his head. 'Nothing for me.'

Jess grabs him by the arm as Craig walks ahead and into his study. 'Is it alright? Is he OK now?' she asks in a low voice.

'I don't think it's going to be OK,' he says to Jess, not wanting to lie to her but feeling sorry despite himself as he sees her face crumple again. Walker thinks about telling her the whole story, the danger she's in, but perhaps she already knows. 'Have you got somewhere you can go? Your family or something? Craig has a lot he needs to sort out and you might be better off out of it for a while.'

She shakes her head. 'No. He needs me here.'

Chapter 48

8 p.m.

'Bedtime, Gabby,' says Dad, coming in and turning off the TV. He helps her walk to the bathroom so she can clean her teeth and then to her new bedroom. Dad's brought her favourite pillow, the one they wouldn't let her have in hospital. It doesn't smell the same anymore, it doesn't smell like home, and she can remember the night she had it in hospital and waking up, panicking, not being able to breathe. But it must have been another bad dream because when she woke up the next morning she was OK, just her throat was a bit sore and it hurt to swallow. Still, it's not her favourite pillow anymore.

She lies in bed with Olly and her two toys from the hospital, Rainbow the unicorn and Kitty the cat. Dad comes in with a glass of water that he puts on the bedside table. He doesn't usually do bedtimes – that was her-and-Mum time.

'Can you read me a story?' she asks.

'Not tonight, Gabby,' he says. 'I don't have any of your books here. But we'll get some tomorrow. I'll ask Granny to bring some.' He leans over and gives her a kiss. 'Goodnight, Gabby. No nightmares tonight. You're safe and sound. I'm right here.'

She nods and he turns out the light and closes the door. She's immediately scared. She misses Mum. She misses the hospital and Matilda and Lucas standing outside her door. This new place is too quiet and too dark.

After a while she can see a bit better. Dad hasn't closed the curtains and there's some light coming under the door. She decides that if Lucas the policeman isn't here to guard her then Rainbow and Kitty will have to do it. She gets out of bed and takes the pillow and puts it down on the floor in front of the door. Then she goes back for Rainbow and Kitty and makes them comfortable on top. 'You can look after me,' she says. 'Make sure no wolves can come in.'

She goes back to bed. Her legs are wobbly and she's very tired. She holds Olly tight but she's still too scared to sleep.

Chapter 49

9 p.m.

On his way home from Craig's, Walker called Anna Jones but the forensics report they're waiting on still hadn't come back. 'I've put in a call,' she said. 'Put a rocket up 'em. They're promising me we'll have it by first thing tomorrow.'

He turned his attention to the Vandals and spent the evening digging out all the background info he could find from the AFP system. He reckons the bald bloke with the face tatts is probably Aaron Adams. With a string of convictions dating back to his childhood, he's believed to be the number two or number three in the club. If he can get evidence of Adams's involvement in dealing and extortion and neutralise him, that would be a real hit to the Vandals.

He's had a text from Craig: the handover is set for just off the M1 near Reedy Creek at noon the next day. Walker checks out the location on Google Earth and finds it's a housing development as yet unbuilt. Private enough, but still open. He does a bit of online reconnaissance and finds a spot where he can observe the location before he turns up, a rise overlooking the development that should give him a good view.

Afterwards, he walks down the highway to a small shopping parade, finds a burger bar that looks a bit old-school and orders a Lot Burger. He takes it back to the motel and sits on the bed to eat it. It's the kind of old-school Aussie burger that Walker hasn't eaten for years. The bun is jammed with fillings – a fried egg, crispy bacon, melted cheese, a slice of pineapple coloured purple by tinned beetroot, and a thick home-made patty, the whole lot oozing tomato sauce when he tries to take a bite.

He's feeling full, wondering if he should take a walk to help it digest and flicking between the news and a replay of the Perth Scorchers vs Brisbane Heat Big Bash cricket final that he'd missed when it played live, when a text comes through from Barbara:

Call me urgently please

He dials immediately. 'Are you OK?' he asks when she picks up. 'Is everything alright?'

'I'm good. Sorry, I didn't mean to worry you. It's about Siobhan Owen. I think I found something,' she says. 'I was looking at her phone records, and at the apps she had on her phone. I looked through the deleted apps too, and I found that she'd had a fitness app. It monitors your steps, your heart rate, and you can check how well you sleep. Things like that.'

'Ah yeah?'

'Yes. It usually connects to a smartwatch. Was she wearing a smartwatch when she died?'

Walker thinks back to the scenes-of-crime pictures, the list of objects that were impounded as evidence. 'Nah,' he says. 'There wasn't a watch.'

'Never mind, we don't really need it,' she says. 'Anyway, this app was deleted on the sixth of March. That's the day she died, isn't it?'

'Yeah, well, she died early in the morning on that day . . .'

'That's what I thought. And I was wondering – why would she delete an app in the middle of the night? So I recovered the data and looked through it, and it says her heart stopped beating at fourteen minutes before one on the night of her death.'

'That can't be right,' says Walker.

'I thought at first it might be a problem with the data, but I don't think so. The app is recording consistently until that time. Her heart was beating much faster than usual for most of the evening. From about nine p.m. onwards. Much higher than other days that week. It peaks at around midnight but stays quite high until it stops, not registering any heartbeat at all, from twelve forty-six.'

Walker thinks about it. 'She was drinking pretty heavily that night.

Her blood alcohol level was very high. That could account for the faster heart rate.'

'Could it be she died of alcohol poisoning before she was stabbed?' asks Barbara.

He thinks back to the autopsy report. 'No, the pathologist said it was the stab wounds that killed her. The way she was bleeding shows she was still alive when she was stabbed.'

'What about the time of death?'

'The pathologist says it was between one a.m. and three a.m. so that fits, but Owen claims the intruders arrived after two . . .'

'Well, I have something else. I did the same check on David Owen's phone. He doesn't have a fitness app, but he has an iPhone and it has a built-in health app that monitors your steps. It's one of those apps you can't delete but he'd removed it from his home screen and hidden it in his app library. I think he forgot it was there. According to that app, he was taking a lot of steps between two and three a.m. There's a really big spike in his activity during that time. He was also active between one and two, but it's in the next hour that he's really busy. Not a handful of steps but over a thousand. Didn't you say he was supposed to be tied up at that time? That the intruders arrived after two? Because it doesn't seem that way according to his phone. Have your team checked this?'

'I don't think they've spotted it – it's not in any of the files,' says Walker. 'Maybe because she wasn't wearing the watch, no one thought to look if she'd ever had a fitness app . . .'

Walker feels his heart hammer hard in his chest. If Barbara is right, this is the proof they need that David Owen has been lying to them about what happened that night. If he wasn't sleeping or tied up, what was he doing?

'Bloody great work, Barbara,' he says. 'I've been looking into it and I don't think it was the Latus who killed Siobhan. I think David Owen had a very coercive and abusive relationship with his wife. There are so many red flags. She didn't have her own money, she didn't have friends, she was estranged from her family and he checked up on her all the time. I think he killed her. I think he forced her to drink the vodka and then he killed her. And when Gabby saw him, he tried to kill her too. Now we can show that this story about being tied up is bullshit and that Siobhan died earlier than he claims. With this phone data we might have him.'

'What about the daughter, Lucas? If he tried to kill her too, she could be in danger, no? Perhaps he will try to hurt her again.'

'Gabby is in hospital; there's a protection team looking after her. She's safe.'

After Walker hangs up the phone, he waits for Barbara to email the fitness data. He looks through it in detail and she's right. Siobhan's heart is racing for a few hours then stops dead at 00.46, whereas Owen is up and about the whole night, his activity peaking between 2 a.m. and 3 a.m. He supposes that the intruders could have held onto his phone during the attack but Owen hasn't said anything about that. Walker wonders where Siobhan's watch is, too. Perhaps Owen disposed of it, along with her new phone. He calls Cummings.

'Hello, DS,' says Cummings. 'Yes, I've seen the new forensics, they just came in. I've called a team meeting – you're welcome to join.'

'I haven't seen them,' says Walker. 'I wanted—'

'The knife was clean, the dishwasher cycle obviously removed any DNA, but the pathologist says it's a match for the stab wounds that Siobhan Owen sustained. I've asked them to take it apart and do some extra analysis on the joinery, see if there are some microscopic DNA traces anywhere that were missed in the wash. The vodka bottle is most interesting for what it doesn't show. It's been wiped clean. There are no fingerprints on the bottle. What kind of alcoholic wipes down their bottle when they're drunk? The same on the funnel.'

Walker's heart sinks. It's what he'd expected, but knowing what Siobhan must have gone through before she died is heartbreaking.

'I've got something else,' Walker says. He can't mention Barbara – she shouldn't have been looking at the phone records – so he takes the credit for this one himself. 'I was looking at the phone records. Siobhan Owen had a fitness app connected to a smartwatch that tracks heart rate. Did we find a smartwatch in the house?'

'No,' says Cummings after a moment's thought.

'Well, according to the app's data, her heart stopped beating at twelve forty-six a.m. And on David Owen's phone, his health app shows that he was moving around, significant amounts of movement, between two and three, the time he said he was tied up and attacked. I've emailed you the data.'

'For fuck's sake,' says Cummings. 'How the fuck could we have missed that?'

'Well, the app was deleted . . .'

Walker can hear Cummings typing on his keyboard. A moment passes, then he hears a loud curse.

'Have you seen the data?' says Walker.

'No,' says Cummings. 'I've just had a message from the team at the hospital. Gabby Owen was discharged into her father's care this afternoon. The officer on watch was told by the hospital that we'd been informed but it's only now that the next bloke's turned up that they've bothered to let us know.'

Walker's heart freezes. Gabby Owen has been alone with her father, who's already tried to kill her at least once, since mid-afternoon. That's almost six hours now. More than enough time for something terrible to have happened.

Chapter 50

Ten days ago

Sunday 5 March
12 p.m.

Siobhan Owen watches her husband David's car pull out of the driveway. He's going to play golf with some prospective clients. They're teeing off at 2 p.m., they'll play eighteen holes, then go for drinks and dinner. Even if he comes straight home after dinner, he won't be back till 9 p.m. at the earliest. This is the best chance she's got, the chance she's been waiting for.

She goes to the utility room on the ground floor. It's a room that David barely checks; there's not much to look at, only the washing machine, ironing board and clothes baskets. But in the cupboard above the dryer is a shelf where she keeps a stack of old towels, neatly folded, to put on the floor if they come home with sandy feet and bathers from the beach. That way they don't trek sand through the house and David has one less excuse to dock her housekeeping money or break one of Gabby's toys or smack her about.

If he doesn't think the house is clean enough, or if he decides she needs punishing for something, an infraction that no one else has seen but he's noticed, he'll cut her money off or hurt her in some other way. Laughing at something someone says at a party, not answering her mobile phone quickly enough, not smiling when he gets home at night . . . It could be anything or nothing that sets him off. She can cope with the occasional smack, but it breaks her heart when he smashes Gabby's toys. She usually replaces them if she can afford it but recently she's stopped doing it. She's explained to Gabby that she needs to save for something very important and Gabby, bless her, has started mending her toys.

The truth is, she needs every penny to make a new start for herself and Gabby, to get them out of this terrible situation before it destroys Gabby's life as surely as it has destroyed hers. She and David have been together for almost eight years. She'd met him shortly after the end of a previous relationship when she'd been heartbroken and lonely and Gabby had been a tiny baby. He'd seemed besotted with her and Gabby. He'd showered her with compliments and gifts, taken her to amazing restaurants, on fancy weekends away, told her he loved her and accepted her fully, new baby and all. She'd fallen in love with his confidence, his charm and charisma, and had been so grateful too. She felt she'd finally met her soulmate, and found a wonderful father for Gabby. He'd filled in all the gaps in her life; he enhanced her. They'd had a whirlwind romance and were married within six months. Not long afterwards, things changed.

He wanted to build up his business so she'd given up the nursing career she'd loved and moved away from her family and friends to the Gold Coast. He'd encouraged her to stop working. They had enough money; Gabby needed her. At first she'd thought it was special, that it proved how much he loved her and Gabby too, how he wanted to take care of them. He was more concerned about her than anyone had ever been. But gradually he'd started controlling every part of her life. From the people she could be friends with to how much money he would give her to the clothes he liked her to wear. It had escalated and escalated, and by the time she'd realised how bad it was, it was too late. He checked her phone and tablet every evening to see who she was talking to, what she was looking at on the internet. He even insisted on going to the doctor with her and would always call and check up on her during the day. If she didn't answer the phone within a couple of rings he'd accuse her of being with another man. And after a party one night he'd hit her. He thought she'd been flirting with someone because she'd laughed at a joke. There'd been four of them in the group and she'd laughed along with everyone else, but he hadn't seen it like that. He was so jealous, so possessive, that eventually she stopped going out. It was easier that way.

Recently he's started using Gabby to hurt her. Two nights after Christmas he'd wanted to have sex, but she'd been on her period and said no. He'd gone into Gabby's room, woken her, smashed up her new doll's house and told her it was Mum's fault. He's broken more of Gabby's favourite things a couple of times since then. He knows it hurts Siobhan and he's hoping to turn Gabby against her.

She's worried he'll take it further, that he'll hurt Gabby physically or begin controlling Gabby's life the way he controls hers. She's talked to Gabby, told her that it's important to be extra good and quiet at home, hoping it will make her as invisible as possible to him. She hadn't wanted to scare Gabby too badly, so she'd turned it into a game, a secret game just the two of them were playing. 'The Big Bad Wolf won't find us, won't even come looking for us, if we're being extra good,' she'd said.

But having to warn her like that and watching him destroy Gabby's toys had been the final straw for her: she knew she had to leave when he started tormenting Gabby too.

He'd gone on an overnight trip when Gabby was little, left the two of them at home alone. She should have run then but Gabby was just a toddler and she had nothing – no money, no friends, no plans. She'd taken the chance, that day he was away, to open her own bank account at a bank that's got nothing to do with him. For the last five years she's been putting money in it whenever she can, whenever she saves a few dollars on the groceries or buys something in a sale instead of at full price. There's close to $6,000 in there now. It's not much but it has to be enough – enough to get them started, at least. To get them to Sydney, pay for a month's rent, give her breathing space to build a new life.

She's been putting it off for too long, worried that she can't give Gabby the same quality of life. They won't have a big house and she can't afford a private school. And if he finds them it will be so much worse than it is now. But Gabby is starting to notice how he treats her mother and to notice that it's not right. Siobhan doesn't want her to grow up like this, to think this is the way a man behaves, to think this is a normal relationship. She's worried, too, that he'll start controlling Gabby, that they'll both be stuck here, with no money, no freedom, no life.

So, today she's taking the chance. She goes to the utility room and reaches behind the towels, where she's hidden an overnight bag, along with the card for her personal account and a new phone, one that he doesn't know about, which she bought on Friday.

She takes the bag up to her room, puts in a change of clothes – just some underwear, a couple of t-shirts. David keeps her passport in his safe and she doesn't know the combination, but she doesn't need it to get to Sydney, she's got her driver's licence for ID. He can't keep that because she drives to pick Gabby up from school. He keeps all the credit cards and bank cards too, but she's got her own secret one and she'll use that to pay for their tickets when she gets to the airport. She didn't want to book in advance in case there's a way he can trace it, find out about it and stop them.

Now that she's actually doing it, that she's decided to go, her heart is beating like crazy. She's sweating; it's hard to breathe. She wants to grab Gabby and run. Run far. Run fast. She forces herself to breathe deeply. They've got hours. There's no rush. She's planned this for so long that she knows exactly what she'll take, the pure basics that they'll need to start with. She doesn't want much. Doesn't want reminders.

She goes to Gabby's room, picks out a few clothes. In the yellow rucksack that Gabby uses for school she packs a book, a Lego set that Gabby loves and her favourite soft toy, the little pink-and-white cat she calls Dotty. It's not much but it will have to do. She wonders again if she's doing the right thing, taking her daughter away from this big house, all her things, a good school, her friends. But the alternative, another decade or more with David, with his controlling and abusive behaviour . . . No, she won't survive it, and it's better for Gabby this way too.

She takes the bags downstairs, sets them by the front door then goes to where Gabby is watching TV in the living room. She sits down beside her, turns the TV off.

'Oh Mum, please, I want to watch that.' Gabby puts her hand out for the remote control.

She shakes her head. 'No, Gabsy, listen to me. We're going to take a trip to Sydney. You and me. I've packed our bags and we're leaving now. It'll be fun – a girls' trip.'

'But I've got school tomorrow . . .'

'I know, I've spoken to your teacher and she says it's fine. You won't miss anything important.' Siobhan doesn't like to lie but she doesn't want Gabby overthinking this either.

'What about Dad?'

'He's not coming. He has to work.'

Gabby looks at her. Perhaps she can sense the anxiety bubbling in Siobhan, because she looks confused, close to tears.

'Darling,' says Siobhan, 'please trust me. We have to go. I'll explain more when we get to the airport, but we have to go now.'

'But I'm hungry. Can we have lunch first?'

Siobhan looks at the time: 12.35 p.m. She's forgotten to give Gabby lunch, her mind so focused on getting away, getting out. She thinks about it for a second. It'll save some money if she makes a sandwich now. They have time. He's not coming back until late.

'OK. How about a ham and Vegemite sandwich?'

'Hmm, no. I want cheese and Vegemite.'

'OK, let's make that and then we'll go.'

They walk into the kitchen and Siobhan sees that her hand is shaking as she butters the bread and makes the sandwich, then pours Gabby an apple juice mixed with sparkling water.

'How long are we going away for?' asks Gabby as she eats.

'A while,' says Siobhan.

'Will I be back for Maddie's birthday party?'

'I'm not sure,' says Siobhan.

'But I want to—'

Siobhan puts her hand up to quieten her daughter. 'Did you hear that? Was that a car?' It had sounded like a car pulling up onto the driveway. But it can't be. David is at golf; no one visits them.

She hears a car door slam and then the front door open. 'I forgot . . .' His voice fades away as he sees the bags by the door. Siobhan feels her hands begin to shake uncontrollably.

Chapter 51

Thursday 16 March
Midnight

It has taken Cummings an age to get an address for Owen and Gabby, but Walker is finally on his way there, driving fast, hoping it's not going to be too late, hoping that Gabby is still OK. Cummings is on his way down too, along with two of his team. They'll be here in an hour or so. They've decided against sending a team of local police to make the arrest. If Owen gets panicked, if he feels under pressure, there's no knowing what he might do, to himself and to Gabby. But Owen knows Walker, so hopefully he can make a quieter intervention, one that won't feel so threatening but will keep Gabby safe. If he's on time. If she's still OK. He adds more pressure to the accelerator, thankful the streets are virtually empty at this time of night. Even so, he wishes he had a siren to expedite his journey.

He can't stop worrying about Gabby. She's been in Owen's care for almost nine hours now, and Walker can only hope that whatever madness caused Owen to stab his wife and attempt to kill his young daughter has passed. But it's a thin hope. Owen has everything to lose and, if he thinks Gabby will talk about what she saw, it's clear what the man is capable of.

He pulls up outside the address, a modern high-rise on Main Beach Parade. The lights are on in a handful of places, dotted across the twenty or so storeys that climb into the night sky above. Owen and Gabby are on the twelfth floor, number 1203. The front door is key card entry only. Walker presses every bell on the long list of apartments beside the door, and eventually someone says a crackly 'That you, Terry?' across the intercom.

'Yeah,' says Walker. He needs to get in, doesn't want to explain, doesn't want delays.

The door buzzes and he's running to the lifts, a bank of three directly ahead of him on the far side of an unmanned reception desk. The lift doors open but won't go anywhere – they need a key card too. Fuck. Fuck. Walker tries the fire exit. The doors open on to stairs, rising high above him. He doesn't know if his leg can take him twelve flights up, but he has no choice. He starts quickly but he's soon limping, his leg aching badly. By the time he reaches the seventh floor it's screaming in agony, demanding a rest that he can't give it. Won't give it. His fear for Gabby helps push him on. By the time he reaches the twelfth floor he is sweating with exhaustion and pain, his heart hammering against his ribs, his breathing rapid.

The fire stairs open into a short corridor with three doors, the furthest left numbered 1203. He goes to the door, no plan for how to handle this, simply hoping that he's not too late. He rings the bell, hears it chime, waits. There's no answer. He rings it again, pushes it twice. Still nothing. He knocks, calls out: 'David? David, it's Lucas Walker, Craig's mate.' Nothing. His blood turns to ice in his veins. Please let him not be too late. He can't let this little girl down too.

He's got to get inside. Remembers the lock pick on his keyring. It's very basic but it's got him into doors before. He looks at the lock more closely; this kind of internal front door, a simple Yale lock, is the easiest of all to open. If it's not secured with a second bolt it won't even need the pick. A piece of card, even a credit card with the right flexibility, will get him in. He finds a card in his wallet, slides it into the gap between the doorknob and the frame, then bends it towards the knob. He gently bends it back and forth, forcing himself to stay calm, to focus on the task at hand. His leg is pulsating with pain, he's nauseous and sweating hard. He wipes his face with his t-shirt and dries his hands. Breathes deep, tries again. A second later he feels the card push against the lock and it clicks. He opens the door and looks down the dark corridor.

'Hello?' he calls out. 'David? Gabby? Anyone home?'

There's a light ahead in a room on the right, the flickering blue of a TV screen, but no sound. The other doors leading off the hallway are closed. He walks towards the light, calling out once more. 'David? Are you there? It's Lucas Walker.'

He doesn't have a weapon, hopes he's not going to need one, as he steps across the lighted doorway and into a big lounge room. There is a wall of windows in front of him, looking out at the ocean, dark now, nothing visible, just his reflection in the glass and the reflection of David Owen, slumped on a sofa, staring at nothing. There's a bottle of bourbon on the table in front of him next to a glass, half-full of the golden liquid. He looks at Walker, his eyes unfocused.

'Whaddaya want?' he says. 'Whaddaya doing in my house?' His voice is slurred with sleep or booze. 'Get out of my house . . .'

'Remember me, David?' says Walker. 'I'm Craig's mate, Lucas. We met on Craig's boat and at the hospital? I want to check up on you, check up on Gabby, make sure you're both OK.'

'We're fine, everything's fine. How'd you get in? What time is it?'

'It's late, after midnight.'

Owen pulls himself into a sitting position, leans forward and picks up his phone and looks at the time. 'Christ, I must have fallen asleep . . .'

'Where's Gabby?' asks Walker.

'She's sleeping, of course. It's the middle of the fucking night, what do you reckon she's doing?' Owen is less charming than usual. He's had quite a few drinks, thinks Walker.

'Yeah, right. Of course. I just wanted to check she's OK.'

'Course she's OK. She's home, safe, with me.' Owen looks at the bourbon on the table, picks up the glass and takes a swallow. 'You wanna drink?'

'Nah, you're alright. I'll just check on Gabby.'

'No. Don't disturb her. She's sleeping. She needs her sleep.'

Walker puts his hands up in supplication. 'Sure, OK, no worries.'

He stations himself at the door. Owen is dangerous and he could have a weapon. If Walker messes this up, it won't only play badly for Gabby – he could be in trouble too. He needs to make sure Gabby is OK but he needs Owen calm.

Owen is watching Walker and there's calculation in his eyes. Maybe he's not as tired or as drunk as he's making out. He rights his drink and says, 'Why're you here again?' with a touch of belligerence.

'Like I said, just want to make sure you and Gabby are settling in OK,' says Walker.

'In that case, you might as well have a drink with me.'

'Go on, then,' says Walker. Owen gets up slowly and walks past him into the kitchen. Walker watches as he opens a series of cupboard doors until he finds one that holds the glasses. He goes back to the sofa, pours a generous splash of bourbon and hands it to Walker. 'Haven't got any ice – we only moved in today.'

'No worries,' says Walker, taking the drink. He picks the armchair to the right of Owen. He's sitting between Owen and the door, still covering him, but it's less threatening than standing. He doesn't want Owen to feel alarmed, it could well put Gabby in greater danger than she is already. And him too. If Walker were fighting fit, he'd fancy his chances against Owen, but right now he's not so sure. He's far from recovered and his leg is hurting badly after the twelve flights of stairs. Owen's a big bloke and he's capable of serious violence.

That's if he's not already too late. What if Owen has already hurt her, suffocated her like he's tried to twice before? It'll be at least half an hour before Cummings and his team arrive. Walker says a prayer under his breath for the safety of the little girl. For half an hour he has to keep Owen away from his daughter. For half an hour he has to keep Gabby safe from harm.

Chapter 52

1 a.m.

Owen is eyeballing Walker. He seems to be getting more suspicious, perhaps as he has the time to sober up a bit.

'Nice place you've got here,' says Walker, in a bid to distract him.

'It's shit, but it'll do until I get my place back from the cops. So, you're here because Craig sent you to check up on us? He worries too much . . .'

'Yeah, sort of. I was on Gabby's protection team, remember? I wanted to make sure you're both settling in alright.'

'Not very bloody protective, were you? Someone tried to kill her. I had to move her here to keep her safe. And you still can't find the bastards who killed my Siobhan. I've lost everything. And your lot, tsssh – they couldn't find a needle in a fucking haystack.'

'Don't worry,' says Walker, 'I reckon they're close.'

Owen shakes his head. 'They haven't got a bloody clue . . .' He stands, walks towards the windows, looks out into the darkness. Walker stays seated, his leg throbbing but every muscle in his body tensed to make a move if Owen tries anything.

'Christ, I'm tired,' says Owen. 'Tired of the cops. Tired of the hospital. Tired of everything. I haven't slept for days.'

'It's hard, keeping up appearances, everyone watching you,' says Walker, pretending sympathy, hoping to draw the bloke out. 'Can't let your real emotions show. I heard Siobhan wasn't the saint they're all making her out to be . . .' He's feeling his way, hoping Owen will open up to him.

Owen turns. 'What did you hear?'

'Ah, nah, nothing. Just that, well, she liked a drink, apparently . . .'

'Bloody right. She was always saying she didn't touch the stuff but whenever we went out, to a party or dinner with friends or whatever, she'd bloody well drink then. She wouldn't have a drink with me at home, though. Trying to make me feel bad, that was always her way.'

'Yeah?' says Walker. He has a feeling that Owen wants to talk, needs to talk. Owen is narcissistic, controlling, ego-driven, and it may be that he needs someone else to know what happened, someone else to acknowledge that he got away with it, that he's cleverer than the police.

'I did everything for her, you know. Everything. And you know how she thanked me? She tried to leave me. One day, I go to play a round of golf, but I'd forgotten my wallet, left it in my other pants. I wasn't going to bother going back for it but I don't like to borrow from mates. And when I got home, there she was, all packed up and ready to go. After everything I did for her. And for Gabby too. And Gabby isn't even my own kid.' He notes Walker's surprise. 'That's right. Not many people know that. She's Siobhan's from another bloke, but I adopted her when I married Siobhan. Should have known she couldn't be trusted – she'd already frightened off the kid's father. Bitch. I couldn't fucking believe it. After all I did for her, she was gonna walk away.'

'Is that right?' says Walker, feeling a stab of pain in his heart for Siobhan, so close to freedom, so close to getting away. Owen is staring out into the dark again. Walker pulls out his phone, makes a pretence of checking his WhatsApp and starts recording the conversation. If Siobhan was about to leave, they have Owen's motive.

'Lucky you got home and talked some sense into her . . .' he says.

'Yeah. I cancelled my game of golf and made her tell me everything. She was crying and begging me to forgive her, but she'd told me so many lies. I knew I couldn't trust her anymore.'

'Fair enough,' says Walker.

Owen turns round and walks back and drops heavily onto the sofa. He takes a mouthful of his drink, then leans back, holding the glass against his chest. 'Why was I telling you this? Oh yeah, the drinking thing, that's what it was. The day she was trying to leave, after dinner, after Gabby went to bed, I said we should have a drink together, make things up to each other. Pretty bloody reasonable, right?'

Walker nods.

'She says no. Says she doesn't drink. But like I say, whenever we go to a party she drinks there alright. Happy to down a glass of wine or two. Thinks I don't notice. She's a lying bitch, but I could see that now. So I gave her a vodka and told her to drink it. Told her the least she owed me was a fucking drink after the way she'd behaved. She took it, but you should have seen her face. Christ, you'd think I was giving her poison. She was making such a fucking fuss that I pushed her down and tipped it down her throat. She spat half of it over me, and that was it. I lost it. Fucking bitch. I'd had enough of her disrespect, of her lies. I forced her to drink the whole fucking lot. She kept saying she was sorry. She was sorry alright. Sorry she got fucking found out.'

Walker feels sick to the pit of his stomach. He's battling a whirlwind of feelings, rage and sorrow and pain spiralling inside him, taking his breath away. He has to look down at the carpet; he can't let Owen see the horror and anger in his eyes. After a while, when he thinks he has himself back under control, he looks up and says, 'So, what – you killed her, then?'

Owen meets his eyes. 'What? Nah, course not,' he says. 'I would never do anything to hurt them. Ever. It was the fucking Latus. They broke in and attacked us, didn't they? They've been dragging my good name through the mud, trying to ruin me. Their sister dying had nothing to do with me. She passed her bloody medical. But they're running around blaming me, setting up protests about me. I lost clients because of them. This women's football team I used to work with, they told me they "prefer to work with someone else". That's bloody good business I lost because of the fucking Latus. Then they went all the way . . . They broke in, they killed my Siobhan.'

Walker realises that Owen has framed the Latu brothers for this from the start but been clever enough not to put their name forward, to let the police form their own suspicions.

'Can't believe the coppers haven't found any of their DNA at your place,' says Walker.

Owen takes the bait. 'Not that hard, is it,' he says. 'You just need a few brain cells operating. Cut the surveillance video, clean things up real good afterwards, get rid of the weapon. If the cops don't find a weapon and they don't find any DNA, they can't really charge them. Or if they charge them, a jury'll let 'em go. All circumstantial, isn't it?'

'Maybe Gabby will remember what happened. She might be a good witness,' says Walker.

'No. She won't.' Owen's voice is final.

Walker's heart drops like a stone. What has Owen done? The man is a monster, unable to feel anything for anyone apart from himself. He has to see Gabby. Right now. He has to know.

He stands. 'I'm going to check on Gabby. I promised her I would. I'm not going to wake her.'

Owen stares hard at him for a moment but says nothing.

Walker goes into the corridor, listening all the while for Owen behind him. If Owen starts moving, if he comes for Walker, especially with a knife or another weapon, Walker doesn't fancy his chances. His leg is still throbbing and aching from the hike up the stairs. He waits, listens intently. But there's no sound from the living room or anywhere else in the apartment.

With a leaden, fearful heart, he starts opening doors. The first is a main bedroom. He flicks on the light. Empty. The second is a bathroom. The third another bedroom. As he pushes at the door something in front of it catches. Fuck.

He pushes harder, and the door opens slowly, revealing a dark bedroom. There's no sound. No movement. As his eyes adjust to the gloom, he can make out a small shape lying on a big bed by the window.

His heart is beating fast. Please let her be OK.

'Gabby? It's Lucas. The policeman,' he says softly.

The shape moves and sits up and Walker breathes again. A wave of gratitude washes over him. She's alive. He's not too late. This time he's not too late.

'Hello, Lucas. Are you here to look after me?'

Walker's eyes sting at her question. He can only imagine the fear she must have been feeling these past ten days, the terrifying ordeal she's been through. 'Yeah, Gabby, that's right. I'm here looking out for you. You can go back to sleep now – you're safe.'

'Can you leave the door open? It's too dark in here . . .'

Walker does what she asks and stands for a moment outside the door, savouring the relief. She's OK. She's going to be OK.

'Lucas?'

'Yes, Gabby?'

'Nothing, just checking . . .'

'I'll be here, don't worry,' he says.

'Hmm.' Her voice is sleepy. He waits a moment longer, listens to her breathing slow into sleep, then walks back to the living room. David Owen has his eyes shut, the booze in the glass he's holding in imminent danger of spilling onto his t-shirt.

He takes out his phone and texts Cummings: *in the house Gabby OK*.

Cummings texts back: *5 mins away.*

He and Owen sit there. After a few minutes the sound of a buzzer reverberates through the quiet.

'Doorbell,' says Owen. 'Leave it. It'll be some hoon downstairs, wanting to get in, ringing all the bells.'

Cummings is here. 'Let me check,' says Walker.

He stands and walks to the door, presses the buzzer on the phone entry system and cracks open the door to the apartment. Then he looks one more time into Gabby's room. He can see her shape under the covers, hear her regular breathing. She's safe. She's going to be alright. But his heart hurts for the little girl, for all that she's gone through, for all that she's witnessed and all that she's lost.

Chapter 53

8 a.m.

The noise of the traffic rumbles through Walker's sleep, filling his dreams with oversize trucks that drive at him, forcing him up against the walls of buildings that seem to want to push him into the path of the vehicles. He's fighting to stand, fighting not to fall under wheels as large as houses, when his alarm clock wakes him. The room is dark and smells musty and he feels lousy. He's had a restless few hours since he got back from David Owen's, his heart heavy with the horror of the story he heard.

When Cummings and his team arrived, David Owen had stopped talking, staring into his glass, refusing to speak. Cummings had asked him to come to the station. 'We need you to answer a few questions,' he'd said. 'We've made a bit of a breakthrough.'

Owen had protested. 'At this time of night? My little girl is asleep. I can't leave her alone. It'll have to wait until morning.'

'It's not a request, Mr Owen. If you don't come voluntarily, I will arrest you for the murder of your wife.'

He'd gone. Not quietly and not willingly. 'You lot – you can't find who really did it so you're trying to set me up for it! I want to call my lawyer. You can't do this . . .'

Walker and a woman constable had stayed at the apartment. They'd sent another PC to collect Owen's mother. She'd been horrified and anxious at the news that David Owen was in custody, asking: 'But why? But why?' but she'd come to stay and look after Gabby.

It was gone 3 a.m. before Walker made it back to the motel. The bed was uncomfortable, his mind and heart bleak and dark with all that had transpired. And now he has to deal with Craig and the Vandals.

He takes a shower, the cool water reviving him slightly, and finds a café nearby for breakfast. He drinks two strong coffees to slack his tiredness and eats a Brekky Roll – bacon, eggs, hash brown and cheese with barbecue sauce. It's greasy and heavy in his stomach and he feels barely more energised as he drives over to Craig's to pick up the money. For once Craig answers the door, also looking pale and tired.

'Jess gone, has she?' asks Walker.

Craig nods. 'Yeah, to her sister in Brisbane.' He hands Walker a red Iron Fitness sports bag, filled with cash. 'There's twenty thou in there,' he says. 'Like they asked.'

'Did they say they'll send the bloke with the face tatts?'

'Yeah, nah, I didn't ask. I just said you'd be there. It'll be him, though. He's the one who keeps coming round here.'

'I'll take your car,' says Walker. 'That way they'll know I've been sent by you.' And, thinks Walker, that way Craig won't be running off to meet Jess and jumping on a plane to somewhere far away.

Craig looks nonplussed. 'You want to take the Range Rover?'

'Yeah.'

'Um, OK.' Craig goes inside and emerges a few moments later with a set of keys. 'Look, mate,' he says as he hands them over, 'be careful, alright? These're bad bastards . . .'

'Yeah, no worries,' says Walker, taking the keys. 'I'll be right.'

He isn't that nervous about the meet. To be on the safe side he's sent Rutherford a brief email outlining the details of what he's doing but this kind of operation, handing over some cash, shouldn't be too dangerous. He's done similar things, and others far more dangerous, on operations in the past. The Vandals will be happy to get the money. As they're extorting Craig they'll be looking to make it a regular thing, so Walker shouldn't be under threat. And he's never met Aaron Adams or any of the Vandals who operate down here other than Markovich, who's not likely to show up today, so there's no way they'll know he's AFP.

The drive to the meeting place takes just under half an hour. He makes a looping circle that brings him out at the slightly higher point behind it, parks the car and pushes his way through the scrub to the edge of a small rise. He can see the empty streets of the development below him, no one in sight. In the distance, the blue smudge of the ocean. He waits, leaning against a small gum tree for shade, brushing away the flies that appear the moment he stops moving, and watches. A few minutes after noon he sees a bike moving along the empty streets and parking up, not far beneath him. Only one bike. As he'd thought, they're making this easy, happy to be getting the cash. He's planning to ask if he can buy drugs from them too. Additional drugs outside of Craig's deliveries, see if he can record them offering to sell, or, more likely, arrange a meeting somewhere else to buy. His plan is simple, if not the most sophisticated or thought-through thing he's ever done. He's going to pose as a potential dealer who wants to start selling in the bush towns out west. He's hoping he can maybe even encourage a conversation about the club's new meth that can be used as evidence against them. Either way, hopefully he'll get an in with their distribution network, like Rutherford has asked.

He walks back to the car and drives the five minutes down the hill to the meeting.

Nathan Brown is standing beside his Harley, roasting like a chook in a bag. The sky is blue, dotted with small clouds, and the weather is hot and steamy; the light is too bright even with his sunnies on. He's jittery and sweating hard, his jeans sticking to his legs, his singlet wet under his arms and across his back. He's parked his bike on a slight rise that gives him a good view across the ten-hectare block they've chosen for the meet: a piece of scrub not far from the clubhouse that's been razed for development. The roads have been tarmacked and there are street lights, even individual blocks marked out, but whoever owns the place has never built a single house and the place is quiet as death. It feels like a scene from a zombie movie and it's giving him the creeps.

He should have done a line or two to fortify himself, but he doesn't want to mess this up. He's finally got an in with the club's top blokes. This is his chance to make a name for himself, get properly into the action. When he hears the car coming, he clenches his fists to pump himself up. This bloke's a pussy, there's nothin' to worry about.

The car that pulls up is a top-of-the-line blood-red Range Rover, the bloke behind the wheel slim but not skinny, with the wild curly hair and broad shoulders that he remembers from the gym. Surreptitiously, he reaches back and touches the blade he's got secreted in his rear pocket. He can do this. He can knock this bloke off, cop or not.

Chapter 54

12 p.m.

When Walker sees the Vandals bikie waiting for him at the meeting point, he recognises the bloke. He's seen him at the gym – broad shoulders and chest balancing on skinny legs. Craig's connection to the Vandals obviously runs deep. But it's not the bloke he'd been expecting, and he curses under his breath. He wants to trap one of the leaders of the club into talking about their drugs, not some street-level grunt, but he should have expected they wouldn't send the top bloke to meet him. He'll have to wing it.

He presses Record on his phone as he pulls up beside the Harley, which is parked against the kerb, and pushes the button to open the window on the passenger side.

'Who the fuck are you?' he says.

The bikie bristles. 'I'm here for the pick-up, that's all ya got to know.'

'No way. I've been told exactly who to give this to and I'm not handing over a bundle of cash to some nobody. I need to meet a bald bloke with a load of face tatts.'

The bikie looks undecided.

'Call your boss and tell him,' says Walker. 'I can wait.'

The dashboard says the outside temp is 36C and, while Walker has the advantage of being encased in the cool of the car's air conditioning, the bikie, standing in the blazing sunshine, is already sweating and puce.

The bikie glares at him then pulls out his mobile phone, turns his back and makes a call. Walker can't hear the conversation but after a moment the bikie turns back. 'What's ya name?' he says to Walker.

'Donnie Young,' says Walker. 'I'm a mate of Craig's. He asked me to bring the dosh, but he says it has to go to the bloke with the face tatts.'

The bikie half-turns away. 'Donnie Young? And he's saying it's gotta be Aaron . . .' he says, confirming Walker's intel. He takes a few steps away – Walker can't hear what he's saying – then turns once more and says, 'Show us the moolah, then.'

Walker leans back and picks up the bag with the money from the back seat, keeping his eye on the bikie the whole time. He unzips it and faces it towards the passenger window, the bundles of vivid-green $100 bills clearly visible.

He can see the bloke saying 'Yeah' into the mouthpiece, then a nasty smile appears on his face. The bikie ends the call and waits, eyeballing Walker the whole time. It only takes a few minutes before he hears the full-throated roar of another Harley coming towards them. He looks in his rear-view mirror and sees not one but three bikes, riding side by side down the empty street. Walker feels a shiver of apprehension run down the back of his neck. He's outnumbered and he has no back-up.

This was a stupid idea. He's rushed in, not thought it through properly. Now he's got four bikies parked up beside the car. He could leave, drive off. He contemplates the idea for a second but discards it. He won't get another chance like this; won't have a way to get this kind of access to the Vandals leadership. There's nothing for it but to bluff it out. He starts the video on his phone, tucks it into his front jeans pocket, camera facing out. It's not much but it'll have to do. He wishes he had his Glock tucked into his waistband and not in storage at the range, some thousand miles away in Canberra.

Nick Mitchell is sitting astride his Harley, watching the others dismount and surround the Range Rover. They'd been waiting at the clubhouse for the call from Nathan that the job was done, but it hadn't gone that smoothly. Nathan had called – apparently the bloke only wanted to deal with Aaron.

'Nathan says it's the right bloke but he reckons his name is Donnie Young. That ain't right, is it?' Aaron had turned, checking with Nick. Nick had shaken his head. 'Nah, the name's Walker.'

'Fucksake,' Aaron had said. 'You want something done, you gotta do the job yourself . . .' He'd thought for a moment then said into the phone, 'Has he got the cash? Alright, tell him to wait. I'm coming to kick his arse, whoever the fuck he is', and hung up.

'Yeah, let's kick his arse,' Shaun, Aaron's sidekick, had said. Nick thinks Shaun's an idiot, but he's big and useful in a fight, good to have in your corner when there's trouble.

'You better come too,' Aaron had said to Nick. 'Gotta make sure Ford's sent us the right bloke.'

Nick is the club's number two and theoretically Aaron reports to him, but Aaron is the enforcer, the sergeant-at-arms, and in situations like this he makes his own call. Nick's been avoiding violence for a long time now, but sometimes you need to show you're still willing, that you've still got it. And with Aaron, Shaun and Nathan in play, most likely he won't even need to throw a punch. Not that there looks like being any trouble now that they're here. Just the one bloke sitting in a Range Rover. Nick stays astride his bike, lets the others deal with it.

The bloke steps down from the car, holding a black sports bag, which he chucks in Aaron's direction. He's got balls, thinks Nick, I'll give him that. One against four.

'Craig wants to make this right, make it all go away,' says the bloke. 'The twenty thou you want is in there.'

He's had his back to Nick, but he steps further from the car now, half-turning to make sure he can also see Nick, sensibly wary of having an unknown menace behind him. As he looks over, Nick scrutinises his face – he's older, his hair longer, but it looks like the same bloke from the ID photo they've got.

'How do you know Ford?' he asks, wanting to make sure.

'He was a mate of my dad's. They played footy together in Sydney.'

Nick smiles: Sydney is the right answer. The cop they're looking for, the one in the photo that was up in Caloodie, the one that fucked up the last operation, he'd come from Sydney. Stefan's been hunting him down ever since and now they've got him.

'Yeah, it's him,' he shouts over to Aaron. 'He's the one who broke the op in Caloodie.'

For a millisecond after he makes the call, nothing happens,

everyone looking over at him. It's the cop who moves first, lunging for the open door of the Range Rover, but he's limping, moving slowly, barely running. Nathan, on the opposite side of the vehicle, goes for the other door, but it's Aaron who's the fastest. From where he's standing in front of the car, he takes three giant strides, slamming his body weight into the driver's-side door, which smashes shut. Aaron doesn't lose much momentum, ricochets from the door straight into the cop. Aaron is shorter but he's at least thirty kilos heavier and he barrels in, arms swinging, punches connecting to the bloke's chest, stomach and head.

The cop covers his head and puts up a good fight – he might even land one or two – but when Shaun joins in and then Nathan arrives, they pummel him to the ground, kicking him, bashing him.

'Stop – for fuck's sake, stop!' Nick is pushing Shaun away, shouting at Aaron.

Aaron aims one more kick into the cop's back, then stands, breathing heavily. There's no other sound. Nick can feel the sun beating down on his head, his heart pulsing in his ears. Aaron is sweating, bleeding from his lip where the cop managed to clock him one. The cop is lying on the ground, not moving, blood leaking from his mouth and nose.

'Fucksake, we can't kill a pig. Are you fucken crazy?' Nick pushes Aaron hard. 'We'll go to jail for the rest of our lives.'

'What are you on about?' says Aaron, squaring up to Nick. 'Stefan wants him gone. Stefan wants him dead.'

Nick puts his hands up. 'Look, you did good, you did what you had to, but we're right next to the fucken clubhouse. We kill him, the pigs'll have us in the frame for it in five minutes,' he says. 'We've given him a proper beating. That'll do it. Leave him, let's take the money and get outta here. We kill a pig, we'll get life, we'll never get parole. We've gotta get outta here.'

Aaron looks down at the cop lying on the road, kicks the limp body. 'Reckon it's too late for that. Leavin' him here is the worst thing we could do. Like you say, when they find a body, this close to the clubhouse . . . Nah, we need to get rid of him proper. No body, no crime.'

'Fuck,' says Nick.

'We'll dump him in the ocean,' says Aaron. He turns to Nick. 'You still got that boat in the water?'

Nick had bought himself a boat a couple of years ago – nothing fancy, just a nice little motor launch. They'd taken it out a few times, him and Stefan, fishing and drinking, but not recently, not since Stefan got angsty and everything changed.

'Yeah,' he says. 'It's in the marina at Coomera.'

'Righto,' says Aaron. 'Shaun, you and Nath go back to the clubhouse and bring a couple of blokes out here to take our bikes back. Me an' Nick'll sort this out. But first, put the pig in the car.'

Shaun picks the cop up under his arms and drags him to the back of the Range Rover. He and Nathan heft him inside, throw him like a sack of spuds into the boot. The cop doesn't move, doesn't make a sound; he's as limp as a doll.

Chapter 55

Nick is driving, taking the familiar route towards home on autopilot, his nerves shot. The cop is in the back, not moving. He's dead. They've killed a fucking cop.

Aaron has the phone on speaker, talking to Stefan. 'We got him. He didn't put up much of a fight,' he says.

'Are you sure it's the right bloke?' asks Stefan. Aaron switches the phone to video, holds the camera over the body in the back.

'Yeah, that's him,' says Stefan after a minute. 'Get rid of him like you said. Leave the car with the keys in it at the marina. I'll get someone to pick it up and take it across the border. This Ford bloke – do we need to put the frighteners on him? Is he likely to talk?'

'Yeah, we'll pay him another visit. But he'll be good as gold. The fire sorted him out.'

'Good,' says Stefan, and cuts the call.

Aaron whistles tunelessly, searches for music on the car radio. Nick resists the urge to drive faster. All they need now is a speed camera to take a pretty picture of them driving Ford's car with a dead cop in the back. He pulls the sun visor down, sits up taller. Can't see so well but it might make it more difficult to ID him if they are snapped. He can't understand that Aaron isn't stressed by this.

'Don't you care that we've killed a fucken cop?' he says. 'That we could spend the next twenty years in the bin?'

'If we get rid of his body, they'll never prove it.'

Nick hopes Aaron's right. It's their only chance of avoiding serious jail time.

When they pull up at the marina, he stops the car at the far end, away from the CCTV cameras. 'They got CCTV up there – we can't park any nearer.'

'We can't carry a fucken body half a mile neither,' says Aaron.

Nick thinks it through. 'There's a park with a boat ramp just up the road. It's quiet, especially during the week. You drive over and I'll bring the boat round, meet you there.'

Stefan hangs up the phone and turns to Wayne, who's dropped in after his visit back home. 'Let's have a JD,' says Stefan, walking over to the lounge unit and pulling out a fresh bottle, cracking the seal. 'I just had some fucken good news.'

'Yeah?' says Wayne.

'We got that pig, the fucker who closed down our site up north. He turned up down here, thought he was too smart for us but now he's dead meat.'

'Which pig?' asks Wayne, his mouth drying up.

'The one Aaron sent round on Telegram, the fucken Fed from out west.'

Wayne's palms are sweating. How did he miss this? What Fed?

Stefan is still talking. 'Tina saw him in Surfers, recognised him, and then one of our blokes spotted him at a gym. We set him up. Aaron and Nick sorted him. He won't be bothering us no more.'

'Nice one,' says Wayne, raising his glass of JD in a toast and downing it in one, hoping the grog will calm the shake he can feel in his hands.

Stefan is in a good mood. He pours them another, talking about his plans for the weekend, this bird he's met. Wayne drinks the second more slowly, wondering how quickly he can get away. He needs to call this in – doesn't know who the cop is, or why they've got him, but it must be someone else who works on Rutherford's team. Fucking Rutherford – he plays things too close to his chest. He's trying to remember the details of Stefan's conversation. A marina? A bloke called Ford?

'Righto,' he says after a few minutes, downing the second JD, 'I gotta get off.'

'Nah, nah,' says Stefan. 'Not so fast. I got a job for ya. Get yourself to Coomera Marina, pick up the car Aaron and Nick left there. Aaron'll send you the details of where. Take it across the border, dump it, torch it.'

'Righto,' says Wayne.

'You got a vehicle?' asks Stefan.

Wayne nods.

'Use that, not your bike. Pick Shaun up from the clubhouse – he'll help you.'

'Righto,' says Wayne again.

He rides home, breaks every speed law there is. Checks his Telegram, sees the bounty messages and swears loud and long. They've even got the ID of the AFP cop, a DS Lucas Walker. Where the fuck did they get that? And how come he didn't see it?

He wishes he was still far away from all this. He'd been needing a break – it's been five unrelenting months up close to Markovich without pause, and recently he hasn't been sleeping, chased by nightmares of being found out, of being surrounded by bikes and gang members with knives, unable to move, unable to defend himself. Rutherford had pulled him out for five days' rest and he'd gone to Newcastle, hung out with his mum and dad, his brother and his brother's kids, had deliberately closed himself off from the club, trying to feel some semblance of normality. He'd managed to sleep a bit better, had come back feeling he could go on a while longer, but in the meantime he's missed this and now a cop is dead. Shit, shit.

He calls Rutherford on the number that is only for utmost emergencies. It will always be answered, day and night. It's the 'Get me out now' line he's never used before.

'What's happening? Where are you?' He can hear the concern in Rutherford's voice.

'They've got one of our blokes. He might be dead already. They're talking about dumping the body out at sea. They're on their way to Coomera Marina.' Wayne can hear his voice shaking, has to sit on the sofa.

'Who have they got?'

'Lucas Walker – DS Lucas Walker.'

'Fuck! Do you know anything else? Any other information?'

'They've got a copy of his ID from somewhere. They sent it round on Telegram, a bounty call, while I was in Newcastle. They must have someone inside the AFP. I could be compromised too.'

Chapter 56

2 p.m.

Aaron sits in the car, watching Nick walk towards his boat. He makes another call to Stefan. 'We're at the marina. We're gonna leave the car up at the Coomera boat ramp.'

'Text Wayne the details. Him and Shaun'll handle it,' says Stefan.

'Righto. But we got another problem,' says Aaron. 'Nick is packin' it. I reckon he's lost his bottle. He didn't want to fight the pig and now he's shittin' it because we're gonna dump the body. I reckon he hasn't got the stomach for it, keeps saying we're gonna spend twenty years in the bin. Doesn't want to do it. I don't reckon he's reliable anymore.'

There's a long silence at the other end and Aaron wonders if he's in trouble. Stefan and Nick have been mates for years, but Stefan needs to know the truth.

'Reckon you can handle him?' asks Stefan after a while.

Aaron feels a surge of relief. The boss has made the right decision. 'Yeah, no worries,' he says. 'He's not expecting nothin.'

'Dump him out there too, then. Maybe there's a way we can pin this cop killin' on him. Take his boat down to Coolangatta afterwards. Wayne'll meet you there, help you scuttle it.'

Aaron drives the car round to the boat ramp. It's in the right-hand corner of a small park on a quiet residential side street. The road is a dead end, so there's no passing traffic. He parks, shuts off the engine. There's no one around. He can hear the river lapping at the edge of the ramp, birds squawking and arguing in the trees. Only one car passes by while he waits, an old silver Holden which turns left away from the park and then down one of the side streets. He finds a wrap of coke in his wallet, takes a quick bump from his key for the feel-good factor, then pulls off his trainers and rolls up his jeans.

When Nick motors into view, he backs the car halfway down the ramp, opens the boot and drags the cop's body down into the water. Nick's come close in; Aaron's barely up to his knees in water when Nick leans over and pulls the body into the back of the boat. Nick motors out again, pulling up alongside the small fishing jetty at the other end of the park. Aaron parks the car, leaves the keys in the armrest console. As he walks over to the boat, he sees a young bloke, scrawny, wearing boardies that look too big for him, using the stationary exercise bike in the park. He glances in Aaron's direction, but it's a lazy look, not an interested one. Aaron can see Nick's angsty as fuck, though, as he climbs on board.

'You reckon he saw us moving the body?' Nick says, glancing back at the bloke, still pedalling slowly on the bike.

'Nah,' says Aaron. 'He just got there. Stop fucken worrying.'

As they head down the river, past the posers at Sanctuary Cove and towards Paradise Point, Aaron fingers the knife in his pocket. His heart is steady. This is gonna be a piece of piss.

It's the water that shocks Walker back into consciousness. For one second it's pleasingly cool, then every nerve in his body begins screaming in agony. He feels himself being manhandled, banging against a hard surface. The pain coursing through him knocks him out again. When he wakes the next time he's lying on his back, still wet, his body on fire, hurting beyond belief. He can't remember anything. Doesn't know where he is or how he got here.

He can feel the floor beneath him vibrating, hear the sound of an engine. The floor is wet and from the unsteady motion, the sound of water, slowly he realises he's on a boat. He hears a voice above him to the left, someone else answering from the right, and an instinct of danger tells him to keep his eyes closed as he tries to fathom what's happening.

'You got anything to drink?' the first voice asks.

'There's probably some water in the Esky.'

Someone stands and steps over him. He can hear the bloke breathing, hear him rattling around, opening the Esky perhaps.

'No beers?'

'For fuck's sake, we're not on a day out.'

As the bloke steps back over him, Walker places the voices and it all comes rushing back to him. The Vandals, the money. They'd known he was a cop. Somehow they'd known he was from Caloodie. His mind works slowly. The pain is debilitating. He's on a boat with two bikies. He needs to pull himself together or this isn't going to end well.

He tries to take a measure of his surrounds. The good news is that he isn't tied up. They think he's so incapacitated they haven't even bothered securing his arms. He can feel his shoulder pressing against a bulwark, and from the proximity of the bikies to his head he figures the boat is a small one. He doesn't dare open his eyes; he wants them to think he's unconscious until the last. It will at least give him the advantage of surprise. Probably they'll tip him over the side at some point. Maybe he'll be able to swim back to shore. A shaft of pain in his back as the boat bounces over a wave dispels this notion. He's badly bruised and his leg is hurting worse than it's ever done since he got the injury. And each time he breathes in he feels agonising pain in his lungs. He won't be able to fight two of them and he'll struggle to swim far.

As if reading his mind, the second voice asks: 'What's the plan, then?'

'Get out of sight of land, cut his throat, dump him over, let the sharks have him.'

'Cut his throat? I haven't got a knife for that.'

'I have.' He hears the bloke to his left move.

'Christ. You always carry that thing?'

'Yep.'

'Fuck me. Put it away, would ya.'

The bloke to his left moves again. Walker can't work out from the sound where he keeps the knife but probably inside the waistband of his jeans. Walker decides he needs to act the next time the bloke with the knife moves. The next time he steps over him, Walker needs to push himself up and knock him overboard. That'd even up the odds a bit.

But the boat motors on and neither of the pair speaks or moves again. Walker occupies his mind by trying to place where he is. He's certain they're not in the ocean. The waves are too choppy, too slight, not the rolling motion of the sea. They're in some backwater, maybe the Nerang River.

He's not sure how long he lies there before he feels the boat turning right and the water getting choppier. They're leaving the backwater. He has to act soon. If he can get the bloke with the knife into the water, he can maybe fight off the other one and then attract attention from another boat, or even from on shore, if they're close enough. But every muscle, every nerve, hurts. He doesn't know if he has the strength, if he can even get to his feet, but he has to try. If he wants to survive he has to push through the agony. If he just lies here, he's heading to certain death.

Chapter 57

3 p.m.

Walker lets his eyes open, slowly and only the tiniest fraction. His head is in shade and he's lying in a well in the stern of the boat in the space that would normally be used for rods and tackle. There's an Esky, a decent-sized blue thing with a white lid, to the left of his feet. Above him, a bench seat, small enough so that the two blokes have to sit close together, under a blue tarpaulin roof. They're both facing away from him, looking in the direction the boat is travelling.

The bloke on his right is steering. The other, the one with the knife, looks relaxed, one arm hanging down the back of the white padded seat, the other holding a bottle of water. He's a left-hander, notes Walker. Neither is paying him any attention. From his position, Walker can see only the sky; he hasn't a clue where they are or if there is land nearby, but the water is definitely getting choppier so he needs to move now.

He eyes the Esky, formulates a plan. He wriggles his toes in his boots, moves his shoulders slowly, clasps his fingers into fists, getting the blood moving, readying himself for action. Moving quietly, slowly, he raises his head, then his shoulders, comes into a sitting position, then a crouch. Pain, pain everywhere. He blocks it out, breathing shallowly.

They haven't heard him, the sound of the motor, the wind and the swell of the waves masking his movement. He was right: they're not at sea but in a shallow channel. On his left is a sandbank with a few trees, on his right suburbia, and up ahead, in the distance, a busy skyline. This must be Southport. They're heading for the Spit, going out to sea that way.

The shore is near enough that even in his sorry state he could just about swim there, so long as they don't run him down with the boat. As he toys with the idea of jumping into the water, the bloke with the knife moves his arm in a stretch. The movement causes Walker's fear to ratchet up, the adrenaline pumps through him and almost instinctively he moves into action. He grabs the Esky, turns, steps forward and swings it with all his might against the head of the bikie with the knife. He has a stroke of luck – taken by surprise, the bloke's head bounces forward into the dashboard with a heavy thud. With any luck, the blow might have been enough to knock him out. Walker immediately swings his arms the other way. As the second bloke turns with a look of shocked surprise, Walker thumps the Esky hard into his face. There's a crunch of bone and a shout of pain. Walker turns back towards the first bloke, who's not as incapacitated as he'd hoped. He's sitting in his seat, shaking his head to clear it, and as Walker swings at him he leans, ducks and then pushes the unwieldy Esky away with the palms of his hands. Walker uses the momentum to swing the Esky back the other way. The second bloke's face is a mess – he's holding his broken nose, blood pouring over his fingers, groaning and groggy. Walker hits him hard on the side of the head and sees his eyes roll back and his body go motionless in his seat. One down.

Walker turns his attention back to the bigger threat, the bloke with the face tatts, who has pulled his knife and is coming to his feet. Walker, standing a few feet below him in the well of the boat, is at a distinct disadvantage. The bikie lunges towards him, knife thrusting at Walker's face. He leans quickly away to avoid it, feeling the steel of the blade whistle by millimetres from the skin of his face.

Without guidance, without a hand on the wheel or the throttle, the boat is slowing and turning in a big lazy curve towards the shoreline. As it comes side on to the swell, it bounces and rolls heavily. Walker instinctively adjusts his footing, a movement learnt from the years he spent sailing in Boston. On the small platform above him, the bikie has less space and perhaps not such good sea legs either. He's lunging towards Walker as the boat shifts and, with a shout, loses his balance, crashing down from the cockpit in what feels like slow motion. Walker sidesteps and swings the Esky one last time. It connects with a ferocious thump to the front of the bloke's head, and he falls, still and lifeless, onto the deck.

Every muscle in Walker's body is screaming with pain. His chest hurts so much it's hard to breathe, and his legs can barely support him. He half-falls, half-sits on the bench that runs along the stern of the boat. In front of him is the curve of a small beach, which fringes a park, and beyond that a suburban esplanade. Two old men are standing on the sand, mouths agape, watching the brawl play out in front of them. In the distance he can see a police launch, siren flashing, the sound ringing over the water, speeding towards him.

Chapter 58

Friday 17 March
9 a.m.

There's no wind. The beach is still. The tide is out. The ocean far away. His feet squeak on the soft sand, leave prints in the hard grains then crunch across shells exposed by the receding water. Great bundles of knotted pale-brown kelp are marooned on a sandbank, emitting a scent of salt and ocean, sun and decay. The warm water laps around his ankles, then his calves. The waves are quiet and the morning sun colours the water aqua green. Only a small set of breakers, easy to dive under, then the gently rolling sea. He can see a vivid-pink buoy in the distance and strikes out towards it, swimming in a diagonal line. The ocean hasn't been this soft and welcoming since he's arrived.

He swims thinking of Kaia, who loved the ocean but couldn't survive on land. He thinks of Grandma and he can hear her voice speaking to him, loud and clear: 'Make sure you come home, Lucas. This is your land, this is your home too.'

He's with Grandma, sitting at the kitchen table. She has her mischievous smile and is dunking a biscuit in her tea. He gives her a hug and she says, 'Go on with you', and he walks outside. The little house is shaded by the mango tree, the galahs squabbling in the poinciana, Ginger on the veranda, her tail swishing with pleasure at the prospect of an early-morning walk in the bush. The sun warm but not yet unbearably hot, the red earth, the land so wide and the horizon so far it seems endless. An endless ocean of land calling him.

Then he's back in the sea, still swimming but now the waves are pushing him gently homewards and soon he's standing on the wet sand of the beach, the high-rise buildings ahead of him gleaming silver in the morning light.

Suffused with peace, he stretches his arms and a sharp and sudden pain in his chest brings him awake. He's in bed, fluorescent lights above him, his chest wrapped in bandages, a drip in the top of his hand. He lies there, discombobulated, trying to return to the ocean, to Caloodie and Grandma, to Ginger and the bush, but the moment is gone.

He breathes and feels the sharp pain in his chest again. Remembers the beating he got, the boat, using the Esky to fight them off, the police launch, siren flashing, then nothing more. He breathes more shallowly and sits up, swings his legs to the side. A shaft of pain runs through his chest and across his back. The pain in his leg is shocking. He looks down; his scar is red and raised and swollen.

A nurse arrives. 'You're up,' he says. 'How are you feeling?'

'Hurts a bit,' admits Walker.

'I'm not surprised. You've got three broken ribs, your leg injury is inflamed and you're badly bruised on your torso, arms and face. Lie down, and I'll bring you some breakfast.'

Walker does as he's told and when the nurse comes back with a tray of food, he's accompanied by DI Ernie Cummings, who is carrying a paper bag and two takeaway coffees.

'Blimey, you don't look too hot,' says Cummings.

'I'm alright,' says Walker, looking with dismay at the poor excuse for a breakfast and the washed-out-looking tea that the nurse has delivered. 'Well, I was until they brought this for brekky.'

'Hospital food,' says Cummings with disgust, plopping the paper bag and one of the coffees on the plastic tray. 'I got you this instead.'

The coffee smells so good that Walker momentarily forgets about his aching ribs. Inside the bag is a bacon and egg sandwich, the egg yolk running out the edges, the bacon perfectly crispy, the bread soft and fresh.

'DI! You're a bloody lifesaver,' says Walker through a mouthful of sandwich. Cummings drinks his coffee and lets Walker eat.

'What day is it?' asks Walker after he's demolished the sandwich and coffee and feels half-human again.

'Friday morning. You haven't been out that long.'

'How did your water police find me? What happened to the blokes on the boat?'

When the police boat had arrived, he'd been drifting in and out of consciousness. He'd been blathering on about the Vandals, drug deals, and the water police had got him into an ambulance pretty quick, or so it seemed. He can't really remember.

'Nothing to do with us,' says Cummings. 'AFP managed the whole op. Your boss, DCI Dan Rutherford, called me last night, asked me to come and check on you. Didn't give me much info, said you'd been caught up in an organised crime op that had gone awry.'

Shit, thinks Walker, another black mark against his name with Rutherford.

'They picked up the two blokes I was with, though?'

'Yeah, couple of head honchos of the Vandals, is what I heard.'

Walker nods. He'll need to call Rutherford. Or probably better to save it for his face-to-face on Monday when the review board hands down its findings.

'How's it going with David Owen?' he asks, turning his mind away from the possibility of losing his job.

'We've charged him. He's in custody and he's staying there until we can get him to trial. When he sobered up and called his lawyer he started getting pushy and saying we had nothing on him, but the evidence is stacking up. We've got enough to hold him. The phone data is gonna nail him. We've got the knife and the vodka bottle too, and your recording of the conversation. It's not a confession but it's close enough, matches enough details. We've got him. I'm certain of it.'

'What about the other DNA? The DNA you found on Siobhan's body?'

'The pathologist says it's small enough to be cross-contamination. We think it might be from one of the paramedics. They were helping someone very intoxicated before they came to the crime scene and that person was grabbing them, holding onto them. We're going to see if we can get a match from that patient.'

'How's Gabby?'

'She's OK. She's staying with her grandmother for the moment. Her mum's sister, her aunt, is coming to stay with them too. They'll work out something together, they say, 'whatever works best for Gabby.'

Walker is happy that the little girl has family looking out for her. He reckons she's going to be OK. She's a strong little cookie – she survived two brutal attacks – and she has a warm heart; she made friends with the nurses and the police who took care of her in hospital. With family to look after her, he knows she'll be OK.

Chapter 59

Walker can't get comfortable in the cramped airline seat. He's probably not well enough to travel but he doesn't want to wait any longer, doesn't want his review hearing to be put off for another week or more, so he's on a flight to Canberra, his body complaining mightily.

He'd checked himself out of hospital on Friday afternoon, figured he could rest and recover equally as well in a hotel room bed with a big telly and decent meals on call from room service. He'd spent the weekend resting and thinking. As always, he'd thought of Grandma, of Caloodie, of Blair and Ginger. He'd thought a lot about his dad and Craig, too. He's decided he isn't going to let Craig define his father for him. Who knows if Bobby would have stayed friends with Craig, if he too would have been tempted by illicit easy money or not. It's all conjecture. His father will always be an enigma to him, and Walker decides that's OK. He doesn't need to know everything; he'll hold in his heart what he does know and let the rest be.

He'd thought about Barbara too. He'd called her to let her know the outcome of the Owen case, to thank her for her help in finding the biggest hole in David Owen's story, the one that might just put him away. She'd been happy to hear that Gabby was safe, Owen in custody. He'd realised how much he looks forward to talking to her. Knows he can count on her, lean on her. Thought of the sound of her voice, its lilting accent, and how it makes him feel warm and good. How she understands him and supports him but is happy to challenge him at the same time. He'd really like to see her again.

He's made some plans, some decisions. Plans that start with going back to Caloodie to say a proper goodbye to Grandma, picking up Ginger, and having a beer or three with Blair. Beyond that, well, some of it depends on what happens with the review board today. But whatever the decision, with the injuries he's got he won't be back at work for a month or so. He'll have time to visit Caloodie for sure. Afterwards, who knows. Maybe he'll bring Ginger to the coast for a swim in the ocean and they can meet up with Gabby. He wants to check up on the little girl, make sure she's doing OK, and he's pretty sure she'll love Ginger. After that, well, he might even go and see Barbara in Berlin.

The plane takes off and Walker drifts into a half-sleep, waking to the bump of the landing, the thrust of the plane as it comes to a halt. His leg is throbbing from the cramped position it's held for the past two hours, his ribs and chest aching.

He grabs a cab at the airport and directs the driver to the Edmund Barton Building, AFP headquarters, in the heart of the government district right on the edge of the Parliamentary Triangle. As they drive over the Kings Avenue Bridge, Lake Burley Griffin on both sides, he feels a sense of homecoming and cranks the window down. The air is cool after the muggy heat in Queensland and the city is low, green and discreet, the antithesis of Surfers Paradise. He's not been a big fan of the capital in the past, but he looks at it with fresh and more appreciative eyes today, enjoying the lushness of its parks and trees, the clean lines of the modern architecture and the calmness of the orderly city.

The driver pulls up in front of the six-storey pale-stone AFP building shortly before 1 p.m. He has a meeting with Rutherford at 2, the review at 2.30. To fortify himself for what lies ahead, he goes to the cafeteria and grabs himself a plate of today's special, chicken curry with rice, poppadoms and chutney, and digs in with pleasure. He's sitting on his own, doesn't recognise anyone in the room, but enjoys the feeling of being back. Back in the buzz, part of the team, part of the service. Maybe he should take some time to show his face around the office after the review board, remind everyone that he'll be back soon and wants to be considered for new ops. Assuming, that is, that he doesn't get fired today.

He lets the possibility of losing the job he loves run through his mind and acknowledges to himself how gutted he would be. He loves this work, loves knowing that he is making a difference, saving lives, helping to make Australia a safer place to live. He's got no idea what he'd do instead, but for sure it would be nothing that would make him feel anywhere near as good.

The thought takes the edge off his appetite, and he drops his plate off, half-eaten, and goes to the bathrooms to change into his formal uniform. He never wears it, but he's hoping it will make the right statement to the board. Then he takes the lift to Rutherford's office on the fourth floor. He's early, so he sits outside in the small reception space rehearsing in his mind what he's going to say to Rutherford and to the board. How he might beg for his job if it comes to that.

It's almost 2.10 before Rutherford's assistant looks up from her desk and says, 'You can go in now, DS.'

Rutherford is standing at the window of his office, looking across the trees towards the park and gardens beyond. He turns when Walker comes in and Walker can see that he looks more stressed than usual. His stomach makes a sudden flip. This could be bad news.

'Take a seat, Walker,' says Rutherford, walking to the desk and sitting heavily on his own chair. 'You look a right mess.'

'Thank you, sir,' says Walker, suppressing a smile. Rutherford's talent for compliments and motivation is clearly unchanged. 'This is mostly superficial. Reckon I'll be back on duty pretty soon.'

'Hmm, yes, well, let's see what the review board has to say about that,' says Rutherford.

'I want to say, sir, that I really am sorry about my actions in Caloodie. I misjudged the operational seriousness of the site, but I've learnt from it and I can promise—'

'Yes, alright, save it for the board,' says Rutherford. 'Tell me about this meeting with the Vandals and why it went so wrong.'

'I really don't know. I've been thinking about it and it doesn't make sense. It should have been a simple handover of some cash. They were extorting a bloke, one of their dealers who owns a chain of gyms on the coast, and I thought it might be a way to get closer to the club, infiltrate their distribution, like you asked. It should have

293

been straightforward. I wasn't planning on doing anything except handing over the money. I definitely wasn't expecting a four-person welcome party and I don't know how they knew I was police.'

'The bloke they were extorting – is his name Ford?'

'Yeah, that's right, Craig Ford.'

'Seems like he might have been the one to sell you out, according to our bloke inside.'

'How do you mean?'

'Apparently, they found out you were AFP and told Ford to come up with a reason to send you to the meeting. The extortion was nothing but a pretext. We've pulled Ford in. We're charging him with accessory to attempted murder.'

Walker doesn't have words to express his anger. At least Craig will pay for his crimes, but it doesn't lessen the pain of his betrayal.

'How did they know I was AFP? Did Craig tell them? He never really knew much about what I did. Maybe it was that constable from Caloodie, Dave Grogan. I don't trust him and he's at the Gold Coast now, working in narcotics. Maybe he tipped them off.'

'No. It's worse than that. It looks like they have someone in here. They had a copy of your ID.'

'What?' Walker is horrified. 'How is that possible?'

'I don't know. But it's very bad news. It means our other bloke is probably compromised too.'

'Is he OK?'

'Yeah, he's good. He helped save your arse. He was with Markovich when he got the call about your abduction and gave the order to get rid of you. He called us and we got Queensland Police on to it. And then we pulled him out.' Rutherford pauses for a moment. 'The two that had you in the boat, Nick Mitchell and Aaron Adams, they're numbers two and three in the club. Adams isn't saying anything – he's ready to do whatever time he's facing. But Mitchell wants to make a deal. He's prepared to give us information on their manufacturing site and their Mafia contacts if we'll protect him. We're evaluating his information, but it could be a breakthrough.'

Walker is relieved that this time his unexpected intervention has had a more positive impact than it did in Caloodie. 'What about Markovich?' he asks.

'He's gone. He must have had a tip-off that we'd picked up two of his top blokes. He flew to Dubai on Friday night.'

Walker has a hundred questions, wants more information, but there's a knock on the door and Rutherford's assistant puts her head round. 'Review board is ready for you, sir.'

Afterwards, dress uniform hanging in his locker, Walker back in his favourite moleskins and boots, he sits in a nondescript bar not far from HQ. It's quiet and a bit upmarket, not like the Durham Castle Arms, the rowdier local that AFP cops usually favour. He should probably go to the Durham and rub shoulders with a few colleagues, but he wants to sit and savour the moment first. His beer is going down a treat. The relief of the review board's decision – poor judgement but made under the stress of operational conditions – means he's kept his job. He won't be next in line for promotion, but he hasn't been demoted or dismissed, and he considers that he's been lucky. He's probably got Rutherford to thank for it; the board mentioned his supervisor's positive review of his abilities and commitment and Walker adds it to the many favours he owes his chief.

The beer is cold, and despite the pain of his injuries nothing can put a dampener on his good mood, the guillotine that's been hanging over him finally lifted. He won't be back at work for a few weeks, and he's going to fly to Brisbane and drive up to Caloodie tomorrow. He'll surprise Blair and the others; the thought brings a smile to his face. Afterwards, well, let's see. He pulls out his phone and sends a text to Barbara: *Review board over, still got my job!*

He doesn't know what time it is in Berlin, but she texts him straight back: *Congratulations Lucas, that is very good news*, with clapping hands and a champagne bottle emoji.

He hesitates only a second before he starts typing. *How would you feel about celebrating in person? I was thinking I might come and visit . . .*

Acknowledgements

Writing can be a lonely business with only a blank page for company, and completing this second book in the DS Walker series was initially daunting, with much tighter deadlines and a whole new world to create. But I was immensely inspired by all the readers who took DS Walker to heart in *Outback* and who wrote kind reviews and emails to say how much they'd enjoyed the book. Thank you so much all for your support and encouragement, it means a lot to me and helped me no end while I was beavering away at my desk on this follow-up. I hope you like it!

I also owe a special thanks to my family for all their support, especially Wolf and Dionne, who always offer me a space to work when I'm in Australia, and along with being wonderful hosts are great cheerleaders for my work.

In terms of policing, any procedural errors or other gaffes are all mine, but I want to say a big thank you once again to Danny and Gary, two Queensland Police officers who helped me with terminology, process and believability.

Thanks as ever to my agents, Jane Gregory and Stephanie Glencross and all the team at David Higham who believed in the Walker series from the beginning.

A big part of a successful novel lies in the quality of the editing, and I owe huge thanks to Jane Snelgrove, my editor at Embla Books, who took DS Walker to heart from the start and who helped me polish the first draft of *Paradise* into this final version.

Thanks also to copy editor Silvia Crompton for her invaluable feedback, and to all the team at Embla Books – a professional, supportive and encouraging group who do all the hard work that enables the book to come to publication.

About the Author

Patricia Wolf spent her childhood in Australia and now lives in Berlin. She likes whisky and strong coffee, busy cities, surf beaches and wild places. A journalist for almost twenty years, Patricia is a regular contributor to newspapers including the *Guardian*, the *Financial Times* and the *Daily Telegraph*. She was formerly a design columnist at the *Independent*, and the Lisbon correspondent for *Monocle* magazine.

 IG: Patricia Wolf, @patricia_wolf_crime
 Twitter: Patricia Wolf, @pattywolfcrime

About Embla Books

Embla Books is a digital-first publisher of standout commercial adult fiction. Passionate about storytelling, the team at Embla publish books that will make you 'laugh, love, look over your shoulder and lose sleep'. Launched by Bonnier Books UK in 2021, the imprint is named after the first woman from the creation myth in Norse mythology, who was carved by the gods from a tree trunk found on the seashore – an image of the kind of creative work and crafting that writers do, and a symbol of how stories shape our lives.

Find out about some of our other books and stay in touch:

Twitter, Facebook, Instagram: @emblabooks
Newsletter: https://bit.ly/emblanewsletter